EDGE OF
ETERNITY

EDGE OF ETERNITY

RANDY ALCORN

WATERBROOK
PRESS

EDGE OF ETERNITY
PUBLISHED BY WATERBROOK PRESS
12265 Oracle Boulevard, Suite 200
Colorado Springs, Colorado 80921
A division of Random House, Inc.

10 Digit ISBN 1-57856-295-3
13 Digit ISBN 978-1-57856-295-4

Printed in the United States of America
2006

10

To Nanci, Angela, and Karina Alcorn,
my unrivaled treasures,
each irreplaceable
and precious beyond words
&
Ron and Kathy Norquist,
travelers who walk beside us on the homeward road,
and whom we count among the King's
greatest gifts to us.

Acknowledgments

As ALWAYS I AM MOST INDEBTED to my wife, Nanci, and my daughters, Angela and Karina, who helped and prayed and made me laugh during the long and occasionally dark days of this project. You are the best—I thank God for each of you.

Special thanks to Thomas Womack and Doug Gabbert, who asked me to write an otherworldly novel. Though this story is not the one any of us envisioned, without your prompting it would never have been written, and without your input it wouldn't be what it is. Thanks also to Dan Rich, Lisa Bergren, and Rebecca Price, whose partnership I deeply appreciate, and to Tim Newcomb and Diane Meyer, who also read and offered valuable comments on the early drafts. I'm grateful too for the fine editing touches of Carol Bartley, Traci DePree, and Ed Curtis.

Thanks to Elmer and Adele Noren, Randy and Sue Monnes, Dave and Mitzie Tillstrom, and Steve and Kathy Duncan, who generously made available their perfect little getaways during and just after the writing of this book. And thanks to Ron Noren for loaning me an armful of books.

My deep appreciation to the past and present staff and board members of EPM and their spouses for their partnership in matters of eternity: Ron and Kathy Norquist (who also read the first draft), Bonnie and Dennis Hiestand, Diane and Rod Meyer, Frieda and Jim Riegelmann, Amy and Rick Campbell, Kristi and Jason Knifong, Steve and Sue Keels, Jay and Debbie Echternach, Don and Pat Maxwell, and Lawrence and Robin Green.

Many thanks to those of you who prayed for me during the writing of this book—you know who you are. If hearts are touched for eternity through it, you played a huge part.

Thanks to C. S. Lewis, J. R. R. Tolkien, Calvin Miller, Stephen Lawhead, and others who have dared to write about other worlds so we could be better prepared for this world and the one to come.

I extend my deepest appreciation to the King, my best friend and constant companion. Your grace is truly unfathomable. May this book bring You pleasure. If it does not, it's worth nothing, but if it does, then that makes every minute invested in it—the fun ones and the not-so-fun—worthwhile. Thanks for going on ahead to prepare a home for me—and for faithfully working to get me prepared for it.

I

THE STORM CRASHED down behind me, lightning bolts chasing me like a pack of bloodhounds, thunder screaming at me. As light flooded the darkness, I looked up through the pounding rain and saw a wall of jutting rocks looming above the road, their long arms poised like executioners.

The wind was a giant hand at my back, driving me on. I tried digging in my heels, but the road was mud, my feet indistinguishable from the swirling brown goo that sucked me downward.

My heart pounded as if I were pursued by a midnight stalker. My body dripped like a deep gash in a dark cloud.

Why did my right arm feel so heavy? My forefinger trembled. My right temple ached from a pressure I couldn't explain. I sensed a cold eye staring at me, a shadowy Cyclops threatening me, pushing itself toward me.

Where was I? What was happening? How did I get on this road alone, bareheaded in this awful tempest?

I remembered driving to my mountain cabin and then…the rest was a blur.

Gusts of wind kept shoving me forward, letting up a little, then pushing even harder. All I saw through dripping, stinging eyes was the ground passing beneath my feet. My jeans were drenched, my hunting jacket a soaked sponge. I shivered.

My knees quaked and my mind started spinning in the gray violence. I could no longer tell ground from sky, earth from heaven.

"Help me! God, help—" Catching myself I groaned. I might as well be talking to the tooth fairy for all the good it would do me.

I heard a violent noise like a huge canvas tarp whipping in the wind. I looked over my shoulder, then dropped to the ground in frozen terror. The sound was the flapping of giant wings on a reptilian creature with flared claws. It looked like a dragon—no, a flying dinosaur, a pterodactyl with dead eyes and jagged teeth.

It appeared too heavy to fly, but it did, and it was coming for me.

I rose from the mud and ran with the wind, but the beating of those wings grew until it filled my ears. I felt the blast of the creature's hot breath. I smelled a thousand matches lit at once—sulfur. I flailed my arms and fell again into the mud as the monster swooped down.

As I tensed, the beast brushed over me. How could it miss? Was it playing with me, terrorizing me before the kill?

I saw the predator circle, keeping its gaze on me like a sniper on his target. Those eyes, cold and brutal—shark eyes. The beast smirked. Did it take pleasure in my terror? I sensed intelligence far greater than mine, ancient and brooding. The thought of a calculating mind in something so grotesque sent an electric wave of terror through me.

Finally the monster turned and disappeared behind the torrents of rain. I stared into the swirling gray where it had vanished. Had I really seen it? I rose from my knees, willing them to be strong. I ran, my feet battling the mire. I had to find shelter.

Behind me I heard again the whipping tarp, louder and louder.

In a heartbeat the fiery breath fell on me again. I threw my arms over my head, and as I fell into the mud I felt daggers pierce me, claws penetrating the base of my neck, ripping through muscle and tendon. Jerked off the ground, I screamed.

The beast dropped me back into the mud, the echo of my cry disappearing into the merciless storm.

Up. I had to keep moving.

I was kept from surrendering to the ground again only by the dim sight of a stone outcropping on a hillside a hundred feet away. I stumbled onward and up, in pursuit of the shelter, evoking memories of pushing across rice paddies in Nam, searching for the safety of a bunker.

As I fought through the storm, a warmth trickled over my right shoulder. I reached my left hand inside my jacket and felt my flannel shirt, now soaked in blood. My neck throbbed. With aching slowness I turned my head each way.

As I did, I saw the winged beast circling. It plummeted toward me like a rock from a cliff. I curled up, pressing my body against the muddy road.

Just as it grazed my neck, I heard a terrifying roar. It came neither from the beast nor me but from an immense dark shape prowling the ground, a beast I could barely see, a mass of fur blowing wildly in the wind. As the roar filled the air, the flying monster's head jerked back violently. It squawked fiercely as it spun away, choking and sputtering, cold horror in its eyes.

I gasped for breath, feeling only a moment of relief. What foe could strike terror into a creature more dreadful than any I'd ever imagined? Would I rather face the flying beast or the prowling one?

I pushed myself the remaining thirty feet to the rocky refuge. Just as I reached it, a burst of wind slammed me into the stone outcropping. Stunned, I fell, throwing out my arms. On the ground my groping hands found a recess, a furrow in the base of the rock. Behind me, just a few feet away, I saw the shadowy image of the ground beast, its great head still roaring up at the sky. Was I the gazelle and this the lion about to claim from the hyena its meal? I reached farther into the recess, pulling my body along, but was still exposed to beasts and elements.

I lay flat on my face, embracing the stony ground. I tried to get a grip, to move myself farther, but I couldn't. My body didn't work, but my mind did. *I'm a realist, a skeptic,* I reminded myself. The dinosaur couldn't be real, the prowling brute couldn't be real. But my stinging neck and pounding heart and the roars of wild beasts said otherwise. I willed myself to wake up, but I couldn't. I pressed my eyelids shut and longed for the relief of dreams or consciousness, whichever I wasn't already in.

When I opened my eyes, I found myself in damp darkness. I spit out sand and heard an echo. Beyond my feet, the barest light came from a two-foot opening. I must have crawled farther than I thought—into a cave. I couldn't remember.

I was spent, twisted and lying in a heap, too sore to move.

My mind slowly grew more alert, despite a torturing headache. I felt paralyzed in this utterly unfamiliar place. All I'd known was far away. Here, there was nothing else besides me and raging beasts and nature gone mad.

I reached into my jacket pocket, feeling the wet fabric for the box of matches I'd picked up at the cabin. I counted them and swore. Only four. Carefully I struck one against the wet box, three times, then once on the side of the cave. Finally a spark. I blew lightly on the flame, and it came to life.

The back wall was only an arm's length away from me, while the cave's height was maybe six feet.

I looked down and saw in the thin ashen dust a boot print

larger than my own. Had I blacked out? Had someone pulled me in here from the storm and the beasts?

A gust of wind forced its way into the cave, blowing out the match. I lit a second one and looked at the ground. The print had disappeared. I stared at where it had been just a moment before. Nothing.

I must have imagined it, or maybe it was my own. Yes, I had pulled myself into this place. I had rescued myself, like I'd always managed to do. I was alone—Nick Seagrave, alone again.

I heard footfalls and heavy breathing just outside. I shuddered. The ground beast was stalking me, so close I could feel its wet heat, smell its animal scent. It couldn't fit through the cave's mouth—could it?

I pushed myself to the back of the cave, but even then I was only four feet from the breathing. I heard sniffing now. Whatever it was, it had locked on to my scent. I couldn't stop shaking. Only my headache and the pain in my neck kept me from yielding entirely to terror.

After a long shivering stillness, I took off my jacket and tore the left sleeve off my shirt. With trembling fingers, I wrapped it around my neck to protect the wounds.

The ground beast fell silent. After a long while sitting against the cave wall, my back and legs cramped. I stretched them. Trying to find the least painful position, I curled up like an old soldier digging in for a long night.

When I awoke again, I listened carefully to the darkness. I heard no movement, no breathing but my own.

I sat up, blew on my fingers, took off my boots, and briskly rubbed my sore feet in my hands. The cave smelled gamy, like wet sneakers. I had the eerie feeling others had held up here. I wondered where they'd come from and what fate they'd met.

My migraine started to subside. My head felt clearer and my fear had loosed its grip—enough to let me reason. Maybe now I could piece this all together.

It was just too weird. I was Mr. Rational, the last guy to ever be abducted by aliens. Yet here I was, chased into a cave by an other-worldly storm and the monsters it had unleashed from who knew where. Was I living out my own episode of *The Twilight Zone?*

I revisited my last memories: changing out of my suit at the office, then driving to the mountains to the cabin, then...

Why can't I remember?

I lit the third match and examined myself. I fingered the blood-soaked collar of my shirt—my favorite blue flannel, ruined now—and reached down to touch my mud-caked boots which I'd last worn while hiking with Amy and Brian months ago. The hike from hell—I shuddered at the memory of the angry words we'd exchanged.

I ran my hand over the right side of my face and felt it twitch. That stupid embarrassing tic had developed over the last few years, showing my hand when the stress got to me, a telltale spasm that threatened my legendary rep as the Iceman. Even with no one here to see it, it angered me.

I breathed deeply, trying to make myself relax in the darkness. I managed to doze off and on. Finally I saw a faint light through the cave opening. Cautiously I pulled myself toward the mouth. The clouds had broken, and a hazy reddish moon peeked through. No, wait. What was that? Another light, lower in the sky and about half the size. A second moon?

Impossible!

I opened and shut my eyes, squinted, craned my aching neck. Each time I looked there were still two moons against a startling deep purple sky. I examined every back corner in the warehouse of my mind, searching for explanations, refusing to let myself believe the obvious. I couldn't be in another world. Could I?

I rubbed my eyelids, then blinked again at the moons. This attack on my sanity seemed more cruel than being pursued by the beasts. Seeing was believing, right? I'd always trusted my senses. But now, how could I? Had I lost my mind?

I retreated from the absurdity and hunkered into the cold, clammy lap of the cave, my back to the opening. Reason was failing me. For the moment, I gave up on it, quit trying to figure it out, hoping it would all make sense if I came back to it later.

Into the mental vacuum fell a tangled, tumbling mass of vivid memories. First came the morning I woke up to discover Marci and the kids gone. It was as unthinkable as waking up now to find myself in a world with two moons.

I relived the shock and anger I had felt as I, in my mind, read and reread her note. And the helplessness, which I hated most of all.

Two years later now, I could understand a little more why they left. My long hours, endless trips away, climbing the company ladder. Enduring—often enjoying, I admit—all that went with it. I did it for Marci, I always said, and when Amy and Brian came along I did it for them.

But wouldn't I have done exactly the same if none of them had been there?

And now they aren't.

Maybe it was something about the air in this cave; I sifted through the ruins of my existence like a man whose life was passing in front of him on the long fall to death.

I saw myself sitting in that corner office, on top of the world, so I thought. I was all the swagger you could stuff into a three-piece suit. A legend in my own mind. I could bark out orders to a hundred people under me. But I could do nothing to make my wife and children stay, nothing to make them come back.

I'd reached the pinnacle of my career. Why had it looked so much better from below? My soul felt empty. *Or do we even have souls?* I wondered.

I'd always outrun those questions before. Now they forced themselves on me, like a hound hot on a scent.

I wished I were thirty again, when nothing seemed beyond reach. Now at fifty I was old, my sore knees forcing me to give up marathons for a treadmill. Treadmills instead of marathons—it had become the story of my life.

I'd lost everything that mattered over the last two years. Now it was too late to chase dreams. Impossible to start over, impossible to unscramble all the broken eggs.

"What happened?" I shouted. The hard echo slapped me, mocking me. Was I trying to make the cave hear me better? I swung my right arm against the cave wall, bruising my forearm. I winced more from stupidity than pain.

Closing my eyes did no good; the wild video played relentlessly: empty days, empty nights, and two years of an empty bed—all the more empty whenever some stranger occupied it with me.

I shouted again, "Is this the best you can do?"

I laughed a cold, caustic laugh that bounced back at me from the cave's low ceiling. I clamped my eyes shut. Then heavy pain shot through me as I saw again the face engraved on the back of my eyelids—Lee Ann, my little Lee Ann, our five-year-old, always five.

Her death seven years ago shredded the last of my optimism. From that day, every cradle I saw swung above an empty grave. Every birth was the beginning of death, a cruelty I could no longer bear. In my grief I'd refused even to look at our family's old videotapes. Seeing her now in wrenching, living color was a twisting knife in my heart.

"Daddy," I heard her say. I felt her smooth cheek against mine. I smelled her baby-powder softness. Roughly, I swept away the warm streak on my face.

Then came my father's wretched end in that nursing home six months later, when I could tolerate his empty suffering no longer, when I told the doctors to… And finally my mother's agonizing death from cancer three years ago, one more outrage heaped on me by a senseless universe.

"Nick, you can be whatever you want to be"—Mom's melodic voice sounded in my mind again, as it had hundreds of times over the years. But was that really what she sounded like? I couldn't even be sure of that anymore. Mom always tried to get us to Sunday school, but every week we stayed home and watched football or baseball with Dad. I closed my eyes and felt my fingers in her long auburn hair, touching her soft reddish cheeks. I smelled her faint sweet perfume.

I wiped my eyes. Why was I pretending they had dust in them? I was alone in a cave—just as I'd been alone in the cabin. Wait…it started to come back. I'd been lying facedown on the cot, wrestling, tortured by the same thoughts that suffocated me now. But I'd gotten up, walked out…and…

Something hovered on the edges of my memory. What was it?

In Nam I thought I'd faced the toughest obstacles life could muster. "Dig deeper," Sarge said as I studied his craggy old face.

"You can always find the will to survive; you can always do what you think you can't. Just dig deeper."

The last few years made Nam seem like kindergarten. I dug as deep as I could. Nothing was left.

Dig deeper. I'd started believing I might be better off beneath the cold, dark ground than on top.

"No!" I was too angry to let Death win the war he always won. Not me. Not now.

A second chance. Is that really too much to ask?

But who could I ask? I'd always heard words about God spoken by that church full of hypocrites, but what did words matter? If there was a God—and I had no reason to think there was—he was irrelevant. Besides, he owed us all an apology for a world of hurt. And I knew better than to expect an apology—or anything else—from God.

If he expected me to come groveling to him, he'd better not hold his breath.

"Did you hear that?" I screamed, jumping to my feet and hitting my head on the cave ceiling.

As I stretched out my hands to keep from falling, my fingers brushed past some indentations on the cave wall behind me. Hesitating, I carefully lit the last match.

Rough letters were scratched on the wall, as if inscribed by a nail. Three lines, one above the other, forming a triangle:

FORWARD

RED ROAD HOME

BE CAREFUL WHO YOU TRUST

They were in plain English—evidence I wasn't on another planet after all. But who put them there? Some lonely lunatic, some desperate prisoner groping in the dark?

I touched every word with my forefinger. Then I flung the match away just as it burned me, and I sank down into the cold, damp darkness.

The throb in my neck yanked me into consciousness. A reddish light from the cave's mouth blinded me. I pulled myself up, amazed I'd managed to sleep on that cold rock bed.

I'd kill for a triple latté.

Once I could keep my eyes open I stared at everything bathed by the warm light pouring into the cave, which now seemed even smaller.

I couldn't stay inside. The light was calling me, inviting me out to something better. Slowly the strength of the morning filled me. I got up on my creaking knees and reached for the wall. I touched the letters again in that cryptic triangle. It wasn't a dream.

But wait—I saw other inscriptions in the wall, a foot above the message. The delicate writing was exquisite, not uniform yet orderly, with a natural beauty that made it appear like artwork as much as language. It seemed more like hieroglyphics than anything else human, but exotic and unfamiliar in form, as if it were alien calligraphy. This wasn't any human language. And yet…what other languages were there but human ones?

I noticed now there were also inscriptions below the English message. Why hadn't I seen them last night? Scrawled out on crooked and uneven lines, sprawled haphazardly across the wall, this was yet another language. The writing was coarse and crude, devoid of artistry. I reached out and started to touch it, then felt a cold chill down my spine. I backed away. I looked up and down from the elegant language above to this one below, and began to see some similarities. Despite their differences they shared some of the same characters.

I spun around, bracing myself. I had the uneasy feeling that whoever—or whatever—had written the alien inscriptions might not be far away. If they returned, I didn't want to be there.

On the floor at the far wall, at the bottom of an eerie shaft of light, I saw something—a dark green heap. I moved toward it, cautiously reaching out my hand. Something darted out from under it—a black snake. I drew back, then reached again—it was a backpack with worn and faded leather straps and a battered frame, bowed and rusted. I emptied it, finding handfuls of dust, a dirty gray blanket, an old black plastic water bottle, and a bent rusty nail. Whose pack had this been? Why had he left it here?

I could have used this blanket last night.

I felt repulsed as I recalled the previous night's wallowing in emotion and defeat and regret. Mom was right, and Sarge was right. It was time to do what Nick Seagrave had always done—take charge.

I pushed aside thoughts of the creatures. I would not spend one more night, one more hour, one more minute in this cave. If I had to fight my way out, that's what I'd do.

I pushed out the backpack and crawled forward on my stomach through the mouth of the cave—out into the brilliance…cast by a huge red sun.

2

IN THE BRIGHTNESS outside the cave, I forced my eyes open into slits and looked from side to side, then, covering my eyes, above me. No sign of the beasts.

I let my eyes savor the gleaming blue Earth-like sky, which for a moment felt like home. But there was no escaping the oversized red ball up above. If my sun, Earth's sun, was a volleyball, this was a beachball, maybe three times larger than the one I'd always known. But I could look at this orb more directly—it wasn't as bright as Earth's, yet because it was so much larger, it seemed to generate about the same amount of light. And heat too; the temperature was maybe sixty degrees and rising. It cast a slight crimson tint over everything, as if I were wearing rose-colored glasses.

I stood, slowly rotating my neck. I was near the base of a great mountain, red and black volcanic rocks strewn everywhere. A tumble of those rocks surrounded me. They were covered with a white mossy-looking overgrowth, the spew of a great mountain once filled with anger or indigestion.

Hope this volcano's not active.

I walked over to a windblown fir tree that had managed to rise up through the lava, its branches dripping with cold dew. I drank some droplets from my hand—they tasted too much like tree and not enough like water. I looked for puddles or ponds but didn't see any, as the rocky porous ground had drained away last night's rain. I drank dew from the branches again and gathered a few mouthfuls into the water bottle, unsure when I would next find water.

A few hundred feet below, a dirt road cut through a grassy valley, the stalks leaning with the wind. Three-quarters of a mile farther, the road began winding its way from the valley floor up a hillside with more valleys and some mountains visible beyond. The road's dirt surface was distinctly red, like photos of the surface of Mars, as if a long piece of rust-colored yarn stretched out over the countryside. Judging from the sun's position and direction, the road appeared to be heading west.

But how could I know for sure what direction was what in this world?

Suddenly a shadow flashed over the ground in front of me. Instinctively I hunched over. I looked up and relaxed my shoulders. An eagle, great wings extended, swooped low, eyes sharply focused on me. I smelled no sulfur, only fresh mountain air. The slight breeze invigorated me, and I felt neither weary nor sore. I slung the pack on my back and took off. When I felt a slight tremor in the ground, I picked up my pace.

Gray smoke rose from the south side of the mountain. I considered following it to see if it led to a city. But that would require going nearly the opposite direction from the red road. I finally decided to head for the red road, at least for now.

I'd walked for an hour, exhilarated but with parched throat, when I saw a tall fruit tree with low-hanging limbs. It was heavy with a dark blue fruit the size of a large orange, though shaped more like a lemon. I clutched one still on the tree and pushed my finger in, working it back and forth. Suddenly a blue juice sprayed my forehead. I laughed and peeled it back, then caught some dripping juice on my index finger. I touched it to my tongue. It had a strong citrus taste but with the flavor of blackberry, only better.

I took a small bite and savored an acidy but sweet tang that awakened my taste buds and made them long for more. Before I knew it, my shirt was wet and stained, and I'd eaten four of them. I stuffed another half-dozen into my backpack. The fruit had been both food and drink, and if the red sun had produced nothing else, I felt grateful for this treat.

I walked farther, seeing familiar flowers—lilies, daisies, lilacs, wild roses—interspersed with the utterly unfamiliar, including delicate bright orange flowers with fragile bells, yellow on the inside, blowing in the wind and making a haunting song. Their different sizes and shapes created different tones, with otherworldly melodies and harmonies.

What is this magnificent place?

A sound erupted from somewhere nearby—what was it? I instinctively jerked my head like a sparrow, looking all around. Laughter! Not a lonely chuckle, but the contagious, unrestrained laughter of a childhood Christmas. But I couldn't see anyone— where was it coming from?

Now I heard myself laughing. I felt almost euphoric, something I'd not experienced since—since I was a boy? I felt intoxicated, overcome by pleasures beyond me yet somehow in me. I breathed deeply the fragrance of wild fruits and flowers I could not see. I could even taste something—as if I'd taken a hungry bite of firm, moist fruit, as if the blue citrus had whetted my appetite for something beyond it.

Suddenly the wind changed, and the stench of burning garbage assaulted me. I winced. In the wind I caught lonely cries, desperate wails. I put my hands over my ears. My tongue tasted sulfur, like the breath of the flying beast.

Then, just as suddenly, I tasted sweet citrus again and smelled flowers. The laughter erupted, and I heard music that grabbed me inside, fueling desire and imagination, bringing me to the verge of singing, though I couldn't find the words.

Then it was all swept away in an instant by the stench, the haunting wails, and the sickening sulfur. My stomach heaved. I jerked my head violently.

Then it was gone. All of it.

I could hear nothing except the quiet of the gentle breeze caressing the valley, the road, and the mountains beyond. I inhaled deeply for the smells. Nothing. I rolled my tongue, searching for the tastes. Nothing. I felt as if I stood in a bland sterile waiting room, a nondescript hallway world between two real worlds.

What seemed undeniably real a few moments earlier had vanished, and the present reality—though beautiful in its own right—seemed empty and lifeless by comparison.

Am I going crazy?

I fell to the ground and started crying. I was as frightened and frustrated by my tears as by whatever was causing them. Nick Seagrave *crying?*

I felt terrified by something I'd never before considered—the picture of myself teetering on the edge of eternity. Dizzy and unbalanced, I wavered between two worlds I could neither see nor touch but which I'd just heard and smelled and tasted.

Had I always lived on the in-between, sandwiched by two universes as incompatible as water and fire, yet each only a shifting of the wind away, each so close as to soak my hair or singe my eyebrows? Was all my life only a split second removed from the long tomorrow, a heartbeat away from the great beyond?

I drove away the questions and forced myself to stop crying. I would not bend to the insanity that pressed upon me.

I stood again, readied myself. If this was a game, I would play it hard until I won. I'd find my way out of here, back to a reality I could take charge of. The business at hand was to get somewhere. But where? I thought of the triangle on the cave wall. "Forward." I wasn't used to taking directions from writing on walls—it could be a trick, leading to a trap or ambush. But I was ready to push on, and the road of red dust stretched out before me. Roads led to people, houses, cities—and other roads. I'd go forward and find my way…somewhere.

While I scoped out the terrain, I carefully removed my shirt-sleeve bandage, starched with dry blood, then gently massaged my neck.

From where I stood facing the valley, the red road appeared to slope down from a narrow, shadowed canyon behind me to my right, then skim across the valley floor spread before me. A river snaked alongside much of this stretch of road—at least I wouldn't die of thirst. Up ahead, just before the road began ascending the far mountainside, it curved around a small, thick grove of oaks. Beyond this shady bend the road was hidden for a while, then reappeared higher up the slope. Whatever lay beyond that, I would soon discover.

Curiously, a long shadow fell across the land, roughly pointing the direction of the red road, but though I turned this way and that, I couldn't identify its source.

A rush of energy and adventure overtook me. I scurried down the rocky hillside to the red road, vaguely aware of a dull clanging in my left pocket, metal against metal. I was too enthralled with my journey to reach in and find out what it was.

The longer I walked on the red road the more my knees loosened. They felt stronger than they had in years. My stride became wedded to this course like a locomotive's wheels to the rails. The drive to reach this road's end gave me a racer's gait. I ran, forgetting everything except shortening the distance in front and adding it behind.

As the road entered the oak grove, a smudge of smoke just a hundred feet to the north brought me to a halt. A small group of people talked and laughed around a fire.

I decided at once to hide and study these people from a distance, to gain whatever advantage I could.

Too late. I'd already been spotted by one of them. He bounded my direction. As he came closer, I could see he was a tall man, muscular and handsome with a neatly trimmed copper beard. He wore sandals and an emerald toga, cinched at his slender waist with a braided red cord. Though his dress was like a statesman's from another era, he somehow appeared modern and fashionable. "Welcome, traveler," he called in a rich clear voice, smiling broadly.

I wanted to grill him with a dozen questions, starting with, "Where are we?" and "How did I get here?" and "Who are you?" and "Where are you going?" But being a veteran negotiator, I didn't want to reveal too much about myself and my ignorance.

"Call me Joshua," he said, extending his arm. I was struck with the strong grip of his big right hand and couldn't help staring into his eyes. They were morning-glory eyes, radiant blue windows of experience and knowledge and promise, deep-set eyes I could get lost in.

"Rough journey so far?" he asked, still smiling.

Self-consciously, I considered my wounded neck, matted hair, torn and bloodstained shirt, splattered pants, and mud-caked boots. If image was everything, I was nothing.

I shrugged, trying to decide how much to say. "I took a fall."

"I understand," Joshua said. He swept his arm toward the others. "We're preparing a meal, and you're just in time to eat with us."

The moment he said it I smelled the rising aroma of baked bread and cooked meat and mouthwatering spices. I was famished.

"Come on over, so everyone can get to know you," Joshua said.

I looked closer at the circle of his companions around the fire. An old woman started singing off-key, "The morning was bright, the burden light." She held a walking stick, swaying it in time with her music.

"Eat and rest with us awhile," Joshua said. "Then we'd love to have you travel with us."

I enjoyed every part of the meal, especially the fresh bread and dessert of wild grapes. The woman, who had sung the whole time I ate, finally ended her song and looked over at me, as did the others.

"Such a wonderful path," she called out in a lilting voice, "so right for this bright day." She gazed down and traced circles with the end of her walking stick in the gray dust of the well-worn trail.

"A splendid path, don't you think?" she asked her companions. They nodded and mumbled their assent, staring down with her into the dust. They all looked glassy-eyed, including the woman.

"You haven't said whether you'll travel with us," Joshua said to me.

"Thanks for the invitation. But I think…for now, I should walk the red road a bit farther." I hesitated, then added, "And I really want to move quickly. I need to get somewhere."

Joshua put his arm around me. "Go if you must," he said, then gave me a solemn look. "But be careful who you trust. Skia is beautiful, but it is not always safe."

His words gave me a shiver. Skia? What did he mean? This was a man with inside information, and I wanted to know what he knew. Still, for some reason I held back from asking him.

"I'll be careful," I said. "I hope to see you again."

"You will. Count on it." Joshua smiled warmly. "Here, take some fresh bread with you."

He handed me a leather sack with drawstrings. I took it and stepped away, enjoying its wonderful yeasty scent.

I headed back up toward the red road. After walking fifty feet, I turned around. Joshua smiled broadly and waved his great right arm, bronzed and powerful.

Did I make the right choice? Will I regret it?

I stepped back on the red road. I kept thinking about Joshua. Three hours after parting, alone and uncertain, I debated whether to turn back. But by now he and the others would be long gone, and I didn't even know which direction they were traveling. Going back would cost me valuable time, while every forward step on the red road at least took me *somewhere.*

I despised the emptiness, the loneliness I felt, and cursed the decision that caused it. I questioned the conquer mode that compelled me to launch out on my own. Still, my instincts had always served me well. Hadn't they?

As I walked, the road became barren, less and less grass and no flowers, but up ahead I saw first one tree, then several, then more and more. The road led me into a grove of thick trees that looked something like mottled oaks and ashes intermingled with taller firs and pines, sharing the same turf, integrated with one another. At first they provided a pleasant relief from the beating red sun. But as I continued to walk, the boughs of the trees dropped lower and lower, creating a living roof so dark and thick it seemed twilight.

The trees encroached farther and farther into the road, pushing me to the middle. I couldn't believe this way had been often traveled, for if it had, surely the branches would not be so untamed, jabbing at me as they were. They kept poking my neck and ribs and got caught in my backpack. The trees gathered in so close I felt surrounded by wooded bullies. I considered turning back, but I'd been walking in the trees for a couple of hours. I'd invested too much to go back now.

The farther I walked, the more gnarled the trees became, knotty and twisted and contorted. They seemed to lean toward me in the darkness, poking and prodding. Wild and unruly, with interlacing limbs, the trees ganged up on me, brimming with attitude, as if I had no right to stroll their turf. Something brushed my face, and I hit it with my arm. It bent back and struck me just as I'd struck it. I felt certain something was there, something more than trees, something over them, under them, or perhaps in them. My spine tingled.

I heard something. What? Faint murmurs and taunts and accusations in some foul language? I shuddered. Turning, I saw behind me two eyes in the dark. Animal? No—these were intelligent but lidless eyes, ever-peering, as if waiting to find weakness and exploit it. I wasn't sure how I knew that, but I picked up my pace.

Twigs like fingers poked at my eyes. I swatted them and cut my hand, feeling blood flow in the darkness. Grit and needles and moss and who knew what else kept crawling down the collar of my shirt and collected on my skin, sticking to the sweat. Suddenly something fell down my collar and moved. I felt things skitter under my shirt, as if little spiders were crawling up and down my spine.

"Get away!" I shouted.

I didn't dare remove my shirt. I hit myself on the back, flailing my arms wildly. I dropped down on the road and rolled on my back, trying to smash whatever it was. Finally I stopped, embarrassed.

If Marci and the kids had been here, I would have teased them, scared them. But now it was I who was terrified. I got up and brushed myself off. I looked around, certain no one could see me in that wooded tomb, yet feeling silly. Nick Seagrave was no coward.

I'd walked another fifty feet when something groped me. I ran. Something grabbed my foot, and I tripped and fell at the base of one of the trees, caught in a root. I felt something cold and slimy on my face. I peered into the darkness, barely able to make out a grayish green moss covering a tree stem. It was covered with slimy, shaggy growths, some of them now attached to my face. I wiped and spit and stood up, drawing up my shirt and burying my face in it. I stopped suddenly when I heard windy whispers.

"Who's there?" I shouted, trying to sound brave. "Show yourself!"

Silence.

I walked cautiously, tempted to force my way through the trees on one side or the other to find another way. Instead, bent low to keep my face from the boughs, I walked forward, shivering and cursing, poising my hands in front of me, ready to engage in martial arts or at least a good fistfight. I found myself wishing not for my shotgun as much as a blowtorch. I pictured myself scorching the trees to keep them off me and get some revenge.

I vowed if I ever got out I'd never go into a place like that again, not alone.

Finally the trees began to thin, and a welcome red glow peeked through the wooden roof. It appeared to be late afternoon. Now I could see the road again under me. I ran the last hundred yards out into the open, pulling off my shirt and falling into the soft plush grass beside the road. A curious hedgehoglike creature with over-big eyes stared at me and cocked his head as I rolled in his grass. I laughed and made a face, and he ran from me.

I'd never felt so relieved to come out of the darkness and into the light. I laughed some more, then looked back at the trees. I stopped laughing. It hadn't been my imagination. There had been something else, something invisible, something sinister, something more than trees. I'd felt it as surely as I now felt the sun on my face.

Hours later, still headed what I'd defined as west, I crested a slope and saw another group of travelers in front of me. I nearly shouted, pausing only to straighten and tuck in my grimy, smelly shirt and try to comb my hair, at least to get the remaining needles and debris out of it. Then I ran to catch them. They heard me, and at the same time all turned and looked. I stopped running and smiled. Friendliness might buy me some information.

The travelers numbered seven. My analytical mind went to work at once, studying each person as if we sat at a negotiating table. The two young women, maybe teenagers, were identical twins, ebony skinned and beautiful. The third woman was fiftyish, tall and elegant, almost courtly.

Of the men, two were young, one middle-aged, one old.

The white-haired old man stood out most. He had the face of February, full of frost and darkness. He was dressed in a tattered, cream-colored toga, stained with sweat and dirt; his heavy beard was unkempt, combed and shaped only by wind and sun and rain. He stared at me as I drew near. I felt the blood rising in my face and reached to hide the twitch.

One of the twins greeted me in a language I didn't understand, her soft cheek lines erupting into a smile. I nodded awkwardly. Her brown eyes flashed curiosity.

"Her name's Malaiki," said a freckled young man whose chestnut hair formed into corkscrew curls. "Her sister's Salama. I'm Mason." He extended his arm and shook my hand eagerly. I liked him.

"You look ready for a change of clothes," he said, trying not to stare at my attire. "We can take care of that."

I nodded, grateful they asked no questions.

Mason introduced me to the others. Quon was a brown-skinned, wiry young man with a haircut that reminded me of Moe in the Three Stooges. He seemed quiet, easy to ignore. David, middle-aged, with a Clark Gable mustache, was sharp looking, fit, and stylish. I picked him as the natural leader. I'd need to get to know him, to position myself.

"And this is Victoria."

"Pleased to meet you," the tall stately woman said, nodding in a way that suggested a curtsy without bending the knees. She touched an earring by her silver hair. Her mouth was delicate, her complexion like a china doll's. Her pants and blouse were elegant. In another era I could picture her attended to by servants. A classy lady.

Finally Mason pointed to the old man. His egg-shaped head was buried under flowing white hair and a beard except for a four-inch bald spot on the crown. What should have been growing there had been rerouted through his ears and nose. Definitely not a candidate for the cover of *Gentleman's Quarterly*.

"Shadrach," Mason said. "We call him Shad—and sometimes other names."

Mason winked, confirming what I'd sensed. The old man was a few sandwiches short of a picnic…maybe more than a few. I looked at Shadrach's gaunt, red-blotched cheeks, flaring nostrils, and blurry eyes, yellowed by infringing cataracts. The lights were barely on, and I got the impression nobody was home. I didn't offer him my hand—I figured whatever he had might be contagious.

Shad asked in a gravelly voice, "What shall we call you, child of clay?"

Child of clay? "Actually," I said, "my dad's name was Will."

Mason laughed.

Shadrach stared at me incomprehensively. "You were born of dust mixed with the water of life. Like all of us you are clay in the Potter's hands."

None of the others seemed surprised at this outburst of obscurity. I smiled. "Uh—sure, right. Whatever. The name's Nick Seagrave." I determined not to say more, though everyone's eyes were asking for it.

"Join us," the old geezer said. It sounded more like a command than an invitation and made me wish again I'd accepted Joshua's offer. Shad turned and resumed his pace down the red road. The others fell in behind him.

What have I gotten myself into?

3

MASON GAVE MY SHOULDER a friendly nudge. "We'll get you cleaned up after we stop for the night."

I nodded but said nothing, staying at the back with everyone in view. We walked past what looked like overlarge plum trees, one of them filled with chirping birds shaped like meadowlarks but half again as large, exotically colored with reds and oranges and yellows and greens. The birds sang like a choir, harmonizing and blending beautifully.

Malaiki handed me a long orange vegetable of some sort, not a carrot, more like a sweet corn but without kernels. I took a bite.

"Tastes good," I said. I hesitated, then took one of the blue fruits out of my pack and handed it to her.

"Senaba!" she said.

I looked at her blankly—did that mean "Thanks"?

"Senaba's the name of the fruit," Mason said. "It's her favorite. Mine too."

I reached into my pack and pulled out one for Mason, not letting on I had four more. As we walked, I continued sizing up these travelers. Who would be my ally? My adversary? Who could I trust?

Gray clouds moved in rapidly on us. Being from Oregon I knew what was about to happen. After a few light drops, the clouds broke open, and we ran for cover under some trees. It was still warm, but already everyone's hair hung lank and dripping on their foreheads. I consoled myself that now everyone looked almost as messy as I did.

I sat near David under a fir tree, while the others took refuge under a thick maple. David handed me a thin, clear rain slicker from his pack. Probably fifty, David struck me as educated, confident, not easily persuaded, a man's man. I imagined him at a big table hammering out a business deal. He wore the best hiking shoes money could buy. His was the finest backpack, large and sturdy, with lots of zippered pockets and two slots holding his water bottles. The others had worn and sagging backpacks, without frames, and fanny packs or little satchels or canteens hanging from their belts.

From David's belt hung one of those elaborate multipurpose pocketknives with assorted tools tucked in with the blades. Another device hung from his belt on the other side.

"What's that?" I asked him.

"A position locator. I like to know exactly where I am."

Yeah. Me too.

After a half-hour of small talk, in which I played some verbal poker with David, doing my share of bluffing, the rain broke. The next moment the sun came out, just in time to begin to sink, its enormous size tripling the duration of a normal sunset. I saw ahead of us, disappearing into the sunset, the strange long shadow, but I was still unable to identify what caused it. I lost myself in the twilight, a stunning bird's-egg blue with tints of green and red. That red sun was an unyielding reminder that I was an alien, a stranger, a pilgrim in this world. So too were the awesome double and triple rainbows I now watched slack-jawed. They had not only reds and yellows and greens but blues and at least three colors I had no names for—and all this on the verge of nightfall!

As the sun set and the frogs and crickets struck up their chorus, David pulled out of his pack an amazingly compact tent of paper-thin but, he assured me, extremely durable fabric. Victoria took out a similar smaller tent from her pack for her and the twins. We set up camp alongside some firs.

Quon built a fire, apparently a delegated area of expertise for him. And while the fire worked on producing some good coals, Quon skinned a small animal on a flat rock, slicing it up, then putting it in a small metal pan he'd pulled from his pack, alongside some red onions. I didn't ask what animal had sacrificed his life for our meal, nor did anyone volunteer. Dinner wasn't a chimichanga with sour cream, guacamole, and salsa, but it wasn't as bad as it looked. On the cuisine scale, it fell somewhere above airplane food.

Quon had loaned me a tin coffee cup, a bowl, and an ancient aluminum spoon, worn and beaten. I wondered how many other travelers had used that pathetic old spoon. When we cleaned up at a nearby stream afterward, I washed the bowl and spoon and brought them back to Quon.

"Keep them," he said. "You'll need them."

We gathered back around the fire and warmed our hands as the evening grew cool and the air slightly damp.

Mason, true to his word, brought me a pair of loose-fitting khaki pants and a thin, light gray sweatshirt much like his own. After changing behind one of the tents, I gladly threw my rags into Quon's fire.

The dull pain in my neck still throbbed, but gentle probing with my fingers satisfied me the wound was on its way to closing up. While I massaged around it, I looked up at the stars emerging in the blackness that hovered over the greens and blues of the horizon. Those same greens and blues spilled over the rolling hills, a breath-taking sight. The larger moon, a red-hued crescent, grew brighter by the moment; its identically lit companion, still close to the horizon, barely peeked out of the darkening sky.

Wait—what was that? Something sparkled on the horizon, a blurry white light that flickered in and out of view. One moment it was there, the next gone. The sight jarred me. I was both spellbound and frustrated as lines of reasoning I'd depended on all my life had suddenly dissolved.

I sent a whisper to the sky: "What is that? What's going on? Why am I here?"

"Caught you!"

Startled, I turned and saw Mason. Why did he say that? As he stepped closer, I tried to turn my neck away. But even in this dusky light, he'd seen the wound.

He stepped around me to look closer at my neck. "What the heck did that to you?"

"A fall."

"Not long ago, looks like."

"No."

"Well, Nick," he said in a low tone, glancing to each side. "This road hasn't been a picnic for any of us."

I felt his thumb and forefinger pressing on either side of the wound. "We'll get a fresh bandage on this in the morning. Meanwhile come on over by the fire."

"How does the economy work here? Where do you get extra clothes? And silverware? And food?"

"You *are* new here, aren't you? Well, we hunt a little, Quon mostly, and the fruits and vegetables along the way are fair game for anyone. We barter for most of the freeze-dried and packaged food. There's an occasional town along the way. The merchants trade with us. I swapped my watch and wedding ring for most of the stuff I have, plus a lot more I've used along the way. Looks like you don't have a wedding ring, do you? Too bad."

I stared at the ring finger of my left hand, then stroked my watch and started making a mental list of what I wanted—a foam rubber pad to sleep on and maybe some sunglasses and a private food supply and more clothes and some tennis shoes and...but I'd have to carry it all on my back, wouldn't I? I wondered if they had Advil in this world. It seemed too silly to ask.

We joined the others sitting around the blaze. Shad gazed into the flames as if he were looking through them. He was hunched, probably three inches shorter than he'd been in his prime. His left eyelid fluttered. I thought he was winking but then decided it was involuntary, perhaps from weariness. He looked like he'd been on the road a long time. Too long.

I heard a sucking noise as he opened his large wrinkled mouth. "Join us," he said.

I thought I did.

"The way is difficult."

Sounds like a barrel of laughs.

"Reward is to be shared and so is hardship. The red road of Thuros is meant to be walked, but not alone."

Thuros? He spoke in one cryptic, fortune-cookie statement after another. I heard demands in his voice, not warmth. I stood to move to the other side of the fire. I had many questions but didn't trust him enough to ask them.

"You're welcome to stay in our tent," Mason said. Inside the tent, on hard ground, we lay too close for my liking, but it sure beat the cave. David was snoring, and Mason lay stone still. I wished I could ask them where we were and why. I lay there thinking again about Joshua and his troupe. No doubt he knew his location. What was Skia? What was Thuros? Why was I unwilling to risk asking the questions that plagued me?

I listened to the soothing sounds of crickets and frogs, which gave me the illusion I was back home on a hunting trip, holed up with my buddies Barry, Jack, and T. J. I held my breath a few times when I thought I heard a flapping tarp. It was only the tent door fluttering in the breeze. I still felt I was being watched, and I looked out in the moonlight to see just a foot away a large frog with bumpy, lime-green skin, four spread-out rubbery toes on both of his front feet, and bulgy red eyes with black teardrop pupils.

"You know more than I do, don't you?" I whispered to him. We studied each other for a minute before I put my head down. Stray stones beneath the tent floor bored into my back. I stood up and stomped them into the ground.

All those hours of hiking in the fresh air settled upon me like a warm blanket, and even without a pillow, I slept.

We rose early, when the light was like rosy honey painting the hillsides, which looked like gentle ocean waves frozen in place. Breakfast consisted of stale biscuits, jerky, and some "potato pearls," as Quon called them, soaked in water over the fire.

"Like the jerky?" Mason asked, smiling too broadly.

"It's okay," I said. "Why? What is it?"

"Possum—Quon trapped it a few weeks ago."

I put it down. After one bite of a biscuit that could have broken a tooth, I pulled out the bread Joshua gave me and shared it with the group. It was the highlight of the meal, along with a senaba fruit from my pack, which I managed to sneak discreetly when getting up for a stretch. It washed away the jerky's taste.

After a quick cleanup, David looked at his Rolex and said, "Time to get moving."

He stepped confidently ahead. I felt relieved the old geezer wasn't leading today. There was too much snow on that old roof to trust it.

We walked up a steep bank and crossed over to a magnificent view of lowlands, dotted with clumps of tall firs and smaller fruit trees, which in the distance melted away into a brownish green woodland haze. I saw faint traces of various roads cutting across the land, crosswise to the long shadow, intersecting the red road.

Shad moved closer to me, and I squeezed as far to the left of the road as I could. He smelled like last year's ham, like the stale air of the nursing home where my father died. Not getting the message, Shad inched in closer like an overfriendly and underbathed stranger on a bus who didn't understand personal space.

"Tell me, Nick," he said, sounding like a creaky gate. "What do you think of your life?"

What do I think of my life? What does a lamppost think of a dog? And while we're asking personal questions, what lunatic bin did you escape from?

I stared at his mottled leather face that looked like it had been hoisted up in the sun and wind and long forgotten. He reminded me of Captain Ahab, and for a moment I felt like Moby Dick, dodging his harpoon. I shrugged my shoulders and said nothing.

Was the old man trying to set me up? I stepped forward, next to Mason, using him as a screen. Mason was laughing about something with Victoria. Her laugh was delightful, her eyes crescents when she smiled.

I walked up next to Malaiki, or was it Salama? No, Malaiki, the friendlier one. Her pixie face peered downward. She studied the red road, examining footprints and marks and stones like an explorer. She periodically uttered animated expressions, still unintelligible to me.

"I think you're hearing Swahili," Mason whispered.

Had she come here directly from Africa? Was there more than one doorway into this world? Malaiki was a follower, I decided, not a leader. If there were a power play in this group, her allegiance might be useful. I determined to gain her trust.

Quon, muscular and compact, came up alongside me, wiping his knife on a rag hanging from his belt. He looked at me from the corner of his eye, then pretended not to notice me. Insecure and moody, I decided.

I saw a bevy of quail, and Quon stealthily pulled a bow off the side of his pack, inserted an arrow, crouched down, and then disappeared into the tall grass, sneaking up on them. I thought there was no way he'd get anything without a shotgun, but he returned ten minutes later, running up to us with one large quail.

"Congratulations," I said. I was relieved to know I could eat dinner tonight without my imagination running away with me.

When we reached a forty-foot swaying rope bridge over a gully, we took it one at a time, not sure how much weight it would bear. The road curved up to more rises ahead. Beyond them I could see more high hills and a few mountains, notably the grim flanks of a jagged mountain to the west, which Mason called Mount Peirasmos. When we hit high spots, I could catch glimpses of valleys between mountains, at times seeing where the red road appeared to cut through gaps in the hills, often alongside the long sourceless shadow. But there was much terrain I couldn't see, my view blocked by the higher hills and mountains, especially Peirasmos. What lay beyond them, where I couldn't see? Where were we going? Was I the only one who didn't have a clue? And how could I find out without giving myself away? I had to try something.

"So," I said, loud enough for all to hear but trying to sound casual, "what's everybody looking forward to most on this journey?"

The moment I spoke, I regretted it—it sounded so silly. But Quon, the quiet one, spoke up with a zest that surprised me. "Home," he said. Malaiki turned to him with a strong affirmative nod. *Home* must be an English word she understood. I wondered what it really meant to her and to Quon.

My question wasn't exactly the discussion stimulator I envisioned. The group seemed to buy silently into Quon's answer, offering no others.

Home? What was home to them? Or to me?

And if it was home we wanted, why were we traveling away from where we'd come?

We trudged up a slope, steadying ourselves on the branches of stout hemlocks. At the top the road began bending through sandstone boulders and rock pillars scattered here and there.

While the others stopped and rested, I stepped out near a wide ledge to take in the view and get my bearings. We were closer to the lowlands, where the many roads were now more clearly etched on the landscape.

Everyone was eerily quiet as a wave of light seemed to wash all around us, as if someone had lifted a veil from the sun, a veil I hadn't known was there.

"Look behind you," Mason said, pointing, his voice quivering.

I looked back to the east, where we'd come from. Rising up beyond the crimson haze of distant ridges were skyscrapers of gleaming glass reflecting the sun.

The skyscrapers must have been out of our sight before, where the road was lower. Or were my powers of vision now multiplying, so I was beginning to see what I never could before and in different dimensions?

Even now surrealistic details quickly fell into focus. I saw that the skyscrapers were the center of a vast city, and in each skyscraper and house and apartment were what appeared to be thrones. People sat on the thrones, each the ruler of his own domain. This place sang to me.

A great mountain, crusted with ancient black and red lava flows, towered above the city, sheltering it. The cave I'd spent my first night in had to have been near the base of that mountain. This must have been the city whose smoke I'd seen. I wished now I had followed the smoke and gone there.

With heightened powers of hearing that startled me, I detected in the city triumphant songs in countless languages. Pride welled up in me as if I myself had been one of the city's builders.

"Behold, at the foot of Mount Hagias: Babel," said Shad's rumbling voice. "The City of Darkness." What was he talking about? I turned and saw him pull an old book from his satchel. He mumbled words from it. "Not all is as it appears."

I looked out again toward the city. But the light was changing, no, the *buildings* were changing into grimy prison towers, decaying and smoking tenements. Chaotic clanging noises filled the thick air.

Then I saw something bizarre—a vast web stretched across the city. From it hung people, some struggling to get free, others poisoned and dying, others bound up head-to-toe in cocoons of death. My blood chilled as I wondered if a gigantic spider was about to crawl over the horizon.

What was happening? I turned to Shad. "You're a hypnotist, aren't you, old man? Or a magician."

He was a kill-joy at the very least. I turned away from him, not waiting for an answer. The others were moving up the road, and I joined them.

Thirty yards ahead, around the bend shaded by the rock towers, we caught sight of another city to the west, rising up beyond rolling green hills graced by the ribbon of the red road. It was high on a mountain ridge, much farther west and slightly south of Mount Peirasmos. Silently we stared at it.

The distant city's buildings looked safe and solid enough, but cold and oppressive. In a moment my heightened vision pierced the walls, but this city was without thrones; no, there was a throne, but only one, there at the center. I couldn't clearly see who sat on it, but my intuition told me it was a dreadful tyrant, intolerant, squashing creativity and initiative. I envisioned him granting his subjects freedom enough to make a mistake just so he could condemn them for it and command their execution.

How did I know all this? I couldn't explain it, but I was as certain of it as I could be.

So this was what awaited us on the red road! I was aghast. I had long ago learned to trust my instincts, and they told me this city was a monument to the pride of some self-proclaimed, glory-hungry sovereign who delighted in robbing men of their dignity.

I smelled Shadrach next to me again and heard him say in a measured tone, "Behold, nestled on Mount Aletheas: Charis, the City of Light."

Light? He was even more a fool than I thought. Why was he unable to see what I saw so clearly?

"Do you hear it?" Malaiki gasped, her face glowing. A few seconds went by before it struck me that I'd understood her words for the first time.

"Music!" she exclaimed with enchanting fervor. "Songs of life and learning, choruses of pleasure and adventure! In a thousand languages!"

I heard nothing. Who was she trying to kid and why?

She broke into dancing, Salama joined her, then Quon and Mason. Shad was dancing too, an unlikely sight to say the least. I thought I heard some distant music myself, then stole a glance at Victoria, hoping she felt like a spin and ready to join her if she did. But she stood back, and I couldn't read her expression.

Malaiki and the others kept looking toward the city even as they twirled and high-stepped. Following their gaze, I saw the coldness of the place replaced by light and warmth and by what seemed to be the radiant energy of people celebrating. I barely heard the music, but now I heard a geyser of laughter exploding from a fountain of joy. It was the same laughter I'd heard when I stepped out of the cave.

For a moment I felt torn between two cities, as if I were the center knot of a rope being yanked from both sides in a cosmic game of tug of war.

A surge of caution overtook me. I could not, would not let that laughter grab me this time. Nick Seagrave wasn't a marionette on a string to be yanked around by someone or something else. I stopped dancing. I had to stay in control.

4

THE BRIGHT CITY SHIMMERED on the horizon, touched by sparkling blues and greens and golds that blended with the sky and sunlight, pulsing in and out of my vision.

Led by Malaiki, who was still skipping and singing, we moved on up the road. I watched Shad. In management, I dealt with my share of eccentric people, including abrasive ones. What was it about this codger that so unnerved me?

"Don't be fooled by him," a voice whispered. I turned and saw no one. What the old man called the City of Light must have been an illusion. Maybe even a trap. If real at all, it would likely prove to be a lair of self-righteous condemners trying to impose their misery on others.

I'd come far enough on the red road now to know it was leading to something I wanted no part of. I'd been wrong about that shimmering slippery city in the distance—I refused to be drawn there any longer. If that place was this group's idea of home, I could live without it. The quicker I ditched this crew and struck out to find Joshua or find another way, the better.

The sun persuaded me to take off my jacket, which I tied around my waist. At that moment, as I trailed the rest of the group, I saw strange movements in the three-foot-tall grass on the south side of the road. I froze. The bent grass came nearer and nearer, not in a straight path, but serpentine. Something was coming my way.

Suddenly it stopped, only feet from the road. Peering intently into the grass, I saw two brown eyes staring at me. I stepped backward. It lunged at me.

It was a snow-white puppy with dime-sized black spots, shoulders no more than six inches off the ground. With a disproportionately large head, the pup had the shape and floppy ears and fur length of a Springer spaniel but the markings of a Dalmatian. His nose looked like a little black wall socket. He frolicked over to me, wriggling back and forth, a furry sausage with legs. I picked him up. He couldn't have weighed more than eight pounds. I looked into his chocolate eyes, and he stuck out his nose to mine. He licked me frantically. As he pressed his neck against mine, I smelled something sweet, like the faint scent of maple syrup.

"What a guy!" I told him. He took the compliment well. "Where'd you come from? There's no one else on the road. You're too little to fend for yourself, aren't you?"

I put him down, and he rolled over on his back, sticking up his legs and kicking. I scratched his spotted tummy until I found the spot that moved his back paws up and down involuntarily, uncontrollably. He groaned in ecstasy. As soon as I stopped scratching, he batted my hand, insisting on more. I complied.

"Looks like you've been adopted," Victoria said, laughing. "He's got you trained already."

We all watched him as he turned circles, chasing his tail, trying to bite it. He finally chomped down on the tail end and squealed, ran to my feet, and pressed himself against me, peering out into the grass as if some horrid enemy had bitten him.

He kept nuzzling my feet until I pretended to ignore him. He lifted his oversized front paws and batted them against my ankle, looking up, trying to meet my eyes. Suddenly a big yellow butterfly flew by over the grass off the road. He froze, pointing at it, picture perfect.

"Look," I shouted, louder than I intended, sounding like a mother whose little boy just won a spelling bee.

"A mighty hunter," Victoria said.

"Maybe I can teach him to hunt quail or rabbits," Quon added.

"We're not keeping him," David said.

"I'm keeping him," I said, picking him up and cradling him. End of discussion.

I hadn't had a dog since I was a boy—Jupiter, my golden retriever, who went and died on me. Maybe that's why I could never bring myself to get another one.

What was it about Jupiter that made me feel more comfortable with him than with most people? He made so few demands—was that it? Or was it that he saw me at my worst and still loved me? No person could ever do that, could they? I could yell at Jupiter, threaten him, send him into ice water to fetch a stick, and swat him when he devoured my lunch bag, and he'd look at me like I'd done him the biggest favor in the world just because I recognized his existence.

The little white dog looked at me Jupiter-like, pledging his undying loyalty.

"What are you going to call him?" Salama asked.

"I don't know."

"How about Jasper?" Malaiki asked.

I shook my head. "Frodo. His name is Frodo."

We started walking again. After twenty minutes or so I picked up Frodo, whose little legs weren't quite ready for the pace and distances we were going. He looked into my eyes gratefully.

Suddenly, Shad was there beside me, his ear hair rustling in the wind.

"Nick, I must tell you about the chasm."

"Chasm?"

As much as I wanted information, I didn't want to be one-on-one with the old man. I jogged ahead to catch the others. With Frodo's arrival, I'd postponed my decision on when and how to leave the group. But I wasn't about to let Shad work a spell on me. The old man came up behind me again, breathing heavily.

"The chasm...a vast abyss!" he called. "It separates roadwalkers from Charis, the City of Light."

His tone was spooky enough to get me to glance out again over the valley.

"I don't see a chasm!" I called back roughly.

"And the blind do not see the sun!" he shouted.

I picked up my pace, leaving him behind again.

"He speaks often of this chasm," Victoria whispered, touching my elbow and giving me a knowing look. "If it was so large, you'd think we'd have no trouble seeing it."

"We're getting closer," Malaiki said. Her voice, so clear and near, was like a splashing stream. "And perhaps soon we'll see the King!" Her dark eyes searched mine. "Have *you* ever seen him?"

Seen the King? I didn't even know there was one.

Malaiki seemed to know instantly why I was silent—she looked disappointed. I felt terrible about having no answer for her, as if I was letting down my own daughter, something I'd had considerable experience at.

Wait a minute. Maybe I *had* seen the King. Joshua! A wise man, a leader, warm, full of experience and insight and generosity and magnetism. He certainly carried himself with confidence and authority, yes, even nobility.

"Actually, I may have met this king," I said to Malaiki.

"Tell me about him," she said.

I didn't get the chance—a captivating melody sounded in the wind, sung by a strong male voice. We all turned. A man walked toward us on the road, alone.

Was it Joshua? I waved my hand and started to call his name. No—my heart dropped. This stranger was short and homely, rough-hewn and weather-beaten. His oversized shirt and pants were stained with dirt and sweat and flecked with what appeared to be sawdust and woodchips. Slung over his shoulder was an old white robe, shed because of the afternoon sun.

Something about the stranger commanded everyone's attention. No sooner had he joined us than he stepped to the head of the entourage as if he were taking over.

Who does this shabby woodsman think he is?

The rest of the group fell in step beside and behind him, so I followed, cautious but curious.

"What were you discussing?" he asked. He looked over his shoulder, and his deep brown eyes—so dark I couldn't see the pupils—caught mine. I felt like a third grader called to the front of the class, not knowing how to answer.

"We were talking about…a king," I muttered.

"And what can you tell me about him?"

"Not much," I answered. "I may have seen him without knowing it. I'm not sure."

"Not sure?" the Woodsman repeated. I heard his doubt, his superior smugness, and I hated it.

He led at a fast pace, but we managed to keep up. Grass and stones and trees along the road faded into a dreamlike dimness while the road itself stayed vibrantly red.

"The King," the Woodsman said, "is the fountain of life." Just then a clear-running brook sprang up beside the road, bubbling and alive, sparkling in the sunlight.

"The King is a rose," he said, "full of beauty but also thorns." No sooner did he say this than the air was rich with the fragrance of blooms lining the brook's banks.

I was stunned by these…coincidences? Or was he another magician, a sorcerer?

"The King is the true vine, the tree of life, the giver of grain," he said. We rounded a corner, and before us spread a vista of golden wheat fields bordered by vineyards and orchards, overflowing with ripened fruit.

"The King is light."

The sun went supernova, then retracted. My knees buckled and I covered my face. A wave of heat enveloped me as if I stood in the mouth of a giant blast furnace. When I opened my eyes again, the blue sky exploded with stars, filling the daylight canopy with points of colored flame before they hid themselves away again.

The road became steeper, but the Woodsman kept his pace. Malaiki stayed at his side, never taking her gaze from him. It struck me as inappropriate, and I resented the stranger's hold on her.

Old Shadrach was on the Woodsman's other side, with Mason and Quon immediately behind. Victoria kept her distance, while David stayed back beside me, studying one of his travel maps.

"The King is a singer and a song," the stranger said. Melody from somewhere filled the air. Keyboards, trumpets, harps, and voices echoed along the ridge as we climbed among evergreens.

"The King is a lamb," the newcomer said. I looked to a nearby hilltop, rising like a bald head out of the woods. On it stood a solitary sheep. I could hear its bleating.

A lamb? Who could respect a king that weak and helpless?

Suddenly a ferocious roar hit me like a hard wind. There on the hillside crouched a huge lion. He looked down at us with head tilted and jaws open wide. The savage beast leaned forward and threatened to pounce. We all jumped away and the women screamed. Everyone ran but the Woodsman.

"The King," cried the Woodsman from behind us, "is a lion!"

I ran at the front of the pack, with frequent glances over my shoulder at the lion. He disappeared from view when we rounded a corner, and after running another hundred feet we slowed down and bent over to catch our breath.

Who would want to serve a king as terrifying as that?

With my hands on my knees, I looked up to see the sky burst into flame with evening colors. Then I heard a whimper and saw something low to the ground running around the corner after us.

"Frodo! I forgot all about you. Sorry, boy!" I strode toward him then bent down. He ran at full speed and leapt into my outstretched arms. His lips curled back exposing his teeth in a ridiculous grin that didn't stop. He insisted I hold him, and when I put him on the ground, he was inconsolable, threading in and out between my legs as I walked, whimpering and begging.

Quon gave me a long strip of cloth which I hung over my shoulder to make a carrier Frodo could rest in, against my chest. It reminded me of the little front carriers I'd used to transport Amy and Brian when they were small.

Before us was a quiet village of only a few houses, the closest one a dark wood A-frame with smoke puffing out of its cracked brick chimney. The stranger finally slowed his pace. The big mahogany door in the closest house swung open, and a light glowed inside. Quon ran ahead and rushed in. Shad and Malaiki followed, while the rest of us approached more slowly. I was relieved to see the newcomer stay on the road, walking on by himself.

Quon stuck his head out the door, took a nervous look, then bolted back toward the road.

"Wait!" he called to the stranger. "Please stay with us! We must hear more."

Speak for yourself.

The Woodsman turned back and entered the door Quon held open for him.

"He would have gone on without us," Quon whispered to me, a look of desperation in his eyes.

Cautiously, I entered the house. In a gray stone-walled room a polished oak table was set for us with a single loaf of bread in the middle and next to it a wooden chalice filled with a dark juice, perhaps senaba. The bread was smooth and well-rounded, but I was certain it couldn't taste as good as Joshua's. We silently seated ourselves in the straight-backed chairs. Did the others feel as uncomfortable as I did?

The Woodsman took the loaf in his hands. I couldn't keep from staring at it. Was I that hungry?

"The King is the bread of life," he said. I held my breath. In the absolute silence I heard the soft sound of the loaf being slowly broken, but the sound resonated differently as it continued, as if it became something firmer, more solid and alive. A fermented scent permeated the room—it was almost intoxicating.

I gasped involuntarily, noticing for the first time that the man's hands were severely scarred. Hearing my outburst, everyone at the table stared at me. The Woodsman's smoked-glass eyes burned into me. My embarrassment was replaced by a wave of fear and guilt that swept over me as if I were at fault for the accident that had injured his hands. But why should I feel that way? It made me angry.

I got up and stumbled from that suffocating room, knocking over a stool. I was not going to eat with this man. There was something wild and savage about him. He was an explosion waiting to happen, an untamed beast. I saw a storm in his eyes, and I did not want another storm. I felt my migraine coming on again and the pounding from that stupid pressure against my temple.

I passed through the doorway and out to the relief of the twilight. I sucked in the night air.

Suddenly I felt roiling pain in my belly and dropped to my knees, holding my upper stomach and lower chest. It expanded and contracted. Something awful pulsated within me. What was it?

Frodo growled, backing away from me, then barked at whatever was lurking beneath my skin.

I sat there on the road, frightened into speechlessness, watching my skin undulate. I tried to cry out but couldn't make a sound.

I heard footsteps on the road, running toward me, then a familiar voice.

"Nick, are you all right?"

"Joshua!"

5

THE IRON-MUSCLED TRAVELER smiled broadly, pulled me up, and slapped me on the back like an old marine buddy.

"It's great to see you," I told him. Already Joshua's presence— or was it his touch?—quieted my pain and stilled my quivering skin.

"Who's your friend?" he asked, pointing at the dog.

"Frodo."

The two eyed each other suspiciously. I laughed.

I looked at Joshua, eager to ask something I'd regretted not asking him before. "You spoke of Skia. What is it?"

"A name for this world," he said. "It goes by other names as well."

"Like Thuros?"

He nodded. "I prefer Skia. How are things on the road you've chosen?"

"Well, I linked up with other travelers…for a while."

"Oh?"

"Yeah—just long enough to know their destination's not for me. I want to press forward, but I'm not so sure about the red road. I'd like to check out some other options."

"Wise words, friend."

He swept his strong arm across the view spreading before us under the two moons in the twilight. "Nick, I'd be happy to serve as your guide to Skia."

"Would you?" I asked.

"No!" A raspy voice came from behind us like a tossed brick. I groaned as I turned and looked at the white-haired man with pachydermic skin.

"Don't listen to him," Shadrach commanded.

"Spying on me, old codger?"

"Nick will be fine," Joshua said gently, putting his great hand on my shoulder. "And he can choose for himself. It's not for you or me to impose our wills on him."

Stooped like an old tree under winter snow and pointing his bony finger, Shad asked me, "What *do* you choose?"

"I'm going with Joshua," I told him. "I've seen enough of your road."

"The red road is not *my* road. It is *the* road. The only road across Thuros that leads to what you truly want, Nick, even if you don't know it."

"What do you know about what I want?" I shouted. "And what do you care?"

Everything this Neanderthal uttered seemed calculated to inflame me. I hated how he got my goat. Only Joshua's presence kept me from doing something I'd later regret. Even Frodo barked at Shad, defending my honor.

"From where you go, few return!" Shad intoned, sounding like a self-important Shakespearean actor.

"Please, let's be civil," Joshua said. "If Nick can find a better way, you won't begrudge him the search, will you?"

"There *is* no better way."

"I'll be the judge of that," I announced. "I was thinking and choosing for myself long before I met you."

"And where have your thoughts and choices left you?"

"Get a life, old man!" I raked him with my eyes, enraged at his insolence and unnerved by what he appeared to know about me.

I waved him off as Joshua and I stepped away into the night, following a dusty gray path that bore down a steep slope away from the village.

"I'll walk with you," Shad called after us, "to offer counsel and remind you of the way back."

"No, thanks, I'd really rather…"

The bandy-legged fossil lumbered down the path like a mountain goat. He stunk like one too. He glared at Joshua, who laughed and shook his head.

Joshua excused himself and took the codger aside, apparently laying out ground rules for the journey. Shad raised his voice and waved his arms, pointing his gnarled fingers, but I couldn't hear what they were saying.

As the two of them talked, I looked at the landscape below and to the north, amazed at how clearly I could see by the soft pink glow of two moons. The roadside was woven with lilacs and primroses and wild blackberries, with heavy ripe clumps bending the vines. I even saw a few senaba trees not too far down the slope, above the mist, and determined to visit them on the way down. Meanwhile thunderclouds came from the east, rolling in the distance where they grazed ridges. The clouds were lit from within by periodic sheet lightning and a soft, silver glow on top from the reflected moonlight. The storm moved closer to the countryside we were about to enter, already shrouded in mist. While I trembled at its coming, it only added to my excitement.

I felt again the adventuresome spirit of my childhood. I remembered being nestled in my cozy house in Oregon, covered in a blanket, watching through our big picture window as lightning bolts pierced the ground, counting the seconds to the thunder—the thrill I felt when I didn't have time to count before the heavens roared and the house shook. I would gladly endure fear and danger for the sense of wonder I felt, grateful that even if I didn't understand what was much bigger than I, at least it wasn't ignoring me.

I recalled being a twelve-year-old, looking through my telescope to worlds beyond and wondering if there was something more, something waiting to be discovered. Sometimes, less frequently as I grew older, for fleeting moments I seemed to hear music, voices, something or someone from another world. When I walked among the towering firs, or smelled the huckleberry, or lost myself in the ocean, or gazed up to the stars, I felt I was on the verge of discovery, of finding I was no longer on the outside of the universe, but on the inside.

Over the years those dreams had died. But now at last I felt hope rising from their ashes. I took a deep draft of cool sweet air.

Frodo swaggered up to me, a pine cone sticking out of his mouth, looking as proud as if he'd bagged an elk. I picked him up, his tail whapping against both my wrists. Joshua rejoined me, with Shad a few steps behind.

"I've told Shadrach about you," he whispered, "and I asked him to respect your freedom. Hopefully, he'll back off." Joshua pointed toward the downward road, heading north, and said, "Lead the way, my friend."

Lead? You bet!

Though Joshua was my guide, he showed me respect by walking to my side, a step behind me, giving me a sense of control. I liked that. I was in conquer mode, so we marched down the terrain at a fast clip. It was a plunging path filled with sharp turns and lined with thornbushes that kept nipping at my pants legs. A few large brown and green lizards stared up at us from the gray path with unblinking eyes, motionless as we stepped over them.

After an hour we hadn't reached a single rise in the trail.

"Does this path only go down?" I asked, careful not to step on Frodo.

Joshua laughed and answered, "To the very heart of things!"

By now storm clouds shrouded the two moons and the stars, but a constant barrage of lightning inside the clouds lit our erratic pathway. I heard low rumbles of thunder. I wondered where the wind was.

I didn't look back at Shad. I nursed the hope that we'd lose him with the clouds and this reckless pace on a zigzag trail.

The path kept descending, and the pace kept accelerating. My eyes began to burn from the strange light. We descended into a basin, walking alongside a marshy creek, or perhaps it was the backwater of a lake. It was shallow and wooded, surrounded by lush reeds and grasses, a bayou of sorts. Not far beyond it we came to a bog, a wetland of soft, spongy ground without a drain. All around us was decayed plant matter with a fetid, musty smell, the scent of peat and rotting logs. The bog was covered with plant debris and water-growing moss creeping out from the water's edge, nearly blanketing the water's surface.

The indistinct connection of land and water unnerved me—I wasn't sure if the next step would put me on soft squishy land or if I would sink under my own weight in moss-covered water. Frodo lapped up the water loudly, but I pulled him away from it. He squirmed out of my arms, insisting on exploring the turf. Next thing I knew he was in tall grass sniffing out the local wildlife, whatever it might be. I just hoped it was badgers or raccoons rather than alligators.

I was relieved to come to an intersecting path that cut sharply away from the treacherous bog and rose over a slope, promising to lead to firmer ground. I immediately stepped onto the path.

"This is not your road!" Shad's crusty head was just an inch behind my own. I threw up my right arm to keep him back.

I walked up the slope, glad when the road didn't give under my feet. Before us lay rugged terrain with little underbrush, dry and solid. Beyond the trees, I could see something in the distance, a tower, tall and looming. I tried in vain to see it through the thick overgrowth.

When I reached the top of the slope, I emerged from the trees and stopped abruptly. There were a half-dozen tall, slender spires of rock, looking as if the mesa had once reached up to heaven in a singular, desperate grasp, now forever frozen. But if the change in terrain and humidity wasn't shocking enough, before us stood a glass-and-granite high-rise, a modern building. Everything had seemed so real to this moment, but this seemed dreamlike, as if somehow I weren't really there—yet it was so vivid, down to the detail, I *had* to be there.

As I walked toward the structure, heart pounding, I stopped abruptly, recognizing what it was. My office building! I'd never seen it like this, isolated from all the adjoining buildings and cityscape, as if it had been uprooted by some alien power and transported from Earth to Skia. I entered the familiar ground-level front door with Joshua a step behind. We took the elevator to the twenty-fifth floor, and I instinctively walked through the maze of work stations toward the corner office, adrenaline flowing.

I knew the people here. I'd seen in their eyes their respect for me. They were here to win, and I was their leader. They were people I understood, people I knew how to motivate and train. I knew how to make them succeed.

"T. J.!" I reached out my hand to one of my vice presidents and member of my golf foursome. T. J. walked toward me and...through me! I actually felt his presence in me for just a moment, as if our molecules had shared the same space. In that moment I read his mind and learned what he thought of me—that I was an arrogant son of a gun and he'd just as soon have me drop off the edge of the world!

I stood still, blinking my eyes as others passed through me, hearing their thoughts as well. I used to think I'd like to be able to read minds, to get the advantage. Suddenly I no longer wished it. I backed away, not wanting anyone else to cross through me. I retreated, and we entered the corner office, my office. Joshua closed the door behind us.

I led him to my bookshelves and reached out and picked up a book to prove to myself I wasn't a ghost. On a large mahogany worktable sat product models and promotional displays. The marker board behind it sported multicolored diagrams and bulleted lists of goals and opportunities. A large electronic screen to one side displayed one sales chart after another.

Excitement and passion welled up within me, a feeling and purpose I loved and understood. The sheer familiarity of it made me want to kneel down and kiss the floor. Had I escaped from the world of the red sun and two moons? My heart sank. No—surely what had happened with T. J. proved I was still somewhere else. I *had* dropped off the edge of the world. And somehow, some way, I had to get back.

Joshua gazed approvingly at the view through the windows towering beside us. "You belong here, don't you, Nick?"

I nodded. This was my world, and I had sailed its waters as expertly as any sea captain had ever commanded his ship and his men. First in my office and last to leave—I'd been proud of that service record.

"I could take you back to Earth, Nick. I have that power."

"You do?"

"In fact, I was thinking, maybe we could go into business together. What do you say?"

"Well...I don't know *what* to say."

"Say yes."

"But how could you get me back?"

"Leave that to me."

"What would I have to do?"

"We can talk about that." Joshua waved his hand across the office. "This is what you were made for, Nick, isn't it?"

Before I could respond, the office door swung open. In walked Shad, his disheveled hair and grimy toga so out of place it caused me to laugh, until I looked at myself and realized I wasn't exactly dressed for success either. Shad moved silently past the bookshelves, the table, and the windows. He stopped at my desk, took something from the desktop, and handed it to me.

It was a photograph, with Marci and Brian and Amy—the only place I'd seen them smile in two years. The picture had been taken three years ago, when we still lived together. But I couldn't get away from the office that day to make the appointment at the studio. It was the second time I hadn't shown, so Marci told the photographer to take the pictures anyway. "It was more realistic with just the three of us," she said to me later, twisting the knife.

I gripped the brass frame with both my hands and, feeling like an empty room after everyone has suddenly left, I stared longingly into their smiling faces. The next thing I knew, I was looking at my held-out hands. They were empty.

We left the office, but as we stepped off the elevator and out the front door, I was suddenly sitting in the office of a counselor I recognized. It was like a movie cut that went from one scene to the next with no transition, nothing happening in between. It was then I realized Frodo hadn't been with me in the office, and I couldn't remember where I'd last seen him.

"Nick, it wasn't your fault," Dr. Druef told me. "You've been misunderstood and victimized. Your intentions were good; your family should have seen that. They should have been grateful for all you did for them."

"Yes," I said, nodding. "They should have been grateful."

"Marci never understood your needs."

"No, she didn't."

"Divorce was better than living together in constant conflict. Much better for the children this way."

I nodded. Suddenly everything went out of focus, and I began to lose touch. Dr. Druef was gone, and immediately I sat with Joshua in my condo listening to classical music. The absence of transition made me think I must be dreaming, yet I was completely lucid, and my blue La-Z-Boy recliner was as tangible as it could have been, right down to the little coffee stain on the right arm.

For a few hours I was immersed in the whirlpool of melancholy and reflection, going wherever the melodies led, over the mountains and valleys and through the deserts of my life. Especially the deserts.

"The music is beautiful, isn't it?" Joshua asked.

"Yes. Beautiful."

After Marci and the kids left me, I'd tried to fill the endless quiet evenings first with bars, then later with classical music, hoping the structure and sound might take me somewhere beyond my broken world. Occasionally it did, but in the end Mozart couldn't lead me to the promised land. I was still Nick Seagrave, a success in the minds of everyone except those I really cared about.

Joshua smiled and pointed to the Monet hanging above the fireplace in my living room. Something about that painting had once moved me, or promised to move me. Joshua stared into the painting and started singing along with the music, some enchanting song about "the great garden in the old world, when time began and art was born."

He sang with insight and authority, sounding as though he'd been there. His voice was powerful, soothing. It seemed to push out of my mind any remnants of negative thinking, and for that I was grateful.

I followed him as he walked slowly down my hallway, which was lined on one side with oak bookshelves. I scanned the titles on the spines. I'd switched majors in college, first philosophy, then business, and I kept every textbook. Over the years I bought and read the major business and leadership titles plus occasional historical studies and top-notch biographies, with a constant supply of westerns and action thrillers. I drifted away from philosophy, but in the past two years I started searching out the best new works by the brightest contemporary minds in the field as well as new editions of old classics. Not that I'd read them all yet, or even most of them, but I intended to. Maybe somehow they would soak in, help me unravel the tangled knots of my mind and find the meaning that had always eluded me.

"Commendable," Joshua commented as he pulled out volumes here and there. "You have a genuine thirst for truth."

"In my college days I searched and probed, thinking the answers were within reach. Then I got more practical. If I couldn't unravel the secrets of the universe, at least I could make some big bucks."

I meant to be witty, but my words rang hollow.

When I saw one philosophy text, a boyish face popped into my mind—Mark, my fraternity brother in Phi Sigma Epsilon. We played intramural football together and went to a few concerts—the Stones and the Grateful Dead. We discussed philosophy after class over joints.

"What does it all mean? What's it all about?" Mark had asked me a few times.

"I don't know," I'd said, "but I want to. If we keep looking, one day we'll find it."

The fall of our senior year Mark didn't show up for school. They found his body in his bedroom—hanging from a rope. I cried at his funeral when I looked into the casket and wondered if he had his answers now or if it was too late. Was death a comma or a period—a pause in our existence or the end? Was he grateful to be dead? Suddenly the pale plastic face I saw in that coffin wasn't Mark's—it was mine.

Mark wasn't my best friend. But he'd haunted my dreams for ten years until I'd managed to shake him off. Now he was back. If only I'd known the answer to his questions…maybe things would have turned out different for both of us.

"It wasn't your fault," Joshua said to me.

I jerked my head toward him. "How did you know what I was thinking?"

"I know. And I also know you can find what you seek on one of the roads traveled by the great minds. Choose any of them. I'll take you there in an instant. And if you don't like one of them, I'll take you to the next and then the next. And perhaps I'll get you back to your world as well."

I thought about it again, intrigued by the possibility of getting home, but for some reason I shook my head, believing there was something more I wanted, something no great thinker could lead me to.

No sooner had I turned down this offer than we materialized back on the gray road. Before us stood more buildings, so many I could almost forget that beyond them was mesa, stone, and sagebrush. I felt eager to see where the gray road, now a city street, would lead us next. What would I find here? Joshua, usually buoyant and upbeat, seemed strangely sullen.

We entered a maze of mall interiors, where my eyes were drawn to displays of power tools, antique guns, shiny knives, snow skis, camping gear, sports clothing. We looked over a balcony to see spotlights zooming over showroom floors filled with the latest-model cars and pickup trucks, boats and RVs, snowmobiles and motorcycles.

I saw a man standing there, hypnotized, a self-made man in a stylish suit, a man with a swagger and graying temples. I watched him walk in a perfect circle around all the things, as if their mass held him in orbit around them. They drew him in tighter and tighter until he was inseparable from them. Finally I couldn't tell where the things ended and the man began. Then he put his hand up to cover his facial tic, just as he disappeared into the things.

I turned away, shaking, feeling my own face twitch. I looked around, twisting in circles. Where was Shad? And why did I care?

The spotlights melted into marquee lights. Joshua and I walked into a fine restaurant filled with people in fine clothes, drinking fine wines. I overheard some of their conversations, whining over poor service and overdone delicacies and complaining of spilled champagne, while others told endless stories of their achievements. I knew the ending of every story. I didn't feel hungry for what was being served here. My hunger was less in my stomach than in my chest.

My heart suddenly buoyed when I saw Victoria alone at one of the tables. I didn't know she'd left the red road.

I watched her from a distance, studied every inch of her. She looked so beautiful tonight, so slight and delicate, dressed so elegantly.

I heard a sound on my chest, a tranquil purr. Startled, I looked down and saw a sort of tiny gerbil, hardly bigger than a golf ball and so fuzzy it seemed almost weightless. Somehow it had attached itself to me with its little claws and was nuzzling softly against my shirt. Where had it come from? Had it fallen on me from a tree back in the marsh without my noticing? Or from something in one of the buildings?

I smiled at the big-eyed creature and thought how Amy would have loved it too. Frodo would be barking his brains out, but he was nowhere to be seen. Joshua looked at the creature, nodding his approval and petting it himself. I stroked it as I watched Victoria. I smiled, mesmerized. The longer I looked at Victoria the more she filled my heart.

"Go sit with her," Joshua said to me. He led me by the arm and took me to her table, then excused himself: "I have other things to take care of."

Victoria seemed pleased to see me.

"He's adorable," she said, stroking the creature's fur. "Have dinner with me—you too," she said to the gerbil.

I couldn't detach him because his claws clutched tightly to my shirt, but he didn't get in the way. Victoria and I dined alone and toasted with champagne. When the music began, I managed to relocate my little friend to my side so Victoria and I could dance. My blood stirred and my senses tingled. We embraced, every song and every dance flowing into another and another. I felt intoxicated. The hunger in my chest deepened.

We stopped, and she kissed me, then smiled and said she had to go.

"Can I…go with you?"

"Not tonight," she whispered to me, but she smiled as she walked away, and her eyes said yes. Another enchanting melody arose, and the desire within me refused to cool. The gerbil-like creature crawled back to my ribs, near my chest. I smiled and petted it.

6

JOSHUA STOOD AT A DISTANCE, watching me with Victoria. He came closer and motioned me down a high-ceilinged corridor, then toward a tinted-glass doorway where other men were entering. I followed. Heading for the door, I pushed it open and entered the building. Inside, it was hot and sticky.

I thought I heard a tarp flapping but looked up and saw nothing. I felt something fall on my shoulders and back. The foul odor turned my stomach. An army of nipping blackflies buzzed around me. At first I swatted at them, but there were so many I finally gave up. The stench overwhelmed me, and I fell to my knees, nearly vomiting.

Yet no sooner had this happened than suddenly I felt fine, alive, energized, eager to move ahead. The foul odor was gone, and instead I smelled sweet perfume, not pausing to consider the incongruity of it all.

"Mason!" I was surprised to see him, pushing ahead with the other men who'd just entered. He looked away from me, then quickly moved farther inside.

Through arched doorways I could see the women. I breathed deeply the perfumed air. It was glorious. My thoughts were on one thing only. I was hypnotized, like a moth fluttering around a blinding light. My longing increased until I knew I would sell my soul for the promised pleasures. I was awash in a tidal wave of passion.

I'd forgotten about the gerbil until I felt it move on my chest.

Suddenly pain shot through my torso, up into my head as if it were a runaway train. I reeled from the blow and tried to shake it off me. The pain was horrid. When I didn't manage to get the creature off me, I continued my quest despite the pain, obsessed with what I wanted.

I looked around at the other men, all of us indulging, none of us satisfied. Some of the men frantically redirected their longings, men looking upon men or even upon children. In a feeding frenzy we became predators, consumers of others, cannibals, no longer men but obscene appetites.

It became a prison riot, and I was in the thick of it. I was ashamed, but my shame gave me no power to resist. I felt helpless, like a junkie enslaved to his addiction. I saw in the men around me lifeless eyes, shark eyes.

Feeling a stabbing pain, I looked down at the creature on my chest. What looked back at me was not a furry little gerbil, but a stone-eyed scorpion. As I watched it with horror, it lifted its tail and brought it down into my chest, piercing my shirt and flesh and wriggling its tail inside me. Stunned by the agony of the moment, I realized the sound I'd thought was the gerbil's gentle purr was all along the scorpion's swinging tail.

Frantic, I tried to remove it. I attempted to beat my hand against it without hitting its tail, but how could I? Panicking, I searched for any hard object. Finally finding a picture frame, I pounded it against the creature, hurting myself more than it.

I heard the purring sound and looked again and saw the gerbil, bloodied by my blows.

What have I done?

I petted the poor creature, warm and fuzzy and harmless. It licked me, rubbed against my hand. I gazed at the women again.

Suddenly a wild rush of pain overwhelmed me, and I looked back on my chest. The scorpion inflicted wound after wound, relentlessly filling me with its poison.

The pain deepened my emptiness, and the emptiness demanded to be filled. I entered beneath an archway, then another and another. I moved from place to place, indulging more and more, satisfied less and less. Still, I came back for more, until I came to one archway, blocked by a silent sentinel.

"Why don't you stop before it's too late?"

It was Shad! His face was lined with pain and disgust, his eyes blazing with fury, a passion of its own sort. I detested this man for daring to judge me and trying to deprive me of what I wanted. I pushed him to the floor.

I went in the door, but I didn't find what I expected. She was there.

"Marci!"

I saw my own wife, but I didn't know who she was. Not really. I'd never stopped to ask her. I'd used her as one more object, one more possession, one more hunting trophy.

I gazed up at swaying women on a stage. Then a shock wave assailed me, followed by a sick emptiness. I screamed in horror.

"Amy. No, not you!"

My own daughter had joined the women who paraded on stage. In the din no one heard me scream. I gazed into the emptiness of my own daughter's eyes. I started pushing and shoving. I wanted to kill the men who lusted after her—vile men whose daughters I lusted after.

Something happened in that moment. In seeing my little Amy, I saw Marci and the other women as they really were—frightened daughters and hardened mothers, desperate souls projecting images of delighted sensuality when inside they felt nothing but disdain for the men and themselves. The raging lust in my blood chilled into shame.

Things were not as they appeared.

I sobbed hopelessly. I thought of tracking down Mason to ask him if he wanted to leave this house of horrors with me, but I couldn't find him.

I heard a soft purring sound and saw the gerbil, soft and cuddly. I reached to touch it then felt the searing pain of the scorpion. Why had I been deceived again? What was wrong with me? Why couldn't I get rid of it? I saw now that the scorpion was connected to me by a sort of obscene umbilical cord, as if it were a part of me.

He stung me repeatedly, and I wanted to kill him, yet I couldn't do it without killing myself.

The scorpion appeared to be growing larger by the moment. And then, to my horror, he opened a fold of flesh in my rib cage and tucked himself into the cavity of my chest.

I froze, feeling the monster crawling inside me, returning to where he must have come from, working his poison throughout my system.

I ran out through the tinted-glass doors and down city blocks of gnawing emptiness. Finally I came to Shad and collapsed in a heap, unable to meet his eyes.

"I know what you're thinking, old man." I wheezed, breathless. "But how can you blame me? It isn't my fault—it wells up within me."

"Walk away from it. The King has invited you to feast at a better table, not on rotten food laced with worms, but on rich food that satisfies. Come back with me, walk farther on the red road. I will lead you to what will fill the emptiness in your chest and give you strength to say yes to what you long for and no to what cannot satisfy."

"Don't let the old man fool you!"

I looked around. Where did the voice come from?

"Nick," Shad pleaded, "you *must* face the chasm."

"Chasm?" I asked dumbly. "You spoke of it before. What is it?"

"Nick!"

It was Joshua. He stepped forward, smiling, and raised a hand to silence Shad. "Come, Nick," he said softly. "There's much more you must see."

"But this chasm, what—?"

"There is no chasm," Joshua said. "The man is sincere perhaps, but confused. Even if there were a chasm, surely it would be the last place you'd want to go!"

I nodded my agreement. Shad closed his eyes and whispered something, I couldn't hear what. Before I knew it, the three of us were walking in a lush hotel hallway. Joshua hesitated, looking as if he'd intended for us to go elsewhere. Shad gripped my arm.

Gilded elevator doors opened across the hall. Out stepped a well-dressed man, accompanied by a woman with the face of a man's dreams. They walked side by side down the hallway, laughing lightly in obvious anticipation.

Then I knew what was about to happen and felt my stomach turn.

Shad tightened his grip on my arm. "Watch," he said, "not with your desire but with your mind."

I backed away from the man and woman who slipped into the room. They didn't seem to notice us as we stood observing them.

Then I watched as the fool torched solemn vows made twenty-five years before and threw ashes to the wind.

"Stop!" I cried. "Don't you see what you're doing?"

He couldn't hear me, or wouldn't. Suddenly I saw the dropping blade of a guillotine, spilling my blood on the clean sheets of a luxury hotel. I saw the face of the woman of my dreams after a night of blind passion, when beauty faded and she became demanding and ugly, one more dried-up carcass on the great web, a revolting reminder of my own condition.

Then I saw the worst of it, hidden from me until that moment.

The drama, everything I'd just seen, was being acted out on a stage—and in the audience sat Marci. She stared at us, at me and the other woman. Marci silently watched me betray her, watched me violate my vows, watched the ugly procession of the lies I had become. I saw her sobs, her grief, her anger, and then watched as her face hardened against me, against life itself.

"Marci, I'm sorry," I cried out. "I didn't mean to hurt you!" She couldn't hear me. Too little, too late.

Just when I thought nothing could be more horrible, I saw Brian and Amy seated beside their mother, observing the same ugliness, watching their father weave his own web. They saw me embrace this woman in our "secret" hotel room that was on center stage of the universe. I ran in front of them to block their view.

"No—you don't understand," I cried. "It wasn't like that; it wasn't as bad as it appears."

But I realized I had no power to reinterpret the truth, for everyone in that cosmic auditorium, including my wife and children, knew it was *exactly* as it appeared.

Brian and Amy could see right through me, right through the

traitor they once loved and now despised. I saw the stunned looks on their faces, the disgust, the brooding anger, felt the heart-stab of their hurt and confusion. I watched them turn from me.

"Amy, Brian—I'm sorry!" I said the words I'd never said on Earth.

I watched them recklessly run away from the auditorium. I knew they were going to choose their own wrong roads—I'd already seen that—because the man they trusted was a turncoat and a liar and a cheat. I saw them hating themselves for having once loved me.

If there was a hell, was I there already? Was this the first installment of what the travelers called Erebus?

I turned to look for Joshua. He was gone. Only Shadrach was there.

"There is no such thing as a private moment," Shad whispered. "The whole cosmos is our audience for everything we do in the dark."

I turned away and ran, hearing the sound of clanging metal in my pocket, too frightened to reach in and discover what it was.

I ran and ran, not knowing what direction I was going, my eyes blinded by tears and wind, trying to outrun my shame.

I lay where I collapsed, outside the slice of city, far from the buildings, in a heap of bristly plants beside the brackish water of a scum-covered pond.

I fought my erupting emotions, trying to reel them in with logic.

Hunger couldn't exist without food, could it? Or thirst without water? Perhaps the arid vacancy of my soul was an indication there *must* be something wet and refreshing, a deep-sourced fountain that could fill me up over and over, something for which my thirst was made.

My guilt feelings were doing me no good—they only increased my pain. If Dad had been there for me, if Marci had been different, if she'd understood…No, it wasn't my fault, it couldn't be. I'd tried my best.

What I'd experienced on the gray roads had only left me thirstier and sicker, as if I'd drunk salt water when I craved and needed fresh.

I wasn't very good at examining the state of my soul. I hadn't had much practice.

As I lay on the ground, I looked up to a plum tree, where a large gray owl perched on a low branch and studied me. He swiveled his head back and forth, without blinking, as if scanning me curiously. His implied question seemed the same as mine—who was I, anyway?

The owl suddenly looked behind me, and I turned to see Joshua walking toward me. Joshua's eyes looked off to my right, and I followed them to see Shad also headed my way, stopping to cough and spit to clear out his old lungs. I got on my feet, trying not to appear as weak as I felt.

"If there's nowhere else to go," I said to Joshua, "I'll return to the red road."

"There are other places," Joshua said, his voice full of optimism. "Lots of them. Don't give up yet."

"I don't want to walk in these parts anymore. Let's go back to the red road."

"To the south, on the other side of the red road, are the roads of religion—they'll take you where you want to go."

"I'll have to think about it. Meanwhile let's head for the red road."

At the word "religion," stomach acid climbed up to my throat.

I thought about that nitpicking church that had embarrassed my family, that money-grubbing, self-righteous minister who had the affair with the organist. I'd sworn as a high schooler I'd never darken a church door again.

Still, as much as I'd been burned by organized religion, I'd always been interested in the great questions religion asked. It was only the answers—and those who offered the answers—I objected to. Religion seemed so irrelevant, so dry, so distant. For me it never had the ring of truth.

No, I thought, religion's roads weren't for me. Once we got back to the red road I'd stay on it, at least for a while. I'd tell Joshua when we got there.

Shad and I hoisted our packs. It struck me odd that Joshua didn't carry a pack, and even odder I hadn't noticed until then. We hiked back up toward the red road.

I heard an excited woof behind us and looked back to see Frodo, his usually floppy ears comically erect, batlike, and his white fur covered with gray dust. He pranced around like a tiny Clydesdale. His tail didn't just wag, it spun like a propeller. He did the doggy dance of joy.

"Hello, fella. You're a sight!" I reached down to pick him up. His lips quivered and he bared his teeth in that outlandish smile.

"Where have you been, boy? I wish you could tell me your story!"

Ten minutes later Frodo nestled into his little sling, soon falling asleep against my chest. It was a far longer journey to climb back up to the red road than it had been to come down. As the hours wore on, every few minutes dirty grit collected on my tongue, and I had to spit it out. My calves cramped up. I sat down and took off my boots, stretched my legs, then rubbed the soles of my feet. I touched two new blisters and wished I hadn't. A dusty sagebrush blew into my face. I swatted at it and swore. What was I doing here? Maybe I'd have been better off to stay on the gray roads down below.

When at last we arrived at the red road, Salama approached us.

"Hello, Salama," Joshua said.

How do they know each other?

"We're going to the southern roads, the roads of religion," Joshua said. "Do you want to come with us?"

"I've been waiting," she said. "I'm weary of the red road. Yes, let me go with you."

Joshua smiled warmly and put his arm around her while Shad tried to talk her out of it.

Before I realized what was happening, I was going to the religion roads by default, without ever making a decision to. Religion? I wasn't optimistic. But…was it possible there was something I'd missed? Maybe here in Skia, Thuros—whatever—maybe here religion would finally make sense. So far nothing else had. What did I have to lose?

As we started our descent, we paused at a break in the pine trees and gazed down into the dusty valley, more like a gulch. I was amazed to see dozens upon dozens, if not hundreds of roads leading out into the distance, as many roads as there were directions. My chest tightened.

"There are so many roads," I said. "As many as on the other side."

"Perhaps more," Joshua said. "But they all have something you can benefit from."

"Is it possible to find…the truth?" I asked Joshua.

"That's a lifetime pursuit," Joshua said. "You need to look far and wide to find bits of the truth that you can weave all together into something that satisfies you."

I pointed at the long narrow shadow reaching to the west. "What causes the shadow?" I asked him.

He stared at it, smiling nervously. "Perhaps I'll show you later. For now we should go forward."

"Forward." I thought about the message on the cave wall. But forward to where? Down below? To which road? Was there such a thing as truth? Would one of these roads take me there? I felt a glimmer of hope. Was I right to hope? Or was I just a fool?

Shad walked behind us, buzzing around like a gadfly, making irritating comments now and then just to remind us he was still there. Strangely, I couldn't really hear most of his words, and those I heard I couldn't make sense of.

What's wrong with him?

We came to a stream running down from the hills in a deeply dug canal with steep slippery slopes on each side. Near the stream we hooked up on a path where we came to a quiet community of people. There a three-sided wood building, open in the front, had candles, incense, robes, books, altars, and offering boxes on display. I kept blinking my eyes because all the colors seemed muted, indistinct, as if everything were beige, like a sun-bleached stage prop. We approached a man in a red robe, meditating in the lovely silence.

"Which religion is true?" I asked him, whispering, as if I didn't want to admit the question had come from me. "And how can we know?"

"We practice all religions here," he said, "for we see truth in all of them."

"And how do I know what to embrace and what to reject?"

"Embrace what you wish and reject what you wish. It's yours to choose."

"Yes, I understand I can choose, but what I mean is, what *should* I choose?"

"You should choose only what you wish. We won't force anything on you."

"Yes, yes, I know you won't force me, but…I'm looking for truth."

"Commendable," the man said, nodding wisely. "There's truth in all religions. You must choose for yourself."

I threw up my hands and walked away, wondering if I was insane or he was. Salama stayed behind to talk with him. My face hot and twitching, I walked to a nearby road where people wore angel pins, collected angel figurines, and read books about angels.

"Talk to your angel," one man said.

"Listen to your angel," a young girl added.

"I know my angel's name," an old woman said. "She speaks to me often."

"Angels are here to comfort us," said a radiant young blonde wearing an angel necklace. "Never be afraid of an angel."

I shook my head in frustration—what was true and how could I know? Who could I listen to? What should I believe? I walked away from the others, kicking the dust with my boot.

A man with a square jaw, a Middle-Eastern complexion, and long, jet-black hair approached me. He asked, "What is different between Thuros and the world you came from?"

How did he know I came from another world? Was it written on my forehead?

"Since I've been here," I said, "for something like sixty seconds each day, I've been able to…see into other worlds. It's as if I've been given eyes that see what isn't there."

"Or is it that your eyes now see what was there all along?"

"I come from a world where seeing is believing," I said. "If you can't sense it, it isn't real."

"I am Marcus," he said.

"Nick," I mumbled.

"In a world where seeing is believing," Marcus said, "men believe much that is not true. And they disbelieve much that is true."

His eyes scanned the great plain spread out before us, full of people walking on the many roads. His gaze pulled mine with it, and I saw a hundred red-winged blackbirds in sudden flight, appearing to flee from something I couldn't see.

The plain suddenly became an immense battlefield, full of great gladiators, with eyes of fire, lifting their swords against other warriors, these with cold shark eyes. The warriors of both sides seemed to be of the same stock, as if it was a civil war—the gray city of the east versus the bright city of the west. Some troops fought on the ground, some above it, as if the air had an invisible floor. Sparks flew off their swords and lightning bolts pierced the sky. Swords clashed against shields, and thunderclaps exploded. Even at a distance the noise was almost unbearable.

People, some of whom I'd just seen, walked on the ground underneath the great combatants. Now they appeared translucent, almost invisible. Most of them stepped casually, unguardedly, apparently unaware of the battle raging above and around them.

One man was out on the battlefield in his underwear, lying on a recliner, sipping a soda. I laughed, but when I saw a huge warrior with a mace raised over him, I turned away, cringing as I heard a sickening crunch.

Behind and above came the sound of flapping tarp. I turned to see a monstrous carrion-fowl plunging at me. Hands on my neck I ran forward as he circled again and came at me from behind. He dived and pursued me, coming at me this way and that, as if he were herding me somewhere. Before I knew it, I found myself on the plain, in the thick of battle.

Arrows shot past me. Then I heard a swoosh and felt something pierce my left shoulder. I saw the arrow just before I felt the pain, as lightning before thunder. I screamed in agony.

I fell to the ground on my right side, alternately covering my unprotected head with my hands and trying to pull out the arrow from my shoulder. I writhed, looking for help but seeing none. I lay flat on my back, clasped both hands around the arrow shaft, and pushed away, screaming as the arrow pulled out of the flesh that had closed around it.

I swooned, the pain threatening to sweep me into unconsciousness. I opened my eyes to see a powerful warrior standing over me, his face contorted. He raised a sword up high, like an executioner. I froze, held by pain and fear. He brought down the sword, and I saw it glimmer in the sunlight just a moment before it sliced into my right arm, just above my elbow. Waves of convulsing agony ushered me into the darkness.

7

WARM BLOOD FROM MY SHOULDER wound awakened me—or maybe it was the deep cut above my elbow that screamed for attention. I tried to stop the bleeding, but my right arm hung limp and useless.

Where was the enemy who'd cut me? Why hadn't he finished me off? Twenty feet away stood the answer. Another great warrior—I saw only his back, with jet-black hair dangling halfway down—battled him with his sword, pushing him away from me.

Surprisingly lucid, considering the pain, I lay motionless, left hand moving from one wound to the other, trying to bind them with strips of my torn shirt. Clanging sounds of battle surrounded me. Several warriors hovered over me, swords clashing. Others had lost their weapons and fought hand to hand. Unable to move, I watched the fighting grow more furious from one end of the valley to the other. Battalions and brigades arrived, bringing reinforcements. Phalanxes of troops moved in from both east and west.

The precision and order of arriving troops stood in stark contrast to the pandemonium in the thick of the battle, which resembled a barroom brawl of galactic proportions, spread out not only as far as I could see, but as high as I could see. I wanted to cry for help, but was too terrified to speak, fearing I would be heard in the din by the wrong warrior and become a target.

Suddenly the black-haired warrior, my defender, fell back on me, pushed by his opponent. The same shark-eyed soldier who'd sliced my arm raised his razor-sharp four-foot sword and laughed sadistically as he swung it down toward my head.

My bodyguard, immediately back on his feet, stepped up from my blind side and swung his sword horizontally, deflecting the blow so it missed my head, instead slicing a quarter inch of flesh off my left forearm. Howling at the white-hot pain, I tried to clutch the wound with my limp right hand. In a cloud of combat dust I crawled to low, soft ground. Two dark warriors flew over me, fleeing from the battle. Suddenly they screeched, facing the swords of their own army's rear guard, who assaulted the deserters and pushed them back to the front lines.

Helpless, with nothing to defend me, I could only hurt and watch. Despite the would-be deserters, I saw that the dark army had a distinct advantage. The people on the ground, walking the roads, seemed oblivious to the battle; they wore no defensive armor, refused to flee and seek refuge, and generally did very little to assist the bright warriors fighting on their behalf. The people fell in battle as steadily as raindrops from the eaves of a house, some screaming, others with no more than a groan or whimper.

In the distance I could see a short young man running in the thick of battle. It was Quon!

"Nick," he called, desperation in his voice. I pitied him, yet felt relief that at least I wasn't the only one trapped in this war zone. He waved at me and tried to run toward me, but he was rolled over by wrestling warriors. I stood up on weak knees, hoping to stagger toward him. So many troops battled between us that I had to keep moving, finding any open space not in front of a dark warrior's sword. In the melee, I got turned around and lost sight of him.

Trembling at the fierce warfare around me, I lay low again. As I looked from east to west, I became aware of two gigantic commanders at opposite ends of the valley, titans surrounded by smaller attendants. Their sculpted powerful faces were almost indistinguishable but for their expressions. The titans looked like identical twins long separated, equals who had chosen opposite sides, the dark commander dressed in gray, his counterpart in red.

But when I looked more closely at the commander of the dark army, when I saw his shark eyes and contorted face, I wondered how I could have thought him the other commander's twin. Cruelty sprung from his eyes like smoke and fire from cannons. He gloated and taunted, now no longer on the edge of the foray, but wielding weapons of destruction, pulled at will from a massive armory cart dragged along by his servants. Cursing the air above and the ground beneath, he fired flaming arrows and poisoned darts into people who did nothing to defend themselves.

My heart stopped when he turned toward me and saw me watching him. He stared at me like a stalker. His eyes flashed, and for a moment, though nothing physical had touched me, my skin seemed to burn under the napalm of his hatred. Why was he looking at me when countless others filled the battlefield? Why should he bother with Nick Seagrave?

Then the dark commander picked up a gigantic harpoon, waved it in the air, hoisted it, and pointed at me. Just as he threw it, I rolled and heard a loud swoosh as it cut through the air with hideous fury. It passed but inches from me, then grazed the black-haired warrior by my side. He cried out and grasped his left leg, but he stood his ground over me. I panicked, got up, and ran, stumbling, unsure where to go.

The dark lord opened his mouth in mocking laughter, a sound so great it rose above the roar of battle. Then he swung a bola in the air, round and round, eyes bent on me. When I could hardly stand the sight of one more circle of those metal balls, he released the weapon. It flew, hitting my legs and wrapping itself around me. I heard the sickening crunch of my own bones. It beat me to the ground, pummeling me even after I fell.

A horrible pain racked my left side, and I heard a sucking sound. I could hardly breathe. My ribs had been crushed, and one of them had pierced my right lung. The eerie gasping sound grabbed hold of me. Broken and bleeding, my breath escaping me, I knew I would surely die.

Shark Eyes glared at me, then marched across the valley, taking huge strides toward me. As he advanced, he swung a great battle-ax with one arm and a mace with the other, cutting and clubbing his victims, people who seemed never to see him coming until it was too late. I could see him coming. But it was too late and I was too little.

A third of the way to me he pulled out a machete, using it first on bright warriors, then on the little people. He wielded his weapons with cruel precision, sporting a sadistic smile, sized in proportion to the suffering he inflicted. He crippled and dismembered and destroyed. I sensed he was warming up for me. At this pace, he would cover the ground between us within a few minutes.

My legs crumbled, arms wounded, torso crushed, air and blood wheezing out of my punctured lung, I tried to crawl away. I couldn't. My head in the dirt, a flood of images raced through my mind, images of a broken life I would never have a chance to fix.

Just then I heard a great voice, speaking a language I couldn't understand. Was it a dialect of titans? I turned my head just enough to see the bright Commander, dressed in red, also marching toward me from the opposite end of the valley.

The face of Shark Eyes's counterpart was rock solid, his chin set and resolute, his eyes loyal and kind, burning with an unquenchable fire. He did not scream or gloat. He entered the foray, and even as he marched toward me I saw him stoop to help a lowly soldier who faltered while trying to protect one of the translucent little people.

I looked back and forth between the titans. I silently pleaded with the commander in red, *Don't stop for anyone else. Keep coming!*

The red-garbed titan wielded his sword with amazing accuracy, as if an extension of his powerful right arm. He cut through the ropes of the enemy's bolas and blocked the poison darts and flaming arrows with the flat of his sword. Always with an eye on me, he called out commands to his warriors. Then suddenly he stopped in his tracks.

He raised his hand to two lieutenants beside him, quieting them, then looked up to the sky as if he were listening to someone. Was it his commander in chief?

The dark commander marched on, gloating and energized when he saw his enemy stop. As he came at me, my spirit felt trapped in frozen flesh. In what I assumed would be my final seconds of life, I became strangely contemplative about this ancient war I had witnessed for the first time.

The conflicting missions of the two armies seemed to have no fog, no gray, only black-and-white clarity. I had lived my life in terms of compromise, rule-bending, trade-offs, concessions, bargaining, striking deals, finding middle ground. In these two great armies, there was no such thing. Good was good, and evil was evil, and they shared no common ground.

Though racked with pain, my thoughts were lucid and focused. I looked at the little people oblivious to the battle, who seemed to fancy themselves neutral and at peace, making choices so as to maintain dual citizenship in the two warring kingdoms. I was shocked at their ignorance and indifference to the gravity of this ferocious war. Above all, I was shocked that I had been just like them, blind to reality.

I turned toward the hideous face of the dark commander, battle-ax raised, only thirty feet from me now. As I writhed, I listened to the eerie gasping of my punctured lung. The irony struck me that the greatest moments of clarity I'd ever known would now be culminated in my slaughter. I would have welcomed death, except...I had a horrible feeling what awaited me on the other side was far worse than oblivion.

Poised above me now was a raised battle-ax. Trembling, I looked into the shark eyes of my gloating executioner.

I watched the ax fall, but just as it came upon me, Shark Eyes disappeared. All the warriors from both sides disappeared. The people on the plain popped back into normal view, as solid as the warriors had been the moment before. Silence.

I pulled my head up out of the dirt and looked from side to side. It took a moment to grasp the fact that the pain in my shoulder and arms and ribs and lung had disappeared, replaced by an aching void in my chest. I looked around, relieved to see an empty landscape.

All seemed peaceful. There was no battle. At least...none that I could see.

Several people out for a stroll stared at me, lying there in the dirt. I started to explain what had happened. They looked at me as though I was crazy, then suddenly I recognized them. I'd seen two of them killed in the battle! And yet…here they were, the walking dead. How could that be? We traded stares, each frightened by the other.

Marcus, his long dark hair dripping with sweat, approached me, haggard and limping, favoring his left leg.

"What happened?" I ask him, but before he could answer, he turned into a raging fire. My face blistered at the heat. Then a portal opened in midair, giving me a moment's glimpse of something beyond. Face grimacing and resolute, like a soldier headed back to battle, Marcus walked through it, to the universe next door.

When he was gone, I felt my body again, barely able to believe my bones were no longer broken, my lung was not pierced, and I could move. I stood slowly, reeling, then sank back down to the ground and clutched the dirt, closing my eyes.

I dreamed a butterfly landed on my face, and I awoke to a slight suction noise, which Frodo always made when he opened his mouth. He was licking my cheek, pressed so closely to my eyes he looked distorted, as if I were seeing him through a fisheye lens.

I nuzzled him, then stood up cautiously, relieved to find I'd regained my sense of balance. Still, I was exhausted. Where was Joshua? Shad? Salama? I found a shade tree, willowlike but burnt orange and with thicker branches, heavy and drooping all the way to the ground. It was a wonderful shelter from the afternoon sun, cool and insulated. Its branches were the roof over my head and the soft grass under it my pillow. Frodo snuggled against my neck. I listened to his rhythmic breathing, interrupted only by a deep contented sigh, as I drifted off again.

It was dark when I awoke to the crackling of a fire. I got up slowly, knees creaking, neck stiff. I pulled aside the hanging branches and saw Shad standing ten feet from the fire, gazing up into the sky.

"What are you looking at?" I asked him. He trembled and stepped back, then looked at me.

"Nick!"

"What do you see?" I asked. "None of the constellations look familiar."

"There," he pointed. "The Lion. See the six stars of his great mane, the red glow of his eyes, the two star clusters of his uplifted paws?"

"No—I don't see it."

He kept trying to get me to see it, quoting from his GuideBook and pointing and waving. I heard a song in the stars, a stirring song, but I couldn't make out the words. The more he talked and pointed the more frustrated I became. I stepped back from him, but still looked up at the stars, searching in vain for what he claimed was there.

I listened to the old man sing into the night sky. "You have made us for yourself, Chasm-crosser, and the heart of man is restless until it finds its rest in You."

I walked to the fire, where Joshua sat, staring into the flames.

"Good to see you again, Nick."

I studied his face, sculpted and powerful and kind. He looked remarkably like the red-robed commander of the bright army. For a moment I felt certain it was him. I almost asked him why he'd stopped, why he hadn't defended me against the dark lord.

"Have something to eat, then go back to sleep," he said to me in a gentle voice. "We have much to see tomorrow."

I considered telling him where I'd decided to go next.

No. I'll wait until morning.

8

JOSHUA SERVED A FINE BREAKFAST of pancakes, eggs, bacon, and wild grapes. The only thing it lacked was a good cup of senaba.

"Where can I take you today, Nick?" he asked me after breakfast. "There are still many roads of religion ahead of us."

I hesitated, looking behind me to be sure Shad wasn't listening.

"I'd like to meet those who believe in the old man's GuideBook," I whispered, "and his chasm, and his king."

"All right," Joshua said, "if you're sure that's what you want. I'll take you to the loyal followers of the RoadGuide, and you can judge for yourself. But he will stay here. You're tired, aren't you, Shadrach?" he called to him.

Shad started to protest, but his eyes drooped and, despite the fact that we'd only been up for an hour, he lay down in some thick grass beside the road and curled up for a nap. "We'll rejoin him later," Joshua assured me.

As we walked, it grew dark. When we came close to a group camped by a narrow road, for a moment I thought I heard again the song of the stars to which my soul resonated as to a tuning fork. Then I realized what I heard was only words without the music.

Joshua took me to a leader surrounded by attentive followers and introduced me to him. I recognized him immediately. Pastor Hepishare. I hadn't seen him since I was sixteen, and I'd hoped never to see him again. He looked just the same as I remembered him, stern and heavy jowled. He moved close to me but did not pollute himself by shaking my hand.

"We are believers in the great GuideBook and followers of the Chasm-crosser."

He lifted a large book, which looked very much like the one carried by Shad, but bigger and stonelike.

"We have 613 rules: 248 commands and 365 prohibitions. We have explained these with 1,521 emendations so we can tell you exactly what you should and should not do."

I stared blankly at him, assuming he didn't recognize me and wishing it were mutual.

"So if I join you," I said, "everything in my life will either be required or forbidden."

"If you find something we have left off," he said in a whiny voice, "bring it to our attention, and we will add it to the list of the forbidden or required or address it with another emendation."

"Uh…thanks. I'll keep that in mind." Just before I turned away, I saw a wave of ripples across the front of his robe, which he patted down quickly.

I watched men standing with clipboards, with page after page of long lists. Some of them stood up on platforms and put megaphones to their mouths and shouted out their rules, and when someone else yelled out different rules, they shouted all the louder. All this brought back my worst childhood memories.

I thought of the old woman who slapped my hand in church because I giggled. One of many reasons why church was the last place I'd go if I were in trouble.

"Your jacket goes against our rules," Pastor Hepishare called to me from behind. I turned around. "It's the wrong color," he said, marching toward me, then jabbing my chest with his index finger.

In an explosion, my right fist smashed into his face. He lay flat on the ground, unconscious. Frodo barked wildly. It felt good. I'd wanted to do that for years.

I remembered why I hated religion so much, why I'd always hated it. When a man came looking for relief from the heavy load he carried, religion laid a pallet of bricks on his back.

"You've seen Shad's religion, the religion of the GuideBook," Joshua said, pulling close to me. "Is this what you're searching for?"

I shook my head.

"I have others who need my guidance now," Joshua said. "I must go to them, but I'll return in a few hours. Just find some shade and relax. I'll be back. Will you be all right?"

I nodded and watched him walk into some thick vine maples with a rich tapestry of fall colors. He disappeared.

Just that moment I heard footsteps behind me and turned to see Shad, fifteen feet away, waving frantically. He ran up to me, breathless.

"Where have you been?" he demanded.

I shrugged.

"Nick," he said, "I still need to explain to you the way of the red road, the way to the chasm."

"Your way's not for me, old man."

"But how do you know if you won't let me explain it—and if you won't walk with me far enough on the red road to see whether my words are true?"

"Joshua already showed me your way," I said. "It's not for me."

"Joshua? What did he show you?"

I told him what had happened.

"The one you've chosen as your guide," Shad said, "did not show you the followers of the King, for those you can find only on the red road. You saw counterfeits. Before you reject something, be sure you know what it really is. Perhaps when you next gain your sixty seconds of clarity, you should look more closely at your friend Joshua!"

I raised my hand at him like a traffic cop indicating "Stop." I turned and walked off by myself. If I couldn't find answers on the roads, maybe I could sort out the voices warring inside me—Joshua's, Shad's, the Woodsman's, the voices on the roads, and fifty years of my own voice.

When the sun began to set and low clouds turned to crimson fire, I climbed a hill to watch. As I reached the crest, I looked down at someone in a black flowing robe, standing on the hillside, looking away from me, down over the roads. Instinctively, I ducked into a thick-branched willow tree and watched as the breeze parted the branches just enough for me to see.

I heard murmurs, voices, songs of weeping. Then I heard what seemed like millions of voices too weary to sing, and I sensed in the quiet distance millions more who'd never even heard a song. I looked at all the roads, where I saw for a moment the landscape littered with human roadkill. Then I saw people walking again, but they didn't strike me as truly alive.

For some reason I thought of my father spending his life affirming his sovereignty, declaring his independence, then slowly dying without so much as control over his bladder, as clueless about the world he lived in as about the worlds beyond.

The ominous black-robed being stood smiling, gloating, taking pleasure in the pain on the roads below him. He took out a lyre and played music and sang an otherworldly song. It sounded like a ripoff of the true song, the song of the stars for which my soul was made. He laughed and pointed his finger down at the sprawling misery and played his music like a cosmic Nero fiddling while a world burned.

He blew smoke out his nose. Then, to my horror, I saw him putting little people into his mouth, smoking men as if they were cigarettes. Now he had a half-dozen in his mouth at a time, a macabre sight that turned my stomach and make my knees shake. He wheezed and choked and laughed like a junior-high boy indulging in a forbidden vice. When he was done, he crumpled the human cigarettes, one by one, slowly, as if taking exquisite pleasure in the undoing of each. Finally, he tossed them to the ground. I watched him lift his leg high, the leg of a tyrannosaur, and smash them, grinding them until they were flat. Even then he did not stop grinding. Throat tight, I shivered in the shade of the willow.

I knew him. I'd seen him on the great battlefield with a battle-ax raised above his head, attempting to remove my head and nearly succeeding. Even at a distance I could see his shark eyes. I chilled at his singing.

At the very same moment, I heard another song in the air, a song in the distance like a pale but ever-growing light behind a dark rain curtain. It was a melody in the wind blowing gently from Charis, the City of Light, barely visible in the west. It was a song of love and might, of grace and victory. The dark prince put his hands over his ears and yelled curses, pacing back and forth. How could such a bright song be sung in the presence of such cruel evil? Yet it wafted its way below through the miserable air of the dead-end roads, reverberating even in the sewer drains that connected them. I saw people here and there, on various roads, responding to it, smiling, then turning to walk up the hillside to the red road.

"That song is a lie!" the dark prince called from the hillside. "You're a fool to believe it. I have better ways, better roads, many of them. Choose what you like. Let me show you. Come my way! Come back to Babel, then follow me to the great kingdom of Erebus!"

He sounded like a carnival barker inviting men into his house of mirrors. A gust of wind blew back the willow branches, and suddenly he turned and saw me watching him. My blood chilled. As I looked on helplessly, he stepped off the hillside like a hang glider, his body transforming into a flying beast, a hell-hawk, claws grasping the air.

He flew toward the willow and circled over me. I saw the weathered scales of his underside. I was overwhelmed with the putrid smell of ancient rotting flesh, caked with blood and desiccated human body parts. I saw on the scales of this filthy, gluttonous beast the dried residue of his sickening drool.

The thunderclaps of his flapping wings deafened me. He parted his razor teeth and descended. I choked on malevolence and felt strangled by doom. Just as the beast opened his mouth, just as I smelled his wretched breath, his head yanked backward, and he disappeared.

Why had I been delivered from it again? And why did I feel so certain this rescue would be my last?

Disoriented, I walked out from under the willow branches, feeling as if space and time had turned inside out. A familiar figure was walking toward me, returning from his obligations.

"Joshua!"

I smiled and walked toward him. I extended my hand. When I

got close and looked at his face, I recoiled, standing for a moment in stunned silence.

His face was a mask with two holes in it. His eyes were not radiant blue. They were the dark dull eyes of a shark!

I turned and ran until I could run no farther. I covered my twitching face. I saw a shadow and felt as if a giant spider lurked behind me. Looking up, I let out my breath when I saw Shad.

"Why didn't you tell me?" I stammered.

"About the one who calls himself Joshua? I tried to. You wouldn't listen. It was as if you couldn't hear my words. You thought me mad and malicious too, did you not?"

I nodded slowly.

"This time he could not keep you from seeing him as he really is. But don't underestimate him. He won't give up."

I didn't know what to say—I was trying to process it all.

"Look at the image-bearers who have forgotten who they are," Shad said. He pointed down to the roads and the people who walked them in a trancelike state, zombies following the crowd.

"You are one of those, Nick, are you not? The Impostor gives them wrong dreams or robs them of the right ones—it's all the same. He gives them hope in the wrong things, then takes away their hope in the right ones. Like a cruel, fastidious nanny, he scrubs the hope out of their bloodshot eyes. And men without hope live their lives in Erebus even before they enter its doors."

"I've tasted Erebus," I said, "enough to know it's not what I want."

"Be grateful you can return to the red road, for few men get so many chances as you have. Thuros has been strip-mined of hope. It is a hollow cavern of broken promises and abandoned dreams, where men eke out an existence, living lives of desperation. The

Impostor gloats over them. The King weeps over them."

"Is the Impostor greater than the King?"

"Greater than the King?" Shad looked at me as if I were insane. "No one is greater than the King. The Pretender is but a creature. He is no more a threat to the King than a mosquito to a lion."

"Then why is there the great battle? And why is evil winning?"

"You have many questions and not all can be answered now. Many I confess I do not understand. But this much I know—not all is as it appears." He paused and looked at me. "Are you ready, Nick, to walk the red road to the chasm?"

"I want to go to Charis, I can tell you that much." Even as I said it, the words struck me, almost as if I'd finally said what I knew deep in my heart. "If the red road will take me there, it's the red road I want. As for the chasm, I'm still not convinced there is one. And if there is, why would I want to go there?"

"It isn't a matter of wanting. No one wants the chasm to be there. But it is. Everyone must face it. You may face it directly by the red road. Or you may waste your life walking the other roads that avoid the chasm for the moment but dump you there the instant you die, when it's too late. Follow me. We must climb up to that ledge." He pointed up a sharp incline of rocks and shale that definitely didn't fall under Climbing 101.

"Ledge? The one halfway up the mountain?"

"Yes. It leads to a higher point on the red road and will afford us the view you need. Once you see the roads and the landscape from above, you'll understand."

Part of me resisted going with him, but I felt certain there was no future here. The red road might be one more dead end—but everything else I'd seen certainly was.

I paused by a stream to refill my water bottle. Then I followed Shad, surprised again at how his goat feet negotiated the mountain. If I hadn't put my feet in the same places he put his, I would have fallen a dozen times. I pushed myself to keep up with him, carrying Frodo in my sling when his little legs began straining.

"Why do you call this place Thuros?" I asked as we climbed.

"Why is senaba called senaba? That is its name."

"Joshua called it Skia."

"Did he? Yes, I suppose he would. When I was young, an old man told me stories by the fire, stories of how this world was first called Thuros, the window land. Then when it was ravaged and spoiled, when the flying reptiles and the scorpions and the great web came, it was changed to Skiathuros, window of darkness. Now some just call it Skia, the darkness. I prefer Thuros, for it is still a window, and the TravelGuide says its darkness will be overcome and light will yet prevail."

We climbed for perhaps eight hours with little rest. We munched on jerky and stale rye bread and a couple of cucumbers. When Shad wasn't looking, I gave Frodo a strip of my jerky, which he didn't chew but swallowed whole, eyes bright and tail thumping alternately against his side and my leg. The highlight of the climb was a lone senaba tree, though the fruit was a faded blue, much smaller and not as sweet as usual. Still, Frodo ate his share, puckering at its tanginess. Even Shad managed to laugh at that.

As we climbed, I kept looking back over my shoulders. "What about Quon and Mason? And Victoria and Salama?"

"I…don't know about them," Shad said. I heard the concern in his voice. Shad kept the lead and reached the top well ahead of me.

"This is the red road," he called down to me, still twenty feet below. "From here we go back down the other side until we reach..." He stretched out his hand and gestured downward.

I stepped up high enough to see over the point. What I saw beneath me took my breath away. It was a canyon so large that it stretched out against the horizon as far as I could see. Way in the distance, on the other side, was the City of Light. It appeared much farther away than before. I looked down at all the roads on both sides. Every road circled around, meandering, until it ended in the chasm. Though they engaged the chasm at different places, each of them wound up there.

On the roads I could see tiny dots I supposed were people or groups of people. Having been on the roads, I could see that they wound around so much that when viewed from the flatlands below they gave the illusion of progress and afforded no view of the chasm. But from here, above, the picture was radically different.

"If the red road goes to the chasm like all the other roads," I said, "why should we walk it instead of them?"

"Because the red road takes you to the chasm before you die, not after. You will see. That is, if you choose to go there with me."

I considered my options. I stared down at the winding roads below, the cul-de-sacs, the figure eights, the circles—all going nowhere. Okay, heading toward a chasm didn't appear to make sense—but I refused to go back to where I'd been. Maybe it was true, not all was as it appeared. The writing on the cave wall, what had it said? "Red road home." I looked at the shining city on the mountain beyond the chasm. Was Charis the home I'd never known but always longed for?

Perhaps it made no sense to walk toward this chasm—then so be it. If a thousand things that made sense to me had turned out wrong, perhaps this thing that didn't make sense would turn out right. If the only way to cross this country was to walk the floor of a chasm, that's exactly what Nick Seagrave would do. Because that shimmering vision beyond the chasm, that place called Charis, was where I wanted to go.

"Let's go," I said. "I'm walking the red road."

Shad smiled broadly, a lopsided grin that drooped on one corner of his mouth. He looked just wacky enough to make me wonder why I'd stopped questioning his sanity.

As I walked behind Shad, I heard a clanging in my left pocket. Frodo looked up curiously. Something told me just to keep ignoring the sound. I did.

It took us most of the day to descend the mountain. At its base, with only a few hours' transition, it became barren desert. It turned arid so rapidly that my nose felt raw just from breathing. The desert was nothing but rock, sand, and salt flats. It was too dry here for clouds to form. The harsh landscape was unforgiving and unsoftened by rains or vegetation—nothing but pitted rocks, sandblasted and wasted. I fingered a few cactuses that had been cut wide open, robbed of their water stores by thirsty travelers. They were hard as truck tires.

We passed a lone mesquite tree, its roots deep, squeezing some hidden drops of moisture out of the rocky ground. The only living things I saw were a few brown lizards and a golden tortoise Frodo pointed to, harassing him until I called him off. I decided the tortoise deserved some credit for defying the odds and surviving where he had no right to.

The only rises in the desert were mounds of formless slag, surrounded by oily black ooze that emitted foul fumes.

Once in the flatlands I couldn't see the chasm. I began to wonder if my eyes had played tricks on me up on the mountain. If it was really there, and we were this close, I'd surely be able to see it, wouldn't I?

I looked in the distance at the shining city. I stared at it, feeling my heart ache when it shimmered out of sight even for a moment and feeling revived when it reappeared. What was it really like there? I had to know. Nothing else mattered.

We camped for the night. The tents were with David and Victoria, wherever they were, so we slept under the stars…except there were none. Which was strange because there didn't appear to be a cloud cover, though in the desert it was hard to be sure of what I saw.

That night I heard no sounds except wolves howling in the far distance and creepy screams I decided must be peacocks. I felt tense and uneasy, relaxing into a smile only when Frodo, inspired by the wolves, lifted up his snout and cut loose with a heartfelt but pathetic howl.

In the morning we'd journeyed only a few hours when I began to smell something foul. The loathsome stench invaded my nostrils and gripped my stomach. Something terrible was in the air. Crook-necked vultures and some unfamiliar birds of prey, hoary and weathered, circled above. They peered down expectantly. I couldn't escape the feeling that this vast stretch of land had fed their morbid appetites for millennia. Were we their next meal?

Suddenly I stopped dead and blinked my eyes. What had appeared to be level land stretching out into the distance was the very thing I'd seen from the mountaintop and hoped was an illusion—it was a vast chasm stretching out farther than I could see, with white rocks scattered around its edges. I should have been prepared for this, but it was very different viewing the chasm from a distance than seeing—and smelling—it at its edge.

I turned my head, looking for some way around the abyss. But it was as wide as it was long. I recoiled at the sight of corpses on both sides of me, on the sloping walls of the chasm where I couldn't see them before. The nearer I got, the more the stench of rotting flesh made me gag. As far as I could see, the fringes of the chasm were lined with corpses. I watched as reptilian carrion-fowl feasted on human entrails, picking bones and pulling tendons with their great beaks.

Upon closer inspection, what I thought at first were scattered white rocks in the sand, I realized now were human bones, picked clean by wind and sand and predators. The chasm before me was not some natural wonder, but an unnatural graveyard, unspeakably vast, with no tombstones or caretakers, nothing but the beating sun and the merciless winds of time.

The air was dry, yet thick with death, so thick I felt like I was breathing through a wet dishrag. Covering my nose and inhaling through my mouth, I moved on the red road to the very edge of the chasm. I scanned it, wondering if there might yet be a way to descend into it and cross. The wound in my neck, oozing again, and the moisture in my eyes drew flies, which I kept swatting, unable to keep them at bay.

As I held it in my hand, I realized that the white sand of the chasm edges was not sand at all, but powdered bone. What did the millions of human bones mean, scattered as far as I could see? Didn't it mean that others before me, many no doubt smarter and better than I, had tried to find their way around and over and across the chasm?

It didn't take Sherlock Holmes to piece it all together. Large piles of bones covering the sloped side of the chasm testified to the distances people had traveled. Some had gone much farther than I would have thought possible, given the steepness of the slope. Groups of bones, some of them gathered on narrow shelves, showed some had tried to cross together, while countless scattered remains showed many had tried to make it alone.

Though some made it a few miles farther down the sheer edge of the chasm than others—either by climbing skill or long falls to their deaths—none came close to crossing it. Indeed, it would be impossible to cross, for as deeply as I gazed into the chasm, I could see no hint there was ground to walk on. It appeared to be a bottomless pit. Even if it weren't, who could possibly cross it? And if by some miracle they did, who could even begin to climb the other side? I *wanted* to cross it—but how could I?

I slapped my forehead, killing a couple of flies and stirring up others.

That sound—what was it? Haunting voices rising from the pit! But…how? The voices were faint yet distinct, full of sorrow and regret and bitterness and self-preoccupation. Voices of those who had no hope, who still had the longings of humanity but no possibility of fulfillment. A chill pierced my bones. Were these the voices of the disembodied souls of the corpses and bones surrounding me? Were they the voices of the damned?

I'd consoled myself that perhaps the souls once joined to these bones no longer existed. But they *did* exist, didn't they? It was not unconscious oblivion—they knew, they *were* aware. A knot constricted my throat, and I gulped furiously for air.

I fell down as a sickening wave of terror welled up from my belly.

I stretched out on the sand, grabbing it with clenched fists. It sifted through my fingers. I could not hold the sands of death. Flies crawled on my neck, picking at my wounds.

"It's hard to accept, isn't it?" a creaky voice asked. I lifted my head, brushing sand from my eyebrows. I looked up at Shad. Beside him stood Malaiki, and next to her was Victoria.

"I *don't* accept it," I said. "I can't. I won't."

I stood and searched the landscape, looking for someone else. Where was Quon? Had he been killed in the battle I narrowly escaped? I remembered the desperation in his voice, and my gut ached. I wished I'd made it to him on the battlefield.

"Where are the others?" I asked.

Shad looked down, and Malaiki said, "We don't know." Her voice cracked, and a tear ran down her cheek.

I gazed again at the abyss, at the battered remains of people who had tried to cross it, hoping to see it differently this time. The more I stared, the more I clinched my teeth.

When I had turned from all the other roads, the roads of emptiness and despair, I'd dared to hope the red road might be different. I'd dared to hope my mother's prayers meant something after all. But here I was at death's end, robbed of any comforting illusions.

"If there's a king," I shouted, "why would he do this?"

"Why do you blame the King?" Shad asked. "It wasn't he who made the chasm."

"Then who did?"

Shad stared at me and pointed his bony finger. "You did."

I paced like an animal, fiercely resisting the absurd notion that I was to blame for this infinite stretch of ruin. I felt sweat pooling on the bridge of my nose. It fell like heavy tears down my cheeks.

My eyes burned as if open in salt water. I felt the same tugging in my chest, the same longing that had pulled me down the road. But now I had no hope the yearning could ever be satisfied. I'd lived as a disconnected soul, and I would die as one. I would never enter Charis—how could I? The City of Light was nothing but a cruel joke—a comfort to the ignorant, an insult to the informed.

My body dropped like a sack of grain on rocky ground. My right temple throbbed, even more when I slapped flies from it without thinking. I sought the solace of sleep—a consolation those in the abyss would never know.

Then, my head poised over the side of the chasm, I heard again the desperate voices of the damned, of those who had abandoned hope. Suddenly I heard another cry, much closer and louder, a hideous piercing shriek erupting as if from a wounded animal.

I turned and looked to see where the howl had come from, clutching my raw throat in terror. No one else was there.

In a moment of horror I realized the scream had been my own.

9

WHERE HAD THIS CHASM come from? Had it been carved out in antiquity by erosion from rushing water? There was certainly no sign of water now. Nothing living, nothing growing. No sooner did I think this than I saw at my feet a single desert flower, bright yellow with seven petals, in full bloom. I shaded the miracle with my hands.

I walked away from the lone flower, and as I did, hopelessness resumed its gnawing at my bones. Where could I go? I looked back to the east. I could return to the mountain. But then what? Should I go all the way back to Babel? Should I try another of the dead-end roads? Every path promised the same destination. I'd sampled enough of the roads here in Thuros and back on Earth to believe none of them would take me where I wanted to go. Where I wanted to go was the other direction, beyond the chasm—to Charis, the place for which I was made, for which I hungered more than I'd ever hungered for anything.

No! I corrected myself. Charis wasn't real—and even if it was, it was a place of relentless demands, of duty without joy, of endless drudgery. Even Erebus was preferable to that.

I felt the battle rage within me, as one moment I believed Charis was the place for which I longed and in the next countered with a dozen reasons why that notion was foolish.

"Nick!" someone shouted. I turned and saw Quon!

He ran toward me from the east, as I stood at the chasm's edge. He threw his arms around me. Neither of us said anything; we just embraced. Quon reminded me of Brian, just a few years younger than my son. When had Brian last hugged me? I'd never been a touchy-feely guy. But Quon's embrace felt good.

"Where have you been?" I asked him.

Before he could answer, the smile on Quon's face froze, then disappeared. He was looking over the edge, into the chasm, at bones and decaying flesh. His shoulders sagged, his eyes drooped. He stared at the abyss, pulling on his knuckles.

"Eeeeooooouuuu."

Guttural screams erupted from the abyss, animal-like, as if from coyotes caught in bear traps. Instinctively, Quon and I both stepped back. He covered his ears. In the abyss I sensed nothing but raw need and horror, undying thirst without a drop of water.

"It's so... There's no hope," Quon said, weak voiced. "Is there?"

I wanted to reassure him, but what could I say? He was right—there was no hope. The abyss was bottomless, fathomless, uncrossable. Charis, on the far side of the chasm, was but a dream, like Camelot or Atlantis or Mount Olympus. Or if more than a dream, every bit as inaccessible.

"I need to be alone," Quon said, voice trembling. He turned and walked away.

Beside me, without footfalls preceding it, I felt a presence.

"Marcus!"

The dark-haired warrior looked like a man, but his face was expressionless, as if he wasn't quite at home in his body.

"I hear no conversation in the chasm," I said, my voice shaking like Quon's.

"There is no one near enough to talk to, nothing to talk about,"

Marcus said. "Erebus is an endless monologue. What else do you not hear?"

"Music."

"There is none and never will be."

"Not even songs of lamentation?"

"Those who have no hope cannot sing. Charis has a song for every star. It is a country of explosion, expanding with every song, becoming ever larger. Erebus is a closet of implosion, the infinitely small becoming smaller. Relationships, even small ones, are too big for Erebus. Music is too big for Erebus. There is no room for it."

"Noooooo!" The hollow echo of the word erupted from those in eternal solitary confinement.

"Erebus is where the King is not," Marcus said.

"So evil reigns there?"

"Evil cannot reign. In the abyss there is no power. It is merely the void left when all goodness has withdrawn, the shadow without the substance. The doors are forever shut, locked and barred. Not only from outside but inside."

"After our hassles with that church," I said, "my father told us he'd rather have fun with his friends in hell than be stuck with the self-righteous in heaven."

"Fun in Erebus? You might as well talk about a cool breeze in a blast furnace. As for Charis, look for yourself."

Marcus stretched out his hand, and the air's fabric ripped open, so I could see above and beyond the abyss and peer into the City of Light as if it were but a few feet away. People laughed, greeted each other, embraced, conversed with animated expressions. I kept hearing the word "Yes!" It struck me as strange, as I'd always believed if there was a heaven it was a place of naysayers.

I sensed their thoughts, not because I was a mind reader, but because they were mind projectors, with thoughts so powerful their bodies couldn't hold them. I sensed no suffering, but clearly discerned the fruits of suffering they had once endured, like ripples in a lake moving outward in concentric circles, growing larger all the time, never dissipating. In the abyss I sensed no fruit of suffering—only suffering itself.

In Charis I saw citizens busily working, learning, and exploring, overflowing with the joy of discovery. They seemed immersed in delight.

Yes, I knew it was Charis I longed for. Who but a fool would not long for it? But how did those people get there? Surely they couldn't have crossed the chasm!

I heard another blood-curdling scream, then gazed back into the black hole of Erebus. I shuddered.

"Those who wish to have nothing to do with the King get their wish," Marcus said. "But they discover too late it is not what they wished for after all."

"How could the King allow us to go to such a horrid place?"

"If you understood his righteousness and your offenses, you would ask a different question—how could the King allow you to go anywhere else?"

"What's that supposed to mean?"

"It is you who rebelled, you who changed Thuros into Skia, you who turned the garden into Babel and made the abyss, which is but a suburb of Erebus. You wonder why the King does not love you more? The amazing thing is that he loves you at all."

I followed his gaze back through the portal to the great gates of Charis, fortified and shut tight, impenetrable. Outside them was a giant pedestal holding an immense scroll, rolled shut. It looked as if it were made not of parchment but of thick metal. Man after man tried to open it. None succeeded.

"What is the scroll?" I asked Marcus.

"It is the ancient book that tells all things, holds all secrets, offers the only way to cross the chasm, to escape Erebus, and to enter Charis."

My spine tingled at the words "enter Charis." My soul felt pulled to the city as iron filings to a great magnet. I realized I had wanted many things in my life—but I'd never wanted anything so much as to enter that place. Yet it was so far away and the chasm so vast.

"The book cannot be opened by anyone with the slightest imperfection," Marcus said. "Only a perfect being, a man with the character of World-Maker himself, could open the scroll and cross the chasm and break open the gates of Charis so that others might enter."

"A perfect man? Impossible," I said. "No one's perfect!" The image of body upon body in the abyss flashed through my mind. Suddenly the weight of worlds beyond fell upon me, and I collapsed. I wept that no one was worthy to open the book and bridge the abyss.

I had been the Iceman, always guarding my emotions, careful not to show weakness. But then and there my image did not matter. Nothing mattered but the tragedy that no one could change my destiny from the chasm to Charis. The tears flowed—I didn't bother to wipe them. It was the darkest night of my soul.

"Weep no more," Marcus whispered, awe in his voice. When I looked up, I saw in the sky a brilliant supernova. On the ground, just ten feet from me, stood a teenage girl, frail and shy. She reminded me of Malaiki and Salama. Inside the girl was a tiny point of light, a circle moving in her midsection. Suddenly a bolt of lightning from the nova pierced her and struck the tiny circle with awesome precision. Thunder exploded like the clash of cymbals.

The tiny circle appeared different now. It was as if two worlds intersected, the molecules of one joining with those of the other. Before my eyes, eternity's door had swung open, and someone had walked through, the incomprehensibly huge becoming indescribably small. I saw infinity become finite, the invisible visible, the universe next door reduced to a pinpoint.

The tiny dot split in two, again and again. Cells divided and multiplied. I heard a lovely melody, held up by the steady harmony of a beating sound within the young woman's chest. As the concerto progressed, the small dot grew at a terrific rate.

Soon I saw a reddish tan form taking shape. Blunt appendages formed into fingers and toes. A child! Now an infant, he moved outside his mother, a cord was cut, and he was welcomed into the world by…animals. A lamb bleated, and his eyes turned toward it.

Just then an ominous shadow eclipsed the sun, and I heard a terrible squawk above. In a mass of flutter and confusion the ancient winged dinosaur dived down at the baby. I knew I should try to protect him, but I was too terrified by the beast. It hovered only a foot over the child, its drool falling upon his tiny head.

But the beast seemed frozen in the air, unable to reach and devour the child. Suddenly the creature's neck jerked backward, and it rolled on the ground. The monster crouched hungrily and prowled fitfully, pacing circles around the child, never taking his eyes off him. Then for a fleeting moment, I thought I saw the outstretched swords of warriors protecting the baby.

The pterodactyl-like creature roared and flailed the air, then flew away from the child. I watched, my throat dry and hands shaking, as it landed again and devoured many other children in its attempt to get to *the* child.

Before my eyes the infant grew into a toddler, a boy, an adolescent, then a man wearing a white robe. The transformation suddenly stopped. He walked right over to me and looked into my eyes, gluing them to mine. I did not know him, but I sensed he knew me. I felt as if he'd come like a delivery person directly to my door, from somewhere far away, a place he missed and longed for. He was a young man with ancient eyes, and as I gazed into them, I saw what he had seen—a million worlds born and die. Rough and sturdy, face windblown and sun-darkened, his skin was tough, like the sole of a boot. His white robe clung to him, stained with sweat and sawdust.

I saw in his eyes the explosions of a thunderstorm, the collisions of galaxies. He sang a beautiful melody, fresh and young, yet prehistoric, far older than even the flying dinosaur—"I am here to do what must be done...and what no other can do...and what I can do no other way."

As he sang, my heart came alive. I'd heard that tune only once before, on the red road when the rough-looking stranger came, the one I thought at first was Joshua. The one who was short and weather-beaten, his shirt stained with sweat and...sawdust.

The Woodsman! Of course. Why hadn't I recognized him immediately?

He sang the ancient song, giving voice to a musical score written on my heart, on every strand of my DNA. He played me with an instrument I couldn't see; I was the sheet music. He sang of

Orion's belt and Lyra's veil, of the hidden worlds on Andromeda's fringes, of the birth of quasars and the conception of children and the flight of electrons. He sang of the great and the small, of the infinite and the finite, the visible and the invisible, the temporal and the eternal. He sang as one who had existed an eternity before time and matter, as one who knew all secrets and offered to whisper them in the ears of those who would embrace his song and sing it with him, those who would join him in the joy beyond all measure. He sang to me.

The song was beautiful beyond imagination, but now he began to sing it in a minor key. He sang of rebellion and betrayal, of the chasm and blood and suffering and death. The same song that had drawn me to him made me cringe and back away from him who was both the singer and the song.

Another man came walking toward us, singing another song I'd also heard on the road. He was tall and bearded with dark red hair, very handsome, his chest bare, showing chiseled pectorals and biceps. His voice was soothing, almost intoxicating. He looked down at the shorter Woodsman and said, "I have a better song for you. Sing a song of pleasure. Eat the fresh bread. Can't you smell it?"

The Woodsman shook his head.

"Sing a song of possessions; I'll give you the wealth of kingdoms, the finest treasures of Skiathuros."

He shook his head again, eyes burning with resolve.

"Sing a song of power; throw yourself from the mountaintop and command the warriors to catch you."

He shook his head a third time. "I will not sing your song, Pretender," said the Woodsman. "Not now. Not ever."

"Then you will pay the price," the handsome one said through clenched teeth, grinding out the words. At that moment a wave of heat made his plastic face buckle, melting the ice of his eyes. Shark eyes.

The handsome man departed, and the Woodsman began singing his song again. It was very intimate, not a performance, but a serenade, as if he sang just to me. He kept returning to the line, "I come to you so that you can come to me."

The song was so familiar, as if it had been sung within me all my life, but I could never identify the words until now. All my life on earth, and all my time in this new world, I'd been longing to hear that song, to understand it…to *sing* it.

Still, something held me back from the Woodsman. He looked so rough, ferocious, untamed, and untamable. His dark yet white-hot eyes were wild—they hit me like a boxer's blows, swift and relentless. And when he sang in a minor key those terrible words…I could not bear to hear it. I backed away from him, intrigued yet wary, doing battle with myself about who this really was and what claim he might have on me.

The Woodsman walked up to the scroll, put his hands upon it, and opened it effortlessly. He read from it as if it were his autobiography. "I made the worlds, I made the image-bearers, I became one of them to fix them and all they have broken."

He rolled up the scroll, and as his hand let go, the scroll turned hard as bronze.

What he did amazed me yet brought me no comfort, because when I turned and looked, the chasm was still there, and I still had no way to cross it. Nothing had changed.

He walked away from the scroll, toward me. There he stood, only three feet from me, a solitary figure dressed in a plain old tunic, spotted with woodchips, not looking like a champion or a hero, just a wandering woodsman. He gazed at the sprawling blue sky above us, then to Charis in the distance, as if looking toward home. Then he grabbed me with his eyes, holding me.

I squirmed away from his hold, then pointed my finger down at the chasm. Despair and anger welled up in me and exploded into a shouting challenge: "How can I cross the abyss? You demand of me the impossible! Is my longing for Charis your way of torturing me? Have you brought me here just to rub my face in misery?"

10

THE WOODSMAN FOLLOWED my pointing finger and gazed down into the abyss. His eyes watered. I could sense wheels within wheels moving inside him, a churning depth of ponderings and musings beyond my comprehension, as if the wheels had been turning ages before I asked my question.

The Woodsman moved away from the abyss, set his eyes, and focused on something behind me.

I turned and followed his gaze. My jaw dropped. Impossible! Why hadn't I seen it before? It was a great tree, reminding me of a Ponderosa pine, yet many times larger than a California redwood, perhaps sixty feet in diameter and rising above the clouds. The reddish bark was unusual, very rough, with splinters so jagged they looked like barbed fishhooks. The tree cast a long shadow to the west, plunging down into the chasm.

When I looked back at the Woodsman, he held in his hand a great sword. He walked to the tree, put his hands on it, and touched his head against it softly. He lifted up the great sword in his hand, felt its sharpness with his finger, then swung it back and uncoiled it against the trunk of the tree. The stringy cedarlike bark exploded, and chunks flew off.

I couldn't imagine how this tree might be cut through, not by the greatest ax and certainly not with a sword.

Why are you doing this?

I watched as he swung the sword again and again with terrible force. He took off his white outer robe and rewrapped it around his midsection, leaving his dark chest bare. His sinewy muscles rippled as he hewed the wood. He thrashed and pounded, again and again. Sweat poured down his forehead and off his cheeks. Small capillaries in his cheeks and brow burst with the pressure, mingling blood with sweat.

I came up close to the Woodsman, alarmed at his exertion and the toll it was taking on him. He spoke as he labored, and I listened to him, hearing things I'd never heard, things I'd never thought of—about himself, about me, about the meaning of life. "I offer a joy that will cost you everything you have, but gain you everything that matters." What did he mean?

"You have fallen short and a terrible price must be paid." I backed away from him, troubled. Was he saying I was at fault for all this? How dare he blame me?

I couldn't explain how a man of normal size could reach into the center of a tree with a diameter ten times larger than his height and continue to swing a sword against it. Nor could I explain why his sword did not break or dull. But I saw it nonetheless, with my own skeptic's eyes.

"Can I help you?" I asked him.

"No," he said, eyes lonesome. "You can't."

Why wouldn't he accept my help? Did he think I had nothing to offer? That I wasn't good enough for him?

He cut on that tree all day and through a long lonely night. I sipped senaba juice from my bottle but ate nothing. I dozed on and off, feeling useless but intrigued by his actions and his words.

In the morning, with one great thrash of his sword, the whole tree wobbled. I ran back, looking up, watching its movement and realizing I couldn't outrun its fall. I moved back and forth, uncertainly, hoping to position myself in the safest place. While I settled on the east side of the tree, the Woodsman stood motionless with a dusky expression, staring at it.

As I watched, he pushed the tree with his right hand, toward the west. It tipped slowly and eerily before gravity grabbed it and began to slam it downward. Mesmerized by the awesome sight, I felt relieved it wasn't going to crush me.

The great tree fell. When it hit the ground, it exploded with what seemed the force of a nuclear warhead. I flew into the air and landed facedown, sprawled on the ground.

The Woodsman lay in a heap, sweating, exhausted, his veins bulging, his worn clothes stained crimson.

Then he stood. He looked across the expanse, to the other side of the chasm, and walked to the base of the fallen tree.

But…why was the tree still there? Why didn't it do what I had expected and plummet into the chasm? It had landed crosswise. This could only mean…its top had reached the far edge of the chasm! Impossible as it seemed, the great tree lay on both sides of the abyss.

The Woodsman slowly took off his sandals and set them on the ground.

Then I heard an eerie buzzing noise coming from below the Woodsman. I walked closer, looked down, and at his feet saw tiny people, the size of insects, maybe half an inch tall. I carefully got on my knees for a closer look.

The little people scurried about and wrapped fragile threads around the Woodsman's feet. To ones so small the threads must have seemed great ropes.

"We have him now," I heard one gloat squeakily. "He can't get away from us."

"He can't tell us what to do."

"We'll show him. We'll force him onto the tree!"

I laughed and called down to them, "With one flick of a toe he would break your threads, and with a stomp of his feet you would all be smashed!"

As I ridiculed the pathetic arrogant men below, suddenly I stopped laughing when I saw them next to me. Standing eye to eye with them now, I saw a huge shadow and looked up. There, far above me was…the Woodsman!

Had I become small or had the Woodsman become big? Perhaps it was both. Maybe that explained how he could cut through the huge tree. I was so much smaller than I'd thought, and he was so much bigger than he looked—things were not as they appeared.

I heard the sound of someone pounding with a hammer, but it was a dull tearing sound, not the crisp, loud sound of nails driven into wood. Where was it coming from?

I heard jingling metal and looked around me and saw people pulling things from their pockets. I reached into my left pocket and pulled out…a handful of nails.

I saw now that each person had a hammer. I watched motionless as person after person positioned nails on the Woodsman's giant feet.

"No!" I shouted. "What has he done to you?"

What horrified me most was that the people seemed so normal, even nice.

"Beautiful day, isn't it?" a woman in a white nurse's uniform asked me as she positioned a nail and hammered it five times until it was buried to its head in the Woodsman's foot.

"Where's your hammer?" asked a businessman in suit and tie. "Here's an extra. Glad to share."

I took the hammer. It hung limp in my right hand. After watching this for a few minutes, it seemed less horrible. Something moved in my chest, and before I knew it, I was thinking about how big the Woodsman was, how distant he was, and how little he cared about me, and how he hadn't made my life go the way I wanted, and how he thought he was better than me and had dared to cast blame on me. I took the hammer and started pounding nails into his heel, first one and then another and another. I felt gleeful, almost giddy.

"Nick! How's it going?"

I looked over at Victoria, pounding her own nails into his feet. I saw David and Quon and Malaiki and Salama doing the same.

I felt the skin of my stomach bulge and saw a pulsating lump move up into my chest and out to my ribs, racing within me, as if I were hollow. Now the fuzzy gerbil appeared on my chest, comforting me. I petted it, then immediately resumed pounding.

I hammered nails feverishly, harder and harder. No matter how many nails I took out of my pocket, it was still full.

Then I thought about the Woodsman, about how much this must be hurting him. The individual nails might have felt like a pinprick, but the cumulative effect of all those people pounding all those nails must have been agonizing.

I began to weep and threw down my hammer and tried to pull away. But I could only get so far—I realized now that I was tied to the others with the sticky strands of a great web, strong and binding, that I couldn't break loose from. I picked my hammer back up and did what everyone else was doing.

"It's he who makes us suffer," someone said, pointing upward, then pounding another nail into his foot.

"Take that," I bellowed, and pounded nails into his heel.

"Nice work, Nick," Quon said.

"You too," I replied, seeing the blood trickle down from the nail he'd just pounded.

"Look out," someone yelled. People scattered, some of them pointing upward. A water droplet as big as a person splashed onto the ground, moisture flying everywhere. It felt warm on my face and had a salty taste.

"Back to work," someone shouted, and we moved in again close to his feet, grabbing our nails and positioning our hammers, as if going back to an assembly line after lunch hour.

For another stinging moment I grasped the horror of what I was doing. I cried. After wiping my eyes, I grew angry at how I'd suffered, how my dad wasn't there for me and how my family had abandoned me. I picked the hammer back up, pulled the replenished stock of nails out of my pocket, and started pounding again.

A thunderous noise came from above the head of the Woodsman. I looked up in the sky and saw a vast army of bright warriors, beating down upon a transparent ceiling. Swords unsheathed, they jammed themselves against a closed portal in the ceiling. Though far below them, I heard their muffled pleas as they called to the Woodsman.

"Let us tend your wounds, World-Maker."

"Let us stomp your enemies and raise your royal standards in their blood!"

"Let us invade Skiathuros, fight the holy war now, and bury forever the twisted ones!"

They paced like caged lions, looking down, searching for permission, longing for a single word to unleash them. I shuddered at the sight of them, legion upon legion, crowding down, pressing and pushing, crying out and begging leave to destroy us who drove the nails into his feet.

"Let us run the cowards through with the sword of your righteousness."

"Let us rid the cosmos of their evil forever."

The more we below drove our nails, the more restless, even frantic, became the warriors above. They pushed against the glass ceiling until I heard cracking and feared it would burst.

The Woodsman raised his hand to the warriors and sternly shook his head. "Hold your place," said the deep, powerful voice.

I felt something under my feet and looked down to see the ground beneath me thin out and transform until it became clear, a glass floor. I saw horrid faces pressing their mouths and snouts against the glass and smearing it with drool and mucus. I moved backward, away from what I saw, but could not escape them because they were everywhere below me. They looked like the warriors above, yet very different, as a rabid dog looks the same as a normal one, yet doesn't. I closed my eyes, hardly able to look at them, but when I opened them again, the twisted creatures were still there, pushing and pressing up.

Their eyes were cold gray, cold as death itself, bloodless, the eyes of predators, while the eyes of the warriors above the glass ceiling were hot and furious and alive.

The shark-eyed warriors below kept pressing up against the floor, searching for every crack, just like their counterparts above. The ground beneath me pushed up, and my heart raced.

Would these dark creatures escape from their pit? What would they do to us? Would it be worse than what the warriors above would do if they got their hands on us? I looked over at Malaiki, hammer in her hand, flesh quivering. I read in her face the same questions. I wondered if she was as terrified as I.

The Woodsman looked down and cleared his throat, as if about to speak. The warriors below shuddered and winced and backed away from the glass, covering their hideous faces, as if anticipating a decree of doom.

I held my breath. What would he say? At last he slowly nodded at the beasts below. "Yes," he whispered, a whisper that blew a powerful wind, forcing me to my knees.

The faces of the beasts lit with malevolent glee. They swarmed beneath me in a circle, like a dark tornado. The land quaked and the glass floor cracked open, and foul-smelling gasses rose. About ten yards from me, right at the Woodsman's feet, the glass shattered and a geyser of putrid chemicals gushed up, creating a stench I could barely stomach, chasing me as I fled. In the midst of the eruption was an army of flying beasts. They screeched and squawked and cackled, celebrating their release like drunken pirates.

Some of the creatures flew low, just feet above us. "Don't let him push you around," one of them cried in shrill but perfectly enunciated words that chilled me.

"You can do whatever you want—he's not your master," said another. Some of the reptiles whispered suggestions, some screamed commands into the ears of the little people who pounded their nails into the Woodsman's heel. The beasts herded in more and more of us, close to his bleeding feet. In one moment I felt outraged at the people piercing him with nails, and in the next I looked down to see my own hand bringing down hammer on nail.

Smaller winged dinosaurs hovered over us, trying to sink their claws into the Woodsman. The flying beasts were much larger than we were, but small enough that the Woodsman could easily have swatted or squashed them with his hand. Several of them pecked at his hands, drawing a little blood, the droplets falling to the ground with a huge splash, though far away enough not to touch me. Still, the beasts seemed limited in their ability to harm the Woodsman directly. They had great success, however, ushering the little people to do their dirty work.

"The tyrant is your enemy," one of them shouted. The monster swooped low and pushed me and several others aside with his slimy jaws. I rolled, then got up shoving and kicking the people who struck and screamed at me. Seething with panicked rage, I pulled more nails from my pocket, held them in my mouth, and in rapid succession drove them into the Woodsman's heel, drawing blood.

"Take that!" I shouted. "No one can tell me how to run my life. How dare you treat me like this?"

The great foot trembled, as if in a spasm, but did not move away from me. For a fleeting moment I wondered why I was punishing the Woodsman for what the beast had done, for what I had done, for what others had done to me. But in the next moment it all seemed perfectly logical. It felt so good to be in control, to determine my own destiny, to choose to do something with my hands, something that made a difference. I was in charge, the Woodsman was at my mercy—and I showed him none.

Another great drop of saltwater fell from above, hitting the bleeding foot and splashing off on me, stinging my eyes. I cursed, then wiped my eyes, blinked hard, grabbed another nail, and started pounding, making up for lost time, drawing more blood. The more I swung the hammer the easier it became, the more automatic. Blood of the innocent, shed at my whim and convenience? It wasn't the first time, I thought, then immediately pushed back nagging memories to the dark corners of my mind. No—what I'd done and what I was doing were reasonable and just. And besides, everyone else was doing it.

I heard voices far above and stopped hammering long enough to look up. I saw in the sky, above the Woodsman, the great red-garbed general of the army of light, the mighty one I'd seen on the battle-field. He parted from his soldiers and came down in front of the Woodsman's eyes—apparently he alone was allowed to pass down through the glass ceiling. He bowed his knees in midair and looked at his commander in chief, eyes pleading.

The Woodsman returned the gaze of his general and for a moment hung his head and winced. He shifted on his feet, and I heard a guttural groan from within him, as loud as thunder.

"Let us destroy them now, Master—*please*." The general's deep voice shook the ground beneath me, causing me to tremble. I felt certain this was the only one to whom this prince of warriors had ever said "please."

"Michael," replied the Woodsman in a tired, hurting voice, "you know if that was what I wanted I could unmake them all in a single moment or destroy them with merely a thought."

"But why, Master, do you not let us protect you and defend your honor? Why do you let them torture you?"

The Woodsman's wet eyes drooped. "Because…it is the only way to save them."

The warrior-lord seemed to search the air for more words. Finding none, he bowed his head and turned away. When he passed up through the glass, the soldiers listened in rapt attention. I heard some of them groan and shout, while others stood in stunned silence. Again they pressed and beat against the invisible ceiling, for them a floor, and for a moment I thought they would surely break through. I clenched my teeth, knowing if they escaped, my comrades and I would be crushed by the weight of their wrath.

They pushed until the ceiling cracked. I cringed and braced myself.

"Noooooo!"

Everything shook at the lionlike roar. At the utterance of the Woodsman's word, millions of warriors were sucked up into invisible regions of the sky as if into the vacuum of space. They disappeared, all of them.

There was only silence above. But from under the ground and on the earth shouts of glee and malice filled the air. The beasts ran wild, serial killers with the restraint of law enforcement completely removed. They swooped and bit at the Woodsman's neck, while prodding the little people to keep piercing his heel, from which blood gushed.

I looked at the blood on my own hands. I gazed up at the giant, certain that in one moment, deliberate or unguarded, he could hurl us into the abyss. Something grabbed hold of my insides and made me stop and wonder.

"Why do you do what you do?" I cried up to him, holding out my hands, with nails and hammer, covered with blood.

He looked down into my eyes, and in the next instant he was looking straight into them—that quickly he had shrunk again to my size. "You are why I do what I do."

My heart was pulled toward him, then I considered his words. Was he blaming me for this again? How dare he? I backed away from him. He stretched out his bloody hand, and I retreated even farther.

A great dark cloud formed and spread. The sky looked as if it had been rubbed hard by a dirty eraser. Within seconds a ferocious wind blew, lightning struck, thunder roared, like the storm in which I first came to this world.

The Woodsman walked alone to the base of the tree. I could not see the nails in his feet now. He climbed up the side of the tree, slowly and deliberately, cutting hands and feet on the barbs. When he got to the top, he stepped on it, his right foot bleeding profusely from the wounds in his heel. The fishhook spurs of the great tree cut into his feet, but he kept walking and wincing, walking and wincing.

He seemed so terribly alone.

The hell-hawks circled over him. The farther he walked on the tree the darker it became. Then, when he was barely visible, I saw him stop, raise his hands, and lie down on the tree. Suddenly he disappeared into the darkness, becoming inseparable from it. For an eternal moment there was nothing, as if all creation braced itself. Then I heard a terrible thud—one, then another, and another, as if hands and instruments from another world fell down on the tree. The force of blows from those great hands must have been much harder to bear than that of the little people.

I heard sounds like flapping tarp and morbid victory shrieks. Then soft weeping. Then nothing.

There was a long silence in which I stared into the darkness of the tree, the darkness of the chasm, and the darkness within me, unable to distinguish one from the others. Then at last the air filled with a solitary scream.

"Whyyyyyy?"

The Woodsman's voice seemed to come not just from the fallen tree above the chasm, but from the depths of the abyss itself. It shook the ground beneath me and the sky above.

The gray sky of death descended on the fallen tree. The longer I looked into the darkness the more I could see. Despite the distance, I beheld the Woodsman pinned to the tree like an insect to a collector's board.

The shark-eyed flying reptile hovered, surrounded by flailing minions, circling as if riding a column of air. Wings outspread, he slowly descended upon the tree. He circled his prey cautiously. He tested the Woodsman with a peck of his beak on his outstretched hands. I heard his deep-throated gurgle of delight as the Woodsman offered no resistance. He pecked and pecked at him, becoming bolder and bolder.

Then a guttural voice, soaked in evil, cried out from the great flying dinosaur.

"Bleed, Elyon! Suffer and die, mighty fool!"

His claws clutching the Woodsman's neck, the flying reptile drove his beak into the Woodsman's eyes. Suddenly the smaller beasts pounced like jackals, picking and eating and gorging themselves on the morbid feast.

I turned away, crying out, partly for his agony, partly for my complicity in it. For though the beast frightened and repulsed me, through the pounding of the nails I had become his partner.

Pacing now, I told myself that the nails I pounded were not fatal, that really they were little more than pinpricks in the giant's feet. But the moisture I'd seen in the Woodsman's eyes and the gut-wrenched tone of his voice said otherwise.

How could I be part of something so monstrous? I'd always believed I was a decent person, sincere, well-motivated, that my good outweighed my bad. Then who was this Nick Seagrave who swung the hammer, who chose to inflict suffering, who served the purposes of the evil beast? Had I just seen the real Nick Seagrave, perhaps for the first time?

Why did I hate the Woodsman so much that I would hurt him so badly? And why, a moment later, did part of me desperately want to love him, so much that I felt I would die if I could not? Who was this person who I would want to hate and love so? I thought of someone else I'd both hated and loved—my father. But this one was far greater than my father, and the love and hate I felt was greater still.

I lay on hard, unforgiving ground, my body aching, my soul tortured by all my questions. Believing the Woodsman was dead already, I was surprised to hear one last word shouted from the center of the tree over the chasm: "Paid!"

The word shook the mountains, from Hagias in the east to Aletheas in the west, from the rising of the sun to its setting. The rocks split; the earth to the far east folded over itself like an ocean wave, molten rock erupting. I heard the rip of fabric, as if the cosmos were a great cloak torn down the center. The sound started far above the sky and hit the ground with a violent tremor. After that, nothing.

The silence of Charis deafened me. Below I heard sounds of glee, the cruel celebration of the bloodless. At last I heard sounds from above and from the west, sounds of weeping.

The City of Darkness rejoiced, the City of Light mourned. Babel partied while Charis wailed in anguish.

I watched the Woodsman—not knowing how I could see so far—through the dark clouds, lying there, lifeless on the tree.

Something dripped into the great chasm. And though the drops were small I could hear them land a million miles below. Their echoes filled the canyon and reverberated inside my skull.

I looked around me, seeing Malaiki, Salama, Victoria, Quon, and David, not knowing how to read what I saw on their faces, knowing only that none of us dared move.

For the King was dead. And we had killed him.

II

BEFORE MY EYES, Erebus crossed in front of Charis and blotted out its light. I beheld the eternal eclipse of hope. The Woodsman was dead. And his blood was on my hands.

My whole body was covered with dirt and blood that had formed into a red clay. Numb, I stumbled around until I found a pumice stone and a small puddle of dirty, undrinkable water that had somehow survived the heat. I tried to wash the bloodstains from my hands. I couldn't. The more I tried, the more the dirt and blood spread.

I grabbed fistfuls of nails from my pocket, again and again, throwing them on the ground or over into the chasm. But still there were more.

Marci always told me I excelled at casting blame and refusing to accept it. But how could I avoid blame for shedding the Woodsman's blood? I'd hammered the nails, hadn't I? I'd stung his feet as surely as if I were a scorpion in the dust.

Still, if he'd been willing to listen to me, to do what I wanted, to use his power to help me fulfill my goals instead of thwarting them… He was asking for it—it was as much his fault as mine. No, it was *more* his fault.

Had I really hammered those nails? Or was it my imagination, fueled by those wretched guilt feelings? I was too hard on myself. Even if I'd driven the nails, I wouldn't have done it without a good reason. Self-defense—that was it. Nick Seagrave was no killer—

even Marci and the kids would have to admit that. I wasn't perfect, but I was a decent person, better than most men.

I heard a familiar purring noise and saw the little gerbil on my chest. I petted it.

Back and forth I wavered, one minute wallowing in grief and guilt, the next in anger and self-defense. I sipped a few more drops from my water bottle, figuring that unless I found some decent water, I would soon die of thirst if I didn't head back toward the mountain.

No! I'd rather die here than go back and try another dead-end road. I'd been lied to and disillusioned and made a fool of one time too many to start it all over again.

Quon chewed his fingernails. David paced, fixated on his position locator. The twins sat near each other but didn't talk, didn't look each other in the eyes. Victoria gazed blankly at the tree over the chasm, a look of disbelief frozen on her face. I said nothing to my companions. After what we'd seen each other do, what was there to say?

In the distance, over the chasm, I heard the predators continue their feeding frenzy upon the Woodsman's carcass.

Did I really help serve them up this morbid meal?

Now I was pacing, kicking rocks, spitting out dust, moving up to the edge of the chasm and looking at it again, thinking maybe somehow it would look different this time. It didn't.

Victoria came up to talk with me, but I backed away, hanging my head, not wanting to hear her excuses or offer mine.

Suddenly I heard the tortured howl of a beast. I looked up to see the great winged reptile retreating from the tree. The howl was quickly followed by hundreds of shrieks from the circling minions.

The lesser reptiles flew toward our side of the chasm, fleeing in chaos from whatever it was they saw. Circling wildly, crashing into one another, they spied the hole in the glass floor and spiraled downward, crowding through and disappearing from Skia.

Then came a booming sound, like an approaching freight train, from the center of the tree. A gigantic stone was rolling on top of the tree with enormous momentum. As the flying dinosaur tried to flee, it was yanked down by some invisible force, and its head was caught on the tree. The great stone ran over it as it squawked hideously. Somehow the beast managed to flail its way toward the edge of the chasm, head mangled and bleeding.

It wove through the air thrashing and falling. It skidded to the ground no more than fifty feet from me. Then it got up, staggering. Its cold murky eyes stared at me, freezing my blood. I felt sure its wound was fatal, but the beast uttered a grisly cry, then wobbled to a hole in the ground and disappeared.

Still rolling, the stone flew off the end of the tree, coming so near to me I had to leap out of its way. Behind it walked a solitary figure—the Woodsman, wearing his white robe, now unstained by blood or sweat or tears.

Then the whole world shifted before me. The land I stood on seemed to sink, and the land on the other side of the chasm rose—Charis with it. The tree was no longer horizontal but vertical, still connecting the two worlds, no longer as bridge but ladder. Against the upright tree stood the Woodsman himself, though he was much bigger than the tree. His feet touched the ground of the lower world, and his head rose above the ground of the upper world. The cosmos had been reoriented, and for a moment the upside down became right side up.

Who was this Woodsman? How had he beaten death?

No sooner had this happened than everything became as it was, horizontal again—two worlds joined by one bridge, the great tree, and the Woodsman normal sized.

All the retaining walls of my mind—carefully constructed to deny the supernatural, to explain away the miraculous—fell to the ground like shacks in a hurricane. Much of what I'd seen in Thuros had beaten upon those walls, but only now did they collapse in ruins. I knew then, in the face of the Woodsman's return from the abyss, that the course of my journey had been charted by an unseen hand, which had led me not just to this world, but to this moment. Yet I felt not only awe, but terror.

I watched the Woodsman go to Malaiki now and talk to her. They were too far away to hear, engaged in private dialogue.

What are they talking about?

Eventually they moved toward the tree. They climbed up and walked upon it. Malaiki seemed to buckle and falter, as if in pain. I feared she would fall. But they walked hand in hand, moving farther and farther away, then appeared to blend into one, until they disappeared from sight.

Despite the distance, it wasn't long before the Woodsman came back, without Malaiki. Next he chose Quon, whose feet shifted and head hung. Quon bit his nails while they talked. What was going through his mind? Did he have the same doubts and fears as I? What was the Woodsman saying? If only I could hear.

Eventually Quon walked with the Woodsman to the tree. I thought I saw him shake and heard him cry out as he stepped onto it. Was the Woodsman pushing him? Forcing him? Or just holding him up? The two of them walked the tree until they finally disappeared into the western sky.

Why did he come for Malaiki and Quon before coming for me? Maybe he won't come for me at all!

What would I do if he didn't come for me? I'd do what I'd always done. I'd take care of myself. Besides, once they were out of my sight, Malaiki and Quon likely fell into the chasm. One false move on that long walk and they'd plunge into the abyss. Perhaps they'd been shoved off. I wouldn't let that happen to me.

Now the Woodsman returned again—was he coming for me? No, he went to Salama. I thought I knew what would happen next. But it didn't. Salama didn't walk with him to the tree. Instead, after just a few minutes of talking, she turned around and ambled away from the chasm.

Salama hadn't gone more than thirty feet when she turned and looked back at the Woodsman. Then, at about a hundred feet she turned back again and once more at perhaps three times that distance. I assumed that from where she now stood she couldn't see the chasm and could barely see the Woodsman.

I watched her hike toward the mountain I'd descended with Shad. Where was the old man now, anyway? And what would become of Salama? Would she rejoin the people she'd met on one of the side roads? Perhaps those who told her she could find truth in all religions everywhere and anywhere? I didn't see her turn around again. I watched, almost hypnotized by her departure, until she disappeared over the plain.

I could run and catch her within ten minutes.

I took several steps her direction. But what would I tell her when I caught her? Would I try to bring her back or go with her to the mountains? Part of me said one, part the other. I didn't know which part I would listen to.

When at last I looked back toward the chasm, I saw Victoria walking the tree with the Woodsman. She appeared to slip and fall, and my heart stopped, until he pulled her up again. I didn't see David anywhere. I assumed he must have crossed before Victoria, while I'd been watching Salama.

Would the Woodsman come back for me? Did I want him to?

The gerbil had disappeared, but something within me moved and pressed against my skin, bulging, causing pangs of torment. In the world's worst way I wanted to relieve the pain and run off and join Salama before having to face the Woodsman. I could provide her company, protect her, help her on the climb. I was flooded with a thousand noble reasons to run away from the chasm and the Woodsman and join her.

I felt my heart in my throat. The Woodsman was returning. I was the only one left. He headed right for me. Though he had the form of a man, I felt pursued by a lion, wild and uncontrollable. As he came near, I saw his eyes, deep and dark, so dark I could not see the pupils, making it seem the large brown iris *was* the pupil. I felt he looked at me through lenses far bigger than a man's. I sensed those eyes—like doorways to another world—saw every inch of me, outside and in.

I looked down at his hands and feet, then shuddered at the scars I saw there. I examined my bloodstained hands and stared at the ground, ashamed.

"Hello, Nick."

I said nothing and didn't look up.

"The deed is done," he said. "The price is paid. The red road continues. The tree is there to cross. Now there is a way to the City of Light. Will you accept my invitation to cross the chasm?"

"But…how can it be crossed? It's so huge."

"The chasm is huge, but the tree is bigger still. And I am far bigger than the tree."

"My friends who went with you—did they make it to the other side? Or did they...fall off and die?"

"They did not fall off. But in a sense they did die."

"What?" My stomach tightened.

"You cannot cross the chasm without dying. If you stay here, you will die. If you walk the tree, you will die in a different way. But the tree is the only way to life. You are already dead. You may choose to die again and stay dead or to die again and embrace life—but in either case you must die again. Nothing that has not died can be raised from the dead."

"I don't understand."

"You don't have to—but to cross you do have to trust me."

"What must I do?"

"You cannot earn your way. You must only receive the gift I freely offer, the gift I paid for. Admit responsibility for the abyss. Acknowledge you pierced my skin with your nails. Affirm I am the World-Shaper who crossed the chasm for you. Ask me to deliver you from the scorpion inside and the web outside and the flying beast above. Invite me to walk you across the chasm."

Objections descended on me like a swarm of flies. I felt a terrible sting within, then saw the gerbil attached to my chest. "Be careful who you trust," Joshua had said to me. Could I really trust the Woodsman? "Things aren't what they appear." Maybe the Woodsman wasn't who he appeared to be. Maybe he only wanted to get me over the chasm so he could push me off the tree.

"I'm not sure," I said. "I don't think I'm ready."

"I have done what was necessary. I have made my choice—now you must make yours."

"Exactly…who are you?" I asked.

"I am the source of your life and of your dreams. I am the dream itself buried deep within you. But be warned—to those who do not embrace the dream, I become the nightmare."

"Then, did I see you before I came to this world?"

"There are fleeting moments when all image-bearers catch glimpses of the eternal. In those moments, it was me you saw, me you longed for." He paused. "Yet you have only now begun to see me clearly—and there is much about me you still do not see. Do you have something to say to me, Nick?"

I sat quietly for several minutes, then cleared my throat, both eager to talk and dreading it.

"I used to be so sure of myself, certain I wasn't to blame, that whatever went wrong, it was someone else's fault—Marci's, Amy's, Brian's, my father's, my coworkers', the church's. And maybe…yours, though I didn't know it was you. I feel now like all my life I've been no more than a little country, surrounded on the north, south, east, and west with nothing but myself, full of self-deception and self-pity and self-preoccupation."

The Woodsman looked at me, nodding, but waiting as if I must say more. I rehearsed to him every offense, every failing, everything I could think of—everything from pride and arrogance to lust and greed and failure to be the man my wife and children needed. It took a long time, because the more I said the more my eyes were opened to what I'd never seen before. Each confession led to the next like falling dominoes.

Finally I said, "That's all I can think of for now. But there must be many other wrongs I've done."

"Yes," he said, "and in time I will show them to you, so at last you may be free of them."

I shuddered, wondering what he was thinking of. Quietly he took my hand, and we walked to the tree. I looked down at the abyss and felt my face twitch and sweat drip from my forehead to my cheeks.

"What if I fall?" I asked him.

I expected to hear assurances, but he said nothing. With his help I stepped onto the tree, which was red with blood. My feet were cut immediately, and I began to bleed. I walked only ten yards before my feet were bloody pulps, and I could go no farther.

I looked at him, not knowing what to do—only that I wanted to cross the chasm but knew I could not.

The Woodsman picked me up and held me in his arms. For a fleeting moment I remembered my father holding me like this when he carried me into the emergency room after my bike accident on my tenth birthday.

The Woodsman walked on, picking up the pace. If he made one false step, I'd fall into the abyss. For a passing moment I wished I'd stayed on the safe ground of the chasm's edge. *Safe?* I questioned myself. How much worse could anything be than to be stranded on the rim of the abyss?

If the Woodsman can't do what he claims, all is lost. But if he can't do what he claims, all is lost anyway.

As we crossed the chasm, he stopped near the middle and with his hands wiped the dirt and blood off me and onto himself. The dirtier the Woodsman became the cleaner I became, until he was completely dirty and I completely clean. He picked me up again, and I looked down into the abyss and shivered at the spiraling darkness below, a drain that seemed to suck ever downward. He drew me close to his chest, and I felt secure in his strong arms. What place could be safer? I gazed into those wide brown eyes and felt I was not just seeing him but seeing the universe itself for the first time.

As we approached the far edge of the chasm, I sensed I was not the same person who'd stepped out onto the tree on the other side.

Before I knew it, the Woodsman had jumped off the tree with me still in his arms, cushioning me from the impact. When he put my feet on the ground, I looked at the terrain, flat and lush with vegetation. I looked back at the abyss and gazed wide-eyed at how far we had come—for in the distance the eastern mountain above the chasm was but a small marker on the horizon, and the mountain above Babel that I'd first descended was only a remote mound of motionless smoke.

I stared at the chasm. Was I imagining this? How could we have crossed something so immense at all, much less in what had seemed only a few minutes?

The Woodsman put his hand on my shoulder.

"I did it all for you."

I didn't know what to say.

"I would have done it for you alone."

I hung my head, feeling both unworthiness and awe.

"And if there was need, I would do it for you again. But there is no need—it is finished. Paid in full."

I reached down to my left pocket. I gasped as I felt the bulge. One by one I pulled out the shafts of pointed metal. On them I saw dried blood. How could this be?

"I still have nails in my pocket."

"Yes. But only for now. There will be none in Charis."

"I don't deserve what you've done for me."

"Of course you don't deserve it." He smiled. "If you deserved it, you wouldn't need it. And I wouldn't have had to die to give it to you."

"But if you knew all I've done, all that's inside me…"

"*If?* I know everything. I am never taken by surprise. There are no skeletons in your closet. I took care of them all. You were wrong—I do not expect the impossible of you. But I have done the impossible for you."

He reached out his hands to me, hands I once thought monstrous. I held them, put my fingers on his scars. I lowered my forehead to his marred hands.

When I looked up, I gazed at Charis, poised beautifully on Mount Aletheas, the red road winding toward it. But it still seemed far away.

"I'm confused," I said. "We're not there yet."

"No. Of course not. Your journey isn't over. Your service for me is just beginning. There was no work you could do for me on the other side of the chasm. But I have much work for you to do on this side."

"And when the work is done?"

"Then you will enter Charis, capital city of my unending country that stretches to the far reaches of the cosmos and beyond—and should you ever make it that far, Nick, I will create for you new worlds that surpass anything you have ever imagined."

I felt my ears move back, pushed by my grin. I wondered if it was as big as his grin. "I long to go to Charis."

"Why?" he asked, surprising me.

"To escape from reality, maybe that's part of it."

He laughed. "Going to Charis is not escaping reality—it's entering reality! You have always lived in the Shadowlands. You cannot conceive what it will be like once you're in the light. Yet in your dreams I have given you faint glimpses of it. That's why Charis has always called to you, why you have always longed for it."

"But why is it still so far away?" I asked, pointing to the west.

"At moments Charis will seem close to you; sometimes it will seem impossibly far. But every day on the red road you will be one day closer to it. I am building a home for you. I'll be there to welcome you when you arrive."

My heart sang and sank in the same moment.

"You're leaving me, then?"

"I'll be inside." He put his hand on my chest. "And I'll give you instructions to show you the way." He reached into his robe pocket, pulled out a big blue senaba, and handed it to me. "I made this for you."

"The place you said you're building for me...what will it be like?"

"A home made just for you. You'll like it." He smiled. "I know how to build." He drew me to himself in a strong embrace.

I didn't blink, didn't move, didn't speak for fear anything I did might end the moment. It was the moment for which I was made. I was embracing the truth I sought, the meaning I desired, the home I'd always yearned for.

Suddenly I felt his firm hug relax. He was gone. At least, I couldn't see him.

But through a portal in the air I saw a gathering on the other side. Hundreds of people were dressed in party garb, while dozens of great warriors served them delicacies, including plates of deep blue, sliced senaba, juice dripping off the sides. They engaged in a great celebration. Then the Woodsman in his white robe joined them.

I heard applause and laughter and saw toasts and festivity, abundant rejoicing. I wondered the cause for their revelry. It was then I realized they were all looking at me.

The portal closed and they disappeared. But though I couldn't see or hear it, I knew the party continued. My party—Nick Seagrave was the cause for celebration!

He'd come to me so I could come to him. I lifted the senaba to my mouth and took a big bite. The dark juice flowed down my cheeks, and I felt like a child, not caring about the stains on my shirt— just savoring the flavor, better than anything I'd ever tasted before.

I heard something, then turned and looked at a great waterfall a hundred yards away—at its bottom, in a river, people were playing and diving and splashing and laughing. I ran the hundred yards, through an open meadow, in what seemed mere seconds, stretching my legs and flailing my arms. I knelt down beside the river and opened my mouth, then splashed cold, clear water into it.

For the first time in my life, my thirst was fully satisfied. I ran and dove into the pool under the waterfall, cool and refreshing, opening my eyes and mouth, relishing every moment.

Still underwater, I felt a hand on my shoulder and turned to see bright eyes that were familiar yet different—Quon! We hugged each other and surfaced together. I looked into his eyes, filled with joy where I'd last seen hopelessness. We laughed together, then cried together. We swam to Malaiki and Victoria and hugged them too.

Then someone from my right side splashed my face with cool water. I turned and gave a great bear hug to a white-haired, stoop-shouldered old codger who was grinning from ear to ear.

12

AWAKENED BY THE WHISPERS of distant suns, I pushed sleep from my eyes. Exhausted from the chasm-crossing and the subsequent celebrations with my companions, I had dozed off just after dinner for a few hours, lying in the softness of the meadow near the waterfall. The night was quiet and warm, and I gazed at the black sky, swollen with stars.

I could see not just pinpoints of light, but visible star surfaces, with planets dancing around them. Red giants, white dwarves, neutron stars, black holes made visible against the backdrop of exploding stars. I saw the swirls of distant galaxies, ringed planets, volcanic moons, giant ice-ball comets, the colored pallets of backwoods nebulae. Each had a story unknown to me, but I sensed they were waiting to tell me, waiting for the day I'd be ready to hear their stories and perhaps explore them.

My eyes were drawn to one section of the sky, where I saw two great red stars and above them six stars forming a shape…a mane! Of course. This was the constellation Shad had called the Lion. I couldn't quite see the two clusters he'd called the Lion's uplifted paws, but the head and mane were strikingly clear.

Why could I see now what I couldn't before? Maybe I'd been too close to the man-made lights of the dark city. Or perhaps, as a chasm-crosser, I'd gained a new ability to see.

I heard in the darkness the whispers of the great music, the truth behind all legends, the object behind all longings. I lay there, tutored and soothed by the heavens.

How long had it been since I gazed so intently at the night sky? Since I was a child, with my little department-store telescope, sleeping out in the backyard with Jupiter, my golden retriever. For the next thirty-five years I lived under fluorescent light, artificial suns that didn't allow me to see the stars, much less listen to them. My attention was absorbed by the counterfeit suns of klieg lights and streetlights and blazing marquees, man-made luminosity. I'd forgotten the stars, those pinpricks in the curtain of eternity, their light shining with the brilliance of the world beyond.

I lay flat on my back, hands cushioning my neck, and watched colliding galaxies a billion light-years away. The universe itself cried out in labor pains, longing for delivery. It was all so enormous, so overwhelming.

I remembered now why I'd stopped looking at the stars. They made me feel so lonely, so disconnected. But not anymore.

Seeing the stars now was like rereading a book after meeting the author—it seemed like the very first time. I'd lived an unconnected life. But I was connected now, to the King, to his creation, and to my traveling companions.

I'd grown bone-weary of playing God. It was a big job, and I'd finally discovered I was too small to pull it off. It was hard to abdicate the throne—but what a relief now that I had.

I saw Malaiki, twenty feet from me, on her knees, close to the fire, gazing back across the chasm. She wiped her eyes. I guessed she was thinking about Salama.

Shadrach stood on my other side, looking into the night as if looking into the eyes of his beloved. He was speaking. I got up and moved toward him so I could hear his creaky voice.

"Cosmos-Maker, you who live beyond the realm where stars are born and quasars sing and the great wind blows the silent stars in the vast explosion of your creation." He paused, then sang. "Architect of the cosmos, Builder of worlds; you became Road-Hiker, then Tree-Walker, making the road red with your heart. You are the Crosser of the Chasm."

Malaiki and Quon and I joined him, though the tune and words were new to me. When I mouthed them, they became more than words. As they formed in my mouth, I felt them take shape in my heart. Quon smiled broadly and looked at me like a child at Christmas dinner.

"The Potter became the vessel that gave its own clay to remake broken vessels, that they might leak no longer and hold at last the eternal waters of their hidden hopes and deepest dreams."

Other chasm-crossers joined us, people I hadn't met, but who I felt closer to than next-door neighbors and coworkers I'd known for years. They opened big bottles of senaba juice, and we took off our shoes and walked barefoot in the long, soft, cushy grass, which cooled and soothed my feet that ached from all the long days in hiking boots. We sat down and drank the juice and shared fresh-baked bread together. Nothing had ever tasted so good. No companionship had ever been truer. The connection warmed my insides in ways I couldn't begin to describe.

One of the women sang, "The abyss is vast, but the tree bigger; the Crosser is greater than the chasm; the amount due greater than men imagine, but the price paid greater still."

I put one arm around Quon, the other around Malaiki. Another traveler began a lively, contagious song: "Tree-walker stared down death and did not blink." People clapped and sang, and soon Malaiki was dancing, and Quon and I, not too great at the dancing, joined in.

The songs went on for hours. I never tired of them.

"World-Maker became World-Saver. Sky-Walker became Tree-Walker. The eternally old became eternally young. And we will never be the same, no never again the same."

I'd never been much of a singer, but when I heard my voice singing those songs, I liked what I heard. Somehow the meaning of the song redeemed the shaky voice that sang it. Perhaps I'd never been much of a singer because I'd never had much of a song to sing.

Shadrach came close to me and pointed westward to lights in the distance. "What do you see?"

I turned in the darkness and beheld Charis, the glowing City of Light. The joy of that place was like a volcanic explosion, spectacular and thrilling, never subsiding. I could feel it from here.

"I see…my home."

I laughed aloud. All my life I'd been a wanderer, a man without a home. Now I was a returning traveler—a man headed home. I considered the joyous irony—the places I'd always been were never my home. And my true home was a place I'd never been.

I went to my tent, still sorting out what had happened to me. I'd lived my life in a dim labyrinth of drudgery disguised as fun and pleasure. I'd sung songs I didn't like, gone down dead-end streets I didn't enjoy, doing things that later haunted me, all in the name of fulfillment. I'd nearly been asphyxiated by the odorless fumes of Erebus.

I knew now that the surest road to Erebus was the gradual one, the one with subtle slopes and turns, without mile markers and signposts. This was the road I had walked, telling myself that around the next corner I might at last find happiness and truth and peace, when all the while they lay in an entirely different direction, a direction I'd always fought against.

But now I knew what it was all about. Surely I would never lose these feelings that now washed over me like a hot bath. I went to sleep with a smile still on my face.

In the middle of the night, jolted by the old man's snoring, I woke up in a cold sweat. I lay there under my blanket, trembling. What was going on? I felt almost strangled by dread.

I've crossed the chasm. There's no reason to fear.

"Maybe you didn't cross it," a voice whispered to me.

"Who are you?" I whispered back.

"Even if you crossed the chasm, what does that mean? You're still who you were. The beasts that walk the night can still devour you—your agony will be just as great, and you will end up just as dead!"

I stuck my head down under the blanket, as if I were a little boy escaping midnight monsters. A few hours before, I'd felt sure I would never know fear again. Or anxiety. Or doubt. But anxiety and doubt assailed me now. Why was I hearing this voice? Would I ever see Marci and Amy and Brian again? Could they ever forgive me? They had never even heard me say, "I'm sorry." How would they ever even know I *wanted* their forgiveness?

I'd been a hammer and the whole world had looked like a nail, including my wife and kids. I'd pushed and prodded and intimidated and manipulated them, trying to remake them in my image. Why had I been such a fool? Visions of my betrayal, recordings of my harsh words, chronicles of my ugliness ran through my mind. It was too late. Too late.

Was there really a king? Or was he a figment of my imagination? Had my longing been so deep that I'd been fooled?

I tried to grab hold of myself—how could I even ask such questions after all I'd seen, all he'd done for me? Fear and anger and images of lust thrust themselves at me like bare fists. I became their punching bag, not knowing where they came from or how to fight them.

"You haven't changed after all," the voice whispered.

It was right. I was still Nick Seagrave. The emptiness I thought was gone had already returned with a vengeance. I got up, put on my coat and went out to look at the stars, desperate to recapture the feelings of warmth and security that had wrapped me like a blanket earlier in the evening.

I stared up at the sky and saw…nothing. No stars, not a single one. In the east were moonlit clouds, but that was all. I looked toward Charis, but it had disappeared. I saw faint lights, like fireflies dancing in the wind, there for a moment then gone.

I turned the other way and saw under the moonlit clouds the towering buildings of Babel, winding about like a serpent coiled to strike, for a moment holding me in its gaze. Suddenly it seemed so lovely, inviting me to return to its embrace. I heard its hissing, then turned around again. I could see no City of Light. Why had I been so sure of it before?

The chill of the night air bit into me. I shivered, longing for the warmth to enfold me as it had before. It didn't happen. Shaken, I returned to the tent. I got back under my blanket, still wearing my jacket. As the cloud-veiled moons rose and peeked out, I watched shadows creep out of the corners of the tent, crawling up the canvas like a dark growth. Night noises haunted me—wind in the chinks of rock, water dripping, the sudden rattling fall of loose stones.

What was that?

"You'll never get home," whispered the voice again, cold and bloodless. "Never."

I lay still, chilled to the bone, numb. I'd thought I'd left behind forever the dark night of my soul, back on the other side of the chasm. But already, even my first night after crossing, I was gripped by a fear and loneliness I'd expected never to know again.

The next morning I got up bleary-eyed. I sat by the fire, not eating much of the bean soup and wild rice, which didn't qualify as breakfast anyway. I kept thinking of waffles and maple syrup and cheddar-cheese omelets with sautéed mushrooms, onions, and green peppers.

"Quon's still hunting," Victoria said, looking at my unfinished breakfast. "He might come back with something yet."

The prospect of varmint-of-the-day didn't ring my bell. I nodded to Victoria and said, "The soup's fine."

I jiggled my tarnished tin cup, swishing coffee around and watching the grounds circle into a pattern, too weary to get up for a refill. I tasted the cold dregs again, remembering why that wasn't such a good idea.

On the other side of the fire, Malaiki asked Shad something I'd been wondering. "How were you able to come to the other side of the chasm when you'd already crossed it?"

"Not all is as it appears," Shad said. "Once you cross the chasm, you cannot return, for it is the Woodsman who carries us, and he will not carry us backward. But he wants us to help those who haven't crossed. So chasm-crossers still share the same ground with the unchanged."

Shad must have read the confusion in my bloodshot eyes.

"There is one chasm," he said to me, "yet each person crosses his own chasm. Before you crossed yours, you met some who'd already crossed theirs. You will meet some on this side who haven't crossed it at all. It seems strange, I know, but so do many things that are true. Some people can't even see the chasm."

"How is that possible?" Quon asked. "How can anyone fail to see that gargantuan abyss?"

"The same way you failed at first to see it."

Quon nodded with the look of a student.

"Will I see Salama again?" Malaiki asked, voice wavering.

"Perhaps…perhaps not," Shad said. "Salama resents that her sister has chosen someone above her. But unless Salama makes the same choice, the two of you will remain on separate paths that end in separate worlds."

I saw the mist in Malaiki's eyes and put my hand on her shoulder.

We packed up and traveled the red road, cutting through richly flowered meadows sloping down from green hills. Soon we came to an intersection of several paths, smaller roads leading off both to the north and south.

I walked up alongside Shad, who was leading. I looked at his face, worn like a weathered rock. "I thought once we were on this side of the chasm there would only be the red road."

"What gave you that idea?" Shad asked.

"Well, I just thought everything would be clear and…"

"Easy? We've not yet arrived. Your heart has been changed, but you must still do battle within, and the world remains the same. All the wrong roads are still there now. On the chasm's other side they distract travelers from coming to the King. Here they distract them from serving the King. If Shark Eyes cannot keep us from choosing the red road, he tries always to divert us from it."

I felt a knot in my gut, wondering if I should say anything about the voice in the night and the black hole of my despair. Instead I said, "I still can hardly believe Joshua was…who he was."

"Even his name he steals from the King," Shad said. "The RoadGuide says he's a liar and the father of lies."

"But he seemed so…real."

"The best counterfeits are the ones that look least like counterfeits. The Pretender succeeds by taking on the appearance most likely to influence his prey. For you it was one mask. For me he wears a different one. Sometimes he fools me still."

"You?" Quon asked.

"Yes," Shad said. I saw an awful look in his eyes and wondered what stories lay behind it. I considered how to probe, but he spoke first.

"Tell me, Nick, what do you see when you look back at who you were?"

I thought for a minute before answering. "I knew the cost of everything. I knew the value of nothing. I searched in ways I didn't understand, but my search for truth was halfhearted, and as the years went on, I became content with too little." I looked down at the road and kicked a rock. "Now I'm beating myself up for walking all the wrong paths, for all the lost opportunities…and especially for what I did to Marci and the kids."

"It's too late to relive your past," he said. "But it's not too late to choose your present and mark out your future. That's why you're here. That's why all of us are here…at least, I think that's why."

"It's like I've always wandered between two worlds," I said, "with blinders on. It never dawned on me when I lived in the Shadowlands that every choice I made cast a vote for either Erebus or Charis." I paused. "Last night something happened—"

Shad put his hand on my shoulder and squeezed tight. I looked up. We all stood still on the road, listening to the sound of approaching hoofbeats from the west. There came a slender girl dressed in black, a cloud of dust behind her, carrying a flag with horizontal and vertical bars shaped into a gold crown. She rode a magnificent blood bay, a stallion wild and rearing up, whinnying and sucking air, its black mane a good two feet long and blowing in the wind. Its skin was scraped and scarred and wet, as though it had run long and hard through a thick forest.

"The King's messenger," Shad said. "None other can ride the wild stallions."

"Greetings, travelers," she called, her voice as light as her frame. She reached into a large pouch hanging from one side of her saddle. "Here, take these sacks. You'll need them on the journey."

She threw down a large pile of brown burlap sacks. I picked one up. It was coarse, plain, and dirty. Unimpressed, I dropped it to the ground.

Victoria kicked at a sack and whispered to me, "If she were the King's messenger, wouldn't she carry something more royal looking than this?"

"The great city is before you," said the girl in black. "The King awaits you. Hear now his words. On your journey you will some-times travel at night. When you do, you may walk over dried-up riverbeds. They will have many stones in them. Pick up the stones, put them in your bags, and carry them with you. When the morning comes, you will be both glad and sad."

"What do you mean?" Victoria asked.

"Farewell," the messenger said. "I'll see you at the city."

We watched her ride down the road, eastward, listening to the departing hoofbeats until she became a sunlit flower against the sky, then vanished.

"How do we know she's the King's messenger?" David asked. "Anyone can carry a flag."

"Her words conform to the GuideBook," Shad said, holding up his worn, gold-leafed volume.

"But it makes no sense," David said.

"The purpose might not have been clear, but the meaning was," Shad said. "Take the sacks, and when we cross the riverbeds at night, pick up rocks."

"But why?" Quon asked.

"I...don't know," Shad replied, shrugging his shoulders. "Still, I trust the King." He turned to a few parts of his GuideBook and read them. I didn't completely understand what he read. I wasn't sure he did either.

"We must take the sacks and continue toward the city," Shad said.

There were dozens and dozens of bags in the pile. Shad and Malaiki and Quon all picked up a bunch of them, but there were plenty left. I didn't see Victoria or David pick up any. Self-consciously, I picked up two, wondering if they would fit in my pack and dreading the idea of filling them with stones. My back already ached.

As we marched forward, I turned and looked at the pile of sacks we had left behind us, wondering why the rider gave us so many. But then something else occurred to me.

"Horses in this world?" I asked my companions. "How come nobody told me? Why don't we get our hands on some and ride them down the road? It'd be a lot easier, and we'd get to the city a lot quicker. I don't suppose you've seen any cars here, have you?"

The old man looked at me as if I were hopeless. "The TravelGuide says we must *walk* the road. There is no quick way, no easy way, no shortcut. And, no, there aren't any cars!"

Well, excuse me for asking!

As we walked, Shad breathed with a wheezing noise and periodically stopped to cough and spit. I tried to keep my distance.

Quon kept stopping and crouching down, searching for signs of varmints. I looked away, not wanting to see dinner in its unedited form. Malaiki kept humming the same repetitive tune. I was running out of people to walk next to, so I stayed at the back by myself, just behind David.

We walked and walked for days, breaking only to eat and to set up camp and sleep. The newness of the road had subsided. The songs were less engrossing, my companions more irritating, the Mulligan stews and tomato soups and asparagus less appealing.

Where's Chinese takeout when you need it?

I sat down beside the road one hot, humid afternoon and shook a sharp pebble out of my boot. There was blood on my sock and I took it off. The pebble had cut deep into my foot, now black and blue. The group had stopped, watching me.

"Go on," I called. "I'll catch up." They didn't buy it, and next thing I knew the women hovered over me.

"You should have told us," Malaiki said, seeing the injury. "We could have helped." I quickly put the sock back on.

My feet screamed at me, my legs were sore, my neck throbbed, my head ached. I would have thought after crossing the chasm that the migraines would be gone. They weren't.

"You've been awfully quiet, Nick," Victoria said. "Is something wrong?"

"No."

"You seem troubled."

"I said nothing's wrong." I knew she heard the edge in my voice. "Okay, I guess maybe…I thought it would be a quicker trip to Charis."

"Yes," she said, looking off into the distance. "It seems almost as far away as it did before we crossed the chasm."

"To me it seems farther," David said from behind me. He walked on, checking and rechecking his position locator.

"Maybe," I said, "I expected the journey would be a bit easier."

"It's not exactly a luxury cruise, is it?" Victoria smiled like someone who'd been on her share of them.

"It wouldn't be so bad if…if the King were here with us," I said. "I'm puzzled by his silence. Why doesn't he just explain what he wants of us?"

We stopped for lunch, my least favorite meal, but Quon hadn't caught anything, and at least I didn't have to worry about seeing a tail hanging out of my sandwich. We'd separated from the rivers some time ago, and pure water was harder to find, so Shad instructed us to ration.

Everyone pitched in something from their packs, and David brought out a variety of freeze-dried packets, or MREs—Meals Ready to Eat. They were the civilian equivalent of C-rations and had nothing going for them but nutrition, and even that was questionable. The fact that we couldn't drink freely to wash them down rubbed salt into my culinary wound.

"I'd kill for some lasagna and French bread," I whispered to David.

"Me too," he said. "And how about some Dutch apple pie à la mode?"

I groaned and rolled my eyes. Shad came our way, and David got up and walked off. Shad reached into his satchel. He pulled out four books, similar to his own, and gave one to Malaiki, Victoria, Quon, and me.

"You each need your own RoadGuide. All who walk the red road must read it. Repeat its words until they flow from your heart like water from a fountain. You must study the map, or you will get lost…or stray from the road…or be unprepared for what you encounter on it."

"You're always reading it," Victoria said. "Can't we just follow your lead? Besides, the red road is obvious, isn't it?"

"The book is your guide, your compass. Don't underestimate your ability to depart from the true road. Don't trust your instinct or your logic—don't even trust me. I don't trust myself. Trust only the RoadGuide."

What do you mean, you don't trust yourself? Now that's reassuring!

I turned through the pages, reading instructions here and there, looking at the maps, scanning the many stories of those who'd walked the red road before.

"It's a corrective lens," Shad said. "It allows us to see Skiathuros as it really is, to catch glimpses of the worlds we walk between. Look here," he said, taking it out of my hands, flipping the pages and pointing to a paragraph on one page.

I lay back on my side, propped up by my left arm, and began to read. I was amazed to find stories and warnings concerning all the different roads I'd walked, all the dead ends I'd pursued.

"Look," I said to Victoria. "It talks about the chasm, the crossing, the scroll. It says the red road is stained with the Woodsman's blood. Why didn't anyone ever tell me these things?"

"Perhaps they did and you didn't hear them," Shad said.

I kept flipping through the pages. It was thick and the print was small.

"There's so much in this book," I said.

"No more nor less than the King knows we need," Shad said. "Let's go." Everyone got up but Quon, already lost in the pages of the book. I had to pull him up, and even then he kept his nose in the book as he walked. I had to occasionally grab his arm to keep him from stumbling. Half the time he didn't even notice.

At twilight the afterglow of the red sun touched the landscape, adding a rosy tint to the predominant blues and greens of the hillsides. As I sat admiring the view, I felt something tickle my right hand.

"What the...? Frodo!"

I picked him up and watched his toothy grin. I threw him up in the air and caught him. "I thought I'd never see you again, boy. You couldn't have crossed the chasm. What's going on?"

"Remember what Shad said," Malaiki replied, petting Frodo. "We cross the chasm, yet somehow we walk in the same land we used to."

I held Frodo up and let him lick my face. "I have to admit it's awfully good to see you again, little fella."

We walked on in the pitch-black night. I'd voted to set up camp two hours earlier, and I didn't appreciate the fact we were still walking—Shad had insisted, saying he thought the King wanted us to keep going.

Does he think he's the only one the King speaks to? I grew weary of Shad's bossiness.

The ground sloped under us, and we all slowed down under the moonless sky.

"Is this one of the riverbeds the King's messenger told us of?" Malaiki asked.

"I'm not sure," I said.

"Yes," Shad said. I heard him low to the ground beside me and felt his hand brush over my feet. "I feel stones. We must pick them up."

With youthful enthusiasm the old man groped about the dried-up riverbed. He bumped into Quon, also on his knees, and both of them laughed.

"Tell Frodo to stop licking my face," Quon said, snickering. "Or he may end up in tomorrow's stew."

"Not even funny," I said, reaching down and picking up a stone. "They're heavy, aren't they?" *And I'm weary*—this I didn't say. A host of pains assaulted me, including the throb in my right temple.

"There are so many of them," Malaiki said, giggling. "Where do you stop?"

"Why pick up any at all?" Victoria asked. "They'll just slow us down."

"The messenger told us to," I said.

"We don't even know the messenger," she replied. "Nor what she meant."

"The stones are rough and heavy," I said. "We need to pace ourselves and not take too many. Don't you agree, old man?"

He said nothing. He was too busy gathering rocks.

I picked up a few more stones, trying to choose the lightest ones.

"Let's move on," David said. "We need to get across the riverbed and set up camp."

I couldn't see Shad clearly, but I heard him still huffing and puffing, picking up more stones than I figured he could carry.

You'll be sorry later. Don't expect me to carry your sack.

After crossing, we set up camp. I plopped my bag containing the few rocks beside my blankets. Then huddling close to Frodo, I fell into a deep sleep.

When the morning came, I found I was the last one up. Everyone was out by the fire with their hands on their burlap bags, straining and appearing frustrated. I went back to the tent and picked up my own sack, anxious to get a good look at what was inside. But somehow the top was secured tightly, even though I could see nothing to keep me from opening it. No matter how hard I tried I couldn't get inside it. I worked at it, sweating and tugging and scraping my skin on the rough burlap.

"What's going on?" I asked, bursting out of the tent.

"I can't get my sack open," Malaiki said, her eyes wet with frustration.

"Neither can I," Shad said. "None of us can."

13

"WE'RE EXPECTED TO PICK UP ROCKS," I said, "yet we're not even permitted to see them?"

"The girl promised that in the morning we'd be glad or sad," Victoria said, smiling. "Well, it's morning. So I guess the joke's on you. I'm glad because I didn't pick up rocks…and you're sad because you did!"

"She must have meant something else," Malaiki said, still trying to open her heavy bag.

"What's the point?" I asked Shad.

"I don't know." His irritation was obvious. "Some things we don't understand."

"Maybe later we will," Quon said.

"Don't count on it," David countered. "If you're smart, you'll leave those worthless sacks behind."

We ate a quiet breakfast of some granola Victoria made, and powdered milk. She kept apologizing for the taste, but I was hungry enough that it seemed a feast, especially with the wild honey Shad managed to talk out of some bees and the delicious fruit, sort of an apple-pear.

Quon seemed mopey and withdrawn, perhaps because he wanted to know what was in his bag and couldn't. Not knowing certainly bugged *me*.

We'd walked a few miles when Frodo started barking. I looked down to see him staring at a weasel as if it were an escaped convict.

Looking immediately at Quon, up ahead of us, I grabbed Frodo and held his jaws together.

"What's he barking at?" Quon asked.

"Oh...nothing," I said.

Quon looked as if he was going to come back and see, but he didn't.

"Good move," David whispered. "I'm not in the mood for sweet-and-sour weasel ribs."

I smiled and nodded.

"If I ever have a brain transplant," David said in a low voice, "I'll ask for Shad's."

"Yeah? Why?"

"Because his brain has never been used." He chuckled.

"He's a man of great learning," I said.

"He's a man of encyclopedic ignorance," David said. "Be careful or you'll end up like him—old and smelly, bad breath and judgmental, never taking any pleasure in life."

"I saw him that way at first," I said. "But now, I don't know..."

"He doesn't embarrass you?" David asked.

"Sometimes. But maybe the problem isn't him. Maybe it's us."

David raised his eyebrows. I felt stupid.

After lunch Quon and Malaiki picked up their hefty sacks, and Shad lifted his nearly full sack, draping it over his shoulder. Even if he didn't let on, it had to upset him that he couldn't even look inside his bag.

I tucked my sack in at my waist, thankful I'd picked up only four small stones and feeling sorry for the old man. Then I noticed the quiet smile on his face.

Clearly, he didn't feel sorry for himself.

I slept fitfully, hearing things in the night, including the clip clop of a horse stopping at our camp, then stealthily leaving a few minutes later. What was going on?

I got up and took a burning stick from the dying fire but couldn't find any tracks. To the west I saw the twinkling lights of what I assumed must be a few villages ahead. What awaited us there? Why did I feel such dread?

I went back to bed, awaking early to whistling starlings and a wonderful breakfast of cooked oats, milk, cheese, herbs, honeycomb, sliced senaba, and today's mystery meat.

"Save some for me," I said to Quon, heading down to the stream to wash up. On hands and knees I put my weary head down in the cold stream water, slapping it to my face, trying to coax myself back to life. Before indulging in breakfast, I fetched the aluminum pot and went to the fire to brew coffee, now my self-appointed job, as I'd learned no one else in this crew knew how to do it right. It wasn't Starbuck's, but it was strong and about as flavorful as campfire coffee gets. It amazed me how delicious a simple breakfast could be out on the road. I was earning and appreciating my meals in a way I never had when I'd spent my days behind a desk.

"Anyone hear a horse in our camp last night?" I asked.

"A horse? No way," David said. "Horses are very rare in Skiathuros. Only the extremely wealthy own them. Have you seen any besides the blood bay ridden by the girl in black?"

"No," I said. "But I heard one. I'm sure of it."

"I hear many things in the night," Quon said. "But often I wonder whether they're part of this world or the surrounding ones."

Sipping my brew, I studied Quon across the fire, his face radiant.

He looked back down in his TravelGuide. The moody, insecure young man had changed since we crossed the chasm. Every chance he had, his nose was in the book. Every time we met someone on the road he spoke of the King. Though he was young, his passion for the King surpassed my own, perhaps all of ours.

Why does Quon burn with a fire I don't?

Did I resent him for his faith, because I found myself questioning what the King had said and done? Perhaps. Still, I cared about him, wanted to look out for him. He was so young and inexperienced, so full of potential, so much like Brian. I walked around the fire and sat next to him and asked him what he was reading. His eyes lit up, and he was eager to share what he'd been learning. We talked most of the day, right into the evening.

The next morning I walked close beside Quon again, and we talked about many things. Finally I asked him, "Have you always lived in Skiathuros?"

His eyes widened. He looked both ways, then whispered, "Have you?"

"No," I replied. "I arrived here in a storm, how or why I don't know. Something was happening to me before I came, something big, but I just can't remember it. It's driving me nuts."

"Did you end up...in a cave?" he asked.

"Yes! Did you?"

He nodded.

"Was there writing on the wall?"

"Yes. A three-line message in Chinese."

"Chinese? The writing I saw was English," I said.

"I only speak Chinese," Quon replied.

"But that's not possible. I hear you in English. How...?"

"Yes, and I hear you in Chinese. Who knows how? Anyway, above and below the words in the cave were other writings in strange languages."

"Yes, exactly! Quon, tell me—why...no, first, where did you come from?"

"Well," he said nervously, "I came from—"

"Out of the way," a man shouted, pushing between Quon and me. I wanted to teach him some manners but thought better of it. Another traveler followed him, then two more, then a group of six. Where were these people coming from? We hadn't passed more than a few dozen stray travelers a day, in groups no larger than four. Why was the traffic increasing? I looked around—the countryside was becoming well-ordered, with tended fields and crops and orchards instead of wild trees and berry bushes.

I looked behind us at the clear stretch of road. I couldn't see anyone headed our direction. Everybody was going the other way. Why? We were always turning our shoulders, trying not to bump into them. This part of the red road was very narrow. As the travelers increased, so did the jostling. I kept waiting for things to calm down so I could resume talking to Quon.

I picked up Frodo, who was gun-shy now that he'd been kicked and nearly stepped on a half-dozen times. He pressed the side of his face against my hand, groaning and licking, playing for my sympathy and getting it.

"We must be getting close to a city," David said. "Or at least a large village."

Within an hour it felt like a shopping mall at Christmas. I wondered if we'd gotten turned around. As a point of reference, I moved to the side of the road and looked to the west for the City of Light. In the midst of the crowd it was very hard to see. We looked at the sun, knew that it rose away from Charis and set toward it, and yet…we still wondered because of all the throngs moving eastward. Did they know something we didn't?

We sat down by the road, reread the RoadGuide and consulted its maps, discussed our understanding of what it said and the meaning of the long shadow that cut east to west across the land. I studied a great gray column in the sky, composed of rings of spinning clouds, one on top of the other like a stack of tires. It made me feel uneasy.

"There's no doubt," Shad said, "we're headed the right direction."

"No," David said, looking at his position locator. "We should go that way." He pointed to a path going off the red road, winding south then appearing to swing back to the east.

"No!" Shad shouted. "That's not right. We keep going this way— that's final!" Malaiki and Victoria backed away. Quon hung his head. David turned red hot and his veins bulged, but when we all followed Shad, he joined us too, walking some distance behind. I checked on him now and then.

Looking at Shad, I couldn't help but wonder if his days as a leader were numbered. In my years in business, I'd taught some leadership seminars—obviously, he could have benefited from them.

Quon was now deep in discussion with Shad, so I couldn't resume our conversation yet. It irritated me. Dust stuck to my sweaty face, my shoulders sagged, and I rubbed my sore neck. I felt like kicking cats. Even Frodo was irritating me.

"Walk on your own, you lazy dog," I said to him, putting him down abruptly. "You have to learn to keep up. I've got too much to carry already."

"Getting rid of your bag of stones would help," Victoria said. She pointed at my sack, which now, after another stop the night before, contained five more stones. Shad was starting his second bag. If this kept up, soon he'd look like Santa Claus. I didn't know how the old guy could carry so much.

"Get out of my way," a man said.

"Excuse you," said a woman, glaring at me.

I glared back at them. It wasn't cats I felt like kicking now.

Another man bumped into me. "Why are you traveling the wrong way?" I asked him.

"What do you mean?" he said.

"I mean away from Charis and back toward the chasm and Babel."

"Who's to say that's the case?"

"Well, look, isn't it obvious? There's the City of Light." I pointed toward it, but he looked at my finger, not the city.

"You're saying I'm stupid and blind, is that it?"

"No, I didn't mean to sound—"

"It's your kind of attitude that convinced me to retrace the red road then get off on one of the side paths. I don't like the company of the people on this road. They're always telling me what to do."

"I meant no offense, I just—"

"Did it ever occur to you that the great majority of us are walking this way, and it's *you* who are walking the wrong way? Instead of pushing against us, why don't you just turn around?"

"But the GuideBook says—"

"I need no GuideBook," he replied. "I know what I'm doing." He scowled and disappeared into the crowd.

Just for the fun of it, I turned around and walked about fifty feet with the crowd. It felt great.

"Nick! What are you doing? Get back here." It was Quon. I turned around, weaving my way back. What a pain.

"Don't do that," Quon said. "The GuideBook says once you

retreat on the road you may not manage ever to turn around again."

Tired of being bumped and bruised, after a while I said nothing to the people walking the wrong way. It seemed pointless. Shad and Malaiki sometimes stopped travelers and spoke with them. But it was Quon who seemed most intent on talking with the strangers. It frustrated me, because the more the three of them stopped and talked, the less ground we covered.

After a couple of hours talking with a half-dozen people in a group headed east, I tapped Shad on the shoulder. "Let's get moving," I said. "We're wasting time."

"I'll be the judge of that," he said, looking at me coolly.

Soon the group was up to a dozen, asking questions and listening as we talked about the King. One conversation led to the next. We set up camp early and invited the group to have dinner with us, seriously depleting our rations. Eight of them stayed up around the fire, talking until the early hours of the morning.

I awoke to a harsh copper-colored sky. Already townspeople sat around the crackling fire, talking, discussing, debating about the Woodsman and the King and the chasm and the flying reptile. Quon was the center of attention—everyone looked at him when he spoke. Large black birds circled above, as if watching us, overseeing the gathering.

David took charge, moved everyone away from the tents, packed them up and announced, "We're leaving. We've got places to go."

Shad held up his hand, watching and listening to Quon talk with the villagers, like a musician watching his protégé perform. I broke off some bone-hard branches of a manzanita tree and drew near to put them in the fire. A stinging cloud of smoke burst out for a moment, watering my eyes. I stayed close to listen, drawn by the passion in Quon's voice.

"There are many false roads," he said, "but one true road. The Woodsman walked the bloody tree for us and bridged the great chasm."

"I've read the stories of the Woodsman," said a young man, who looked like a college student. "He inspires me. He was a fine moral teacher. But no more."

"Read the TravelGuide," Quon said, turning roast marmot on a spit over the fire. "The Woodsman claimed to be the World-Maker. If he was, you should believe him. If he wasn't, you should reject him as a liar or a madman. Either way, the one thing you can't believe is that he was just a fine moral teacher."

"Don't tell us what we can't believe," said someone standing on the edge of the circle, a man with a fist for a face, hard and pinched. "We've already heard this story, and we're weary of words. It's time to party."

When he said this, a few dozen people outside the circle, far enough back I hadn't noticed them, erupted into a cheer. A party sounded good to me too, though morning seemed a strange time for it. But what happened next made me squirm. They sang songs mocking the King and the GuideBook. They began to look at each other and dance in ways I had seen on the dead-end roads. A surge of memories assailed me.

I felt a pronounced drop in temperature and watched dark red clouds swirl and gather. Quon, seemingly oblivious to everything but his conversation, continued to talk with a small group of villagers. Fistface marched up to him and yelled, "Didn't you hear what I said? It's time to party. That means, stop talking that nonsense."

"If we're in your way, we can move," Quon said. "If anyone wants to talk more, let's go where it's quieter."

"You think you're better than us, don't you?" asked a petite blonde next to Fistface. "Hypocrites, that's what you are."

Quon opened his GuideBook and flipped the pages, then started to read. "The Woodsman says—"

"We don't care what the Woodsman says." Fistface slapped the book from Quon's hand. He screamed and cursed and held up his hand, limp, as if he'd hit hard metal. "You hurt me!"

"It's you who hit the book," Quon said. "If you'd listen to it instead of striking it, you'd learn that the book gives the guardrails to guide us and protect us from veering off the road. They aren't there to hurt us, but to keep us safe."

"Maybe we don't want to be 'safe.' Maybe we just want to have some fun. The girls would like that, wouldn't you?" He leered at Malaiki and Victoria. "Think you're too good to party with us, is that it?"

"We have our parties," Quon said, "celebrations full of joy. We sing songs of the King, of his sovereignty and grace, and our hearts overflow. The meaning and pleasure that elude you, that you try to find in all the wrong places, we have found in the King."

"You presume to judge us, you self-righteous bigot?"

"The only righteousness I have is a gift from my King. It's his righteousness that consumes me, not mine."

"So you *do* claim to be better than us." Fistface spit on the ground, and his bloodshot eyes bulged as he stared us down. "Ever since you bigots arrived, people have stopped coming to the parties. Everything was fine until you came. Your poison is spreading. And you're bad for business."

"Is your business darkness?" Shad asked. "Light is always bad for darkness."

"Why are you here?" asked a heavy, muscular woman with

pouchy chipmunk cheeks, her hair a wild red tangle. "We didn't invite you."

"The King sent us down the road to your village," Quon said, "to tell you about him and his pleasures. He's a gracious king, and in his kindness he causes his sun to shine and rain to fall on all men."

The woman spat on the ground. "Kindness? The burning sun is kindness? The soaking rain is kindness? I see no kindness."

"There is much you don't see," Quon said. "But I can tell you firsthand the King offers you eyes to see. He did it for me."

"Are you calling me blind?"

The big woman stepped forward suddenly and slapped Quon's face so hard she knocked him to the ground. The crowd laughed. I started to restrain her, but Shad put his hand on my shoulder and stepped forward, arms outstretched, urgency in his voice. "We don't want to fight. We're just beggars telling other beggars where to find food."

"Now you call us beggars," an elegant woman said, handling the fine fabric of her dress. "Are these the clothes of a beggar?"

"Self-righteous bigots," said Fistface. "That's what you are, all of you."

"Isn't it possible," Quon said, wiping a trickle of blood from his mouth, "that the truly self-righteous are those who imagine they don't need the righteousness of the Chasm-crosser, that their own righteousness is enough?"

"Now you call *us* self-righteous?"

In unison, like a basketball crowd jeering the free-throw shooter, they waved their arms, then put their hands over their ears.

For just a moment I saw through a hole in the air great warriors clashing in combat. One stood in front of Quon, his sword raised in defense. Two comrades stood at his side, but dozens of shark-eyed warriors charged at them, wielding swords and battle-axes.

"No more!" shouted Fistface.

"Shut up!" screamed the muscular woman.

Fistface shoved Shad to the ground. Someone kicked him, then others did the same. I ran to Shad, put my body over his, taking the kicks in my side. A boot hit my face, and my vision blurred. But even from the ground I saw through the hole in the air—the warrior in front of Quon looked up as if listening to a voice from above. Then with a pained expression, he lowered his sword.

Everywhere people were throwing things and yelling. In the midst of the riot someone shouted, "Let your king save you now!"

Frenzied men and women grabbed Malaiki and Victoria, but I managed to snatch them and pull them outside the circle. While everyone watched Fistface move toward Quon, I hurried the women beneath two adjoining willows on the edge of our camp.

"Stay put," I pleaded.

I ran back to see a dozen men encircling Quon.

Before I realized what was happening, Fistface, his shark eyes showing, raised a stone and threw it at Quon. It hit him in the shoulder and deflected off to his ear.

Quon moaned, and the side of his head turned red. He looked at the crowd and spoke quickly, as if trying to beat a ticking timer.

"Cross the chasm, meet the Woodsman, that you may walk the red road all the way to the City of Light."

For a moment Quon's face looked different. It reminded me of someone…the Woodsman.

Another man threw his rock and then another and another.

I tried to stand, but my knees wobbled and I fell. I heard old Shad praying for Quon.

Prayer—of course! "Save Quon, mighty King," I asked. "Deliver him."

I felt a sudden, overwhelming peace. I knew the King would answer my prayer. Quon would be spared, and come nightfall I'd gratefully be eating his stew.

Fistface picked up another stone, huge, probably four pounds. He raised his big arm and hurled it at Quon, only eight feet away.

The stone hit Quon in the head with a horrid dull thud. He fell to the ground limp, like a marionette whose strings had been cut.

I shoved my way through to him while the angry crowd pummeled me. I put my hand on his wrist and felt his weak pulse. Shad crawled up beside me. I stared at Quon's disfigured head, blotched with blood.

Searching the crowd for Fistface, I found him and charged the ten feet between us like a wild bull. I planted my head in his stomach and knocked him to the ground. He punched my ribs, and I felt them crack. I hit him twice with my fists and watched the blood spurt over his tight, hard face. I put my hands around his neck, squeezing with all my strength. I shouted, I didn't know what, as his eyes rolled back inside his skull. Seeing this, I released my hands. The flow of air revived him, and he swung his left arm up against me.

As I held his flailing limb with both of mine, he reached for his belt with his right hand and pulled something out. I saw it glimmer just before I felt it pierce my shoulder.

"Ahhh!" I screamed as he twisted the knife in me. My right fist fell on his face like a trip hammer, and I heard the crunch of breaking bone. I pulled the knife out of my shoulder, screaming again—the second pain worse than the first. As he still struggled beneath me, I lifted the knife in the air and started to bring my arm down.

Then someone grabbed my fist, I don't know who—I didn't see him. Three men were on me, trying to get the knife from me. I refused to unclench my fist or get off Fistface.

"Nick—stop!"

When I recognized David's voice, I hesitated, then rolled off Fistface. David pulled me up, and as I stood, knife still in my hand, the crowd backed away in an ever-widening circle.

I stumbled to Shad, who knelt over Quon.

The air was deathly still. Quon's eyes were wide open, as if staring off to something beyond. But his eyes began to fade, like dying embers of a fire. He gasped loudly, and for a moment he seemed to smile. He whispered a word I could not hear, then his lips froze stiff. Just then I felt a distinct updraft, a brush of wind rising from Quon's body.

"Ichabod," Shad whispered. "The glory has departed."

I looked at the old man, searching his face.

"The temple has been deserted," he said. "Quon has stepped out the door of this world and entered another."

"No," I cried. "It can't be."

I wrapped my arms around Quon, hoping to feel something. I didn't. I sat back and looked at his lifeless body, then up at the sky. I raised my bloody fists, knife still in my right hand, and screamed my challenge upward.

"Whyyyyyy?"

14

THE COLD FRIGHT of the young man's death dispersed the crowd, who hauled Fistface away to tend his injuries. Though my left shoulder burned, I carried Quon's body to the cool of the willows, where the women peeked out, stunned and weeping.

I laid Quon down, then backed away to the trunk of the largest willow, huddling against the darkness. I fingered Fistface's knife, cleaned it in a patch of long grass, then slipped it under my belt.

Maybe I'll give it back to him—between his ribs.

I must have sat a long time, all my jumbled thoughts threads in one vast fabric of pain. Malaiki finally convinced me to join them in the camp and let her tend my wounds.

Reluctantly I emerged, light assaulting my eyes. I sat against a large rock in silence, staring at a circular white cloud wrapped around a jagged peak to the west, a stocking cap on a cold bare head. The southern face was a weather-shattered cliff on which I watched dark shadows play. This was Mount Peirasmos—the closer we got to it, the more it obscured my view of Charis. The thick red clouds had blown south and never dropped their rain on us. I wished they had, so that I wouldn't need to hide the wetness on my face.

"I don't get it," I said, as Malaiki wrapped a bandage around my bruised ribs. "Quon served the King. He was so young. And he was my friend. Why would the King let him die?"

"All men die," Shad said. "Most live and die for nothing. Quon lived and died for something."

I cringed and turned my back on him. "He suffered," I spit out. "The rocks, they…I should have…" I clenched my fists.

Malaiki crushed some leaves in her hands and rubbed them against my lifeless left shoulder. I flinched but inhaled deeply the sweet yet pungent fragrance of the herbs. After putting water on the fire and mixing in leaves, she pressed a cool, wet rag against my forehead, then gave me a cup of senaba. When the leaves had boiled, she dipped a towel in the water and packed the hot towel on my shoulder.

Meanwhile, just thirty feet away, Victoria washed and prepared Quon's body, and ten feet beyond her David dug a shallow grave, using a trifold shovel from his pack.

"The GuideBook promises suffering," Shad said, apparently in response to my words several minutes earlier. "It also promises comfort and relief. But most of that comes in the next world. Here we are but aliens and strangers and pilgrims. We're not citizens of this world."

I could feel my flesh burning as he quoted from the GuideBook, "In the new world there will be no more crying or pain."

"Quon was in pain," I said. "And I'm in pain!"

"As am I—because we are not yet in the new world." He shrugged, as if it were that simple.

"The King could have stopped Quon from suffering," I said, "saved him from dying. Why didn't he? Does he lack power? Or…does he lack love?"

Shad looked at me, eyes watering, then said in a firm voice, "He lacks neither. The TravelGuide tells us so."

"He picks a strange way to show love," I said. "If I had the power, I'd *never* let a friend die."

"Are you better than the King, then?" Shad said, pacing, his voice raised. "Would you have Quon live forever in a world like this? He lives now in a far better place, the one for which he was made."

"If the King is all-powerful, doesn't that make him Quon's killer, as surely as if he'd thrown the stones himself?"

"And if he did bring about Quon's death, was not Quon his to do with as he pleased? Quon was not his own—he was bought with a price, the shed blood of the Sovereign. He knew this. You must learn it too!"

Without thinking, I reached to my belt, fingering the knife I'd taken from Fistface. Quickly I withdrew my hand.

"I miss him already," Malaiki said, sobbing, removing her healing hands from my throbbing shoulder.

"We'll see him again," Shad said, as if that made everything all right. "It's not the end of our relationship, only an interruption." He stared at me—I hated his words of cold comfort. "If you had the power, Nick, would you take Quon from the unspeakable joy he now experiences?"

"Yes, I would!" I shouted. "I don't care what you say. It's a waste."

"There's no waste of the life wholly given to the King. Our friend has lost the life no man can keep. He has gained the life no man can lose. Weep for us, yes, but do not weep for Quon—he is immersed in pleasures beyond our wildest imagination."

Smelling pine and herbs I stared at the fire, then felt a hand on my right shoulder.

"Get your hand off me," I screamed, jumping up and pointing my finger at Shad. "You pushed him into it! You egged him on to preach at them and make them mad. You figured you were safe, right? That they wouldn't beat up a crazy old man. You should have known what would happen to Quon! You think you know so much—why didn't you know that? Or maybe you did and you let him die anyway!"

Shad slunk down onto the ground, as though I'd hit him with a baseball bat. He lay in the dirt and sobbed.

"Will we die like that too?" Malaiki whispered, drawing close to Shad.

"I...don't know," he said. "I just don't know."

I saw the pain in his eyes. But I didn't care. I was furious. I heard in the distance the terrible roar of a lion. I shivered, partly from fear, the rest from rage.

I stood up and walked away. I didn't want to hear one more empty reassurance. I retreated again under the two brooding old willows whose branches overlapped. It wasn't just the travelers I was angry at—it was the King. I stayed there in the shelter, hiding from the light.

After burying Quon in a meadow and piling on gray rocks from a nearby quarry, we sat on a hillside, looking at grand vistas across the open country ahead, between us and the looming Mount Peirasmos. We talked about Quon and what he meant to us.

"He reminded me of my son," I said, choking on my tears. My fellow travelers embraced me. On earth I couldn't ever remember crying in front of a group—or being hugged by one.

We staged a dinner in Quon's honor, taking the light metal pans from his backpack and cooking some wild geese he'd bagged just that morning, along with some mushrooms he'd picked. Malaiki made his favorite cornbread, and we drank gallons of senaba juice—I polished off a half-gallon myself. We talked about Quon and remembered his love for the King.

David sat next to me, shaking his head.

"What?" I asked.

"If only Quon hadn't been so pushy, so zealous. He didn't have to make them so angry."

"Zeal for the Woodsman consumed him," Shad said. "But the King honors such zeal."

"Right," David said. "No doubt Quon felt honored to be hit with those stones."

"And what would you have had young Quon do differently?"

"Hold his tongue," David said. "Try not to offend people. Be more...normal. We can't win people over unless we're more like them."

"If we are like them, what do we have to offer them? Darkness doesn't need a little less darkness. It needs light."

"This wouldn't have happened if Quon had been more positive, more upbeat," David said. "If we do what we should, the King promises us health and wealth." He pulled out of his backpack a very small book and read a few sentences from it.

"You read part of the truth, not the whole," Shad said. "He promises us health and wealth in Charis, and sometimes he graciously gives them in Thuros. But he also promises persecution and trial and suffering—you didn't read about those, did you? He didn't say it would be easy to walk the road. He said it would be hard. Your king is too small, David, for your book is too small. You need all of it."

Shad pulled a full-sized TravelGuide from his satchel and handed it to David.

"Mine is all I need," David said, clutching his little book. He walked away, mumbling.

After dinner, I went off by myself. I stared blurry-eyed into the dark silence, held in its stony grip. I looked ahead on the red road gradually raising us from the lowlands toward the mountain, now barely visible in the moonlight pressing through the clouds.

Shad approached me cautiously, Malaiki at his side.

"There's more that bothers you, isn't there?" he asked. "It isn't just about Quon, is it?"

I looked away and felt my chest tighten.

"I wanted to kill the man with the fist face. I almost did. And part of me still wants to."

Shad nodded. "Fistface is an evil man."

"He deserves the chasm," I said.

"Of course he does," Malaiki said. "And yet the King walked the tree for him just as he did for us. The book says we deserve Charis no more than he."

"If I'd killed him, he would have gone to the abyss," I said. "Part of me wanted him to go there. That's what bothers me—I thought I was beyond the anger and the hate. I thought I'd really changed."

"You *have* changed, Nick," Malaiki said.

"I prayed for Quon. I believed the King would answer my prayer. He didn't."

"You prayed for Quon to survive," Shad said. "So did I. We thought it best for him. The King answered that part of our prayer—he did what was best for him. It's just that the King knew what we didn't."

"Quon whispered something just before he died," I said. "Did you hear it?"

"Yes," Shad said. "It was just one word—*Home.*"

I choked.

"I grieve because of what happened to Quon," Shad said. "But I do not pity him, I envy him. He has already entered Charis, the home I've yearned to enter since long before Quon was born."

"The Woodsman knows our doubts, our struggles, Nick," Malaiki said. "Let's talk to him." Malaiki bowed her head, as did Shad.

"I wish we still had Quon, mighty King," she said. "We don't understand why you took him. But we trust you nonetheless."

"I don't understand either," Shad said, voice quivering. "But I ask you to make me as faithful as young Quon."

At first I resisted, but when I heard their words, I melted a bit, though I did not pray aloud.

"You died," Malaiki said to the King, "so we know you understand. You lost your beloved when you didn't have to. And you did it all for us."

For a few minutes I breathed pure air from a life-support system that gave me strength to keep going in a world gone mad.

Shad and Malaiki went back to join the others, asking me to come also. But I insisted on retreating again. There was too much on my mind. I had no more illusions of an easy road this side of the chasm. I had no reason to believe that what had happened to Quon would not happen to me.

You killed Quon. Will you kill me too?

Just when at long last I thought I'd found life, I stared into the eyes of death. I put my right hand on my wounded left shoulder, stretching my broken ribs and feeling the tears run down my cheeks.

I looked around me. I didn't know who I was or where. But I knew I had to get away. I refused to surrender to fate or providence or luck or circumstance. Nick Seagrave vowed to regain control.

The next day I walked alone, saying nothing. The previous night's dreams and whispers and unrest boiled down to this—it just wasn't working. I'd be better off walking by myself, perhaps even turning around, at least for a while. I needed to launch out and call my own shots, not wind up the victim of someone else's bad decisions. If I could, I'd make my move before we started up Mount Peirasmos.

We stopped at dusk and set up camp, eating a dinner of roasted rabbit, which David managed to trap, taking up the role of hunter in Quon's absence. The rhubarb and black-eyed peas weren't bad, but the rabbit was delicious.

"Where'd you get the spices?" I asked David.

"I bartered for them with two of the roadwalkers we met this afternoon, remember?" he said. "Shad insisted I take a RoadGuide from him, so I finally did. I managed to trade it for some salt and pepper." He laughed. "At least I got some practical use out of it!"

I slipped away from the usual round of fireside stories and lay down in the tent, huddled under my blanket, thinking about Quon behind us and the great mountain ahead. It was hard getting warm, so I borrowed the blanket from Quon's pack, thinking I should give it to Victoria or Malaiki, but deciding to wait until later.

In the distance I heard soft big sounds, which grew louder and closer. The mountains to the north rumbled. Soon there were flashes of light illuminating the tent, and oohs and aahs from those sitting around the fire. The flashes were followed by explosions of thunder ten seconds later. Soon the interval was five seconds. I heard one tick on the tent, then another, then a thump, then another, and suddenly it was deluged by raindrops.

I heard laugh-filled screaming and drew back from the tent door, knowing David and Shad were running my way. I felt left out, alone. I pretended I was asleep as they loudly settled in, droplets flying off their clothes onto my face. Then, to the background of the hard and heavy rain, I moved my head back to the tent flap to watch as the glowing remnant of the fire washed out.

Great bolts split, dividing into vertical and horizontal. Each line of this cosmic script was painted on the canvas of the black sky, so vivid that when I closed my eyes I still saw the bolts exactly as they'd been five seconds earlier. I counted seconds between lightning and thunder and now it was less than two. A massive lightning bolt struck some nearby fir trees and an explosion followed, then a smash on the ground just before the thunder crack. Frodo whined nervously and pushed himself against my stomach. I rubbed his ears.

Another eruption of light followed, and for a long moment the entire tent was lit bright, right through the concussion of thunder. The bolts were so thick and brilliant I could see them through the tent canvas.

What was that?

In the moment of light I saw the shadow of a man, but after a brief darkness, lightning flashed again and it was gone. I stared at the same place. Three light bursts later I saw another shadow—a great beast prowling the ground, either hunting or guarding, I wasn't sure which. I didn't know whether to feel comfort or dread. When the next bolt glared, it too was gone.

The wind pushed against the tent flap, and I held onto it, still watching the fireworks. The clatter of the pounding rain was so loud that when I heard David or Shad raise his voice and say something, I couldn't even make it out. I snuggled in, grateful for the tent and the blankets, strangely feeling more secure now than I had the night before when there'd been no storm. The storm was a blanket of comfort, though I couldn't understand why.

Frodo nuzzled in against me, pressing his warm body against mine, surprising me when his cold nose touched my cheek.

"You don't understand the storm, do you, boy?" I whispered. "But you just want to be close to your master, don't you? That's all that matters to you, isn't it?"

I lay back, enjoying the fireworks, thankful for the reminder there was something in the universe far greater than I. Something fierce and out of my control, yes. But also wise and comforting.

As the storm raged, I sank into a peaceful sleep.

The next morning we awoke to much cooler temperatures. As pale strips of blue emerged from the remnants of the previous night's storm clouds, we sat at the foot of a tall fir tree and attempted to build a fire. David finally got a good light from his flint, and we managed to ignite a few dead sticks and pine cones. Then we tried to coax the fire to take hold of damp, icy logs. After an hour the fire finally took. I watched with fascination the light snow fall on the fire. Eddying blasts of wind caused it to swirl and turn to drops just over the flame, making a hissing sound. I looked to the north side of Peirasmos and saw mists of fog creeping up it, the tall trees drifting on a sea of mist.

We watched the fog lift to the southwest, uncovering a deep blue mountain lake with large chunks of snowfields and parts of glaciers that had slipped down from the surrounding cliffs, now floating like barges. A lone dark elk, clearly visible against the white-snow canvas, drank deeply from a stream feeding the lake. Just above the lake, not far from an alder thicket etched against the snow, a geyser let loose and blew white steam a hundred feet into the air. The elk loped off over a slope and vanished.

"Let's go take a closer look," I said. "Wouldn't it be great to warm our hands on that geyser?"

"There may be some warm springs," Victoria said. "We might be able to get a hot bath, a real one."

"You've got my vote," I said.

"We're travelers, not tourists," Shad replied. "We need to stay dry. We've got a mountain to climb."

"So much for other people's ideas," I muttered under my breath.

"We need to collect light wood to make fires on the mountain," Shad said, "in case we can't find anything up there. Come up with what you can, but not too much, and we'll start the climb in half an hour."

I wandered off by myself, picking up sticks here and there. Suddenly Marcus appeared beside me, startling me.

"It is hard for you," the warrior said, with that never-changing emotionless expression. "You wonder about yourself, do you not?"

"I'm still the same person," I cried, clenching my fists. "It took me years to become what I was, and I just can't shake it. I'm a walking bundle of habits. My mind has been programmed by a hundred thousand images, from magazines and television and movies, locker rooms and business luncheons. I'm the cumulative product of small choices, minute compromises, little frauds, and white lies. They added up to the big lie—my life. After I crossed the chasm, I felt so different, so changed and yet…images and thoughts and feelings of rage haunt me. I'm filled with doubts. It's as if something calls me back to what I was before."

"Something does call you back. You must refuse it."

"But how?"

"The King has given you resources—the soaring bird within, the TravelGuide, the family of light."

"The bird? Yes, I feel his presence inside me." I hadn't been aware of it since Quon's death, but I felt a soft ripple under my skin. It didn't hurt like the scorpion. It soothed me.

"The bird is stronger than the scorpion," Marcus said. "He helps you understand and obey the book. The book is stronger than the words of men. The family of light is stronger than the web. The King is stronger than the Impostor. The King's warriors are stronger than the turncoats." When he said the word "turncoat" his lip curled, the only change in his poker face.

"There's so much I hate here, so much that's wrong," I said.

"Not all is as it shall be. One day the silent planet will sing again."

"I feel like turning back, leaving the group."

"I know. But you must not do it, no matter what."

No sooner had he said it than he disappeared. I picked up some more wood, then went to our meeting spot, the first to arrive. I sat and read the TravelGuide, then looked up the mountainside before us. Peirasmos was directly west, between us and Charis. It would be a hard climb, but its beauty drew me nonetheless.

Near the top was a raw edge of snow on an ice field. It looked like thick, untouched frosting on a huge cake. Perhaps that was where some of the barges on the lake had broken off. Pine trees decorated the snowy lower slopes, like birthday candles, some of them entirely covered in white, like tall vanilla ice cream cones, their ice-covered coating causing them to gleam in the sun. The effect was of a masterpiece, as if Mount Peirasmos had been perfectly fashioned by a skillful artist.

"I traded a pheasant, some oats, and powdered milk for more blankets," David announced, pulling me back to the moment. "We'll need them up on the mountain."

Malaiki suggested we hold hands and ask the King's help before we started the climb.

Far above us we watched as a big-horned sheep scaled the mountainside with ease, as if his feet were made for such terrain. Of course—the World-Maker had designed them for this place, just as he had fashioned me for another. I breathed deeply. It felt good to see with clear eyes again. The mountain cut a swath in the blue sky, pointing me upward.

The pack felt light on my back—I'd started to feel its weight less since I'd lost some weight of my own. As we began our ascent in earnest, I felt intoxicated by the piercing purity of pine-scented mountain air. Even as our altitude rapidly increased, the oxygen was still so plentiful my lungs scarcely knew how to handle it. It wasn't city air, not suburban air, not even country air, but otherworldly air. Fresh and cool, enriching to the mind.

I liked the challenge of the climb, and every step helped me crawl out from under the ballast I'd carried since Quon died. Walking on the flat road had gotten to me—I wasn't made for passivity; I couldn't wander aimlessly and wait for death. I needed a tangible goal, a bull I could take by the horns. This mountain promised to provide it.

As I walked, I recited words from the GuideBook. As the breath of the spoken words hit the brisk air, I watched the swirling steam.

"The snow's getting so deep we can't see the red road," Shad said. I heard worry in his voice.

"Look!" I pointed down to the right.

A mule deer foraged on the other side of a white-capped stream. I watched it as I leaned against an old hemlock plastered with wind-blown snow, bare brown on one side and thick white on the other.

Shad walked quietly beside me.

"Old man, I have a question."

"Yes?"

"Where did you come from?"

"From...the other side of the chasm."

"That's not what I mean. Were you born in this world?"

He didn't answer for a long time. "No," he finally said.

"How'd you get here?"

"I once lived on the planet with a yellow sun and one moon." He said this as if he couldn't remember its name. "I followed the King when I was young. But then I took control, went my own way, did things I'm ashamed of. I made such a mess of my life, I thought it was over. I lost all hope."

"And then?"

"Then...I woke up here in Thuros, in a dark cave on Hagias, the volcanic mountain above Babel."

"How long ago?"

"I don't know for sure. At first I tried to keep track, but the years are longer here...or shorter—I don't know. It's impossible to measure time."

"What about the others? Victoria and Malaiki and David? What about Quon? Did they all come from Earth?"

"I don't know. I haven't asked them."

"But...why not?"

"Perhaps because they would then ask me why the King snatched me from Earth and brought me to Thuros. And I would have to tell them." He flinched. "You don't understand what I was."

I wanted to ask more, but after seeing the hollow look in his eyes, I didn't. As we trudged on, I said, "Maybe I do understand."

My back muscles burned as the terrain got steeper and the path harder to see. The crunch of hard-frozen snow under my boots, which at first had energized me, now tired me.

"Are you sure this is the red road?" I asked Shad.

"We have to follow the GuideBook. Even when we can't see the road, we must believe it's there." He insisted the book said we needed to cross the mountain near the summit. I wasn't sure, but Shad was so pigheaded there was no convincing him otherwise. As living things became scarce, I began to wonder if we also would disappear one by one.

I leaned forward so much that at times my head seemed only a few feet above the ground. Hot sweat dripped from my face, cutting little holes in the soft snow at my feet. Frodo traipsed on below me.

"The snow's getting too deep for you, boy," I said to him. "Pretty soon you'll have a free ride in your sling."

I heard my comrades' heavy breathing and strained movements. No one talked now. It was one thing to stand back and admire the mountain's majesty and contemplate the power surge of the ascent. It was another to actually climb it. Perhaps I really didn't want to climb the mountain after all—I simply wanted to *have* climbed it, accomplishment without struggle.

The air that was so rich and fresh before now became thin and deadly.

"How can anyone climb such a mountain?" Victoria asked, wheezing.

"One step at a time," Shad grunted. Victoria shot him a look he appeared to miss. At least it seemed to warm her up a little.

We hit icy mud, and traction became difficult. My feet couldn't dig into solid ground. Malaiki slid back. I managed to catch her and get her back on solid footing. No sooner had I done this, and congratulated myself for it, than I slipped and Shad caught me. Ten minutes later Shad lost his footing, and Victoria and I helped him. That surprised me—I didn't expect old goat-feet to ever slip. And I certainly didn't expect to be able to help him.

We hadn't been out of the mud long when we came to loose shale, partially covered by the windblown snow.

"It's treacherous," Shad said. "We need to tie ourselves together."

"Bad idea," David said.

"The GuideBook says in the hard places with difficult footing we must link ourselves to each other," Shad said. He opened the book and read several parts. "If one of us slips, the strength of the others can pull him back to secure footing."

"But we could all crash to our deaths," I said.

"We must make sure we don't slip at the same time. We need to pay close attention to ourselves and also be alert to help each other at the first sign of trouble. I know—this is not my first climb."

We tied ourselves together, with only Frodo walking on his own, his four feet and proximity to the ground giving him a distinct advantage. I felt uneasy, vulnerable. If the others blew it, I would pay the price.

For more than three hours we climbed on the shale, some loose, some tentatively glued to the ground by ice. We weren't lined up vertically, but more horizontally, with Malaiki and David on my left and Shad and Victoria on my right. Once I felt more sure of myself I stepped a little faster, to show the others I could lead.

I looked back at Malaiki and David and flashed a confident smile.

Just as I did, I felt nothing beneath me. My feet slid out from under me, and I was facedown on the shale, skidding down Peirasmos as if I were a fifth grader on a Slip 'n' Slide, except this fall wouldn't end on soft grass.

I was certain I'd lost it, when suddenly I came to the end of the rope. I looked up and Malaiki and Shad were holding the rope firmly, their feet dug in.

"Are you all right?" Victoria shouted. A moment before she'd been five feet away. Now she was forty.

"Yeah, I'm fine. No big deal." I got up and pretended I wasn't hurt. I didn't reach to my throbbing right side, cut and bruised by the shale and ice. It was all I needed—one more injury. I walked forward and upward, steadying myself on the rope as the others pulled it toward them, trying not to favor my sprained right ankle, though by now Frodo was sniffing at it as if he sensed the damage.

When I got near my comrades, I saw all their hands were bleeding, especially Shad's and Malaiki's. I almost said something, but I didn't want to make a scene. Shad tried to look me over, but I brushed him off and resumed the climb. We took it slower. Finally the shale ended, and we untied the ropes. It felt good to be free and yet...without the connection, I felt more vulnerable.

The air had gone from brisk to bracing to bone-chilling. Freezing rain formed a thick solid layer on my jacket. Any enjoyment of this climb was quickly disappearing. I picked up Frodo and held him securely in his sling, drawing from his warmth and giving him mine.

My jaw ached, as if it were set in concrete, my teeth clenched in the stone cold. My right ankle throbbed. The air was raw—it felt like a power outage at a North Dakota morgue in January. I longed to warm my hands around a hot cup of anything. I blew on my fingers but couldn't feel my breath. The days of electric heat seemed a distant memory—right then I'd have settled for a little propane stove or even a cigarette lighter.

My fatigue came not just from the steepness of the slope—I wasn't as fit as I'd believed. Not only was I carrying a load, I was winded, my back strained, legs cramped, my left shoulder killing me, my right side bruised, and my ankle sprained. Aside from the sprain, these were not new ailments created by the climb, but old ones exposed by it. The climb showed me I was weaker, more needy than I'd supposed. I didn't like the feeling.

Darkness fell like a huge icicle from a roof. The swirling wind and the narrow ledge made it impossible to build a fire. We were too cold to sleep, and we didn't dare try. We had to keep moving. Images assaulted my semiconscious mind. I was a sailor on the Bering Sea. Then I was a prisoner in a drafty Scottish dungeon in the dead of winter. I was an explorer in Antarctica. Lapland. Siberia. The Yukon. Green Bay. Duluth. The hood and pockets of my jacket offered no more warmth. I longed for a ski mask and decent gloves. I should have been better prepared.

Where's the King? Why isn't he helping us?

I wished I had a magic lamp, so I could rub it and make a genie appear to grant me wishes. But the Woodsman didn't work that way. He was unmanageable, unpredictable, unruly. Not only did he not do what I wanted, he never seemed compelled to explain himself to me.

Frozen air stung my face like a horrid insect. My body felt like a freezer bag, my internal organs frozen artichokes, cauliflower, and peas. I prayed, reminding myself the King was listening. The book said so. Shad said so. It was true—wasn't it?

What was fresh air a minute ago suddenly reeked. I heard thunderous flapping above. I thought I saw a shadow. Was it the beast? Glancing up, I nearly lost my balance. I looked down the mountainside and thought about how the slightest misstep could send me crashing to the rocks below. Suddenly that was not so fearful—it seemed almost a relief. I pictured myself jumping off the mountainside and plummeting down below. Who would know? They'd think it was an accident.

No sooner had the sound and shadow gone than I felt another beast, the one within, stinging me, also coaxing me to jump and punishing me if I refused. I moved closer and closer to the edge, surprised when my leg stopped against some sort of guardrail.

"We have to turn back," I cried out suddenly, not even recognizing my voice. "We're going to freeze up here. There must be another way. I'm going back!"

15

"I HAVE TO TURN BACK," I said to the group crowded around me.
"I have to."

"The flying beast wants you to turn back," Shad said. "The
scorpion wants you to turn back. The web tries to pull you back.
But you must go forward—to Charis."

"I can't."

"You can, for the Woodsman says to, and he only commands what
he also empowers. You have his book, you have the bird within, and
you have us, your family. You must draw on our strength now as in
other times we must draw on yours."

As he said this, I felt two forces fighting within me. I kept trying
to remember the words of the GuideBook, repeating them over and
over. After a few minutes the scorpion stopped its stinging. I still felt
fear but was determined now not to show it. Nick Seagrave was
not a coward or a weakling. Now I fought not only fear, but
embarrassment at how I'd panicked.

We moved on, the old man close beside me. His breath whistled
in his nose. His neck creaked like a rusty hinge. The breeze clinked
the icicles in his beard against each other. The sounds annoyed me.
Malaiki hummed a gentle song in the frosty air.

Don't waste your energy.

When I saw her face, the frost on her eyebrows, the fear in her eyes,
my heart melted. I took my second sleeping blanket from around my
coat and wrapped it around her own two blankets, now stiff as boards.

I looked at her and smiled, seeing my daughter, Amy. She reached out her hand. It was permafrost. Immediately I forgot the condition of my own chapped hands and rubbed them briskly against hers. After I'd done this for a minute or so, she bent her fingers.

"I feel them again," she whispered. "Thanks." She sang again, so softly I couldn't make out the words. I felt a surge of warmth in my own hands. Funny, I hadn't thought about making myself warmer, only her.

"Here," I said, picking up Frodo and handing him to her. "He'll warm up your hands. When he gets too heavy, I'll take him back."

Malaiki took him in her hands close to her face. He licked her frosty cheek, and she giggled. Then she tucked him under her blankets and coat.

"Colder than a well-digger's knee." My dad always said that. I never knew exactly what it meant. I wished now that I'd asked him, one of those cold days I visited him for five minutes in the care center, trying to check off one more box on my duty list. Why didn't I ask him to tell me his stories? Why didn't I give him a reason for living? Why did I let him go?

I put my shaking water bottle to my mouth. My lips froze to it. I pulled it back and felt the blood, thankful for the fleeting moment of warmth. I shook the rock-hard water bottle. No more.

"Chew ice," David whispered, his face cold-reddened. I did. After managing to get a few swallows of water, I fed slivers of ice to Frodo, now back from Malaiki, situated in the sling.

Malaiki stretched out her hand to me. I took her water bottle, not expecting it to produce anything when I put it to my lips. I tasted cold senaba, not yet frozen. I drank more, forcing myself to stop. I gave it back to her, trying to smile. We plodded on as darkness descended.

I was at Valley Forge. Winter 1777. George Washington. I was a weatherman pointing to a colorful chart with numbers, talking about blizzards. Cold fronts. Arctic air masses. I drank lime green antifreeze, winterizing my body.

Not much sanity left. Better use it while I can.

"Chili," I said in my loudest voice. "My mom used to make the best homemade chili. With cheddar cheese melted on top. Onions. Ritz crackers."

The words met with silence, dropping to the frozen tundra.

After five seconds, I heard a weak voice. "Coffee," Shad said. "A large mug of coffee."

"Dark Colombian roast," David added.

"A bubble bath," Victoria whispered.

"Hot tub," Malaiki said.

"Sauna," I grunted.

"Vegetable soup," Shad said. "And, for dessert…no ice cream."

We laughed weakly. I felt the coat of ice crack on my jacket. My body temperature seemed to rise slightly for the first time in hours.

"A barbecue," Malaiki said. "Rotisserie chicken."

"Put me straight on the rotisserie," Victoria said.

"We're all in a Jacuzzi," Malaiki said, "filled with Shadrach's vegetable soup."

The old man reached his hand to me, and I grabbed it. Instinctively we rubbed our hands together, warming each other with sheer friction.

The soft snow on the ground whispered to me, inviting me to curl up in it and fall asleep and awake into warmth. I heard it and obeyed, dropping down in a snowbank. My ankle no longer hurt. As I closed my eyes, I felt Frodo's hot breath, but it wasn't enough to bring me back. Then I felt the sharp point of a stick in my ribs.

"Get up," Shad said, poking me again. His hand and three others reached down to me. I stretched out my frozen right arm, and they pulled me up.

I ran the mile in college. Never the relay. In tennis I preferred singles over doubles. I never wanted to depend on someone else. I had more confidence in me than anyone. I was never a passenger, always the driver. I took pride in my rugged individualism. But when I pulled on the outstretched hands of my comrades, I stood by their strength, not mine.

Ten minutes later I'd regained some energy and walked on my own. Just then, Shad collapsed without warning. I picked him up and put my arms around him, massaging his body as I had massaged his hand and Malaiki's. The others drew close. We all embraced each other, moving our hands on each other's backs and faces. The warmth from our bodies merged and sustained each other like glowing coals piled on one another in an Arctic squall. Frodo's eyes drooped, as he pressed hard against me. He didn't understand. Me neither.

"I feel better," Shad said at last. "Let's move on. Soon it will be morning. We can make it till then. We have to. Ask the King to help us."

Shad was too weak to talk anymore, so Malaiki prayed. So did I. I could hardly hear her voice. And I didn't recognize my own.

Morning fog in the eastern lowlands, hit by a sudden red sunburst, created a frozen explosion of light reflecting off the snowy slopes. We squinted at the sunrise, and despite our sleepless night stopped to absorb the reviving hope it brought.

I looked down to an incredible view of evergreen trees divided by meandering streams, where hills stood like islands in a rolling green sea of forested valleys and low ridges. How could any place with a view so beautiful be so deadly? Or was this the price that must be paid to gain perspective?

We reached a bend where the path was extremely narrow, where only one could walk at a time. Fortunately there were portions of a guardrail, consisting mostly of cables and shafts of metal and poles, driven into the ground at the most treacherous parts. The day was dark and overcast, and thick mists shrouded sections of the trail. At times we leaned on the guardrail, feeling our way, with it as our reference point and guardian.

We heard a loud rough voice up ahead, coming our direction.

Shad was leading—suddenly he stood toe to toe with a tall, heavy man with a double chin and puckered lips and a scowl that could curdle milk. Peeking over the big man's shoulder was a chinless man with a large crooked nose and corn-kerneled teeth, wearing an orange stocking cap. There was room for only one on the ledge—passing each other wouldn't be easy.

"Who are you?" the big man demanded of Shad. "Why are you going this way?"

"We're walkers of the red road, servants of the King. We're going this way because…it's the right way. Why are you traveling the wrong way?"

"Don't test my patience, old man. I could toss you off this cliff." I put my hand on Shad's shoulder and tried to look intimidating. Frodo, poking his snout out my jacket, let out a low sustained growl.

"Are you the ones who put up these stupid rails?" the big man asked.

"Stupid?" I asked, looking at the guardrails. "What do you mean?"

"They keep getting in the way," he said. "They bruise my legs and hips. The steel cables cut my arm. And when I touch them, my fingers stick to the icy metal. Look, it tore the skin off me."

He held up his hand. I didn't need to look, since my hands were in the same condition.

"But what's the alternative?" I asked. "They've saved our lives—if not for the guardrails we'd plunge over the cliff."

"Do you think I'm stupid? I can stay on the path without these rails. All they do is get in the way."

"Have you crossed the chasm?" I asked.

"Chasm? I should have known. You're one of those. Funny, you didn't strike me as a total imbecile."

Thanks.

"Why would you want to believe in a chasm?"

"*Want* to believe?" I asked. "If a sword were poised over my neck, I wouldn't want to believe it. But if it was, I'd better believe it! The chasm is real. You'll know that eventually. The question is whether you'll find out about it too late." I pulled the book out of my coat pocket and opened it, fumbling with my frozen fingers. "The TravelGuide says—"

"I've lived here all my life. If there was a chasm, don't you think I'd have seen it?"

"But there *is* a chasm. It was hard for me to see at first too. But I crossed it with the Woodsman."

"I'm sure you think you did. Anyway, stand aside and let us by. We have to keep moving."

"Keep moving, yes. But take the time to make sure you're going the right direction! Wait just long enough for me to tell you about what really matters. Give me five minutes, okay? Here goes—all men die once, are judged once, and are relocated once. Now the Chasm-crosser—"

"I said let us by! We have no time for myths. And don't try to scare us by talking about death. We have major building projects and long-term plans as soon as we're out of the mountains. We intend to go right on living, thank you."

"Look around you, man!" I said, trying to catch my breath. "Feel your frozen eyelashes. We may all die on this mountain. And even if we survive, we'll all die eventually."

The man stared sternly. David whispered from behind, "Just shut up and don't hassle him!"

I thought about Quon. Perhaps the King arranged this appointment with them. Or perhaps I was being a fool. I looked at Shad in front of me and Malaiki behind me, their heads bowed, lips moving.

"You know what bothers me about you people?" asked the chinless man in the orange stocking cap. "It's your wishful thinking. You want there to be a City of Light, so you pretend there is. Me, I'm a realist. I don't play games."

"Wishful thinking?" I said, trying to keep my voice from shaking, yet feeling warmer the more I spoke. "If I were to wish for something, do you think I'd have wished for a flying beast so deadly, a scorpion so horrid, a web so hideous, a chasm so vast, a cost so great? Never in a million years would I have believed or wanted to believe such things. I would have wished for something easier, and if I had made it up, it would be a lot more attractive and a lot less costly. But the universe isn't governed by my wishes. It's *you* who practice wishful thinking."

"Me? What do you mean?"

"You believe there's no King because you wish there to be none, correct? If you're like I used to be, you wish you could make up your own rules and get away with it; you wish you wouldn't be held accountable for your choices, that you wouldn't have to answer to someone after this life. You wish there was no creator because you don't want to face a judge. It's not my belief that's wishful thinking. It's your unbelief."

The man in the stocking cap started to retort, then stopped abruptly. He said nothing, but I could see his wheels turning.

"I've had it," the big man said. "Get out of my way or I'll toss you off the ledge. Do you hear me?"

I pulled Shad toward me with my left hand, shoulder aching, then I yanked out my knife with my right, hiding it behind the old man. The big man squeezed by, taking shots at us with knees and elbows, and swearing at us for being pushy. He stared at me coldly, and I stared back. Who would blink first? Not Nick Seagrave. I didn't. I wondered if before I could act he would grab someone and push him off the cliff. I almost waved the knife at him, but resisted the urge.

Then the others, eight of them, passed us single file. They waddled cautiously, like penguins on a narrow ice ledge, following their leader.

But the man in the orange stocking cap held back. He pressed against the mountain between Malaiki and me, telling the others to pass him.

"I'm Shaun," he said. "Tell me more of the chasm. And the Chasm-crosser."

"Get back in formation," one of the penguins commanded Shaun. He ignored the scolding.

The penguins stopped to rest maybe sixty feet behind us. I talked with Shaun, telling him what the Woodsman had done, about Charis and why we were headed that direction, and warning him about the Pretender. Finally, he went off to rejoin the penguins, but he promised he'd consider what I'd said. Though I'd expended a lot of energy, I felt less tired than an hour before.

Back behind us, where the penguins had started moving again, I heard a strange noise, like someone kicking hard against metal. I turned and saw a dozen warriors in battle. I couldn't understand how they all fit on the narrow walkway, then realized they didn't—they were standing on air. There was only one bright warrior against a gang of dark ones. I prayed, and so did Malaiki and Shad. When I looked up, out of the air there appeared one more bright warrior, then another, then another. They were still outnumbered three to one, but at least it was a fight.

"These stupid guardrails!"

It was the voice of the head penguin, and when I focused on it, the warriors disappeared. But the noise continued, metal crashing against metal. Then I heard a scream and squawks and the sound of something careening off the mountainside, falling onto the rocks below. It was the sickening crunch of bouncing flesh and broken bone. I listened breathlessly.

"I told you those rails were dangerous," said a whiny voice. "Look at what they did to him."

"Let's get rid of the railing so it doesn't hurt anyone else." The air filled with grunts and groans and kicking and hitting and pulling.

"Please don't," Malaiki called to them. "You'll just make the road more dangerous for yourselves and others. Without the guardrails, more people will fall off the cliff—or jump!"

We heard no answer. Then another scream bit the air, followed by thuds below and another silence.

After thirty seconds or so, I heard Shaun's voice.

"Maybe it's time to rethink this. Maybe the guardrail isn't the problem. Maybe we are the problem."

We stared to the east, down at terrain we had walked through. The large lake we'd seen, near the geyser, was one of at least three dozen glaciated basins. Some of them were surrounded by rust-colored larch trees coming down from the snow-dusted slopes. The temperature was bearable now. We were thawing out, but there still wasn't any room to set up camp except on the road itself, which was just too narrow. We had to push forward. The way was difficult, and my ankle hurt so bad I cringed and bit my lip.

"Let me help you, Nick," Shad said. He put his thin but strong arm under mine and around my back, taking some weight off the ankle.

"You need to learn how to ask for help," Malaiki said. "We want to be here for you."

"It's not that bad," I said. What I didn't say was that it would kill me to ask for help—I'd had a lifetime of experience not doing it.

As we moved ahead, I heard Malaiki groan, sounding distressed. I looked back quickly to see her push David's hand away from behind her. I pretended not to notice and turned my head slightly to watch out of the corner of my eye. He whispered to her, and I saw him touch her again.

"Pass me, Malaiki," I said, pressing against the rock. Eyes down, she did.

"What do you think you're doing?" I challenged David through closed teeth, my nose two inches from his.

"It's no big deal. Mind your own business."

"Malaiki is my business. She belongs to the King, not you."

"Who do you think you are?"

"Her...brother," I said.

"You don't understand," he sniveled.

"I do understand. I've ruined my life and my family's and more than one woman's. I won't let you do it, not to Malaiki." I pointed my finger at him. "Do you hear me?"

He stared at me, and I braced for a fight. Finally he relaxed his shoulders, then turned his eyes to his position locator.

Watching my back, I moved forward again and caught up with Malaiki.

She turned and whispered, "Thanks for your help. I was scared and...confused."

"No problem," I said.

"You mentioned you have a daughter, didn't you?"

"Yes. Her name's Amy."

"She's lucky to have you for a dad."

I looked down at the blurry mud on my boots.

No, she's not.

After a long tense descent, the path widened. At last there was enough room to safely set up camp. After spending two hours defrosting at the fire and drying our blankets, we went to our tents. David wasn't speaking to me, which was just fine. I lay down between him and the tent door. The ground was hard yet welcome. I heard Frodo's gentle sighs, then faded into dreams.

Early the next morning I drank strong coffee heated on the fire. David examined charts and consulted a strategy manual for roadwalkers. Shad sat next to him, reading the GuideBook. I heard faint sounds on the mountain slopes above us. The beautiful snow seemed to quiver slightly.

"We must go," Shad said. "We're in danger."

We quickly packed and continued our descent. I could see where the ground leveled out only five hundred feet below us. Then I heard a sound, like a huge hungry stomach growling. Everything seemed deathly still except high on Peirasmos where a large slab of snow wavered. I watched it slowly break loose from the slope, beginning to pull away. It shattered into separate blocks, the blocks smaller and smaller but spreading out so as to create a cloud of snow and ice. I was almost hypnotized by its beauty when I heard Victoria scream.

"Run!"

Oblivious to my throbbing ankle, I ran forward, my pack slinging back and forth, the sack of riverbed stones pummeling my right shoulder, and Frodo swinging against my chest in his sling. Everyone else was in front of me. The noise grew like an approaching locomotive, but I couldn't resist turning back to look over my shoulder as I ran.

A river of snow and a cloud of icy particles rose high into the air, hundreds of feet above the surface of the slope. The cloud of what must have been thousands of tons of snow and ice chased us. Up above, where we'd just come from, faint screams emerged from the massive momentum of falling snow.

"Run, Nick!" Malaiki yelled back at me. I turned to see my companions much farther down the mountain than I. From the corner of my left eye I saw snow slipping over the bare rocks and onto the path. I moved to the right, snug up against a guardrail, still hundreds of feet above stony ground.

As I ran, I slipped on ice and slid, feeling my back crunch into my pack, which became a makeshift sled, sliding me faster than I could run. I spun and lost control. My last image was of a great hand of snow pushing me into the guardrail and trying to thrust me off the cliff. I felt my head slam into something, and before I could even feel pain, a black hush overtook me.

16

I AWOKE TO AN EERIE SILENCE, inside what appeared to be a log cabin. Malaiki hovered over me, tending to my leg. She didn't see my open eyes. Through the doorway I saw a tall, mustached gentleman with a big smile and a woman I didn't recognize, wearing an apron and talking with Victoria. Looking out a window, I saw what appeared to be the fringes of a small town. Between us and the western slope of Peirasmos was a stand of evergreens, a natural barrier shielding the town from the mountain's wrath.

The faint scent of maple syrup nudged me. Frodo licked my ear.

"Welcome back, Nick," Victoria called, running to my side.

"How…?"

"Relax. We carried you here. Cal and Helen say we're welcome to stay as long as we need to."

Malaiki put senaba juice to my lips, and I gratefully accepted. I caught a scent from behind me, familiar and comforting—Shad.

He came around my bedside and took my hand. His callous grip reminded me of my father's, a hand I'd held far fewer times than I wished, but now longed for. Shad smiled broadly. I watched a single tear flow down his weather-beaten cheek. Before I knew it, he'd bent over and his arms were around me. I heard and felt him sob— I kept thinking of my father and didn't want him to let go.

We stayed in the cabin two days, enjoying wonderful meals and conversation while I began to recover. I had no broken bones but was sore in places I didn't know I had. My ankle had a chance to heal along with everything else. I had time to think about the penguin hikers, especially Shaun. They surely must have perished in the avalanche, all of them. I couldn't get Shaun off my mind.

I would have liked to stay a week, but Shad was eager to move, so we packed up our things. After a wonderful breakfast of bacon and sausage and fresh bread and strong rich coffee and senaba, we took off, moving slowly in the cold but bright red sunshine. My ankle throbbed, my calves burned, and my shoulders ached. Once I got in a groove, though, it was actually a pleasant gradual descent.

It warmed up rapidly, and by midday we hit level ground, where we drank from a cool stream and basked in the sun. We lounged in tall grass and flowers, feeling like we'd come from the bitter frigid winter to the bright blossoming warmth of spring. We laughed and rested. I clenched and unclenched my sore but warm hands. Just before the avalanche I'd told myself if I ever got warm again I would never take it for granted. I thanked the King again.

I found a bed of ferns and thick grass, deep and soft and fragrant. I lay down, not caring that it was midday and not wanting to be found by anyone. "Thank you," I whispered, as I closed my eyes and eased into sleep.

"Time to get up," Shad said what seemed to be just minutes later. His wasn't a welcome voice. I'd been hoping for a good nap.

We traveled on gentle, slow-climbing slopes, the road moving alongside the long, narrow shadow on the land.

"Hello!" called a traveler in a blue raincoat. We chatted about the weather and turns in the road, and I told him about the mountain and the avalanche.

I asked him about himself and told him a little about me. I

considered asking him why he traveled east instead of west and whether he had crossed the chasm. I wondered how I might bring up the Chasm-crosser. My mouth started to open, but it froze.

What would Bluecoat think of me if I questioned his direction? Would he be insulted, as some of the others had been? Would he think me a fanatic? Perhaps just by being friendly I could be a good example. I might dispel any of his negative impressions of chasm-crossers. A voice inside me told me this was not the time to speak. And I remembered what happened to Quon.

After a pleasant conversation, Bluecoat waved good-bye and disappeared down the road.

We pressed on day after day, Shad pushing us to get in extra miles. The stay at Cal and Helen's was a fond memory but now seemed long ago.

We met and passed many travelers carrying loads of baggage. They didn't carry burlap bags of stones but hauled large wagons with boxes of valuables, everything from crafts and wall hangings to appliances and entertainment systems and gas engines. Their possessions were so heavy, the carts and wagons kept sinking in the mud, toppling over, and rolling back on their toes. Some limped from more serious injuries. There was a lot of yelling and whining and some scuffles.

We passed more and more people as we came to a steeper upgrade. I was thankful to be carrying so little. A frazzled-looking woman, her back arched against the weight of her cart, sighed and said, "I can't go farther; I can't make it up the hill."

"You can," Shad said, pointing to her wagon full of artwork, jewelry boxes, shoes, and clothes. "If you just leave your burdens behind you."

"Burdens? These aren't burdens. They're treasures."

"Your treasures have great mass, and mass creates the pull of gravity and holds you down. It's not the hill that's the problem, it's everything you're trying to carry up it."

"I can't go on without them."

"Of course you can. You *will* go on without them, because you cannot take them with you. You may or may not separate yourself from your possessions now, but you will surely be separated from them later. Do it now and you'll be free to serve the King."

"If you have less," Malaiki said, "you'll have less to worry about."

"Who are you to talk?" asked a dour-looking man. "You carry heavy sacks, without even a wagon to aid you!"

"We carry these stones because the King tells us to," Malaiki said. "I can't explain it, but the more I carry, the stronger I get, and somehow it feels lighter. What you carry grows heavier each day, and you become weaker."

The frazzled woman looked at her things and fingered them. "But my art, my music, my books, my collections," she said. "These are good things, aren't they?"

"Many of them are good," Malaiki said, "and we should thank the King for them. But even the best things can't endure the journey. They're expendable. The GuideBook says we shouldn't hold anything too close in the short today that will not be ours in the long tomorrow. It commands us to travel light."

The longer we walked, the more people and possessions we encountered, the more tired I got, and the less enthusiasm I felt for the road. That night we let the fire die early and withdrew to our tents with little conversation.

Words in the dark pulled me out of sleep. These were not the murmurs of some unknown being, but a man inside the tent. A dark image just three feet from me fervently whispered in a hoarse creaky voice. Then I heard the distant sound of clanging metal. The more the shadow whispered and the more intensely, the louder the clangs.

Vicious but unintelligible words filled the air. As the whispers in the tent continued, there was a shriek, followed by one last clang, and then a shout of triumph in some glorious unfamiliar tongue. As I watched, the shadowy figure crawled back under his blanket. Within a few minutes he began to twitch, then snore.

The next day we walked for hours alongside a magnificent, well-tended estate that sprawled across the south side of the road as far as we could see.

"Who owns all this?" David asked. "I'm impressed!"

We heard approaching hoofbeats and a jet-black thoroughbred with hints of blue appeared, ridden by a distinguished and finely dressed gray-haired gentleman, accompanied by several attendants also on horseback. I stared at the black horse, obviously bred for speed and intelligence.

"I'm Mr. Timothy Bartholomew," he said, extending his hand down to me. When he saw me admiring his mount, he added, "And this is Thunder."

We chatted about the weather and a half-dozen other inconsequential items, then Mr. Bartholomew said, "You've obviously been on a hard journey. I invite you to stay with me at my estate. I believe you'll find it refreshing."

"Can we?" Malaiki asked Shad. "We've been pushing so hard. We could really use a rest."

We all nodded our agreement. Shad hesitated. Finally he said, "Well—all right."

Bartholomew sent one of his attendants back to inform the chef we'd be joining them for dinner. He walked Thunder at a footpace and told us about his estate, which he said was more than a thousand acres. He pointed to landmarks along the way.

Particularly captivating were the green fields where I saw at least a dozen horses running. We'd walked next to his property for half a day when at last we came to his mansion. It was the size of a corporate headquarters but with a warm blend of ivy-covered brick and polished wood, sloping roofs and arches, large picture windows and ornate lattices and doorways.

"It's the house of my dreams," David said. I knew what he meant. I'd owned a couple of beautiful houses, but they were shacks compared to this.

When we entered the mansion, he escorted us to large bathrooms where we could clean up.

"I know you're famished," Mr. Bartholomew said, "so we'll eat before I show you to your rooms. Meet me down the hallway at the waiting area outside the dining room."

When a servant escorted us into the dining room, it took my breath away. It was the size of a house, with intricately carved cedar paneling and a thirty-foot-high, gold, frescoed ceiling. In the center of the room was an oak table with seating for sixteen, seven chairs on each side, two on the ends, one occupied by Bartholomew, the other by his wife, who wore an exquisite Victorian dress.

The high-back walnut chairs were ornately carved and had soft, embroidered cushions. Above the table was a fine cut-glass chandelier with at least forty candles. I got dizzy trying to count them. On the far side, thirty feet from the table, was a white marble fireplace with a fine cherry clock above it. Suits of armor, shields, and busts of various luminaries, most of them foreign to me, were spread across the room.

To say the least, it was all overwhelming to a band of pilgrims who slept in tents, ate on rocks by an open fire, and on a good night complimented the chef that the porcupine meat wasn't as stringy as usual.

There in Bartholomew's fabulous dining room we feasted on an exquisite dinner with seemingly endless courses, including Caesar salad, shrimp cocktail, and filet mignon. The only thing I didn't touch was the escargot. After mouthwatering strawberry cheesecake, we spent two hours on a tour, going from room to room—two libraries, drawing rooms, dining rooms, an enormous kitchen and pantry, recreation rooms with pool tables and exercise equipment, an entertainment room with a huge screen, and an indoor swimming pool.

"There's the sauna you dreamed of on the mountain," Malaiki said, pointing and giggling.

We spent the night in gorgeous private bedrooms, each with its own bath. On Earth I'd always been a shower guy, never taking time for a bath. But now I stayed in the tub until the water started to get tepid, then turned on steaming hot water, soaking in the warmth, as if it were a commodity I might store up for the journey. I slept soundly, with no dread of noises in the night.

Over the next few days we swam in Bartholomew's lake, fished in a gray cold river, and hunted with bows in one of his forests. I kept thinking how Quon would have loved the hunting.

"I could stay here forever," Victoria said after dinner on our third evening.

"We must leave tomorrow," Shad said. My heart sank.

"How about one more day?" Mr. Bartholomew asked. "You can ride my horses and see more of my estate."

We all looked at Shad like little children at their father, begging with our eyes.

"All right, then," he said with a slight smile, "but tomorrow will be our last night."

We rose early, brimming with anticipation. Bartholomew led us to the stables, where we were greeted by dozens of horses. All the mounts were well-fed and most were frisky, front hoofs rising at our entrance.

"Choose your horse, Nick," Bartholomew said to me. I looked past a proud pinto and a striking blood bay that reminded me of the one ridden by the mysterious girl in black. Then I fixed my eyes on a magnificent blue roan.

"That's Megan," he said.

A powerful white stallion, deep-chested and restless, reared up and whinnied. "He's Pegasus."

"And this is Missy." He pointed to a lovely chestnut mare with a flaxen mane.

"What's his name?" I asked, nodding at a dapple-gray Arabian with dished face, wide-set eyes, and a high tail set. Sleek and shiny, he was unusually large, at least sixteen hands, and built for strength, with powerful hindquarters. He eyed me, not the others, and blew air out his flared nostrils.

"Sauto. You've chosen well, Nick," Bartholomew said, smiling. He'd read me right—I'd already picked him. "Sauto's one of my most refined steeds. He'll take you as far as you want to go—and farther."

I saddled and mounted Sauto. He pranced in a circle outside the stable, while my companions made their choices. Bartholomew took the lead, riding Thunder, black and beautiful. We rode the vast and strikingly beautiful countryside. Even the houses of Mr. Bartholomew's servants were beautiful.

As we passed various orchards and ponds and lakes, Sauto snorted as if expressing his opinion of them. He was class on four legs, strength under control. After a long, wondrous day riding, when I cooled him out and brushed him down, he nickered with delight and moved his head against mine.

After washing up, we sat in the great dining hall and settled down to a Greek salad with fresh tomatoes and olives and feta cheese. It was followed with veal cutlets, steak tartare, warm French bread, and fresh asparagus under hollandaise sauce. I raised my eyebrows at David when the server brought in Dutch apple pie à la mode.

"Today you saw only a portion of what I own," Bartholomew said to all of us after the last bite of pie. "Tell me, now, after being here these days, what do you think of my houses and lands?"

"I think they're spectacular," Victoria said.

"They're very…impressive," I said.

"Fantastic," David said. "I've never seen anything like it."

"I feel refreshed; I've enjoyed our time here," Malaiki said. Did I hear a slight hesitation in her voice?

Bartholomew turned to Shad. "And you, Shadrach, what do you think?"

Shad thought long and hard. Finally he said, "I think…you're going to have a hard time leaving all this."

David turned crimson. "Mr. Bartholomew extends us every kindness, and this is how you repay his hospitality?"

"He asked me a question. I answered it honestly."

"So you did," Mr. Bartholomew said. The remainder of the dinner was very quiet. As the rest of us left, David stayed and talked to Bartholomew.

The next morning we gathered in the great living room, packs in hand, ready to head for the road.

We thanked Mr. Bartholomew warmly, then followed Shad toward the front door. He seemed anxious to get us out. David lingered, talking with two of the servants.

"Come on, David," I said. "Let's go."

"I'm not coming."

"What?"

"Mr. Bartholomew offered me a position. I'm staying to manage his estate."

"But...what about the red road? You're a traveler, aren't you?"

"I'm tired of the road. It's time to settle down, do something worthwhile, something I can measure."

"But we're headed home," Shad said.

"So you say. I don't know about Charis. I look to the west and see nothing but sunsets. Besides, I doubt anything could compare to Mr. Bartholomew's estate."

"Momentary ease isn't the answer," Shad said to him. "The daily hardships of the road sharpen and deepen the man."

"No doubt," David said. "And the chill winds of an arctic winter are better than the tropical breeze of an island paradise!"

"If the winter is about to become a glorious spring," Shad said, "and the island is about to be buried in hot lava, then yes, the winter *is* better!"

"*If...*," David said, emphatically.

"Please come with us, David," Victoria pleaded.

"Mr. Bartholomew has given me liberty to hire anyone I choose. Stay, Victoria. Your elegance and experience would serve us well."

Victoria's eyes grew big. She looked at David, at Mr. Bartholomew, at the house. She walked to a large picture window and gazed out at the horses, the flowers, the land.

I heard to my right the sudden clang of metal, then turned. Nothing.

"It's a great estate by this world's standards," Shad said to Victoria. "But by the standards of the King, it's a ramshackle old hut soon to be reduced to ashes." He opened the front door and pointed down the red road toward Charis, nestled in the foothills of Mount Aletheas. "Now *there* is an estate, one that will survive the coming holocaust of things."

She walked out front and looked back and forth between the two homes, Bartholomew's and the King's. Slowly she walked back inside.

"I'm afraid I can't stay," she said to David, eyes falling. "I have somewhere else to go."

"Malaiki?" David asked, looking at her fondly. "I can certainly find a place for you."

She backed away, toward the door, shaking her head.

"How about you, Nick? You've got savvy. You could be in charge of dozens of employees—eventually maybe hundreds."

I stared at him, stunned and thrilled at his offer. What a prospect. I was eager to take charge, face the test of responsibilities, use again the skills that had served me well in business. Even if David and I had our differences, I could work around them.

"Think about it," David said, smiling. "You could ride Sauto whenever you wanted. And I was just told there's going to be lasagna and French bread for dinner tonight—and senaba sorbet."

"Give me a few minutes," I said. I glanced at the old man and saw fear in his eyes. I walked out one of the back doors to breathe in the fresh air and look over the estate that beckoned me to stay.

I walked for half an hour, at least, Frodo at my heels, looking as far as I could see. I visited the stable and talked to Sauto, who nodded and nickered and gratefully ate carrots from my hand.

I wanted to do something, longed to succeed, to make a difference in some tangible way. This was the chance I was looking for. Why not? There was so much promise here. I had no reason to believe I'd find a greater opportunity. And even if it didn't work out, I could always walk the red road again, couldn't I? Why hurry? It would still be there tomorrow.

I was tired of dry sandwiches, bean soup, varmint jerky, and raw cucumbers. I was tired of the way my backpack bit into my shoulders, of having to drive on despite all my wounds, tired especially of packing the stones. I felt like a snail, carrying my home on my back. What kind of home was portable, anyway? It felt good to have a door between me and the night. Why should I give it up? Most likely the King was behind it all—maybe he'd prompted David to offer me the position. Yes, I was sure he had.

I walked back to the mansion. Everyone was waiting out back, by the pool.

"What's your decision?" David asked.

"I'm staying here at Mr. Bartholomew's."

The old man's eyes widened.

"Look, before you preach at me," I said, feeling my face flush, "I can serve the King anywhere, can't I? I don't have to walk the red road."

I was prepared to argue with Shad, but he hung his head and said nothing. It was Malaiki who opened the TravelGuide and read, "We are aliens, strangers, and pilgrims in this world. It is not our home. Our citizenship is in Charis."

I looked at Malaiki and Shad and Victoria and then at David. I started to speak, still not sure exactly what to say. I thought a few moments more, and for the first time I quietly talked to the King and considered the words from the book. Then I looked back up, in a surge of clarity. I knew I'd rationalized myself into the easy way out.

"It's all going to burn," I said, my voice sounding more certain than I felt. "Perhaps I should go back to the red road. All this is beautiful, but you can't take it with you."

"Well, then, I'd better get as much out of it as I can now," David said with a fixed smile. He waved his hand at us. "Look at you," he said through his teeth. "You're homeless. Tramps and bag ladies."

"Homeless is exactly what we're not," Shad said. "We're away from home, yes, but we are headed there. You too are away from home, but you're headed nowhere. If you stay here, you'll not only be homeless, you'll be worldless. The whole globe is going to burn—the TravelGuide says so. All will be homeless then, except those whose home is in another world."

"The treasures here are greater than any I've ever seen," David said. "I won't leave them for a journey with a destination I'm unsure of. I won't let myself end up like Quon—I wouldn't have thought you would either, Nick."

I swallowed hard. He was right. I didn't want to end up like Quon.

"Quon knows the truth better than any of us," Malaiki said. "He's already home."

"Listen to the TravelGuide," Shad said, not opening it, but reciting it, looking into my eyes. "Each day every man comes closer to the day of his death. Those who lay up their treasures in Thuros spend each day moving away from them. Those who lay up their treasures in Charis spend each day moving toward them. He who spends his life moving away from his treasures has reason to despair. He who spends his life moving toward his treasures has reason to rejoice."

I finally stopped wrestling and gave in to what I knew was right. When I had first joined this group, I'd have never believed I would choose with old Shad and against David. But, as I stood on Mr. Bartholomew's estate, I weighed my own houses and cars and possessions and treasures back on Earth in the scales of eternity. And I saw how little weight they carried. Yet the certainty, the clarity, I thought was forever mine in one moment suddenly wavered in the next.

"Come," Shad said. "If David won't walk the road to Charis, we cannot force him."

"Are you staying or going, Nick?" David asked.

"Going," I said weakly.

David handed me his backpack. "I won't need this anymore. If you change your mind, the offer's still open—but not forever."

I nodded, hung my smaller pack over a hook on his, and slung them on. I gingerly positioned my left shoulder, better but still sore, then tied David's pack at my waist. Though the weight was heavier, his pack was so balanced the overall load seemed less. Then I sighed, remembering my sack of stones, still in the living room.

We walked back to the house quietly. I picked up my stones, and when we stepped out the front gate, I looked back. I thought about that soft bed, the warm bath, those wonderful meals, the chance to work my way up again, and Sauto. I wanted to swallow my pride and run back.

We'd walked fifty feet on the red road when I heard Victoria's muffled cries next to me and saw the longing in her eyes as she looked at David and the estate.

I stopped and stared at David, standing alone inside the gate. Trying to make the best of it, I waved to him.

He didn't wave back.

17

"WHAT HAPPENED TO DAVID?" I asked as we sat around the evening's fire after a long, silent day of walking.

"Perhaps it's not what happened as much as what didn't," Shad said.

"What's that supposed to mean?"

"You can't be the King's bride without giving up your other lovers."

"But he crossed the chasm," Victoria said.

"Things aren't always what they appear," Shad said, warming his hands on his old tin coffee cup. "Whether a man has crossed the chasm is between him and the King. But sharing the same ground and air and meals with chasm-crossers doesn't make you one, any more than pouring oil into a coffee cup makes it coffee."

I thought not just about David, but how close I came to staying behind.

"David's window of opportunity will soon close," Shad said, "as will ours. But for now he can still choose his path—so can we all."

As we walked, I looked to the east and noticed how Mount Peirasmos slowly shrank behind us. Just then Marcus appeared beside me, startling both me and Frodo, who barked and growled. Marcus gazed at him, and the pooch suddenly calmed down, falling into step beside us.

"Do you remember," Marcus asked, "the man you passed on the road, the one in the blue raincoat?"

"Sure."

"What was his name?"

"I never asked."

"His name was Ed. You considered telling him of the King, did you not?"

"Yes, and I almost did, but…the time wasn't right."

"And did you expect to have another time?"

"Maybe. I might bump into him later." I hesitated. "I guess I just didn't want him to think I was a fanatic."

"Are you not a fanatic, then?"

"I mean, I didn't want him to think I was pushy."

"And so you did not offer him the most important gift in the universe? You did not sing to him the music his songless heart longed to hear?"

"No. I guess I didn't."

"You will stand before the Audience of One," Marcus said. "Men's opinions of you will not matter to you then. Knowing that, why do they matter so much to you now?"

"Something told me I shouldn't bring it up."

"Something or some*one*? Tell me, Nick. If the worst happens, if men reject you, what have you lost?"

I thought of the bad feelings, the insults, the embarrassment— then made a quick comparison to the life awaiting me in Charis. "Nothing," I said, throat scratching. "Marcus, tell me about Bluecoat, I mean, Ed. Will we cross paths again? Will the King send others to speak to him?"

"There was a rock slide this morning," Marcus said. "Ed was killed."

At a color-cloaked meadow lined with fruit trees heavy with senaba and apples, we stopped for a break. Victoria squeezed the senaba and filled our water bottles, while Shad cautiously inspected some combs dripping with honey—as the bees inspected him.

"Ouch! You miserable creatures!" Shad shouted.

Titters of laughter rippled through our corner of the meadow where red, blue, yellow, white, and orange flowers were so plentiful we didn't even feel guilty disturbing them. Having filled every nook of my backpack with senaba, I stretched out in a clump of soft grass, cutting a small hole in the fruit and putting in a straw as Malaiki had taught me.

Just then I heard strange voices at the far edge of the meadow, out in a clump of oak trees.

"I'm taking a walk," I called to Victoria, who hadn't heard the voices or was too tired to care. I got up and followed the voices and finally came to an old wooden structure that appeared to be a makeshift jail, made of thick, tightly meshed oak logs, with a locking metal gate built into the wood.

I saw three men inside, threadbare and ragged, wearing handcuffs.

"How long have you been here?" I asked.

"Twenty-five years for me," said a crotchety voice coming from a short, muscular man in a blue denim jacket. "Name's Zed. Gordy, there, now he's been here what, sixteen years? Roy's the newcomer; nine years for him. Ain't that right, Roy?"

"But…what's this all about?" I asked. "How could you possibly live here all those years? And how did you get locked up?"

"Seen a lotta things these twenty-five years," Zed replied, picking his teeth with a sliver of wood. "Got some stories to tell, I reckon."

I looked at Gordy and Roy, hoping they might answer me. Roy

never looked up. He just kept dealing cards, a bit awkwardly due to his handcuffs. Gordy, his long blond hair in a ponytail and his pale chalky face strewn with red splotches, was extremely thin and gaunt, dangerously so. Sucking his teeth and staring at the dirt floor, he appeared to be watching spiders and centipedes and chiggers and beetles, all of which came and went as they pleased through the small cracks in the logs and the four-inch spaces between the cell door's iron bars. I heard him call some of them by name. I had the uneasy feeling he was waiting for his next meal to walk through.

A hundred questions assaulted me, like how they got food and especially water, and what they did in bad weather, and who provided them clothes, but answers wouldn't come easily from this tribe. I decided to check the metal door. I looked for rust and possible weak spots but saw nothing. I stooped and examined the lock and the latch. I leaned forward for a closer look, then lost my balance and fell against the door.

It swung open, and I tumbled into the cell. The prisoners barely looked up, as if this was a casual occurrence. I jumped up and yelled, "It's unlocked. You're free!"

"Another one of them 'you're free' jokers, hey?" Zed asked. "Don't that just beat all, boys? We sit here year after year; he pops in, and lickety-split he tells us, 'You're free.'"

Gordy, his brown britches cinched at his narrow waist and his long handcuff chain dangling, moved over suspiciously. He looked at the open door, then me, then the others. Gordy slowly put one foot out of the cell and waited tensely. When nothing happened, he put the other foot out.

"It's true, Zed. Look, I'm standing outside. I'm a free man!"

Zed kept his back to Gordy and the jail door.

"You may think so, Gordy, but I reckon I know when a door's locked or not. Been here twenty-five years, remember? Ain't much, but it's home; it's where the likes of us belong. You know as much. Fella learns not to believe these quick-fix artists that come along and say, 'You're free,' like everything's all right, just like that. Ain't it so, Roy?"

Roy just kept playing solitaire.

"Roy, the door's open," Gordy said. "Come on out." Roy didn't look up.

Gordy stretched and jumped up to a tree limb, then started climbing, all smiles despite his handcuffs.

"I walked the red road years ago," he said. "But things happened, and I ended up in this jail. I owe you big time, mister. Thanks for unlocking it."

"But I didn't do anything, it was already..."

He dropped down from the tree and put his outstretched hand-cuffed arms around my neck and gave me a tight hug, which was more than a little uncomfortable.

He laughed, then swung the gate open and shut. "Look, boys," he called. They still wouldn't look, so I went to Zed and tapped him on the shoulder.

"Been here twenty-five years, did I mention that, partner? Everybody knows me in these parts. Ol' Zed. Roy, his pappy and grandpappy both spent most their lives in this jail. He knows he's stuck here. No use fighting a losing battle."

Zed babbled on and on. I kept trying to interrupt, to come up with a new and more compelling way to deliver the simple message: "The door's open—you're free!"

When nothing else worked, I decided to drag Zed out. He fought me off, as if I were trying to put him in jail instead of take him out. I felt like I was wrestling a greased pig. He kept giving me the slip, using his cuffed hands to ward me off. Finally I gave up and sat down, getting back my breath.

"I don't get it," I said, hearing the frustration in my own voice. "If you stay here, you'll die in jail. Needlessly. Is that what you want?"

I watched ripples move across Zed's stomach. He put his hand on them and grinned. "Got me a toucha heartburn. Comes from eatin' some bad critters, I reckon."

Standing only three feet from a wide-open cell gate, Zed talked to the wind, telling story after story about his jail-room exploits. I kept trying to convince them they were free, that the King had paid for their release, the chasm wasn't uncrossable, and the gate wasn't locked. I sang songs of the Chasm-crosser, hoping maybe the music would get through to them. Gordy remembered some of the words and sang with me.

Gordy got a blanket and foam-rubber pad from his cell, which he rolled up tightly, tied with a strap, then hooked on an ancient backpack he must have worn when he came to the jail sixteen years before. He and I walked off together, leaving the gate wide open behind us. I looked back and saw Zed move toward the gate. I stopped and watched. Maybe…No—he shut the door. Roy said nothing and kept playing solitaire, occasionally pausing to curse and stare at the spiders.

As Gordy and I walked back to the road, I felt overwhelmed by frustration with Zed and Roy. But suddenly I heard in the wind, coming from the west, the sounds of a great party, a celebration, filled with laughter and feasting. I wondered what the party was about, and then I looked at Gordy. Of course.

He breathed deeply and stretched out his legs and swung from tree limbs and soaked in the sunshine like a man who'd been locked up sixteen years and now was free. He seemed oblivious to the party held to celebrate his liberation, but he was having his own little freedom party and enjoying every minute. I laughed and hugged him and slapped him on the back.

When we made it to the red road, I finally got Gordy to take off his handcuffs. Of course, they'd been unlocked all along.

After nightfall it cooled down quickly, and we dropped our bags, not bothering to set up tents. We just sat around a blazing fire, laughing and singing. While dinner was cooking, Shad, the fire glowing on his face, told us tales of those who'd walked the red road before us. After the last story, eyes red and heavy with moisture and voice breaking, he said, "They passed the baton to us, and we must pass it to those who follow. May those who come behind us find us faithful—may our footprints lead them on the path of the King, to the very gates of Charis."

Shad's words inspired yet weighed heavily on me. Meanwhile Malaiki spooned stew into our bowls. Gordy raved about the squirrel meat, making me feel a bit guilty I wasn't so appreciative. Then he told us his own story, which held us spellbound. Finally we threw a party for Gordy, to honor the King for what he'd done in him—it was my idea, stolen from the universe next door. We laughed and celebrated for another two hours.

When I thought we were about to set up our tents and go to sleep, Shad said, "Let's travel tonight! The GuideBook says there's another dry riverbed ahead. You know what that means." His eyes glowed. Mine dropped. We hadn't crossed many riverbeds, and I wasn't carrying a lot of rocks, but I didn't feel like adding to my load.

Malaiki explained to Gordy about the King's messenger telling us to pick up stones. He listened attentively, sucking his teeth and nodding. She gave him a burlap bag, which he fingered as if it were a fine garment.

We plunged forward into a deeply cut track between tall oaks that rustled their dry leaves in the night, as if trying to talk to us, welcoming or perhaps warning us.

"What's that?" Victoria asked.

"It sounds like an animal—something sniffing," I said. I felt like we were being watched. Or followed.

After I hummed a few songs from the GuideBook, it seemed pleasant enough walking in the cool darkness, until we came to the riverbed.

"We're here," the old man said. I heard him and Malaiki and Gordy already down on their knees.

"I don't haul rocks," Victoria said. "That's where I draw the line. I'm walking on ahead, and while you're feeling your way in the dark and groveling in the mud, I'm going to set up my tent, get under a blanket, and have some senaba. Who's with me?"

"Be there in a little bit," I said. I stooped down and halfheartedly felt for stones.

"There's plenty," Shad said gleefully, like a child with his hands in a big bowl of candy.

"You're already carrying nearly three sacks full," I said. "I don't see how you can haul what you have now—much less any more. My half bag's weighing me down." It was closer to a quarter bag.

"But don't you find," Malaiki said, "the more you carry, the more strength you have?"

"Yes," Shad said.

"Yes," Gordy said, not knowing what he was talking about, since this was his first time gathering stones. The three of them kept laughing and crying out, "Here's another one."

Hearing the joy in the voices of this unlikely trio on their knees, I put my aching body on the ground. Soon I opened my bag—puzzled at why I could open it in the dark but not in the light—and I was laughing too. I got carried away and picked up more stones than I'd intended.

The road was lined by deciduous trees with reds and yellows and oranges against a backdrop of evergreens. Walking up and down gentle slopes, we came to a populated area. At one home, a man in a green polo shirt busily constructed a fence around his garden.

"Have you heard of the King?" Malaiki asked him.

"Certainly. I'm his follower. The name's Alec."

"Come, Alec," Shad said, "walk the road with us."

"Not today. There's too much to do. I have urgent business. A fence to build, tomatoes to tend, corn and cucumbers. And some prize-winning roses." He pointed at the beautiful flowers. "I can't leave them unattended, can I?"

"Something will always be urgent," Shad said. "But anything that matters can be done on the journey. We see many beautiful wildflowers. To walk the road is what's important."

"I plan to—I'll have time for it as soon as I'm done with other things."

"Will you ever be done, Alec?"

"Sure. I'll finish by tomorrow. The fence, I mean. Then there are the melons—a week at the most. No more than a month."

"And between now and next month won't you find more things to postpone the journey?"

"It's not as if I don't walk the road. Most days I get out on it, a half-mile down, a half-mile back. I prefer to walk it alone. It's a private thing, between me and the King."

"The road is to be walked to its destination," Malaiki said. "You have to leave some things behind. And the road isn't meant to be walked alone."

"I do all right by myself," Alec said.

"That's for the King to judge, isn't it?" Shad asked. He opened the TravelGuide. "It says here travelers must stay with a group of the King's followers, to help and encourage each other, to keep each other on the path."

"I'd never have made it this far alone," I said.

"Perhaps tomorrow," Alec said. "I'll catch up with you."

"Don't procrastinate obedience," Shad said. "Don't put off to tomorrow what the King calls you to do today."

Alec thought for a moment, then went to a storage shed next to his house and took out a backpack that didn't look like it had been used in years. He held it in his hands, looking it over, moving it up and down as if weighing it. Finally, he tossed it back in the shed.

"I'll join you soon," he said. "Really." He turned and knelt down, resuming his urgent project.

On the other side of the town we found the rusty hues of tiger lilies on the south side and the comforting sound of a brook on the north. Straight ahead of us, perhaps four days' journey, was a broad, gray, snowless mountain the red road seemed to lead directly into. Farther to the south stood a profusion of wild peaks, including three shark-fin crags, casting eerie shadows. Near them was a single mountain that looked like a melted vanilla ice cream cone, soft and sagging, dripping on the edges. I had thought I'd never want to climb a mountain again, yet here I was, my heart tugged toward adventure and exploration—a stark contrast to my years spent on a recliner in the evenings, my biggest adventure punching the remote control.

We traveled this beautiful terrain for three days, passing no one on the road. Finally, nearing the gray mountain, we met an entourage with somber faces, each wearing dark, formal clothes.

"Where are you going?" I asked.

"To a funeral. Our friend died."

"All men do," Shad said. "But that makes it no easier, does it?"

"He was so young," an old woman said.

"He had great plans," a young man said.

"Yes, we'll miss him," she said. "I always thought I'd die before dear Alec."

The red road led straight into the side of the gray mountain, a protruding, hollowed-out rock formation serving as an archway. It looked like a monstrous eye socket with a pitch-black hole in the middle. The closer we got, the more uneasy I felt. Ancient rock carvings surrounded the black hole, presumably a cave. On the archway were pictographs, prehistoric drawings suggesting this cave had been used for ages. Were these mute testimony to those whose journey ended here in a rock grave?

The longer I gazed at it, the more confused I felt. Why did the red road not go around or over the hillside? Why did it lead into this foreboding darkness?

Shad opened his GuideBook and looked at the maps. I opened mine and pored over it. I didn't understand everything I read, and I didn't like what I understood.

"We must enter this cave," Shad said, "and the tunnel it leads to."

"I don't want to go into a cave," Victoria said. Her voice shook, suggesting she'd had a bad experience in another cave.

"The King doesn't ask our opinion," Shad said. "It's not subject to popular vote."

I checked the GuideBook again and reluctantly agreed—this was the way it said we should go.

"Thirty minutes in a cave or a tunnel won't hurt us," I said. "Compared to crossing Mount Peirasmos, it'll be easy." I tried to sound confident. I didn't mention my claustrophobia or my stomach's flip-flops at the thought of being trapped in a tunnel. The prospect of being stuck on an elevator, something I'd thought about every time I traveled to and from the twenty-fifth floor at work, seemed mild in comparison.

We walked up close to the mouth of the cave. I heard faint drumbeats and chanting in the wind, as if primitives had stood here and voices from the past were inviting us in.

Or were they warning us to stay out?

We bent low and walked cautiously into the mouth of the cave, about five feet high. It was dark and dank, cool and clammy. Something flew by my ear and squeaked. I couldn't see anything. I took a deep breath and walked into the darkness, bracing myself.

18

IT TOOK A LONG TIME for my eyes to adjust. Three feet inside its mouth the cave opened into a huge chamber, dwarfing the cave I'd been in my first night in Thuros. It appeared to be limestone with large sections of marble. The rock ceiling, covered with stone daggers pointing down, must have been a hundred feet high, and it glowed slightly. Whether it was luminescent rock or caked phosphorous, I couldn't tell.

Huge mounds of rocks and spires jutted up from the cave floor, some of them thirty feet high. Icicle-shaped pieces of dripstone hung from the ceiling, sometimes in pairs, looking like giant open scissors. In a few places the dripstones met spires below to form a continuous column, as if sky had reached down to touch ground. It was stunning. The longer I looked the more I realized the cavern was much larger than I'd thought, at least a football field deep and almost that wide. Fantastic shapes were everywhere, including baconlike draperies hanging from the ceiling.

From the icicle rocks above, water dripped onto the cave floor, much of it accumulating in a large oval-shaped pool perhaps fifty feet across. I knelt down and touched the green and white water, mildly acidic, filled with dissolved limestone and tiny calcium particles.

Instinctively, we all stood still, listening to the awesome sound of water dripping into the great pool. There was an implicitly agreed-upon minute of silence as we united in our attention to the wonders before us.

Near the edge of the pool, I reached down and picked up some small spheres that looked like pearls.

"They're made from the water splashing from the pool," Malaiki said. "It forms coatings around grains of sand, and they get bigger and bigger."

I looked at her with surprise. "You sound like a girl who's spent some time in caves," I said.

She looked at me defensively, and I was sorry I'd said anything.

I wondered how long it had taken the acidic water to hollow out this cavern or to form the many rock doorways and the channels I imagined beyond them. Or was it all made this way originally by a master artist wanting to enjoy his handiwork, a living artwork that looked different today than it had last week? The fact that it was illuminated reminded me of paintings and sculptures in an art gallery—apparently the artist wanted men to enjoy his handiwork. I did.

We sat and absorbed the wonder, spending two hours exploring and pointing. "Look! Over here!" someone would call, and we'd all come over.

"What's that? Help!" Victoria screamed, waving her arms. I rushed over as two bats dive-bombed her. I swatted at them, laughing.

"It's not funny," she said, straightening her hair, then laughing herself.

Shad led the way to the back of the cave, which lowered and narrowed. The farther back into the cave we went, the darker it became. Fifty feet ahead of us now was a wide, darkened area where the ceiling gathered much closer to the floor. It was mouth shaped, with the dripstones above and the spires below giving the effect of jagged teeth.

"Looks like you're leading us right into the jaws," I said to Shad. "Are you sure you know what you're doing?"

Shad said nothing—his lack of assurances and the uncertain look on his face unnerved me.

A half-dozen caves, ranging from three to eight feet tall, were cut into the back wall. "It's probably a system," Malaiki said. "A network of caves connected by passages and tunnels. It may not matter which we go in first—and even if it does, there's no way to know."

Shad took out his TravelGuide, examined the maps and directions, and we discussed it. We finally chose the second cave from the right, leading into a tunnel about four feet high.

"I'll take up the rear," I said, as if it were an act of bravery. I heard my voice crack and hoped no one else did. I stretched my neck for one last look at daylight. Then I turned to face the darkness. I swallowed hard. I saw no phosphorescence. It was damp and pitch-black, like a tomb. Frodo was uneasy. He wasn't the only one.

Within an hour the tunnel was even narrower, and I couldn't stand at all, even bent over. The best I could do was squat once in a while to get relief from crawling on my hands and knees. I dragged my sack of stones behind me. The tunnel grew very narrow, like a labyrinth. I smelled wet, sweaty fabric, like a locker room right after a game. I felt something brush my face. Cobwebs? It seemed unlikely. I trembled and pushed on, feeling more and more closed in.

My neck and shoulders ached, while my knees screamed at me. I couldn't stretch out anything to full length, but I kept trying, putting weight on my wrists and contorting my legs. I let myself fall back from Gordy, who crawled in front of me. I gasped for air, not wanting him to hear. The scent of bat guano didn't help. Neither did the fact that my hands had come down on a couple of beetles and what was probably a millipede, judging from the way it felt when I squished it. I couldn't see my companions in front of me, but I could hear their breathing. Frodo stayed close, sometimes too close, startling me.

"What was that?" Victoria squealed.

"A cockroach," Gordy said, and at the word Victoria squealed louder. I remembered the jail—Gordy knew his cockroaches. I heard a shell crack.

No one said what we all knew—where there was one there were hundreds more, if not thousands. The skin on my back tingled at the thought. It was one thing to face big bugs in daylight in an open room. It was something else to be in the dark where they could sneak up on you.

My claustrophobia spoke louder and louder. I longed to move freely, breathe fresh air, and see the stars. I had to try not to think about it for fear of losing my mind. My face twitched, and I attempted to calm it with my right hand, now covered with smudge and wet grime. I felt like a soldier in Nam again—the thought was actually a solace. At least soldiers had a purpose and a mission.

"We're rats caught in a maze," Victoria said from up ahead, as I kept pulling my hands away from cockroaches. "I can't see anything," she added, stating the obvious.

"You don't have to," Shad said. "Just stay close to us. We're in this together."

"I thought you said it would only be thirty minutes," she groaned.

"I didn't say that," I retorted, feeling the blood rush to my face and glad the darkness covered for me. If I hadn't said that, how did I know she was talking to me?

"Look out for sharp sticks on your left," Gordy called back. "I cut myself." My left hand came down on one of the sticks. Wait. This one felt smooth. What was it? I reached inside my damp coat pocket and pulled out a match, one of five I'd traded for on the road. I struck it on the wall. It lit up the stones and showed them to be white, some smooth, some jagged. I held the match up farther and saw a large white stone with holes in it. Frodo started growling.

"No!" I backed away from the thing staring at me—a human skull.

"What is it?" Victoria cried.

"These aren't sticks. They're bones. Human bones." I pinched the match to the tips of my fingers and looked at scattered bones, some of them nearly fossilized, ancient layers of history over which we'd crawled without knowing. It struck me that this journey didn't begin with me or our group. Many others had gone before us. Some fared well, others didn't. Shad was right—a baton had been passed to us. We could drop the baton or finish our part of the race and pass it on to those awaiting it. Time would tell which we'd do.

Just as the match began to seer my fingertips, I saw on the wall a few names. Others had been here and wanted those who followed to remember them. The match burned me and I dropped it, wondering if I'd been a fool to use up precious oxygen.

"Not everyone who enters this tunnel comes out," Shad said. "The GuideBook warns of it."

Victoria began to sob. Frodo worked his way forward, attempting to console her.

"The tunnel's wider up here," Shad said. "Let's stop for a while. I'll read from the TravelGuide."

Read? In the dark?

I heard Shad flip pages of his book, then he spoke, quoting what he'd memorized from it. As he spoke, I saw a faint glow. Maybe my eyes were adjusting to the dark. But I could have sworn the words from the GuideBook had a physical presence in the air, generating a soft light. Malaiki began to speak the ancient words too. I reached into my satchel and touched my own book. I tried to repeat what I could remember. I wished I could recite more.

Now there was just enough light that I could barely see Gordy in front of me.

"We never should've come in here," Victoria said. "We're trapped."

I couldn't help but think we'd end up fossilized remains awaiting some paleontologist to exhume us for a museum.

"Do you have any more matches?" Gordy whispered to me.

"Yes. Why?"

"Why?" It was Victoria's voice, ahead of Gordy. "Because we've been crawling in the darkness, that's why! And maybe light will chase away the roaches!"

Striking awkwardly four times, I finally lit the match. Apparently fueled by mineral vapors, it flared up out of control.

"Ahhh!" I heard the groans, one of them my own. Needles had pierced my eyes. The brightness was an explosion that lasted only a moment and left me blinder than before. Now I couldn't see the TravelGuide.

"Our eyes had adjusted to the darkness," Shad said, "and the soft light of the TravelGuide led us. The bright light of the match was to make us see better—but now we can't see at all."

Sheepishly, I put away my matches. Finally the tunnel widened, and we crawled side by side.

"I can't stand the darkness or the bugs," Victoria said. "Please, Nick, light another match!"

"No," Shad said. "Everyone take out your TravelGuide."

We all fumbled around and found them.

"Now, open them."

Everyone opened the book at the same time and suffused light filled the tunnel.

"Look, here on the wall," Gordy said. He pointed to scratchings and held up his book to them. Pictographs. A horizontal line cutting through a vertical. One looked like a child's drawing of a fish.

"Are those words next to the pictures, Gordy?" Malaiki asked.

"Yes. Three lines," he whispered. "I...I saw these once before, long ago."

"What do they say?" I asked. "Read them."

FORWARD

RED ROAD HOME

BE CAREFUL WHO YOU TRUST

I crowded close and looked up above these words. I saw writing in the elegant otherworldly language. I stooped down. Yes—there below were words in the foul tongue. I trembled, then felt Victoria next to me, studying the markings. I saw the look of recognition on her face.

"Why us?" I asked. "Why were we chosen? Why were we brought to Skiathuros?"

No one said anything. I wanted them to tell me their stories from the other world. Yet I did not offer them mine. I wasn't ready for them to know what I'd done, what I'd been.

We crawled a few more hours. My back swayed, then convulsed with muscle spasms. My wrists were sprained, my shins tortured. I'd lost feeling in my knees, my thighs were stiff, and I could feel blood inside my socks. I kept trying to stretch out my cramped legs, but in trying to relieve existing injuries I kept incurring new ones. The claustrophobia plagued me worse than anything. I stopped and picked stony grit out of my raw elbows, trying to control my breathing.

"You okay, Nick?" Gordy asked.

"Sure," I said. "Why wouldn't I be?"

Why was I so concerned about maintaining my Gary Cooper–*High-Noon* image? Nick the loner, brave, self-reliant, powerful, incredibly competent. Who was I kidding?

The cool damp had gradually disappeared, replaced by a sticky humid heat. Sweat poured from me, and my clothes smelled. My shoulders burned. I felt I could go no farther. But my companions were still moving. If they could, I could. I pushed on, like a good marine, thinking of what was behind me—the chasm-crossing—and the hope of what lay ahead—Charis.

"Ow!" Two of my fingers were smashed beneath the toe of Gordy's boot, or was it the edge of one of his stone sacks? I swore and yelled, "What do you think you're doing?"

"I'm really sorry, Nick," Gordy said.

"Just be more careful!"

"Maybe *you* should be more careful." I heard Malaiki's muffled voice in front of Gordy. "It's your fault if you don't stay back far enough not to get your fingers smashed. Don't blame Gordy."

Who did she think she was, taking Gordy's side and preaching at me?

We stopped to rest. I laid my head down flat on the grimy stone. The next thing I knew I woke to Victoria's voice.

"We've been in darkness so long. I'm beginning to wonder if the City of Light is really out there."

"We've seen it...haven't we?" I groaned, trying to convince myself.

"I'm not sure if we really did," Victoria said. "Maybe David was right."

"The TravelGuide says it's there," Shad said. "That is enough."

"Maybe for you," Victoria said. "I need to see it to believe it."

"Have you ceased to believe there's a sun just because you've not seen it recently?" Shad asked.

"Why is the King punishing us?" Victoria replied. "We walked the red road—how did we end up here?"

"Not everything difficult is a punishment, is it?" Shad asked, his voice much less confident than I sensed he wanted it to sound. "And what makes you think we're not on the road? It was the red road we followed into the cave. We're still on it. At least...I think we are. Things aren't always what they appear."

"This is no road," Victoria said. "It's dark and damp and miserable. It's horrifying. The red road is bright and warm and safe."

"The road is the road," Shad said, "and it is not always what we expect or want. We cannot change it. We can only travel it. Or not."

The ground trembled and we froze. None of us had to comment about the implications of a quake inside a narrow tunnel. After the tremor subsided, we heard a fierce roar right in front of us.

I felt bodies push against me. Gordy peeled out in reverse, his feet in my face. I back-pedaled as quickly as I could, hearing bodies shuffling and scuffling and slamming into each other.

"Move!" "Hurry up." "It's coming." Words were exchanged, panic took over, and cramped chaos reigned. Had this been a soccer stadium it would have been a trampling.

We'd retreated probably sixty feet when Gordy no longer pressed against me. I listened carefully and heard heavy breathing, hoping it was ours.

"What was it?" Victoria cried. "A bear?"

"More like a lion," Gordy said, huffing and puffing.

"Yes, a lion," Shad agreed. "But a good lion or a bad one?"

"Why does it matter?" Victoria asked. "Does it feel better to be devoured by one than the other?"

"It may not feel better," Malaiki said. "But it is better. I'd rather be swallowed up by good than evil."

"And I'd rather not be swallowed up at all," Victoria said. "It frightens me to think of the King as a lion."

"What would you prefer?" Shad asked. "To think of him as a lap dog?"

"Well, yes, I suppose. Lap dogs don't roar and chase you and scare you to death."

"Neither do they create you and cross the chasm for you and go to war for you," Shad said. "But, still, the GuideBook says there is another lion, a pretend king, one who prowls about seeking to devour us. I'm not sure which…"

Then came another roar, even louder, this time from behind me.

"Move it!" I yelled, pushing against Gordy, hitting my head on a sack of his stones. Before I knew it, we'd scrambled and regained the sixty feet and maybe another sixty. We sat again, catching our breath, listening. I tried to breathe more softly but couldn't. I heard my chest pounding and put my hand on it. Then I reached to my knife, wondering if it would do the slightest good against…against what?

"Is there one beast or two?" I asked, gasping in the oxygen-deficient air. "And if one, how could he be on both sides of us?"

No one offered an answer, not even Shad. I rubbed my skinned knuckles and bruised shins, wondering which way we would have to shuffle next and what beast sat watching us in the dark. We waited silently a long time, not knowing what to do now. Go backward? Forward? Stay where we were? I didn't have a clue. I smelled hot terror in the air. Frodo whined.

Finally I heard a soft voice like the fluttering of a hummingbird. It grew louder. Malaiki sang, "Architect of the cosmos, Builder of worlds; you became Road-Hiker, then Tree-Walker, making the road red with your heart."

I started singing too. Then Shad. Gordy sang, "The abyss is vast, but the tree bigger; the Chasm-Crosser is greater than the chasm; the amount due greater than men imagine, but the price paid greater still."

Victoria joined us. "How high and how wide, how deep and how long, how sweet and how strong is your love; how lavish your grace, how faithful your ways, how great is your love, oh Lord."

"World-Maker became World-Saver," I sang. "Sky-Walker became Tree-Walker. The eternally old became eternally young. And we will never be the same, no never again the same."

For the first time, I smiled in the darkness, buoyed by the songs. I'd been paralyzed by the roars, tired of the dark, sick of the tunnel—I would have taken any ticket out in a heartbeat. Yet here I was, uncertain which way to even move, yet smiling—not because I knew I wouldn't die, but because I knew if I did die the best part of my life would be just beginning.

At long last we crawled forward. We sang and talked and even laughed. We took frequent breaks because of the difficulty and lack of oxygen. We passed around two water bottles with senaba and told stories. I took off my saturated shirt and tried to wring it dry. My jeans were sopping wet, and I felt holes in both knees. I was a miserable sight, I was certain, and took some solace in the fact that no one could see me.

Yet I did see something—the walls of the tunnel seemed to glow slightly, a gold hue here and a silver there. I reached up to touch the rock ceiling—yes, there were precious metals hidden in the heart of this mountain, waiting to be mined.

"Look, up ahead," Malaiki said. "Is that light?"

I couldn't see it. But then...

"That tiny pinprick? Yeah...I think it is!"

We crawled quickly, and the spot of light now looked the size of a dime. It kept getting bigger and bigger.

Two hours later we emerged from the darkness. I stood up, wobbling, shading my eyes. We embraced, laughing as we covered each other with sweat and grime.

"Look...the city!" Gordy said. Once again, Charis appeared much closer than before.

We found a pond and bathed, then relaxed and ate and drank and celebrated—even though the main dish was a rubbery pasta with no sauce. We set up camp for the night although it was midafternoon. I lay down near the old man.

"Why did the King allow us to go through all that groping in the darkness?" I whispered. "It's another mystery, isn't it?"

"Is it? Let me ask you—have you ever heard anyone say he learned his greatest lessons and developed his strongest character in times of ease?"

"I guess not."

"What did you do in the darkness?" Shad asked.

"At first, I managed, but after a while I despaired. I came to the end of myself. Then when you spoke from the TravelGuide, I could see a little, even in the darkness. I wished I'd studied it more, that I'd been more ready to speak its light into the gloom. I longed for more light, more space, but told myself that even if we died in the tunnel, it wasn't the worst thing, because we'd end up in Charis anyway. And when we sang...it was beautiful. I felt strength from the King and from all of you."

Shad's neck creaked like an old gate as he turned to look at me. He sounded like a man in need of a new body.

"You've answered your own question, Nick. Perhaps it's not such a mystery after all."

"Wake up," a creaky voice ordered.

I groaned and fell back asleep until I felt something poking my ribs. I looked up and saw a stick, with Shad on the far end.

My anger woke me.

I stumbled out to the fire, after Gordy, and grabbed coffee and a stale cornmeal biscuit, brooding as I gazed at the washed sky of thin blue. Victoria was nowhere to be seen. Malaiki, eyes bloodshot and hollow, stared into the fire.

"The road seems to go on forever," Malaiki said. "I can't. After that tunnel, I need to rest."

I heard the defeat in her voice, and I was relieved that she'd spoken—we all needed rest.

"No," Shad said. "When we rested last, we wasted time and...lost David. We must move on."

"But doesn't the GuideBook say we need rest?" Malaiki asked.

"We rest each night. That's enough."

"But look," Malaiki said, turning the pages of her book. "It says right here that—"

"I said we're moving on!" Shad shouted. Malaiki winced, and the book dropped out of her hands. I picked it up and handed it to her, glaring at Shad. Irritating was one thing, mean was another. Under the great snowy brows of his aged face his dark eyes were coals that could leap into fire at any moment. I was tired of being under his thumb.

We traveled two more days, walking slowly and stiffly. Though the voice of adventure kept telling me to press on and discover what was around the next bend, the voices of my burning shoulders and aching knees and throbbing calves cast dissenting votes. We still hadn't recovered from the tunnel. The silence of the road was interrupted only by sighs and grumbling.

We spent the night on a slope just outside a large town that appeared to stretch for a few miles down the road. After a breakfast of red onions and fried zucchini and packaged rolled oats boiled on the fire, I took Malaiki, Victoria, and Gordy aside and convinced them we all had to stand up to Shad, for his sake as well as ours. When Shad approached us, the conversation stopped. He looked at us suspiciously.

"We're taking a day of rest," I said.

"No. We have to keep moving."

"Didn't you once say we shouldn't trust you? Well, guess what— we don't. You're off base on this one. Our legs feel like lead, we're sore, tired, and we need a break. It's not negotiable. End of discussion."

Shad marched off, pouting. The others looked on wide-eyed and slack-jawed. This was new territory for them. I enjoyed myself. The moment I did it, I knew I should have done it long ago.

19

WHILE SHAD WANDERED off by himself, the others went to the tents to go back to sleep. Over a third cup of dark campfire coffee, I savored the way I'd finally taken control.

Weary but curious, and enjoying these rare moments of independence, I decided to walk through the town, to scope it out. I entered a general store and bartered with a merchant, trading my last dozen strips of Quon-made jerky for some gloves and ground coffee.

Strolling aimlessly and looking in storefronts, I came to an abrupt stop in front of a building of dark red brick. My stomach churned—something was uncomfortably familiar about this place. Had I seen it in a dream? Had I been here long ago? Or both?

A teenage girl brushed by me and walked in the front door. She wore dark glasses and carried a baby. Why did she seem so familiar? I shuffled my feet. As I peeked in the window, I saw the girl sit down with a middle-aged man in a white coat. She listened nervously to Whitecoat, looking at the window where I stood, as if expecting someone to join her. Whitecoat then handed her some white forms to sign on a clipboard. Her hand trembling, she signed and gave him a handful of cash.

Who is she?

From behind me and to my left a young boy strolled to the door. He wore a letterman's jacket and acted cocky and in control. I knew him well but had never seen him from the outside until now. How was this possible?

I looked back at the girl. Marci! Of course—she was just as I remembered. Why hadn't I recognized her immediately? Walking toward the back room, she hesitated, turning around to the waiting room, her eyes pleading with the boy. He looked at her sternly, this take-charge young man, and insisted that Whitecoat would take care of everything. I couldn't hear him, but I knew exactly what he said—I retrieved it from storage in the back room of my mind.

The door shut behind her. While the young man sat in the lobby reading *Sports Illustrated,* I went to the side of the building. I heard through a window desperate cries. I stayed outside for at least an hour, heart racing, until I saw the young couple walk away, the girl in dark glasses now carrying nothing but white forms, the boy pretending what they'd done was no big deal.

Hearing a door open, I walked all the way to the back of the building and saw what I hadn't thirty-three years earlier. Whitecoat walked out the door with a black garbage bag and put it in a big Dumpster full of other black bags.

I turned away, reeling. The thirty-three years seemed like a day. I remembered it all, unearthing every forbidden detail buried in that unmarked grave in my mind.

Desperate to get away, I walked quickly through the town, looking in storefronts but seeing nothing, thinking only of a past that haunted me worse than any sounds in the night.

At the far end of town I was about to turn around when I saw one last large building, a professional center, well landscaped and manicured. It too seemed strangely familiar. I stepped in the door and sat in a corner of the waiting room, pretending to read a magazine, certain I had been there and not that long ago. I could almost remember. The office smelled mediciny, like it'd been swabbed with a ball of camphor.

In the front door walked a middle-aged man in a sharp business suit, escorting a white-haired man who seemed anxious and confused. My jaw dropped as I watched them. I recognized the old man immediately—my father. But the face of the middle-aged man was so hard, his eyes seemed so gray and cold...like shark eyes. I'd seen that face in the mirror for many years—but I'd never realized it looked like this.

I stood up and watched through the receptionist's window as they sat down and spoke with a woman in a white coat. Whitecoat explained things to the son, and the son explained things to the father. The father nodded, eyes wet. They filled out some white forms on clipboards. I put my fingers to my twitching face, grieving at the sight of Whitehair, sickened by the sight of Whitecoat, and enraged and frightened at the self-made man in the business suit.

Whitecoat escorted Whitehair to another room, while the businessman paid at the front desk, then walked out the door, talking on a cell phone. I got a clear look at his face. I saw it twitch. I felt for the knife in my belt. Part of me wanted to kill him. He didn't deserve to live.

I followed him out the front door then went around to the back of the building and heard a cry, a resigned whimper from inside. It haunted me. A few minutes later the back door opened and someone pushed out a gurney covered with a white sheet. A young man with big biceps picked up Whitesheet and threw him like a sack of concrete into a hole in the ground.

That was something I hadn't seen—it wasn't how it had happened, not exactly. Yet it *was* what happened, the details had changed somewhat but were accurate in all the essentials.

I ran away from the building, tears flowing. I ran all the way through town, past people giving me strange looks, but I didn't care.

I'm sorry, Dad. I'm sorry, my child... I don't even have a name to call you. I'm sorry, Marci, so sorry. Brian, Amy, forgive me.

I finally stopped running, sat down by the road, and spoke to the King about two things—two *people*—who weighed so heavily on my shoulders. I'd never told him about them. He knew, of course. I remembered what he had said, that he'd bring more things to my mind—and that he'd paid the price for everything.

Everything? Even this?

Yes, even this. Still, nothing I could do now would change what I had done to those who most needed my protection and care. Like a barbarian, I had sacrificed them on the altar of my convenience, sanitizing my barbarism with white coats and white forms and sugarcoated words in a futile attempt to cover the blackness of my heart.

I poured out my insides to the King and wept. I wept for the evil I had done, for those I had betrayed, for the opportunities I had lost, and finally for the grace he'd shown me—that one such as I could be headed for Charis after all.

As we walked, Marcus suddenly appeared alongside me. I shuddered—some things I never got used to. Without a word, the warrior pointed, and a portal opened in the air. I peered across far reaches of nothingness and saw a spattering of shriveled souls, husks of humanity. On one of these desert islands of misery, I saw a pathetic being with contorted face and body. He was familiar. I cringed when I saw his chestnut curls and realized it was Mason, buried to his neck in boiling sludge. The stench was awful.

Had Mason died already? Or was I seeing into the future? I couldn't tell.

I heard a shrinking man mutter on and on about theology and what the King had really said and what he hadn't. "I had degrees. I wrote books. I taught classes," he said.

"I fed the poor," a nameless woman cried, then muttered about medicine and rehab and going to church and bazaars and soup kitchens and saying her prayers. She stopped, as if waiting for applause. Hearing none, she recited her virtues again and again, but her words were only words, met with eternal silence.

"I recognize some of them," I said, pointing to famous people here and there.

"Erebus is full of the once well-known," Marcus said. "Physicians and scientists in white coats, businessmen and educators and politicians and celebrities and clergymen with white collars, smooth-shaven faces and manicured fingers."

Reading my dismay, he said, "When your stories say 'they lived happily ever after,' it all depends on where they end up living, doesn't it? For in Charis all live happily ever after, and in Erebus none do."

As I scanned the wretched faces of Erebus, I noticed two philanthropists I'd seen on television. One had given away a billion dollars.

"They donated so much money," I said.

"They believed they deserved Charis—and therefore failed to accept the only gift that could get them there. Erebus has its own peculiar clarity. In the face of truth, illusions and lies collapse. But too late."

Then another portal materialized, right next to the first, and I beheld a wondrous realm of delight and discovery, excitement and exploration. I saw people embracing, walking, talking, working, and playing. I felt its bursts of joy, experienced the adrenaline rush of the great adventure. I heard the music, and my heart rode upon it.

Suddenly I recognized a man whose face had also been on the television news—a molester and murderer of children. Revulsion welled up in me, and I couldn't hear any music now.

"What is *he* doing in Charis?"

"What everyone else is doing," Marcus said. "Enjoying the presence of the King."

"But…it's not right."

"Because he doesn't deserve to be there?"

"Yes!"

"Do you think you deserve it in some way he does not?"

I shrugged.

"None of your bent race deserves the King's gift. Every sin is a capital crime requiring World-Maker's death to atone for it—and atone he did. No sin is greater than the provision. Do not be scandalized by his grace."

"Still, it…troubles me."

"Would you instruct the King whom to offer his grace to and whom not? Those who know their unworthiness seize grace as a hungry man seizes bread; the self-righteous resent grace. Those you thought 'good' men are far worse than you suppose, just as you are far worse—did you learn nothing about yourself when you looked in those buildings in the town? Evil men are the objects of God's grace—be glad for that."

"It's troubling enough that evil people can end up in Charis," I said. "But it bothers me even more that decent people end up in Erebus."

"You think they are decent only because your standards are so low. You thought *you* were decent until you saw the chasm, did you not? And you thought so again until you saw what you did to your child and your father. And already you think yourself decent again, do you not? By thinking men better than they are, you make the King's grace seem less amazing than it truly is."

"I'm sorry. I didn't mean to."

"Erebus is earned, Charis is not. You take for granted the King's love and are amazed at his wrath. Yet it is his wrath, not his love, which you deserve, every one of you." Marcus paced and gestured furiously, speaking with an intensity that frightened me. "Do not wonder why he might despise you—he has every reason to. Wonder why he would love you. It is not his wrath that should amaze you, but his grace. It is not Erebus that should astound you, but Charis!"

He paused, his brow furled. "Do not think I say all this with understanding. Indeed, the King's grace is something I long to understand but do not. Perhaps I never will. Yet I know it to be true. Had it been up to me and my comrades, things would have gone much differently for you." He stared at me, eyes burning. "You are most fortunate it was not up to us."

The others all in front of me, I was lost in thought as we walked toward a huddle of green hills covered with mounds of yellow daisies, so thick they seemed to be painted. The red road swept round the feet of the hills, out of the midst of which tall stones pointed upward, like jagged teeth jutting out of yellow gums. As I walked, I recited the words of the book in my hand over and over, trying to wash my mind, cleanse it so I could think the King's thoughts.

I kept seeing needy people on the road and beside it, far more than before. Were there really so many more now, or was I seeing with different eyes?

When I saw people, I knew their stories, certain my intuition was correct—hungry children, a wife beaten by her husband, a husband deserted by his wife, a follower of the King who bore the scars of torture.

"How do you help a billion needy people?" I asked out loud. I hoped Marcus would appear again and answer me. He didn't.

A man walked by, pale and shriveled, ravaged by disease, dry blood on his face. I looked away and walked faster on the red road, crossing momentarily under the long shadow, turning briefly to look for its source and as always, seeing nothing. I walked faster still, determined nothing should distract me from my journey to Charis.

From the side of the road, in the ditch, I heard a groan—one disturbing sound among many. A body lay there, motionless.

A well-dressed man strolled by, looked at the body in the ditch, and said, "They need streetlights here to curb crime." He walked on.

A woman came by and said, "They need to teach self-defense courses for the elderly." She, too, walked on.

Next came a man reading a GuideBook. He kept his nose in the book and appeared not to notice the person in the ditch. He walked on.

Another came by wearing a T-shirt with a saying from the TravelGuide. He called loudly into the ditch, "Trust the Chasm-crosser!" and walked on.

I looked into the ditch where the groan came from. Afraid, I forced myself to approach and knelt beside him, a wrinkled old man, bloodied and beaten. He was missing several teeth, and the others were brown and yellow. His dull, hollow eyes reminded me of my father's just before he died. I wiped my cheeks.

I lifted his head with one hand, quivering as I touched nearly dead flesh. I took my water bottle, hesitated, then put it to his lips. He swallowed senaba and choked, then opened his lips for more.

"My name's Nick," I said. "What's yours?

"Cliff," he whispered.

I held his head, gave him more senaba, and helped him to sit up. I took bread and fruit from my pack, pinching little bits with my fingers and putting them in his mouth. I called on travelers to help me get Cliff out of the ditch and onto the road.

"Sorry," said a young man. "I'm on my way to Charis. No time."

"I'm going to worship," said another.

"I'm preparing to speak," said another.

"I'm writing a book," said another.

I stopped asking for help until I saw a familiar face coming back to get me. "Gordy!"

He helped me pull Cliff up and carry him down the road. The first few inns had no room. When we saw a house with a banner of the King hanging on the front porch, we knocked on the door. A woman answered.

"Can you put up our friend for the night?" I asked. "We'll stay and tend to him."

"The only extra bed we have is in my daughter's room. She's away, but…she has some nice things. We're not really comfortable having strangers here." She turned us away.

Finally we found an inn with no vacancies, but they offered a mattress in a storage room with an adjoining sink and toilet.

Gordy and I gave Cliff a sponge bath, washed him, helped him use the toilet. At first I was uncomfortable and embarrassed. But as the night went on, all I did seemed very small. Especially when I thought about the misery the Woodsman endured to relieve me of my suffering for all time.

I took Gordy aside. "You can spend the night with the others," I told him. "Tell them I'll rejoin you when I can. But I don't expect you to wait—you can go on without me."

Cliff fell asleep. At first I curled up in a corner, but I was so exhausted I was afraid I wouldn't hear him if he called for help in the night, so I lay beside him on the mattress.

I awoke several times to his moaning and put a cool washcloth to his head.

A wound on his forearm kept weeping. I wiped the blood away, but it got all over my hands. When I washed them off, I discovered I'd cut myself on my right hand. Cliff's blood and mine had mixed.

In the morning I went to a merchant and traded my hiking boots for some older ones and a set of decent clothes in the old man's sizes. There my traveling companions found me.

"I spoke with some chasm-crossers who'll be here for a while," Gordy said. "They offered to look after Cliff until he's strong enough to walk."

Gordy introduced me to them, and we spent most of the day in their company. When I was finally satisfied, I said, "Take good care of him."

"As soon as he's better, he'll walk the road with us."

Gordy shook hands with old Cliff. Malaiki kissed him on the cheek, and his eyes sparkled. I put my arms around him, and he hugged me with surprising strength.

"Thank you," he whispered.

"Thank you," I whispered back. "Don't forget what I told you about the King."

"I won't," he said, eyes bright. "And I won't forget you."

Cliff's lips spread into a broad, gap-toothed smile.

By then it was late in the day, and we pitched our tents just a few hours up the road. I lay awake hours after we retired, reflecting on the last few days, thinking about Cliff and all that had happened. Suddenly I saw a large misshapen shadow cast on the tent by the moonlight. Frodo lay beside me, and I expected him to wake, but he didn't. The only sound I heard was his light breathing. But I felt something outside brooding, watching, waiting, planning.

Why was the night so still? Where were the sounds of frogs and crickets? Why were they quiet? What were they afraid of?

Finally I peeked out the tent flap. I saw nothing. I got out of the tent and peered into the darkness with only the aid of the second moon, which was dropping low on the horizon. I smelled the scent of death. Then ten feet away in the bushes I saw a reflection...eyes! Windowed eyes, three feet off the ground, catching the moonlight. I heard the creaking of great joints. Was it a giant spider? Was it a spinner of the great web of Skia? Was it he who hated the singer and lived to rid the whole world of song? Or was it one of his foul servants? Or some loathsome beast he had nurtured and set out to prowl the camps of men?

Trembling, mind racing and terror-struck, I returned to my bed, grasping my knife. I sensed I was still being watched and heard in the wind the whispers of phantoms and specters, goblins and gremlins and ghosts. I felt something light brush my face and tucked my chin against my chest under the blanket. I stuck my neck out of the covers again. I saw and heard nothing. Finally the terror lightened to dread, then dissolved into tolerable fear.

Exhausted, I slept fitfully, dreaming that I sat before Brian and Amy and Marci and poured out my heart, confessing all the wrongs I'd done. I opened a TravelGuide and told them what had happened to me. In my dream, first Amy, then Brian, then finally Marci forgave and embraced me. As the dream started to fade, I reached out to hold on to it, to reel it in, but it vanished like smoke from a fire.

My eyes popped open and I lay there, arms stretched upward, biting my lip, robbed of my dream and believing that a dream was all it was and ever would be. The darkness of the night seemed indistinguishable now from the darkness within me.

The next morning I awoke, my head pressed against a warm pillow with black spots. The pillow licked my ear. I got up and rebandaged my aching right hand, pushing away Frodo who kept trying to lick it.

When we set out on the road, I was startled to see the City of Light appear so close. I saw it, heard it, smelled it, tasted it, felt it.

"It looks like it can't be more than a week away," I said to Shad. "How could we lose two days' journey on the road but be closer to our destination?"

"Sometimes you travel farthest when you're not aware you're traveling," Shad said, "when your thoughts and efforts are on the King's business, not your own. Because you were willing to delay your journey to help Cliff, the King has accelerated your journey. Tell me, Nick. What did you learn the last few days?"

I thought a long time before answering, looking at my feet walking the red road.

"When I first started out in business, I was an investment

counselor. I always told people not to be shortsighted. I told them not to look just three months ahead, but thirty years, to their retirement. I advised them to consider how their investments would be paying off in another thirty years. I see now I was shortsighted. I should have asked them how their investments would be paying off in thirty million years. I believe our investment in Cliff will pay off like that, I mean for the long run, in the world beyond."

Shad smiled. "And you've learned the answer to your question."

"What question?"

"How do you help a billion needy people?"

I thought about it, then nodded. "One at a time."

Feeling on top of the world, I picked up my pace and came alongside Victoria, Frodo nipping playfully at my heels.

"It was wonderful how you cared for Cliff," she said. The glow in her eyes warmed me.

I thought about all I'd done for Cliff and how I'd played such a critical role with Gordy. It felt great. I couldn't help but wonder why most people were unwilling to serve the King.

Mason was a fool to be caught on that dead-end road. Why hadn't he returned to the red road like I had? Salama had been so blind not to cross the chasm. I'd seen the truth and eagerly crossed. How could anyone fail to see it? And how had David gotten so distracted? And what about that fool Alec? And all those people on the road who didn't help Cliff?

What was wrong with them all?

I'd never be so selfish and stupid.

I'd never turn my back on the King.

20

THE BRIGHT CITY spread out across a great broad mountainside above the foggy mist. But my thoughts were less on Charis than on the tasks at hand and taking my proper role with the other travelers.

What was that?

For a moment I thought I saw troops assembling, preparing for battle on the plain between us and Charis. No. There was nothing. I'd seen so much of other worlds I was beginning to imagine things in the mist.

Just that moment Marcus appeared, as if beamed down from the starship *Enterprise*. Frodo greeted him warmly this time, nuzzling his feet, proving a dog could get used to almost anything. Marcus looked at me, and I saw in his eyes a consuming fire.

"We must speak of the other worlds," he said urgently.

"Do you mind if we talk about something more immediate?" I asked. "I'd like to discuss the King's plans for me. I feel like he's preparing me for something, maybe to be a leader. What do you think?"

"Today you will be given sixty minutes to see beyond, instead of sixty seconds. I have much to teach you, and you must pay close attention." He seemed anxious, almost nervous, as if I were embarking on a dangerous mission and he must give me a full briefing.

"Behold, Charis and Erebus."

I looked into the other realms, one on my right, the other my left. I saw faces of joy and grimaces of misery, heard cries of delight and moans of regret, smelled pleasant fragrances from one, foul odors from the other.

"Erebus is the imploding pinpoint of death, Charis the exploding universe of life. Both are retroactive to Earth so that Earth is the suburb of each. Men without the King live their lives on the outskirts of Erebus even before they enter its doors. Men with the King catch glimpses of Charis before they ever arrive. The King has put eternity in your hearts." He spoke so rapidly his words ran together.

"Wait, hold it, slow down, Marcus. What's the hurry? I've got more on my mind today than other worlds. Right now my concerns relate to this world. How about we take it one world at a time?"

"That is a luxury no man can afford. Charis and Erebus are the worlds next door. You can hear them when you put your ear to his book." Marcus looked at me sternly. "If you are to be of use in the visible world, you must pay close attention to the invisible worlds."

"I don't like to think about Erebus."

"For good reason," Marcus said. "Charis is a vast estate in which galaxies are but steppingstones. Erebus is an abandoned mine shaft on the back acreage of the most remote estate of Charis. Erebus is the only uninteresting place in the universe. Its inhabitants are gripped by a sleepless, unsmiling obsession with self. They have become so heavy with themselves that they fall as the Impostor did—from the sheer gravity of self-preoccupation. The pit is bottomless, and hence their fall eternal."

"Erebus looks much smaller now than it did the first time I saw it."

"Erebus is but a footnote of Charis. It is an asterisk, what you call a 'blip on the screen.' It is not a palace, but a crack in the tile of

Charis's palace. All Erebus is smaller than the smallest particle of Earth, which itself can fit into a blade of grass in Charis. Erebus is microscopic and getting smaller all the time. Charis is cosmic and getting bigger all the time. The inhabitants of Erebus are shrunken and ever shrinking. The inhabitants of Charis are great and ever growing."

I stared into the abyss, experiencing a shift of perspective. "The people in Erebus literally do look tiny, don't they?"

"Tiny people who were once bigger and could have been magnificent. Small and petty people, with nowhere to go, nothing to explore but their own grievances and missed opportunities. Life in the Shadowlands is full of choices. In Charis, right choices are forever celebrated. In Erebus, wrong choices are endlessly reviewed and regretted—especially the choice to refuse the greatest gift ever offered."

"Is it impossible then to escape from Erebus?"

"No man can get out of Erebus. But each man can keep out of it. There is a choice—though even choice is governed by the King's sovereign will—but the opportunity to choose always ends at death."

"Surely those in Charis can't know about Erebus?"

"Why not?"

"How could we have joy in Charis if we know there's such misery in Erebus?"

"Do you imagine the joy of Charis is based on ignorance?" Marcus asked, sounding appalled. "Do you believe the self-imprisoned will hold the universe for ransom, blackmail it, so if they do not choose joy no one else should be able to have it? You give Erebus a power over Charis it does not have. Erebus can never infect Charis. Misery will never veto joy. The key to Charis is not ignorance but perspective."

"I do long for Charis," I said. "But there are things I'd like to do before I arrive. I want to do more, make a difference, play my part, find my role in the story."

"Each character is placed in a setting by the novelist; each expands or contracts his part through the choices he makes. Play your part gladly, but do not waste your time trying to make your role more important. The more a player in the drama elevates his part, the less he fulfills it. And the less is written of him in the Book, no matter how much is written in the Shadowlands."

"Can a person go back and alter his role?" I asked.

"Once written, the story is finished. It cannot be revised. Death is every man's final signature on his life's self-portrait."

"If only there were a second chance," I said. "With Marci and Amy and Brian, for starters. What have I left them? An inheritance? But no heritage, no legacy. Only money. Nothing. I know I'm not going to Erebus—but what I feel when I think of how I failed them, that must be a taste of it. If a mere taste of Erebus is so horrid, what's it like to actually be there?"

"The heights of the mountains of Charis are measured against the depth of the valleys of Erebus."

"Every time I've seen the sixty seconds of Charis and Erebus, I've walked away convinced I'll never forget it. Yet every time, the vision dissipates like smoke in the wind."

"The GuideBook is a knothole into eternity. It gives you glimpses of what lies beyond—and you may go to it again and again for more than sixty seconds a day."

I looked from Charis to Erebus and back.

"The stakes are so high. Higher than I ever dreamed."

"Charis and Erebus are the high stakes that give meaning to life in the Shadowlands. The roads men choose in the beforelife lead to infinite joy or infinite misery in the afterlife, to surpassing glory or surpassing tragedy. Everyone you pass on the street will one day be a creature of unimaginable greatness or unimaginable horror."

"It's as if life on this side of the door is the preliminaries," I said, "and on the other side is the main event. Like this is the tune-up and that's the concert."

Marcus nodded. "On Earth, I was not sure you would ever learn these things."

"You saw me on Earth?"

"What is important is that you not forget what you have seen."

"We live our lives in eternity's lobby," I said, "walking toward a door that will forever seal our destiny."

"Yes," Marcus said. "Exactly."

I couldn't shake what I'd seen. The sky over the plain seemed at eye level, vast and perspective-giving. I felt like a man who'd been a hermit, closed in by the hills, who now walked on an open plain, able to see forever.

That night we camped in rock-strewn hills of chaparral, eating prickly pears, breaking acorns, and chewing some kind of gum Gordy got from a tall plant. I felt like Gary Cooper again, the cowboy, no permanent home, owning just his horse and what he could pack into his saddlebags. A decent man who defended the honor of women and stood up for the underdog. Not seeking a fight but never backing down from any man. A natural leader who everyone looked to. I felt good about myself.

We stayed up late around the fire. Gordy pumped me with questions, and so did the others, even Shad, late into the night as the fire crackled with dry shrubs flammable as matches.

"Nobody's gonna fall asleep around this fire," Gordy said. "Not with those dried shrubs and not with Mr. Nick's stories of what the warrior told him!"

I knew this time I'd never forget what I had seen. I'd never lose sight of the worlds beyond. It felt so good not to just listen to the stories, but to be the storyteller.

Morning's first gesture was the stretched-out top of the rising sun, so broad at first it was a flat red line, then transformed into the beginnings of an oval, then a full circle. Singing meadowlarks and cooing doves welcomed it, as did our party, watching it with awe. But all I could think about was how yesterday Marcus had revealed all those important things to me and not the others. He must have had a reason.

We trussed up our packs and got started on the road. The chaparral led into a stretch of desert before hitting rolling hills twenty miles ahead of us—we hoped they were the final hills before reaching Mount Aletheas and ascending to Charis, now shrouded in mountain mist.

"I'll lead today," I said to Shad.

The old man stared at me. What did I see in his eyes? Resentment? Jealousy?

You think you're the only one capable of leading?

I stepped forward, took the lead, and didn't look back.

After a long silence Gordy said, "I'm glad you're leading. If it wasn't for you, I'd still be back in jail with Zed and Roy."

"What'd you say, Gordy?" I asked.

I hoped when he repeated it, the others would hear.

"The King's given you these great visions, Mr. Nick," Gordy said. "Tell us more about Charis and Erebus, would you?"

"Glad to, Gordy, but would you mind carrying my sack? I'm still tired from my time with Marcus. It was so draining—an incredible experience."

"Sure, no problem, Mr. Nick."

He picked up my half-full bag of stones and slung it alongside his own bag and a half, which awkwardly hung from his unbalanced pack.

As the day heated up, I kept up a good pace, faster than Shad ever had, despite the demanding terrain. As we walked, I told stories of what Marcus had shown me.

"So naturally," I said, "I took full advantage of the opportunity to find out all about Charis and Erebus. A man doesn't get many chances like that—I suppose most men don't get any chance at all."

"Not me," Gordy said. "I've caught a few glimpses, but nothing like what you've seen. Tell us about Charis, Mr. Nick."

"I like to think of it as the main event, with this life being the preliminaries. It's as if we're in a cosmic waiting room," I said.

"Cosmic waiting room? Wow. That's a good one."

"Eternity's lobby, that's how I put it. Marcus really liked that one."

The heat pounded us, and we wilted like rootless flowers. A prairie dog ran by five feet from Frodo, and he barely even barked. The sweat dripped, and we all dragged, especially Gordy.

"We should have traveled this stretch by night, not day," Shad said.

"Easy to second-guess now," I said. "Why didn't you mention it earlier?"

It began to cool in the afternoon, and as the sun lowered, we saw a large solitary tree a mile ahead of us, the sun's lower curve resting on its top branches.

"We should camp by that tree," Gordy said. "There must be water."

We came close to the tree, a twisted mass, thick but carved and sandblasted by the desert winds.

"It's a bristlecone pine," Gordy said. "It's a survivor. They can be buried in Alpine blizzards and stand up to desert winds and drafts. They say some are thousands of years old."

"How can it survive all by itself in this thin rocky soil?" I asked.

"The roots dig deep in search of moisture far underground," Gordy said. "If the roots can't find water, they just keep digging deeper until they do. All's you see is what's on top, but most of this tree is underground. That's the only way to survive when you live in a desert."

"I'm just glad the hills aren't that far away," I said, drinking less water than I wanted and giving more to Frodo than I should have.

I was tired, and I'd almost lost my voice, but as it cooled off, I felt great—I'd had that unforgettable guided tour from Marcus and had done well on my first day leading the troops.

Gordy set up the tent and spread out my blanket on top of his foam-rubber pad, to which Frodo laid immediate claim. The pad felt great. I liked it as much as Frodo did. Once I got Gordy to stop asking questions, I went right to sleep.

I slept in, and when I peeked out of the tent, I saw the others eating stewed tomatoes and soybeans and fried zucchini and reading the GuideBook. Waffles and omelets haunted me. Even cold lasagna would have drawn me out of the tent. Not this.

Rummaging through the items in David's backpack, I picked up his mirror, staring into it, craning my neck until I could see my whole face. I couldn't believe I'd let my hair get so ragged. I was spending so much time looking at the TravelGuide I'd forgotten to take care of myself. I'd first noticed it in the bathroom mirror at Bartholomew's mansion; now I couldn't stand letting it go a moment longer.

I took David's scissors and cut my hair. My beard had grown rough, so I shaved it clean. Hair had even begun to grow out my ears and nose. Yuck! I was beginning to look like Shad. That was a scary thought. If people were going to respect me as a leader, I needed to pay more attention to how I looked.

After Gordy packed our stuff, I led the way. Later we came across some traders, and I tried on some new clothes. I offered to swap a few of David's items, but they weren't satisfied.

Gordy stepped up to the traders. "Here, take a look at this." He handed one of them a shiny quartz rock with a distinctive reddish tint. "Zed gave it to me. Here, it's yours if you give Mr. Nick his choice of new clothes. What do you say?"

They looked it over, nodded, and agreed.

"Get something for yourself too, Gordy," I said.

He picked out a couple of shoestrings. I walked away with two pairs of pants, two shirts, a sweater, and some tennis shoes. I threw away my old clothes. I should have dumped them long before.

"You look great," Victoria said to me.

"Thanks. I feel great."

"I like it when you lead," Victoria whispered to me. I saw the admiration in her eyes. "You're more sensitive than Shad. And more like us. He's just too…demanding."

"I hear you," I said, glancing back at Shad, who walked by

himself at the rear, looking even more unpleasant than usual. I walked past Gordy, who carried his bags of stones and mine and also a bag with some of my new clothes hooked on his pack. He'd insisted.

"If your sacks weren't so full of stones," I said to Gordy, "you could carry a lot more."

"No problem," Gordy said. "The stones aren't that heavy."

I approached Malaiki, took her hand, and squeezed it, wincing because of my wounded hand, which I'd momentarily forgotten. The cut was bandaged, but it had become infected.

"You've been quiet today," I said.

"I'm praying for Salama…and David."

"David? The man's a mess. I can't understand why he couldn't see what's so obvious," I said.

"It's not always that obvious to me," Malaiki said. "I'm afraid any of us is capable of letting the King down."

"Well, I'm not perfect. But with what I've seen, I'm certainly not going to walk away from him. And neither are you. You're a wonderful young woman, Malaiki."

I squeezed her hand again. She smiled.

In the middle of the night I was restless and hungry. I kept thinking about lasagna and French bread and Bartholomew's dining room, hot baths and horses and the position David had offered me. Suddenly I heard someone outside. I saw a shadow cast on the tent by the moonlight. I groped in the dark for my knife and crawled cautiously to the entrance. It was a very large shadow. I squeezed the knife.

"Who is it?"

"My name is Gabriel. Marcus sent me. I'm his comrade."

I walked out cautiously, pointing the knife. In the starlight the tall, broad-chested warrior looked a lot like Marcus, strong and noble. I lowered the knife—if he meant me harm, I was a goner anyway.

"You show great promise, traveler," Gabriel said. "I am sent only to those important to the King. Come, warm yourself by the fire. I don't need it, but you do."

I stirred up the coals and put on a few branches that flared up.

"Nick," Gabriel said, "we have decided it is time for you to be the permanent leader. The group needs your direction."

"I'm not sure if Shad's ready for that."

"The others are. And he will come around in time."

"I think he's jealous that the others followed me."

"He is used to commanding their respect. But Shad is old and stubborn. You have learned much from Marcus, and the King has given you great wisdom."

Gabriel's words warmed me as much as the fire.

"Gordy and the women seem to really respect me. They've said they're grateful for my leadership."

"With good reason," Gabriel said. "I have seen your heart. So has Marcus. So has the King. You deserve to be rewarded. He who crossed the abyss for you would not deny you small pleasures—especially not when you have served him faithfully. He has chosen you above the others."

"I've been wondering about that."

"Remember, the King came to free you from guilt, not saddle you with it. The TravelGuide says he offers his children pleasures beyond their dreams."

He opened the GuideBook and read passage after passage to back up his claims. I nodded, fascinated at this perspective.

"I must go now. Don't delay. Marcus has told you of windows of opportunity. You have such a window of opportunity now. Strength and passion are qualities of the King's great leaders. The others need your leadership and your love. Do not hesitate to give them both. You owe it to them and to yourself."

He smiled warmly and disappeared, just as Marcus had.

I sat by the fire a long time. Planning. Strategizing. Choosing the steps I would take the next day.

As we walked in the morning, I beckoned to Victoria to come up alongside me as I led. I looked at her. So elegant and beautiful and alive. I wondered what it would be like to hold her again. I put my hand on her shoulder.

"Victoria."

"Yes, Nick?" She smiled, her white teeth shining.

"Beautiful day, isn't it?"

"Yes, beautiful," she said. "The King is an artist. He paints each day new." I saw the look in her eyes.

"Last night I sat under the stars, after the fire had burned low. Talk about artistry. It was breathtaking."

She smiled again and nodded.

"Victoria, I was thinking. After everyone's gone to bed tonight, how about joining me out under the stars? You'll love the view."

She looked down, her face flushed. "I'm not sure. I…"

"It's all right. We'll talk about the King." I felt movement in my chest, the soaring bird within, I told myself.

"Okay. Sure," Victoria said.

"Then it's a plan. After everyone's turned in, come out and join me by the fire."

I kept watching her and thought about how young she made me feel, about the way she looked at me. All I could think about was being close to her. A flood of images and sensations warmed me, stirred me. I could hardly wait for tonight.

I picked up Frodo, lifted him up to my chest. For some reason he growled and insisted on being put down.

"That's a first," I said. "What's wrong with you?"

He looked up and continued to growl, as if at some lurking enemy.

"Lighten up, fella," I called down to him. "Trust me, there's no danger here."

21

AS I LED THE WAY in the midafternoon, the sky turned ashen gray. Then darkness descended like a falling rock. I turned, and my comrades were gone. I called back to them but heard no answer. I stood alone on the road, on the fringe of a valley. A frigid wind blew from the east—none of my garments or blankets could keep its icy searching fingers from touching my skin.

I heard a noise above like a flapping tarp. A midsize flying reptile swooped down at me, and I saw its dead eyes. As I ran, I held up the knife with my right hand and put my left on the back of my neck. But this time it swooped around and went for my eyes. I heard a dull thud and felt searing pain as its beak penetrated to the bone of my right eye socket.

"Get away," I shouted, terrified at the prospect of my eyes being pecked out by this hell-hawk.

Suddenly I saw something shine in the darkness. A warrior stood beside me. Marcus lifted his sword against the beast and held it at bay. I thought I'd been rescued when suddenly a much larger beast, the great flying dinosaur itself, swooped down. With a hard swipe of a claw he knocked Marcus to the ground. The warrior got up, limping, then staggering back in front of me, he raised his sword again, like a Secret Service agent standing in the line of fire.

The smaller beast, emboldened, returned to attack me, but Marcus struck him with his sword. They fought viciously. I stumbled back, terrified.

The larger dinosaur saw me by myself and dove. It knocked me to the ground and tore into me. I screamed. It went for my eyes, and I covered them. Its beak punctured the skin on my hands, and I felt the blood spurting but didn't dare uncover my eyes to see it. I writhed on the ground, helpless.

"Stand up and defend yourself," Marcus shouted, still battling the smaller beast.

"How?" I cried.

"The TravelGuide!"

While the great beast circled above, readying to dive again, I yanked off my backpack and reached in to search for it. Where was the book? Finally I found it at the bottom, where it had been for days. I pulled it out and opened it, holding it in my wounded right hand. As the beast dove at me, the book transformed into a sword.

Stunned, I slashed air with it awkwardly, missing him. Swordplay was new to me—I wished for a shotgun. The dinosaur swooped, eyes on the sword, keeping his distance from it. He circled above until I couldn't see him, but I felt sure he was preparing to dive at any moment. I didn't believe I could survive his next attack. But I held up the sword, determined to go down fighting.

Just then another warrior emerged from the darkness on the valley floor.

"Gabriel!" I yelled.

"I've got you," he said. He picked me up as if I were a child and ran swiftly, across the misty valley, carrying me to a solitary hill and into a cavelike dugout, a shelter in the hillside, that covered our backs and sides. He set me down.

"Are you all right, little one?"

"I think so...thanks to you."

Gabriel applied his healing touch to stop my bleeding and tended my punctured hands and the injury beneath my eye. I heard fighting in the distance and wondered about Marcus.

"We're safe here," he said. "No need to worry. We must stay here until we're sure the evil ones are gone. They attack you to rob you of the King's blessings."

"What blessings do you mean?"

"The King offers you power, possessions, and pleasures. He has sent me to be sure you have them."

He reached into my pack and pulled out the TravelGuide. It had transformed back from a sword and somehow reappeared in my pack. He read to me from several places.

"You see, Nick? He offers you power to lead your comrades. He promises you great importance and influence. What made you so successful in business will make you successful in the King's work."

Yes. That makes sense.

"He also offers you great possessions. The present world is his, not just the world to come. He promises treasures for you to enjoy."

I nodded, as Gabriel read other parts of the TravelGuide.

"He offers you great pleasures, all you yearn for, as your reward for serving him. The TravelGuide says so, does it not?"

"Yes," I said. "It does." He read other parts of the book, skipping from here to there—I hung on his every word.

Suddenly a large figure stuck his head into the dugout. I lurched back against the rocky lining, hitting my head.

"Marcus! Are you all right?"

"Do not listen to him, Nick!" Marcus cried.

"What?" I looked from Marcus to Gabriel. "He rescued me from the beast!"

"He is not what he appears."

"Marcus, my friend, please let's calm down," Gabriel said.

"You are not my friend, nor his, name-stealer. You are a traitor, the sworn enemy of the King."

"But…he reads from the GuideBook," I said.

"Yes," Marcus replied, "and he twists it to make it say whatever he wants you to believe."

"But he speaks the King's own words—he taught me about power, possessions, and pleasures."

"Read the GuideBook, *all* of it," Marcus said, voice loud, eyes burning as he stared at Gabriel. "Power comes later in Charis to those who forgo power now in Thuros by serving others. Possessions come later in Charis to those who forgo possessions now in Thuros to invest in the King's work. Pleasures come later in Charis to those who forgo pleasures now in Thuros and live in purity."

Marcus quoted from the book, passage after passage, countering the claims of Gabriel, who then turned to still other parts, reading sentences here and there, weaving them together eloquently and persuasively. It was a war of words.

"I'm not sure what to believe," I said.

"This Impostor wants you to serve yourself and to serve him, not the King," Marcus said. "He tempts you to sacrifice the eternal on the altar of the immediate. Are you so blind you cannot see that?"

"But Gabriel has been kind to me. He rescued me!"

"He *appeared* to rescue you—but from whom? From himself! Search your heart—you know who he is!"

I backed away from Marcus, terrified. I'd observed fire in his eyes but had never seen him so angry as now. He pointed his finger at me, his mighty arm shaking, his voice shouting.

"Did you think I was not there by the fire? Did you think the King was asleep? Did you imagine all Charis was blind to Thuros, that we did not all see when this one you call Gabriel enticed you to seduce the woman? Do you think we do not know your plans to commit the great wickedness this very night?"

I dropped to my knees as an awful clarity fell on me like a meteor from the sky. A white-hot dagger stabbed my chest. I felt warm blood in my mouth, the taste of death. The acts I had already committed in my heart flashed before me relentlessly, without mercy. I had fallen, and the depth of my fall overwhelmed me.

I looked up at Gabriel and saw his eyes. Shark eyes.

How could I have been so stupid? So blind?

"I'm sorry," I cried. "Forgive me, Marcus."

"You have betrayed—and plotted to further betray—one far greater than I. He rules the universe. Ask his forgiveness, not mine."

"Forgive me, my King," I cried out to one I could not see. "I have wronged you and Victoria and Malaiki and Shad and Gordy. And Marci, Amy, and Brian."

"You've done nothing wrong," Gabriel said in a soothing voice.

"I've done everything wrong. I've been proud, impure, selfish. I've dishonored the one who crossed the chasm for me. Forgive me, Lord," I cried, looking up. "I wanted too much."

"No, you wanted too little," Marcus said. "You settled for momentary power, possessions, and pleasures that would rob you of eternal ones."

"I forgot there is no private moment," I said, choking on tears. "The GuideBook says what is done in darkness is shouted from the rooftops. I forgot."

"The GuideBook is your sword," Marcus said. "You had put

down the book—you were unarmed, helpless to fight the battle. My strength was not enough to defend you against the mutineers."

As Marcus spoke, he staggered, shifting weight from his badly hurt leg.

"I'm so ashamed," I said. "How can the King forgive me? How can he use me after what I've thought and done? And come so close to doing? How can I face the others?"

"Come now," said Gabriel…Joshua…the Impostor. "Say nothing to the others. You need to maintain their respect. Image is everything."

"Image is nothing," I replied, opening my GuideBook. "Character is everything."

"Appearances are everything," Joshua retorted, his voice as cold as death.

"Truth is everything," I countered. "Virtue is everything. Appearances are falling leaves, blowing in the wind, here for a moment and gone forever. Truth and character are what remain."

"Truth and character? They do not matter!" His voice oozed with scorn.

"Truth," I said, "is something you know nothing of. Character is what you are in the dark, when no one but the King is looking. You, Pretender, what are *you* when no one is looking?"

I smelled sulfur. I tasted bile. I felt the burning fire of dry ice put to my face and violently ripped away. Despite my bold words, I shook with fear. I heard howling, saw an insatiable beast, a wild animal more intelligent and vicious than any man, flies swarming around his head.

Suddenly, I saw Gabriel again, calm, warm, attractive. "Do not sell yourself short, my comrade," he said to me in an enchanting voice with a melodic lilt that drew me to him. I felt that he earnestly wanted to be my friend, that perhaps I'd misunderstood him.

"Let me sing you a song of how the King taught men to find the best in themselves."

He sang a haunting seductive melody: "Adam's choice fulfilled destiny, allowing man to become the best he could be. Thuros was transformed to a paradise of choice, so that man might forever speak in his noblest voice."

His words drew me in like the swinging gold watch of a hypnotist. I felt my TravelGuide in my right hand. I held it up to him and shook it in his face. I saw him flinch, and it emboldened me.

"Impostor!" I shouted. "You hold out the skin of truth stuffed with the guts of lies! You are the bender of men. You make lie-tellers teachers, life-haters doctors, King-betrayers religious leaders! You train them to mouth your lies."

"You believe this slander about me...and you?" He sounded genuinely shocked and hurt. I backed down, wondering for a moment if what I'd said was unfair.

"Don't you see?" he said. "The King knows your potential and is threatened by you, as he is by me. He doesn't want you to succeed. The most you will ever be is the King's errand boy. I offer you a captaincy in my army...and upward mobility from there!"

I paused, feeling the struggle within my chest. Finally I spoke.

"What choice should I make?" I asked, then laughed aloud. "Would a starving man choose to eat a banquet or choke down dirt and gravel? I am the King's son, and he promises I will reign with him. But even if not, I would far rather be his errand boy than a four-star general of the doomed troops of Erebus!"

"Nick," the Pretender said, holding out his smooth hands as if in good will. "I'm speaking the truth." A fly crawled across one of his eyeballs. He didn't blink.

"I've worked for you before. I know the wages you pay your servants!"

"I offer you power, possessions, pleasures, the delights of Skia."

"You offer rat poison wrapped in taffy."

He sang another lovely song. I put my hands over my ears, but still the music wormed its way inside my head. I felt movement within, the scorpion. I called upon the soaring bird to fight him.

The words of the TravelGuide filled my mind, and I sang them out, dueling with the Impostor's song, Marcus at my side singing with me. Covering his own ears now, the Pretender sang louder and so did I. Finally he shouted the words, pacing like a madman.

The words I sang pierced his armor. The song of the Chasm-crosser fought the song of the Counterfeiter, whose words were now reduced to the mindless blabbering of a raving lunatic.

"You pretend to be his follower," he screamed at me, pointing his finger. "But look at your thoughts about Victoria. Beautiful, isn't she? Picture her as you did before, hunger for her! And what about your jealousy of the old man? And how you've made Gordy your servant? And your anger at the King? You are part of my rebellion. Admit it. An hour ago I controlled you. An hour from now I will do the same. You are mine!"

"I am the King's, Accuser!" I said, holding up the book because my mind was not strong enough to resist his logic. "The TravelGuide says the Woodsman defends me in the court of Charis. I stand pure, cleansed of my guilt, for he has paid the price for me."

"You killed your own child and your own father. Do you deny it? I know what you really are and so does all Charis. You'll *never* enter there."

"The King says I will! He promised to welcome me there. I deny none of my evils, none of the abominations you deceived me into doing, but the book tells me when Charis looks at me, it sees the King. You see him in me too, Pretender, for you try to hurt him by hurting me, don't you?"

"You presume to know *my* thoughts? I was ancient before the first of your kind was created—the two idiots who served me in the garden. Listen to me and learn!"

"I *have* listened to you, Shark Eyes. I listened to you all my life, when you enticed me down dead-end roads. I listened to you even after I crossed the chasm—I nearly let you talk me into jumping off that mountain and ending what the King was trying to accomplish in me. I even listened when you told me not to speak to Bluecoat."

"Yes, Bluecoat. I'm so sorry for him. What an unfortunate rock slide—ill-timed, wasn't it?" He laughed long and hard.

"No matter how you try to hide it, your true nature eventually surfaces, doesn't it? Whenever you speak, you lie. Whenever King Elyon speaks, he tells the truth. I choose to follow truth, not lies."

"Truth? What is truth?"

"The King is truth."

"The King takes everything from you and demands everything of you." Smoke rose from the crown of his head. "Is that love? What does he give you in return? Sorrow, suffering, shame, ridicule. Remember your friend Quon? That is how the King repays his servants. The more you yield to the tyrant, the more he demands of you. Turn from him while you still can!"

"To turn from the King is to turn from life itself. You, Pretender, feed men gravel, telling them it's bread. And when they break their teeth and wail, what do you do? Feed them larger rocks until they choke and die."

Talking back to the Impostor seemed to drain him of the power to disguise himself. His bloody head, smashed long ago by a rolling stone, hung and bobbed like a boxer about to go down. His eyes were empty, like two holes in a mask.

Suddenly, I felt his mighty will grab hold again. He rose up before me, muscles bulging, much taller and stronger than Marcus, his head nearly hitting the ceiling of the dugout. Seized by evil strength, he raised his fists to the sky. He hissed long and hard, then screamed, *"Baal jezeb ashnar mordol nuhl—keez gimbus molech nargul dazg!"*

He spit the words as if he could not bear their weight on his tongue. I reeled backward at this foul, dark language. My vision blackened, I groped for sight.

Marcus, his eyes ablaze and the tendons of his great neck stretched, stared at the evil prince, then raised his right fist and cried to the sky, *"Elyon miriel o aeron galad—chara domina beth charis o aleathes celebron!"*

His speech was loud as a deafening waterfall yet soft as a gentle brook, the words sweet as honey. The raging beast covered his ears, wincing and shouting vile foreign slurs in a fruitless attempt to drown out the cascading echo of the golden words. I heard, though I could not see, a multitude of the King's warriors take up the words of Marcus in a glad shout that then became a mighty song.

"Do not speak again in the fallen tongue," Marcus warned. "For though my power is as nothing to yours, fallen star of the morning, I can still speak Elyon's truth in the ancient language…and in the face of those words you shall surely wilt—just as you must in the final day!"

"Speak not that name," the Usurper snarled frantically. "I cannot bear to hear it, I who have made myself equal to the Most High!"

"I will speak the name of Elyon freely, for the Most High reigns—and *you, Fallenstar, do not!*"

A hideous scream erupted from the twisted titan. He pushed Marcus aside like a rag doll and slapped his large hand against my injured left shoulder, causing an explosion of pain. I flinched but refused to cry out.

"When I conquer your King, puny one," he raged, "I will not forget your blasphemy against me. My arm is long—I can crush you at my will."

"At *his* will only," I said, drawing my knife and holding it out at him. He laughed loudly.

"Do you believe you can hurt me with that?"

Moved by gut-felt hatred, I stepped forward and thrust the knife into his chest, surprised at how easily it pierced his skin and sank all the way to the handle. I felt his skin, cold and sticky, the skin of a snake. Black blood flowed, staining my hands and burning them. I stumbled backward.

"Fool! Such weapons only give me more power over you!"

Hitting me with the back of his hand, he batted me to the ground, sending me sprawling. "I am your King's equal opposite, the heir apparent. I will defeat him!"

I pulled myself up and faced him again, book in hand, my only recourse.

"*Equal?* You are the equal opposite of the King's general, not the King. He is creator, you are creature. Conquer the King?" I laughed all the more when I saw how angry it made him. "You are more powerful than I, but what does that mean? The dung beetle is more powerful than the grubworm. But does either pose a threat to the Lion? Your minions are a small cloud of gnats to be smashed with the clap of his scarred hands. You are no more than an inconvenience—no, you are his tool, which he may use for whatever purpose he chooses and dispose of when he wishes!"

I was stunned at the words, marveling they'd come from my mouth.

"Shut up, runt!" he screamed at me. "I am no one's tool. Do you not know? I *killed* the King!"

"Yes, and I helped you do it! But do you think we could have done anything against him unless he chose to endure it? And did you keep him in the grave? No. You bruised his heel. But he came back to crush your head. You're a murderer on death row, ranting about your prowess. I've read the book, I know how the drama will end—you're a cancer about to be removed and cast into the burning garbage dump of the cosmos!"

I heard a terrible scream. Before my eyes, fire consumed the Pretender and burnt off the remaining layers, mask after mask, until I saw evil unveiled, a putrid dripping mass of blood and pus. I smelled the stench of rotten flesh.

"I am royalty," he screamed hoarsely. "I was chief of all creation before your kind was made!"

"The King is Lord of the cosmos," I cried. "You are lord of the flies!"

At that moment I heard distant cheering, as if some crowd was rooting for me.

"I will drink your blood and skewer you like meat, miserable image-bearer!" He shrieked the words, veins in his temples bulging.

"I brought civil war to Charis itself. I turned Thuros into Skia! What mighty works have *you* done?"

"None. You are a fallen titan; I am but a reclaimed man. What you were makes what you are all the worse."

The Impostor lunged at me, and I braced myself for certain death. But he stopped in midair, as if he'd hit a cement wall. He clutched at his throat. I saw what I'd never seen before—a tight collar around his neck. Something dangled from it, hung horizontally and disappearing into space. I couldn't see the other end. Suddenly I realized what it was.

"When I first came to Thuros, you pursued me, Pretender. You ripped into my neck. And just as you were about to carry me off to your lair, your head jerked violently. Now I see why. You're on a leash!"

I stepped into the opening and pointed to the sky.

"All your flying reptiles, they're on leashes too, aren't they? They're held by an unseen hand. But now I know the one who holds the other end of your leash, Pretender. I've heard his roar. I've met him. I crossed the chasm in his scarred hands. You can't move an inch farther than he permits!"

He screamed in rage and lunged at me again from the dugout. His outstretched hands were but a foot from my throat. I was frozen with fear yet determined to hold my ground. His fingernails stopped within an inch of me, his head jerking back on his neck. Whiplash. He raised his fists and glared at Charis on the mountain-side, screaming and cursing. He looked like a rabid marionette trying to loosen itself from its strings.

The one I'd known first as Joshua and then as Gabriel—that intelligent, charming, thoughtful being who sang so beautifully and spoke so eloquently—was a ranting, raving lunatic, a mass murderer, a great impostor, a miserable wannabe.

I despised myself as I contemplated how this beast, patient and skilled as a fly fisherman, had waded out into the river of my blindness and pride and lured me in. He was an operator, a flatterer, with millennia of experience in sweet-talking ignorant children to their destruction.

"You are a miserable fool, child of Adam," he cried, quieter now, gasping for breath. "I could kill you with one squeeze of my hand."

"You can do no more to me than the Leash-holder permits. And even if he permitted you to kill me, my death would be the doorway to joy unimaginable. You will not win, Pretender. You cannot win."

Flies buzzed around him, crawling again across his lidless eyes. Like a decrepit old field bull with a rope tied around its neck, tethered to the fence, he didn't have the energy to swat them off.

I walked away, an exhausted soldier, finding a stretch of grass on which to rest my head. The beast did not follow me. I saw Marcus nowhere. I lay quietly, speaking to the King. There was much I needed to say to him. After I spoke to him at length, I sat up and read the TravelGuide and listened to him. He too had much to say. I listened harder than I ever had before.

I smelled something on my right hand, like the residue of a snake. Hearing the chatter of water falling on stones, I walked to the stream, bent down, and washed my hand, rubbing it against mossy rocks, finally ridding it of the stench.

I walked back toward the red road as the darkness surrendered to daylight. Soon I saw my comrades sitting by the road, as if they were waiting. When they saw me, they stood, looking uncertain.

I walked toward them, then broke into a run. I heard something at my feet and looked down to see Frodo's puckered lips and white teeth—a warm welcome home.

"I'm so sorry for the way I've acted," I said to all of them. "Forgive me, please."

Shad embraced me. Gordy did too, insisting I hadn't done anything wrong. I knew better. Malaiki hugged me. I looked at Victoria.

"Never again will I speak like that," I whispered to her. "Please forgive me, sister."

She looked at me, an odd expression on her face. She nodded.

"Please," I said to Shad, "lead us."

"I'm returning the clothes you got me," I said to Gordy. "They're rightfully yours. And please, let me carry some of your things."

He refused, but I insisted. I hoisted my own half-sack of rocks and his two sacks, one full, determined not to complain about their weight. Surprisingly, the whole load seemed lighter than what I'd carried before.

"Wait," Shad said, after we'd traveled just a few minutes. "Even though it's midafternoon, in honor of your return, let's set up camp now and throw a party!"

"Are you all right, Shad?" Victoria asked. "I don't think I've ever heard you say the word 'party.'"

"Perhaps I should say it more often," he said, smiling.

We cooked up our best rations, including a fresh chicken and mashed potatoes, and I stayed by the fire, close to my friends, not making excuses to get away. I didn't want to get away. I'd had the props kicked out from under me. I needed these people. Frodo and I were the last to go to our tent and retire for the night.

———

The next morning I traveled behind the others and opened my TravelGuide. I read it as we walked, putting it on like a myopic man putting on corrective lenses. I sang its words, consumed them, and filled my hungry soul. Thinking no one was behind me, I was startled when I saw a shadow—Marcus.

I waited for him to talk, but he said nothing. I swallowed hard.

"Thank you," I said. He looked at me strangely, as if he'd never expected to hear those words. "I was so sure I wouldn't fall."

"That's why you did," he said. "The man who thinks he can't be robbed leaves valuables in plain sight. The one who knows he can be robbed puts them somewhere safe. If you know you can fall, you make wise choices to keep yourself from falling. But if you tell yourself it can't happen to you, that ensures it will."

"I'm so disappointed in myself."

"To be disappointed in yourself is to have believed in yourself. Be careful whom you trust. Trust the King, not your ability to follow him."

"The Impostor was so persuasive. I believed he'd been sent by the King. Or at least, I wanted to believe it. He kept quoting the TravelGuide. I think that's what fooled me."

"He's a master at denying the TravelGuide to those who don't want to believe it and twisting its meaning to those who claim to believe it. He wears the mask of friendship and benevolence, and with smiling face and soothing voice and concerned nods and compassionate counsel he leads men step by step into the eternal flames of the damned."

I trembled. "Yes, and when I listen to him somehow the voices that speak truth seem harsh and intolerant, or naïve and foolish. He's so persuasive, he appears to be so good. But he's so…corrupt, so malignant."

Marcus nodded, his eyes sad, as if I'd said something that hit too close to home.

"As a good man is much better than a good dog, a vicious man is much worse than a vicious dog," Marcus said. "And one of my kind who turns evil is far worse than either. Nothing is evil in the beginning, for Elyon creates only good. I knew Morningstar and admired him. He was the very best of all creation. Now he is Beelzebub, the very worst. I see in him what I could have become. It frightens me. The greatest evil is done by those created for the highest good. He will never give up trying to draw you from the King, Nick. Not until he is bound or you are home, forever out of his grasp. For now, you must keep up your guard. So must I."

That night sleep eluded me. The Impostor's bony finger pointed at me, accused me, gloated over me. I felt so dirty and stupid, such a great fool. Finally I fell asleep, hoping for rest, but my dream erupted into horrible nightmares of betrayal and filth, as if a bulbous boil within me were lanced and my dream was its wretched discharge.

I vaulted out of my dream and crawled to Shad to wake him.

"I'm so unworthy," I whispered.

"Yes, you are," he answered. "As am I."

"I'll never try to lead again."

"Let that be the King's decision," Shad said. "He must soften the clay before he can sculpt the work of art. Sometimes he must first hurt those he would use. For he uses those who learn from their failures."

"Learn what?"

"To trust him more and themselves less. He who would lead others to the King must first learn to follow him humbly." Shad paused. "I confess this is something I've often failed at. I, too, need to ask your forgiveness."

Surprised at his words, I nodded. "I know he's forgiven me," I said. "But I can't forgive myself."

"Are your standards higher than his? Don't raise up yourself or bring down him by refusing to believe what he's told you. Don't pretend your tolerance for sin is less than his. I speak from experience—for every failure of yours I have committed many more, including the sins of pride and self-righteousness that pursue me like bloodhounds on a scent. Whenever they catch me, I must go back to the King again, as he tells us to. And acknowledging my unworthiness, I must receive his gift of grace. You and I both must learn to accept his atonement—not try to repeat it."

I stepped out of the tent. The night was silent as a crypt. Tiny burning holes appeared in the black canopy above the sinking moons. I walked for an hour under the stars, exhausted yet restless. I looked up into the face of the King. I gazed at the great city on the hill, now so close I could see the different colors of its shining buildings.

Never had I wanted so much to go home. To *come* home.

I returned to camp and rekindled the fire and read the book by its flickering light. I mulled over the King's words, soaking them in like a dry sponge. "Those who appear to be foul sometimes prove to be fair, and those who appear to be fair often prove to be foul."

Half of me was chilled by the dark night air, half comforted by the fire. I stared into the flames that stood in a row on the crackling fir branches and licked the air, reaching higher, ever groping for something above them and warming me by their pursuit of it.

I marveled that I'd come this far without electricity, pumped water, or sewer, without my car or computer or cell phone or even a schedule, without the stock market and gadgets and entertainment systems that had been so central to my life on earth, a place that had never been the home I'd tried to make it. I smiled, realizing this was the longest I'd gone in thirty years without calling out for a pepperoni pizza!

I came to Skiathuros with nothing but the clothes on my back, stripped of the things I'd depended on, things that had insulated me from seeing my true character, my deepest longings, from life itself. And yet here I was, my life reduced to my character, the road before me, the travelers beside me, the people we met on the road, the worlds beyond and the King above—and Charis, the destination that loomed ever larger by the moment. I'd been laid bare here. I'd seen myself as I really was. Now, perhaps, I could see myself as the King was refashioning me to be.

My eyes drooped. Overcome by fatigue, right there by the fire I laid my head gently on the book, which felt surprisingly soft.

Then I saw the Woodsman. He held in his hand something tiny and round, like a blue-green marble. He rolled it in his palm, and suddenly the ground lurched and heaved. I fell backward.

His footing firm, he stared down at the marble, deep in thought, seeing things in it I could not.

I looked up, terrified to see a giant eye peeking down from above the clouds. Was this the Cyclops I'd thought was staring at me, poking at my right temple all the time I'd been in Thuros? I turned to the Chasm-crosser, searching his face for an explanation. I heard him whisper something to the tiny sphere in his hand. Simultaneously I heard from above a terrible thunder.

Chasm-crosser gently laid the marble down, then walked away. I looked back up at the sky, but I could see and hear nothing. The eye was gone. So was the thunder.

I awoke by the dying fire, trembling.

22

EARLY NEXT MORNING, eager to travel, we broke camp, munching on yesterday's biscuits and sipping senaba as we walked. We hadn't gone far before five enormous soldiers, with straight posture and military formality, approached us. They all had placid faces, sculpted jaws, deep-set eyes. The one I recognized, Marcus, stepped toward me and each of the others toward one of my companions.

Marcus led me away from the others to the north side of the road. After we'd gone a half-mile, we descended into a storm of wind and lightning. The horizontal rain pelted me, washing my eyes. I turned to Marcus, trying to see him through the blur. He'd disappeared.

As the rain beat down on me, I stood at the foot of a hill, wet leaves slick under my feet and blowing in my face. I didn't want to climb it, but if I'd learned anything here, it was that what I wanted wasn't reason enough to do or not do something. I climbed for an hour and, soaked to the bone, arrived at the top. There stood a lonely, gaunt tree, about nine feet tall. It had only two long limbs, spread horizontally about five feet, in macabre stick-man fashion. Wet leaves blew against it haphazardly, hanging on for a moment until they were blown off. As I came near it, mud grabbed at my feet. It thickened with every step. I tried to plod to drier ground but couldn't.

The mud rose to my ankles. With every effort to get out, I sank deeper. It was now at my knees.

"What am I supposed to do?" I cried, hoping to bring back the warrior who'd abandoned me.

I reached out, grasping for branches that weren't there. Then I saw someone in the distance watching me. He sat on a delicate white mare. Was it Marcus? No. It was a gentle rider with fierce eyes. The King!

I felt like a child at bat whose father just showed up at a baseball game. I was determined to pull myself out of the mud, to show him what I could do and how much I'd learned. I tried harder and harder, yet the mud kept swallowing me. It came to my waist now. For a few minutes I stopped trying altogether. Perhaps that was what he wanted. But I continued to sink. So I redoubled my efforts to escape, while the churning mud rose to my chest.

Why doesn't he come for me? I've traveled so far; I'm so close to the city. Is this where I'll end, buried alone in muddy quicksand?

Finally the King got off his horse and approached me. He stopped about twenty feet away. I waited for him to speak, but he said nothing.

"What can I do?" I cried.

"You're not using all you have to get out," he said.

"But I am," I whimpered. I flailed my arms and wrenched my back and twisted my body to prove I was using all I had. The mud was now at my neck. I quaked with fear.

"No," he said again, "you are not using all you have to get out." He spoke with infuriating certainty.

"I am! Can't you see that? What else do I have? What do you want me to do?" I spat out mud with my question. The King I'd come to trust was letting me choke on mud? Why?

"You are not using all you have to get out," he said, "for you have not asked me to help you."

He said it slowly and clearly. He gestured to the barren tree with its shaft crossed by the thick ugly branches.

As mud oozed into my mouth, in desperation I cried, "Help me, Lord, please help me!"

As soon as I spoke, he put his left hand on the tree branch and leaned out toward me, one foot stepping into the goo. He stood on the mud, reached down with his right arm and pulled me up.

A moment later I stood on the mud beside him. He drew me to him, embracing me, his white tunic now covered with my mud.

"I'm sorry I got you so dirty," I said.

"It isn't the first time," he said. "I know what it is to be made dirty. I planted this tree for you, long before you were born."

I looked at his left hand, which had held on to the thorny tree limb. It was covered with red mud. I reached down into my bulging pocket, full of nails. I spilled them at his feet. Maybe I'd find them in my pocket again, as I always seemed to, but here, now, I was determined to have nothing to do with them.

"There are two kinds of people," he said. "Those who deny they carry the nails and those who admit it. My followers admit it and empty them often at my feet, just as you have done."

He stretched out his disfigured hands, twisting them from side to side.

"Without reaching for my hands, you cannot succeed in anything that matters. If there was any other way besides the tree, do you think I would have done what I did?"

"I thought I'd learned so much," I said. "But I forgot to call on you when I needed you most. I tried to rescue myself. But you are all I have. If I don't remember your grace, the price you paid, if I don't reach out to you, I'm not using all I have."

He nodded and smiled. "When the Impostor whispered his lies to you, I was there all along, waiting for you to call on me. You never asked for my help, though finally you quoted my book to him. You resist my help because accepting it requires change and self-denial, and both are always painful. The only thing more painful than obedience is disobedience."

He pointed at the solitary tree, perhaps the ugliest specimen I'd seen in all Thuros.

"To walk the road you must never forget the tree that defines the road."

The King cleaned me off, lifted me up on his white horse, and walked beside it, holding the reins as he guided us down the hill. The sun wore through the dark cloud cover, and I saw the eerie shadow outlining the road.

The King helped me off the mare and pointed to the road and the city, so very close now.

As the King rode away, he gazed reflectively at the hill behind me, as if he'd spent an eternity there. I turned and looked up at the skull-shaped hill. At the top, where we'd just come from, I saw the rugged tree, nine feet tall and five feet wide. From it came the shadow that led to Charis. But how could anything so small, situated in this remote place, cast a shadow across this entire country? This was not the great tree that fell across the chasm—or was it? Could the great tree crossed by many be the same as this small tree planted just for me?

Perhaps things were not as they appeared.

I stared at the tree. It gave connection and meaning to those isolated shadows across the land. Its vertical reach united those above with those below. Its horizontal reach united me to my traveling companions. It divided history, nations, families. It divided Charis and Erebus. It was death. Yet it was life.

I looked at where shadow and road both pointed, to the City of Light. I was captivated by Charis. I wanted to step forth as Columbus or Magellan on new ground. I yearned to meet its inhabitants. I longed to be lost in the new world…and to be found there.

I saw smoke ahead, and when I arrived back at the red road, I found three of my companions waiting there, sitting by a fire, clothes covered with mud.

"Nick! Malaiki!" Gordy shouted, popping up from the south side. "Shad! Victoria! You won't believe what happened and who I saw!"

We all told our stories, much the same, yet each unique.

"I'd asked the King to remove a great burden from me," Malaiki said. "I couldn't understand why he hadn't answered. He showed me that what I had asked him to take away was exactly what he'd given to make me more like him."

She laughed delightfully, her voice sounding like the whispers in the wind from the City of Light. I loved her as if she were my own little sister.

Shad told more stories around the fire, wonderful tales of those who had served the King in many times and lands. "They walked the red road long ago and paved the way for us. We have followed in their footsteps as others follow in ours. Perhaps, someday, those who come behind us will sit at a fire and tell stories of us."

Even though it was in the west and the sun had set hours before, the city glowed in the night like the breaking of dawn.

"You can almost reach out and touch it," Gordy said. "It can't be more than a day's walk."

"It's the world I've lived for," Shad said. "Charis has been my beacon through so many dark and stormy years." Tears streamed from his eyes. "Lonely years."

Malaiki put her arm around him, and I squeezed his hand.

"Why not just walk through the night?" I asked, so eager to enter the city I couldn't imagine stopping now.

"If we have a full day's journey left," Shad said, "we must renew our strength with one last night's sleep in Thuros."

We lay down. But with visions of the city in our minds and sounds from the city in our ears, how could we sleep? I peeked through the tent opening, chin on the ground, staring at the city, Frodo's head beside mine. When I finally dozed off, hours after midnight, Charis invaded my dreams as it had my whole life without my knowing it.

But now I knew where the dreams had come from. And I knew I was a day's journey from what my empty soul had always longed for.

I woke up deeply refreshed and intensely eager to walk the road. A swift sunrise fueled our sense of urgency. We ate quickly and broke camp. As we pulled up each stake and washed each utensil, I wondered if everything we did was for the last time.

While we climbed up from the valley toward the city on the hill, I could see hundreds of people on the hillside, some sitting in lawn chairs outside their cabins, binoculars in hand, some with easels and paintbrushes. Several pointed at us, waving their arms, as if discussing the comings and goings on the road.

"Why do they discuss the road," I asked Shad, "and make paintings of it…but not walk it?"

"It's safer. Less at stake, for the moment. But where is the reward?"

I pointed at the City of Light, so close now it dominated the horizon. "It isn't a picture to paint," I said. "It's an ocean to dive into, a galaxy to explore."

Suddenly I heard a voice whisper seductively, "Don't go there; don't fall for the self-righteous lies of the city of hypocrites; go back to the great city of human achievement, where the road is broad and the opportunity for self-advancement endless."

I shook my head and talked back to the liar, whom I could not see except in my mind's eye.

"Save your breath, Pretender. I won't fall for it. Your voice is soothing, but I hear the hiss—and your smell betrays you."

I shifted my sack of stones and reached into my pack for the TravelGuide. I listened carefully to another voice, stiller and smaller but far more powerful and true.

By midmorning we could see the city's gates. Between us and them we saw a flag hoisted high, with bars shaped into a gold crown. At its base, mounted on her great blood bay, sat the young woman in black and with her a platoon of the King's army, camped by the road, standing around a raging bonfire. We approached cautiously.

"Welcome, travelers," said the girl. "We meet again. You are about to enter the city. Present to us your gifts for the King."

"Gifts?" Malaiki asked.

"Yes. The stones you picked up in the riverbeds."

My heart pounded. I put down my worn sack, just over half-full. Though I'd often tried before, for the first time in the daylight I managed to open it.

I pulled out a stone. It glimmered in the sunlight.

"It's gold!" I said. I reached back into the sack. "Silver! A ruby.

Look—two diamonds. An emerald! And this one…I've never seen anything like it!"

I was vaguely aware of the others shouting. I looked to see them rifling through their bags, holding up precious stones in the rosy sunlight.

I reached farther into my bag and found what I'd thought were some light stones. I pulled them out and stared at them.

"They're not stones at all," I said. "They're just crumpled balls of straw."

I turned the bag upside down. One last gem fell out, a small one. The rest was straw and stubble.

The girl in black picked up my stones and straw and placed them on a grate connected to a long pole. She held it over the blaze. The fire immediately consumed the straw, while it burned off impurities from the gold and silver and gems. They glowed with an otherworldly beauty, and I stared at them breathlessly, held captive by their radiance.

When I came out of my trance, I turned to Malaiki, now opening her third and final sack. She had dozens of precious gems, perhaps twenty diamonds and chunks of gold and silver. Her eyes danced as she watched the sunlight play on them. The grate was large, and a big warrior affixed it to the pole and held her stones over the fire.

"Well, if that don't beat all!" Gordy said, bouncing around like a child in front of Christmas presents, sucking his teeth and gazing wide-eyed at the precious stones from his two bags. I was amazed at how many stones he'd picked up in such a short time. Gordy had always struck me as being not too quick on the uptake. Yet here he was with three times as many precious stones as I.

So when it comes down to it, who's smart and who's dumb?

For the next hour we all watched Shad go through the rest of his sacks. He stopped to laugh and dance a jig. Then he stood still and solemnly handed each stone, one by one, to the King's envoy. She nodded her approval and put them on a large grate. It took two warriors to help her swing the pole out over the fire. The old man's eyes watered as he watched the straw burn away and the precious metals glow in the fire.

I stared at all those stones. How could one old man have carried them all on our journey? In his own strength it would have been impossible—of course, that was it. He'd carried them with the strength of another.

"Thuros, like Earth, is the womb of Charis," whispered a familiar voice beside me. "Choice and consequences. What is done in one world has profound effects on the next."

As I nodded at Marcus, a warrior carrying the fine tools of an artisan stepped forward. He went to the grates where the stones were cooling. He picked up gold and jewels from each grate and masterfully forged them together into crowns of stunning beauty. Then he handed them to my companions, one by one.

"You will cast these at the King's feet," said the girl in black. "And sometimes you will wear them. The King and all the citizens of Charis will be forever reminded of your faithful service. You will remember the meaning of every stone, and so will he. Elyon's book says, 'A scroll of remembrance was written in his presence concerning those who feared the King and honored his name.' All your works are recorded here—every cup of cold water given in his name."

I looked at the stones on my grate, not yet fashioned into a crown. In each of them I saw animated images. I saw in a diamond the moment I first met Gordy in the makeshift jail. I saw in silver the dark, cold day I stood up to David on the mountainside and protected Malaiki. In one very large ruby I saw myself caring for Cliff. But something was very strange—Cliff looked different now. His smoked-glass eyes burned into me, the scars on his hands...and feet.

"The Woodsman," I said, voice trembling. "Cliff was the Woodsman? The King?"

"Yes," Marcus said. "The King is not gone, you know. He walks the planet, disguised as the needy."

I stared at him.

"Do not think it so strange. I sometimes do the same thing myself."

Dumbfounded, I looked back at the other gems. In one I protected Shad from being beaten by the mob that killed Quon. In another, on the perilous ledge of Mount Peirasmos, I told Shaun about the King.

In the other stones I saw many different things, some I'd completely forgotten. Several gems contained images of things done while I was alone, including prayers to the King.

"But no one was even there," I said.

"I was there," said Marcus. "And the King is always there."

"There's no such thing as a private moment," said the girl in black. When I'd heard that before, it had terrified me. Now it thrilled me.

"I have no stones," Victoria said to the messenger, her voice breaking. "Can I not enter the city?"

"Entrance to the city is the King's gift," she said. "He paid your full admission and you accepted his gift. Therefore you may enter freely." She paused and looked at Victoria curiously. "It is sad, though, is it not, that you bring nothing to him?"

"Sad," Victoria mumbled, her eyes drooping. "Yes, very sad."

I remembered then the words spoken by the girl in black when she first told us to pick up stones by night. "In the morning, you will be both glad and sad."

The long night was over, and morning was here at last. I looked at the stones I'd picked up, knowing they were my tribute to the King. Seeing them, I'd never felt so glad.

Then I thought about all the stones within my reach, all those I could have picked up but didn't.

I'd never felt so sad.

23

WE STOOD NOW within fifty feet of the gates of Charis. I looked back to get a panoramic view of Thuros. I saw the dark city looming in the distance. Grayness and dimness rose from her like smoke from a fire. Even from this far away, I could see the web and the people caught in it, thrashing, stomachs bulging and quivering as the scorpions moved freely within. I heard them cry and moan. I saw shadows move upon the great web that trapped and connected all men, and I heard the screeches of the hell-hawks. Frodo's gaze followed mine, and as I held him, I felt him quiver. Seen from Charis, Babel had no lure—it appeared as it really was.

I turned away from Babel and looked back into Charis, standing right on its threshold.

Up in the sky far above the city, but headed down to it, I saw someone magnificent, mounted on a great white stallion, a man who shined with the brilliance of a thousand quasars. I didn't know how my eyes could tolerate the brightness. I beheld the naked glory of the King—or perhaps it was only a faint reflection of his glory.

With his bare hands and a column of wood he had punched a hole in the fabric of the universe and turned it inside out.

Darkness fell so quickly I thought I'd been blinded by the light. But then I saw the stars, and my eyes fixed immediately on the constellation of the Lion, the great red eyes, the six stars of his mane, the two star clusters of his uplifted paws that I had not seen before, and star after star outlining every contour of his great form.

Suddenly a great star, a supernova, exploded at the lion's open jaws. It had appeared once before, long ago, I knew, and this was its encore. He who came once as a pinpoint in a peasant girl, now readied himself to come again with ten thousand galaxies as the train of his imperial robe.

This time I did not hear the tentative bleating of a lamb. Instead I heard the relentless roar of a lion.

A mighty army came from the far end of the cosmos, progressing across stars and planets, through Orion's nebula. Vast hordes of warriors moved in an explosion of colors. The army advanced toward Thuros—or was it Earth?—in rumbling cadence, shaking me to my very core. They rode great white thoroughbreds without saddle or bridle, proud stallions that seemed to know their mission as well as they knew their riders. Some of the mounts pulled chariots of fire, streaking like meteors across the dark sky.

The warriors' hands moved to the hilts of their swords, the fire of righteousness in their eyes exploding into infernos. Then I realized that spread among the tall warriors like Marcus were men and women, crossers of the chasm.

This time the warriors looked confident that the King would unleash them to fight the legions of Erebus and vindicate Charis's cause. They sang songs of triumph, ancient hymns of battle written before the world drew its first breath. They were not only an army of retribution, but liberation, coming in response to millions of suffering voices crying out from the darkness of the charred planet, once a garden paradise.

I saw all this not merely as an observer, but as a participant, heart pounding, passionately immersed in the great events unfolding before me.

The army of warriors and chasm-crossers waited impatiently behind the King. Hovering over the City of Light, capital of Charis, they positioned themselves toward the dark city of Babel. They watched attentively for a hand to rise, listened for a trumpet to blow.

There among myriads of riders, mounted on a great steed, I saw Marcus. Next to him rode a man with a face familiar, yet not. This face was noble, valiant, filled with truth and grace. It bore a strong resemblance to the face of the King. And yet he was only a man, a small man, but one made great.

In a moment of stunned silence, I recognized the face. *It was mine!* A man who had once been a mile wide but only an inch deep. A man who now had a full chest, a purpose for living, eyes that burned with calling and significance, unclouded duty and unswerving loyalty. I who had served as a marine and fought in Nam and never dreamed that one day I might go to battle again, much less as a righteous soldier in the ultimate cause—I, Nick Seagrave, was one of the King's warriors!

I whirled back toward the man-made city and saw the Usurper assembling his own armies, hordes of darkness. Though they fancied themselves dressed in battle regalia, they were in fact a scraggly pack covered only with dirty rags. They rode pitiful nags—beaten down, overridden and whipped, droopy eyed and lame.

"Throw off the Woodsman's chains," yelled one of the enemy generals, fingering several jagged medals on his chest; the medals looked like they had been cut from old soup cans. "We are mighty princes, and Joshua Beelzebub is our valiant king!"

The voice was hollow, lacking not only honor but conviction. Across the stage swaggered Shark Eyes, dressed in a filthy robe, a scroungy old bedspread that had covered ten thousand wanton acts that now hung open in shameful clarity. He pranced and strutted like a washed-out vaudeville performer, gesturing dramatically, taking himself with utmost seriousness, while to the eye of the outsider, he dripped with absurdity. I was shocked by how he'd changed, how he'd lost his allure. Or was it that I now saw him as he'd been all along?

He sang a song, horribly out of tune, bragging that he'd destroyed the Sovereign's most treasured works of art—earth and man and the Prince himself. He gloated as an enemy of da Vinci might gloat if he had torched his house, burnt his *Mona Lisa,* and murdered his only son.

The Impostor, his face contorted, seemed oblivious to the collar around his neck and the chain leash that grew taut even as I watched.

The sun was blood red in a smoking haze. Mount Hagias surged and throbbed above the dark city and billowed a canopy of white and black smoke that separated Babel from the light of heaven. I looked at Babel's shelter, where forgotten winters had gnawed and carved the sunless stone.

Then, through the mountain's black skin of long-cooled lava, streams of red-hot molten rock broke through. Hagias spewed up a bright red river of heat and light that burned, through trees and stone, a new path down the mountainside. The devouring river headed straight down to Babel, great city of the east, where the screaming inhabitants only now realized the full measure of the volcano's descending doom.

Then earthquakes and tidal waves and floods assaulted the city writhing on its deathbed, as if a tormented earth could finally exact revenge on the fallen stewards who had caused its ruin. What was once a beautiful blue-green planet turned black and white with soot and ash. I looked back across the countryside I'd traveled—hills and lowlands, marshes and bogs, mountains and rock spires, plains and valleys, woods and rivers, cities and towns. I watched as they quaked and trembled on the verge of destruction—or was it childbirth?

Then came four horses and their riders—war, famine, sickness, and death. I saw a land numb with pain, sick with its own wickedness, tired of being what it was never meant to be. Earth—yes, it was Earth—strip-mined of hope, a hollow cavern of broken promises and abandoned dreams. The rebel planet awaited its last battle, its final defeat, its day of doom…and deliverance.

The King held up both his scarred hands. In one he held a writ of pardon, in the other a sword of justice.

"Every man must accept the pardon or be devoured by the sword," Marcus explained from atop the steed beside me. "There is no third option. Bow to him now in repentance and service, or bow to him later in judgment and condemnation. In either case every knee *will* bow to him."

"Come deliver us," I heard aliens and strangers and pilgrims cry from the red road. "Take us home!" they pleaded.

"Stay away," countered the citizens of the dark city. "Don't trespass on our turf, or we'll teach you a lesson you'll never forget!"

They reminded me of junior-high boys armed with slingshots and threatening a police SWAT team armed with assault rifles.

Then a cry from the heart of Charis sounded: "How long, O Lord, before you bring judgment upon the dark world for what they have done to your children?"

I looked at the man on the great white stallion, the man with the face of the lion. My eyebrows were singed by the awful heat of his anger.

"No longer," was the reply I read in his fire-hot eyes. He thrust up his hand to the sky, and the battle cry of millions of warriors erupted from one end of the heavens to the other.

There was war in Charis. War in Erebus. War in the narrow isthmus between them called Earth.

I was in the middle of it, inside the soldier I would one day be, riding on a great spirited thoroughbred beside an army of comrades, my sword raised to the sky. So quickly did we descend on Babel that within moments I could smell the rottenness of that city so long infected by the cancer of Erebus.

Suddenly the air was filled with clashing weapons and the cries of marauding warriors and flying reptiles. I felt my sword land upon the enemy and heard the din of war—the wails of oppressors being slain and the joyous celebrations of the oppressed that at long last we, their liberators, had arrived.

Some of the warriors sang as they slew, swinging a sword with one arm and with the other pulling victims up onto their horses. I too sang as I drew up a bloody little girl onto my horse and then with my sword cleaved the vile man who'd hurt her. I gazed into her wide eyes and saw her wondrous grateful smile. I felt a warm flood down my cheeks when I promised her she would never suffer again—knowing one greater than I would keep that promise.

I felt I was not just singing a song, or listening to one, but was inside a great song being sung by another.

The long arm of the King moved with swiftness and power. The hope of reward that kept the sufferers sane was now vindicated before my eyes.

It was a rout. This time none of Charis's blood was spilled. It was as if the universe could not tolerate the shedding of even one more drop of righteous blood.

The flames and shrapnel of combat scourged the Earth with burning debris. The ground exploded. The air itself was consumed in flames.

Charis released fury, and Earth bled fear. I beheld the world's last night.

Then I saw something very strange. Even as he conquered the twisted planet and made it his footstool, the Commander on the white stallion wept. I rode near to him, set down the little girl at his feet, and saw the tears myself.

The remaining rebels cried out to the King, "Withdraw from us. Give us a place all our own, where we need never see you."

"It is done," the King said, sweeping them away in answer to their own ignorant prayers—away to the one place in the universe in which the Lord of the Cosmos would never again set foot.

As I watched, the melting city of darkness slid down the river of lava into the abyss. Michael, the general, looked at his King, asking an unspoken question. The King nodded and said, "Yes."

Michael raised his great sword and brought it down upon the flying reptile. He was decimated by the blow, his head split and crushed, or rather his already crushed head shown to be what it was. The Impostor looked like a large spider—stepped on, then crumpled to a fraction of its original size. By the power of his commander, Michael—his muscles bulging at the strain—picked up his evil twin and cast the writhing beast into the chasm, all the way down to the fiery waters of Erebus. The vast army of warriors around me cheered, and I with them.

"And now, you shall reign with your King!" Michael shouted to us. I looked over my shoulder. Surely he couldn't be talking to me.

I still couldn't believe I would walk the same ground as the King, much less share in his rule. The thought was too vast, too fantastic for me to absorb.

I gazed down to where Mount Peirasmos had been. The ground was leveled—Peirasmos was gone. So was the broad mountain with the great cavern and tunnels. I searched for the land that had been Mr. Bartholomew's estate—nothing but scorched soil. I looked carefully about the decimated face of Thuros. Nothing had survived the fires of this holocaust of things.

Nothing but the followers of the King and the stones they had picked up during the world's long night.

Suddenly I was yanked back to the present, where I stood outside the great city. I had seen beyond the moment to a time and place yet to come.

Warriors who appeared to be palace guards ushered us into a courtyard fifty feet from the gates of Charis.

"What's this about?" I asked one of them. "Why can't we enter Charis now? That's why we've come, isn't it?"

No one answered me. A warrior sat me down—I could hardly bear it when we were so close to our destination.

My chair, like the others around me, had in front of it a portal, almost like a television screen. When the program began, it showed the events of my life on Earth, seemingly happening in real time. It was unedited—every choice, every incident intact. Yet somehow it moved very swiftly, and I was able to assimilate it all. I viewed it, fascinated, with the objectivity of an outsider, yet the feelings of an insider.

I saw some good things, some wonderful memories. But overriding them I saw how my mind had become the cumulative product of all I'd chosen to feed it and all the lies I'd chosen to believe. I saw how I'd betrayed my wife and children, the never-ending deceptions, the squandered opportunities. I wanted to look away but could not.

There, sitting on the threshold of joy, I felt the pangs of misery.

My mind raced through my life like a fallen leaf down powerful rapids. I thirsted for the undiscovered country that beckoned me. But I also yearned inconsolably for a second chance, an opportunity to do it all over, to make things right, starting with Marci and Amy and Brian and so many others. But I had squandered my opportunities. I had missed my chance. I wiped my eyes and stared at my feet.

Before I knew it, my companions stood around me, presumably having finished the retrospectives on their own lives.

"Come on, Nick," Gordy called, slapping me on the back. I walked forward, now only a stone's throw from the enormous open gates, Frodo weaving in and out between my legs as I walked.

Shad led us to the gate. After standing before a great book, he stepped into a room at the entryway, full of muddy and discarded shoes and clothes, as if it were a mud room. Shivering, Shad stripped himself of his dirty clothes. Carrying only the crown of precious stones forged in the fire, Shad walked farther in, eyes wide, through long soft grass, past a few senaba trees, and stepped into a steaming lake.

"Oh...," Shad cried, delight rising with the steam, his arms around his body soaking in the warmth, his eyes rolling back in sheer ecstasy.

Shad splashed and laughed, so hard and so long he seemed mad with delight. His head went under the water, and he came back up again and shook the water from him like a carefree spaniel, white hair strung down between his eyes. He peered through the strands like a little boy peeking through vertical blinds. Under his mustache

I saw what looked like piano ivories, a young man's teeth.

Young? Yes. It was Shad, but he was young. His once-wrinkled body rose above the steamy water. It was smooth, muscles firm, sags and scars gone. He kept splashing and blowing bubbles and giggling. I saw others in the steaming lake too. Malaiki and Gordy swam and sucked in air as if they'd just walked out of a garbage-lined ghetto into the freshness of a mountain resort.

They looked at each other, heads bobbing above the water, and grinned and slapped each other's hands. They laughed the laugh of insiders, those who knew the joke because they'd walked together and finally arrived together. Victoria joined them, her laughter merging with theirs.

Why haven't I been brought in?

I waved, and they gestured for me to join them.

Yes, I'd gladly come. I longed to strip off my muddy clothes and immerse myself in the clean warmth of Charis. I'd spent my life on the outside, out of the only loop that mattered. Now I wanted to come in.

I turned to Marcus, thinking he might escort me in, but he stood still, watching my companions.

Shad got out of the lake, and a warrior put new clothes on him, clean and beautiful. They appeared to be uniquely made for Shad, different from all the other clothes I saw on the hundreds around the lake.

"Those clothes were woven by his service in the Shadowlands," Marcus said.

Shad ran his hands down the front, as if he'd never felt such material. He raved at the comfort and the style. He skipped away with the lightness of youth, stripped of the heaviness of age and burden. Then he bent down and stuck his face into a fountain of water splashing up from the ground. He drank and drank.

Shad, with a young man's legs, ran back to the mud room and picked up his old TravelGuide. He opened it up to the middle and read, "You give us drink from the river of your pleasure!"

Malaiki cried, "In your presence is fullness of joy, at your right hand are pleasures forevermore!"

Shad ran farther in, greeted by applause and backslaps. Malaiki was embraced by loved ones, and Gordy and Victoria soaked in the world of wonder and delight. I smelled the aroma of wonderful cooking. Warrior-servants carried big platters covered with sliced senaba, juice dripping off the sides. My mouth watered. I inhaled deeply, wanting to enter, only wishing I had picked up more stones so I could present more gifts to the King.

Then I trembled as I saw the Woodsman approach Shad, who fell to his knees before him, setting his crown of jewels at his feet. The King picked up the crown, put it on Shad's head, pulled him up by the hand, embraced him, and cried, "Well done, my good and faithful servant!"

Next the King came to Malaiki and lifted her high above his head as if she weighed nothing.

"Welcome, my daughter," he said. He put her down and took the crown from her extended hand. He examined it carefully, as if peering into each stone. Then he grinned and cried, "Well done, my girl!" and embraced her.

The smile on Malaiki's face was like nothing I'd ever seen, surpassed only by the King's smile. In fact, they appeared to be the same smile, his joy hers and hers his.

People surrounded all four of my travel companions, like

midwives delivering babies into a birthing room and family members overwhelmed with joy at their arrival. A chorus of welcomes sang out in a thousand languages.

My friends looked like miners rescued from a collapsed cavern and emerging to well-wishers in the land of the living.

Malaiki's eyes glowed wonder and delight. She turned circles, dancing with the King and then with Shad and Gordy and Victoria.

"What's it like?" I cried out to them, standing on my tiptoes just outside the gate, feeling thrilled and left out at the same time, eager to enter but sharing in their joy.

"I've been born," Shad cried, arms flailing. "All my life on Earth and on Thuros was but a series of labor pains preparing me for this."

"This is it," Malaiki shouted. "The country for which I was made!"

"At last," Victoria said, voice trembling. "The *real* world!"

"What were circles before are now spheres," Gordy cried. "Squares have become cubes and triangles pyramids!"

"This is joy itself," Shad said. "Every foretaste of joy in the Shadowlands was but the stab, the pang, the inconsolable longing for this place!"

"The TravelGuide was right," Gordy called. "We were aliens and strangers and pilgrims. We lived in temporary quarters, on borrowed time. How could anyone be satisfied with less than this?"

"The best reason for loving the old world," Malaiki said, "was that sometimes, in its grandest moments, it seemed just a little like this one."

I stared at them, filled with wonder and envy. Even Frodo, at my feet, gazed in respectful silence at what he seemed to realize intuitively was the cosmic center, the core of all that mattered.

I knew then that if the atmosphere of Earth is nitrogen and oxygen, and the atmosphere of Erebus sulfur and acid, then the atmosphere of Charis is joy and delight.

I looked at Marcus, my eyes begging him to take me into Charis.

"Be patient," he said. He pointed, and I saw across a broad expanse a blue-green planet I recognized as Earth.

"The people there live between Eden, a world that has ended, and Jerusalem, a world that hasn't yet begun," Marcus said. "Earth is the walkway between two kingdoms. Its most horrible nightmares are of Erebus. Its most wondrous dreams are of Charis. Erebus is the worst of Earth multiplied a thousand times; Charis, the best of Earth multiplied a million times. Earth is a place to preview both, to sample each, to make the final unalterable choice between them."

A vast fabric stretched across the sky. Bending back my head, I saw on the fabric countless lumps and knots, like thick, rough yarn with frayed strings.

Suddenly, Marcus beside me, I was yanked up into the sky and pulled through a hole in the center of the fabric. Now I was on the other side, the top side. I looked down and saw a beautiful work of art, like needlepoint or cross-stitching, a magnificent tapestry more exquisite than any I'd ever seen. The yarn and threads had been perfectly knitted together in elaborate design by the hands of a master craftsman. I saw in the center of the tapestry the Woodsman on a tree. I saw how a senseless murder, history's worst act of betrayal, was the centerpiece of a glorious design. Surrounding it I saw other tragedies, other absurd and incomprehensible events that now had clear meaning and purpose.

"It's stunning," I said to Marcus. "Before I saw only the underside of the tapestry, the knots and frays. I never saw the design, the beauty."

"No wonder," Marcus said. "You have always lived on the wrong side of the tapestry."

"Charis and Erebus were both at my elbows every day," I said to Marcus. "My choices cast a vote for one or the other. And even in what seemed like chaos, there was purpose. How clear it all is now. How cloudy it all was then."

I stood back on Thuros again and saw a dying cosmos hold out its weak right arm, longing for a transfusion, a cure for its cancerous chasm. I saw the Woodsman, holding what appeared to be a tiny lump of coal, the same size as the blue-green marble he'd held before. The Woodsman squeezed his hand, and the world around me darkened. I fell to my knees and grasped my throat with my hands, felt the squeeze against my right temple. Just as I felt I would scream from unbearable pressure, the crushed world emerged from his grip a diamond and I gasped air in relief.

All around me I saw soldiers drop their weapons, the crippled toss their crutches and run, the blind open their eyes and see and point and shout and dance, throwing their arms around each other and me. I saw children sit on the King's lap and watched him wipe away their tears while his own fell upon them. I saw a new world, once more a life-filled blue-green, the old black coal delivered from its curse and pain and shame, wondrously remade.

It looked so easy for the Woodsman to do all this. But then I saw his scars and remembered it was not.

Suddenly I saw again through the eyes of the man I would be, mounted on the magnificent white stallion. I rode back west with my fellow warriors, returning from the front lines of the battle we'd just won. We rejoined our comrades in the great camp of Charis, embracing and shedding tears and slapping each other on the back. Then warriors around me turned toward the masses of untold millions gathered in Charis. The army began to sing, perhaps hundreds of thousands, perhaps a million.

"Elyon miriel o aeron galad, chara domina beth charis o aleathes celebron!"

I added my voice to theirs and sang the unchained praises of the King. Only for a moment did I hear my own voice, amazed to detect the increased intensity of the whole. One voice, even mine, made a measurable difference. But from then on I was lost in the choir, hardly hearing my voice and not needing to.

As we sang to the gathered throngs of Charis, the sheer power of their voices, *our* voices, nearly bowled me over.

Then suddenly the multitudes before us sang back to us, and our voices were drowned by theirs. We who a moment earlier seemed the largest choir ever assembled now proved to be only the small worship ensemble that led the full choir of untold millions, now lost to themselves. We sang together in full voice, "To him who made the galaxies, who became the Lamb, who stretched out on the tree, who crossed the chasm, who returned the Lion! Forever!"

The song's harmonies reached out and grabbed my body and my soul. I became the music's willing captive.

I knew now that all my life I had caught occasional strains of the music of Charis. But it was elusive, more like an echo. All that clatter, all those competing sounds, all the CDs and sitcoms and ringing phones and blowing horns and nagging voices drowned out the real music. I'd spent my life humming the wrong tunes, dancing to the wrong beat, marching to the wrong anthem.

No longer—for at long last I heard, undiluted, the song for which

I was made. And I not only heard the song, I sang it!

The galaxies and nebulae sang with us the royal song. It echoed off a trillion planets and reverberated in a quadrillion places in every nook and cranny of the universe. The song generated the light of a billion burning supernovae. It blotted out all lesser lights and brought a startling clarity to the way things really were. It didn't blind, it illuminated, and I saw as never before.

At long last, things *were* as they appeared.

Our voices broke into thirty-two distinct parts, and instinctively I knew which of them I was made to sing. "We sing for joy at the work of your hands...we stand in awe of you." It felt indescribably wonderful to be lost in something so much greater than myself.

There was no audience, I thought for a moment, for audience and orchestra and choir all blended into one great symphony, one grand cantata of rhapsodic melodies and powerful sustaining harmonies.

No, wait, there *was* an audience. An audience so vast and all-encompassing that for a moment I'd been no more aware of it than a fish is aware of water.

I looked at the great throne, and upon it sat the King...the Audience of One.

The smile of his approval swept through the choir like fire across dry wheat fields.

When we completed our song, the one on the throne stood and raised his great arms and clapped his scarred hands together in thunderous applause, shaking ground and sky, jarring every corner of the cosmos. His applause went on and on, unstopping and unstoppable.

And in that moment I knew, with unwavering clarity, that the King's approval was all that mattered—and ever would.

24

PULLED BACK TO THE MOMENT, I eagerly stepped toward the warrior who stood before the great open book, guarding the gate of Charis. If Marcus would not escort me, I would go there myself!

In front of me a man argued with the warrior, the palace guard.

"I did good things," the man said. "I was a better man than many I see inside. I gave generous gifts."

"But you did not receive the gift offered you," said the guard. "The only gift that qualifies you to enter. Your name was among those invited, but not among those who accepted the invitation. Your name is not written in the book. Depart."

As I watched, the man was sucked through a portal into another world. I heard his scream, and I trembled.

I stepped forward, standing now with no one between me and the warrior who bent his head in silence, searching the book. I looked behind him and saw a crowd gathering just inside the gate. A welcoming party!

Shad and Malaiki and Victoria were laughing and dancing around someone. Who was it? I leaned from side to side trying to get a clear view. It was a short young man…with a huge smile.

"Quon!"

He looked out and waved me in. "Come on, Nick—get in here and join the radiance! I have so much to show you. You just won't believe it!"

He laughed uproariously, as if his troubles on Earth or Thuros had never been—or as if they had helped make him the man he now was.

Then I saw another familiar face, one I'd seen in another context. A man with a large crooked nose. I pictured him…wearing an orange stocking cap.

"Shaun?"

"I beat you here!" he called, waving and smiling broadly, showing perfect teeth.

Shaun survived the avalanche?

No, of course, he *hadn't* survived. But I realized now he'd embraced the Woodsman's gift before the snow buried him. The avalanche ushered him straight into Charis.

Then I saw long auburn hair and a soft reddish face. I gazed at her, thinking this must be a dream.

"Nicholas!" She smiled and stretched out her arms.

"Mom?!"

I closed and reopened my eyes, fearing she'd disappear like a cruel mirage. I never believed I'd see her again. The faith this woman tried to teach us, a faith my father and brothers and I always rejected…at last, it was vindicated.

Why didn't I listen to her? Why did I come to love him so late?

Tears streaming down my face, I waved at Mom. Then my heart stopped as I saw someone beside her. A young woman, whose lovely face had haunted me a thousand nights, a face I hadn't touched since she was five years old. She looked so much like Marci and Amy.

"Lee Ann!" I shouted, seeing the look of delight in my daughter's eyes. I stared at her, speechless.

"Please, I have to enter," I said, turning to the palace guard. "What's the delay? You have to let me in *now!*"

At that moment someone stepped forward inside the gate. The milling crowd made way for him, as flimsy huts make way for a hurricane—but happily.

I saw him, no stranger to tears, wipe teardrops from people's eyes. I wanted to cross so he could wipe mine. He was coming to welcome me in, as he had my comrades. I couldn't wait.

I saw the banquet table just on the other side and inhaled its delightful fragrance. I hungered for the meal. This time when the scarred hands broke bread, I would see them differently.

I stepped forward, right to the threshold of Charis, past the guard with the book, who did nothing to restrain me. I longed to be freed from the throbbing pain in my temple, the ache in my neck, the injury under my eye, the bleeding sores on my hands, but more than any of those, the stinging scorpion inside, the web that entangled, the flying reptile that hovered and stalked.

I wanted to throw myself in unreservedly, to pour out myself into the cosmic celebration, to join a great river of water drops and be part of the great waterfall descending into a magnificent pool of praise—to lose myself and in so doing find myself.

I turned back and looked once more at the keeper of the book.

"Please. I don't deserve to enter. My only claim is the price paid for me by another. The Woodsman. The Lamb. The Lion. The King!"

"Your name is written in the book," he said at last.

"Let the labor pains end," I cried. "Let the birth take place, let the umbilical cord to the old world be cut at last!"

I stepped forward to the open gate, ready to come home.

"No!" someone roared just inside the gates. "Not yet."

It was the voice of the lion.

———

The King stepped from the great city, just outside the gate, and put his hand on my shoulder. I was aware of no one and nothing but him. I saw before me an aged, weathered King, thoughtful guardian of an empire. But I also saw a virile Warrior-Prince primed for battle, eager to mount his steed and march in conquest. His eyes were keen as sharpened swords yet deep as wells, full of the memories of the old and the dreams of the young. He studied my face, then opened his mouth, his voice rich and resonant.

"A moment after a man dies he knows exactly how he should have lived."

I nodded, saying nothing, my words unworthy to share air with his.

"But it is too late for him to go back and live differently. After death, there is no second chance."

He paused. Now I felt I should say something. "Yes. Those in Erebus can never come back. They cannot go back and live life over again and this time accept the gift you offered them."

"True," he said to me. "But it's more than that, isn't it? Something else haunts you—those in Charis can never go back either. They too have no second chance. They cannot go back and do it over again, this time pick up the stones, obey the TravelGuide, live for me instead of themselves."

I hung my head and nodded.

"Earth is the dressing room. It's where you put on clothes you'll wear on the other side."

I swallowed hard.

"I've given you my GuideBook. Do you know why?"

I wasn't sure what to say.

"So you need not wait until you die to learn how you should have lived."

"Have I not died, then?"

"Soon...but no, not yet."

He clasped my wounded right hand in his wounded hands.

"My wounds will last forever," he said, "but yours will not. Yet what I shall do in you through your wounds will."

"Wouldn't I serve you better without a wounded hand?"

"You would not serve me at all without a wounded hand. The hand that offers help is always a wounded hand."

The King looked away from me, and his face turned more fearsome than I'd ever seen it—fearsome yet gentle. For the first time, I saw simultaneously the face of Lion and Lamb. Suddenly Charis, a moment ago just a few feet from me, was eclipsed by a dark cloud. I heard the thunder of a great door closing. The sky boiled and darkened. Great crashes filled the air.

"What is it?" I asked.

"The sound of battle," he said. "Not the last battle, but nearly. The time has come. You must go for me."

"Go where?"

"Back to where the need is greatest and the battle rages. Back to the one place in the universe that disputes my claim on it. Back to Earth."

I fell at his feet and covered my face. "Please. How can I go back to the Shadowlands when Charis is so close? How can I live without being able to see and touch you? And how could I ever face the disasters I created there?"

"What you've seen in Thuros will equip you to face what you've done on Earth. I send you back for the short today; we will meet again in the long tomorrow. I give you, Nick, the second chance you long for. A chance to enter Charis after serving me faithfully on Earth. A chance to hear me say, 'Well done.' To rewrite your obituary, to give your family not just an inheritance but a heritage. Each day I grant you is a gift of grace, a window of opportunity. Use it wisely. Pick up the stones, even when you don't understand why."

"Yes, my King," I said, both thrilled and terrified.

"You cannot, must not try to walk the road alone. To walk with me you must walk alongside my people. Find them. Join them. Walk with them."

I nodded, for the first time truly understanding.

His voice roared thunderously. I groveled before him, afraid of his anger. He pulled me up with one hand and looked into my eyes, smiling. "You must learn to recognize my laughter, Nick. My roar is not always anger, you know!"

He roared again, and it was laughter indeed, so powerful, so grabbing that it evoked my own laughter, sounding light and frail beside his, but growing stronger by the moment. He laughed at my laughter, and I at his. Frodo jumped up and down at our feet, doing the doggy dance of joy. The Woodsman picked him up and held him, roaring when he saw the lips curl back and the toothy smile emerge. He put Frodo down and embraced me tightly, a bear hug.

I had always ached for something more, something better. But all along it had never been something, it had always been someone—the one who now embraced me. He held my shoulders and my eyes locked into his.

"Charis is a trillion different colors, Nick, Erebus only the eternal gray. All in Charis are wonderfully different, united by their differentness. All in Erebus are horribly alike, divided by their sameness. Charis is an unending story, each chapter more wondrous than the one before. Your time in the Shadowlands is the first paragraph of chapter 1. Every day there you will move people toward me or away from me, toward Charis or toward Erebus. Your life in that world is but a dot. From it extends a line that will never end. So, Nick, will you live for the dot or for the line?"

"For the line," I wanted to say but was afraid to.

He held a water bottle I hadn't even noticed. He lifted the opening to my mouth and squeezed it. I gulped and gulped the senaba, wanting more and more. Then I looked at him, took the bottle from his hand, and held it to his mouth.

"Thank you. But I will not drink it again myself until we are all together in Charis." I saw wetness in his eyes. "I was unashamed to die for you. Will you be unashamed to live for me?"

"Yes," I wanted to say. But I knew myself well enough now to hold my tongue.

"Remember, Nick, you were the cause of my journey. I loved you as you were, but I loved you too much to let you stay that way. Rather than give up on you, I gave myself up for you. I chose to go to Erebus for you rather than go back to Charis without you. The gift I extended to you is free but not cheap. It costs you nothing. It cost me everything."

I looked at his hands.

"Do you understand the extent of my gift?"

I started to say yes, then hesitated. "No," I said.

"Good answer," he said, smiling thoughtfully. "Any who thinks he understands does not. But understanding is not necessary for belief and worship and obedience."

He put his hands on my shoulders again, rubbing them firmly

with his hands. "It will not be easy for you where I'm sending you, Nick. But one day you'll understand that a short period of difficulty is a small price to pay for a clearer view of your King." My spine tingled at his words.

"Friday has passed," he said to me. "Tomorrow is Sunday. I send you back to the world's Saturday. Know that the never-ending Sunday comes, and even until it does I am with you. I listen to you, and I weep with you that you may one day laugh with me."

My eyes burned.

"Listen carefully, Nick, for in a moment I send you back to the true Skiathuros. Before I do, I want you to look once more at Charis. I am preparing this world for you—and I'm also preparing you for it. Charis isn't just a world I make for you, it is the world for which you were made. Every part of it resonates with who you are, who you *really* are, not the old Nick Seagrave, but the one I've made you to be. I have a new name for you. You're not ready to hear it yet. But I will give it to you when we meet face to face in our home."

The darkness parted just for a moment, and I saw and heard and smelled and tasted Charis with Mom and Lee Ann and Shad and Malaiki and Gordy and Victoria and Quon and Shaun and the others.

Then it was gone. No, not gone. It was there. I simply could no longer see it.

"You cannot control me, Nick," the King whispered to me. "But you can learn to trust me, even when events are too big and your mind is too small. Live each day as if it were your last day there. One of them will be. I'll be on the other side, waiting for you. And then at last, I will give you joy unsheathed—Charis the unfathomable,

Charis the unbridled, Charis the boundless adventure."

"But…I want to enter Charis *now*, my King."

"Soon, but not now. You have your orders—I send you to battle. You are a soldier, and I would not promise a soldier ease. I promise you difficulty but with it resources and purpose and joy. Go back now to where men die of thirst a stone's throw from pure water…go back as my water-bearer."

Marcus appeared beside me, dressed in full battle armor, bowing his knees before the King. When the King took his hand and gave him leave to rise, Marcus grabbed my arm, a portal appeared, and he led me through it. Behind us I heard barking, then singing, then nothing.

For a moment I thought I was floating over someone wearing my hunting jacket, then I felt like liquid being poured into a container. The next thing I knew I was sitting on an old stump outside a familiar mountain cabin, dripping wet, eyes blinking at the light of a yellow sun peeking through the clouds.

I looked for Marcus but couldn't see him. For an instant I thought I might have imagined him, until I saw large footsteps in the mud beside me. Rainwater filled the prints, the mud rose, and I watched the impressions dissolve into nothingness.

The pressure against my temple came back with a vengeance. My right arm felt tense and fatigued, as if I'd held it up for hours. I started to move my hand, began to peek at it out of the corner of my right eye, but stopped, afraid to see what was there.

I stood slowly, knees creaking, arm still in the air, and walked to the cabin window only ten feet from me. I looked at the table inside. On it I saw a picture. Staring at me were the faces of a woman

I had betrayed and a daughter and son who no longer trusted me.

Through blurry eyes, I saw beside the picture a scrawled note. I recognized the handwriting—my own. But I was too far away to read the words.

Then, finally daring to look, I stepped back and saw in the window my grotesque reflection. My spine tingled, and I held my breath. I hesitated, then moved my eyes to the right, toward my frozen arm. I strained to focus.

I saw my bent wrist, held in the air, and at a sharp angle the face of my wristwatch. For a moment the digits weren't moving, but as I looked the seconds began to tick off. I felt the flat rod pressing on my temple. Slowly, I managed to move it back. I felt the gaze of the Cyclops.

I looked out of the corner of my eye at the hard, cold metal in my hand and saw a few words, a blurry insignia, five inches away on blue steel, just above the checkered walnut grip. One word slowly came into focus.

Luger.

I gazed at the weapon, breathing shallowly. My fingernail was white as it pressed tight against the trigger. I looked at the rod that had pushed against my temple, the Cyclops staring at me—the barrel of a gun.

I smelled sulfur.

Trembling, I lowered the gun, flipped on the safety, and carefully placed the weapon on the stump.

Falling on my knees into the mud, I cried out to the Audience of One. "My King—thank you for your grace; help me, please. I can't do this without you."

I thanked him that as hard as what lay before me was, he would be with me. I asked that he would help me find chasm-crossers to walk with me on the homeward road, for I knew I could not walk it alone.

I reached to the back of my right hand and gently touched the weeping wound.

My eyes fell on something half-buried in the mud—a key ring. I picked it up. I fingered the keys to my office, my club locker, my cars, my apartment. Then I grabbed the key to our home, a key I hadn't throw away when I'd moved out from my family.

I thought about going into the cabin to dry off and clean up. Instead, I ran to my truck. I had to get home.

Home? My true home was a place I'd not yet set foot in. And the place I'd always been was not my home. But Marci and Amy and Brian...I had to go to them, I had to weather the dark storm over our lives. Tell them what had happened to me. Ask them to forgive me for the fool I'd been.

My body aching, I drove the truck down the muddy, red-clay road, following a long shadow. The mountain peaks pointed me upward. A black thundercloud eclipsed the sun. A shadow passed over me, and I heard the squawk of an unknown creature. Then lightning struck, and the thunderclap sounded like the roar of a lion. I rolled down the window, fresh rain blowing on my face, and heard in the wind two foreign tongues, one sweet and sacred, the other foul and coarse.

How long before I will hear them no longer and, still worse, imagine I never heard them at all?

I cried out to King Elyon, asking that I would not forget, but that if the memories faded I would cling to what is true even when I could no longer see or hear it.

The clouds broke, and I saw the sun again. I'd returned to a world of death and darkness but with windows to life and light. As I drove west toward my family, I searched the sky in vain, looking for Charis. In my mind's eye I could see a great shining city on a hill, and beyond it a country of unimaginable wonder. It was there when I saw it, I told myself, and there when I did not.

Things are not as they appear.

I walk between two worlds. I stand on the edge of eternity.

I thank the King for whatever time he's given me.

Here, in this brief window of opportunity.

Here, in this land of second chances.

About the Author

RANDY ALCORN is the founder and director of Eternal Perspective Ministries (EPM). Prior to this he served as a pastor for fourteen years. He has spoken around the world and has taught on the adjunct faculties of Multnomah Bible College and Western Seminary in Portland, Oregon.

Randy is the best-selling author of eighteen books (over one million in print), including the novels *Deadline, Dominion, Lord Foulgrin's Letters* and the 2002 Gold Medallion winner *Safely Home.* His ten nonfiction works include *Money, Possessions and Eternity, ProLife Answers to ProChoice Arguments, In Light of Eternity, The Treasure Principle, The Grace & Truth Paradox, The Purity Principle* and *The Law of Rewards.* His two latest books, *Why ProLife?* and *Heaven: Resurrected Living on the New Earth,* will be out in the fall of 2004.

Randy has written for many magazines and produces the popular periodical *Eternal Perspectives.* He's been a guest on over 450 radio and television programs including *Focus on the Family, The Bible Answer Man, Family Life Today* and *Truths that Transform.*

The father of two married daughters, Randy lives in Gresham, Oregon, with his wife and best friend, Nanci. He enjoys hanging out with his family, biking, tennis, research and reading.

Feedback regarding Randy's books and inquiries regarding publications and other matters can be directed to Eternal Perspective Ministries via e-mail at info@epm.org.